NEXUS : ASCENSION
ROBERT BOYCZUK

ChiZine Publications

For Sandra, who did a helluva job editing this book

FIRST EDITION

Nexus: Ascension © 2010 by Robert Boyzcuk
Jacket design © 2010 by Erik Mohr
All Rights Reserved.

This book is a work of fiction. Names, characters, places, and incidents are either a product of the author's imagination or are used fictitiously. Any resemblance to actual events, locales, or persons, living or dead, is entirely coincidental.

LIBRARY AND ARCHIVES CANADA CATALOGUING IN PUBLICATION

Library and Archives Canada Cataloguing in Publication

Boyczuk, Robert W. (Robert Wayne), 1956-
          Nexus : ascension / Robert Boyczuk.

ISBN 978-0-9813746-8-0

          I. Title.

PS8603.O979N49 2010   C813'.6   C2010-902882-1

CHIZINE PUBLICATIONS
Toronto, Canada
www.chizinepub.com
info@chizinepub.com

Edited by Sandra Kasturi
Copyedited and proofread by Gemma Files and Helen Marshall

NEXUS : ASCENSION

THE TWINS

The ship drove toward its hellish perihelion.

On its cramped flight deck spun a simulacrum of a binary system: two white dwarfs locked in a vicious gravitational embrace, a combined orbital period of two minutes, twenty-five seconds. Their luminosity had been muted to make them bearable. Even so, the display cast double shadows throughout the cabin that slashed across walls and deck like whirling blades.

Too late, he thought from the confines of his narrow cell. *Too late to change anything.*

A bright green designator appeared at the periphery of the display. His ship. Then, before he could draw another breath, seven red indicators appeared like flotsam in his wake. Drones.

His ship had no weapons.

A heavily armoured gravity-whip vessel, it was shielded only against the temperatures and tidal stresses of the stars it skirted. The drones' particle weapons would be useless, the fan of his exhaust consuming anything they might fire at him. But their warheads...

If he could lock into the gravity well before one detonated, then he could kill his telltale plasma-fusion drive and wink out of existence—at least as far as his pursuers were concerned. A millisecond-long power manoeuvre at perihelion, and he would be flung out of the system at twice his current velocity.

Two of the furthest indicators shifted to orange.

Out of range. Even if those warheads detonated now, their expanding shells of radiation would be beaten back by the furious solar winds, what was left damped by the powerful shielding of his ship.

Another indicator turned orange. Four viable drones left. The corner of his mouth twitched up. But the smile collapsed almost immediately under the weight of a bilious memory: the face of his betrayer. Years of meticulous planning had been unravelled by one weak man chosen for his political acumen as much as for his overweening ambition. That man was still dying, painfully. A death that would go on for days, perhaps weeks. It was far too small a consolation.

Another indicator turned.

The cabin temperature had risen sharply in the last few moments. Sweat sheathed him. His body had been enhanced in every conceivable way, yet there were limits to what even he could bear. Soon he would have to seal his cell, order protective agents to pack around his body, turning off his metabolic processes, insulating him. He watched the display, unwilling to surrender to the oblivion of stasis just yet. As soon as he was out of range of the last drone—

Where will you go?

The words thrust into his mind, a jagged edge of glass. He sucked in a sharp breath.

You cannot survive. Cold this time, malevolent. *What do you hope to achieve?*

He squeezed his eyes closed, concentrated on shutting out the intruder's words.

Please. An abrupt change in tone, a sad whisper in the back of his mind. *Do not abandon me.* Surprised, he relented—until something exploded in his skull, like a pinpoint charge had been detonated in his medulla. He screamed, clutching his head.

You see. The words tore through. *I can still hurt you.*

Dizzy and nauseous, he clutched the sides of his cell. He sensed a rising wave of anger crashing toward him, and gasped beneath its weight—but it hadn't the strength of the first attack. This time, it broke against his will, receding quickly. He wiped sweat from his eyes and checked the display. A lone red indicator remained. And then it turned orange.

Too late, he answered, triumphant.

A howl of outrage filled his mind.

The cabin temperature continued to climb. He ordered his cell's lid to coalesce. A prominence rose from the chromosphere of the sun, sending his instruments momentarily off-scale.

His display wobbled, then refreshed, a new red blip ahead of him. Another ship. It had been hiding, its engines shut down.

In seconds he would hurtle past it. But for the next few heartbeats, he would be exposed to its weapons. He cursed aloud.

I can't let you go. This time, the other seemed almost apologetic. *You're too dangerous.*

His ship shuddered, pitched violently, and he was thrown into the cell's transparent cap. He fell back onto his pallet, stunned. The ship rocked again. Through a fog, he saw the forward bulwark buckle, vaporising in a fiery cloud. Smoke swirled madly, tore past him, rushing toward vacuum. Vaguely, he was aware of his ship intoning its warnings, shutting off a damaged engine and jettisoning its leaking deuterium/helium-3 reaction mass.

His head spun and his ears rang; his cheek burned, like it had been splashed with acid. Tasting blood, he felt tiny fragments of tooth swimming in his saliva. Darkness swirled around him, tried to pull him down. Pressing his palm against his shattered cheek, he screamed as bright pain drove it away once more.

He was sealed in his cell, a red smear of blood on the lid's underside. The cabin was dark, display gone, most of the instruments off-line. Debris tumbled listlessly through vacuum, rebounded off walls and his cell with dull clicks and hollow thumps. Through the ragged tear forward, he could see stars.

The ship seemed to stagger. Two engines down, it reported flatly, the third partially operational, magnetic field fluctuating. A steady stream of figures detailed its imminent collapse. The display flickered back to life. Incredibly, they were suddenly past the red indicator, yet still well within range of its weapons.

The last engine cut out altogether, taking with it the protective plume of exhaust. He sucked in his breath, waiting for the final blow which would transform him and his ship into an expanding cloud of radioactive debris.

But there was nothing.

What happened? he asked. *Why hasn't the drone fired?*

When I jettisoned the reaction mass, his ship replied, *I directed it at the other vessel.*

You're alive. The other voice was astonished.

For a moment, he felt astonished too. Then despair supplanted relief. Before, he had hoped to reach those sympathetic to his cause—but now he was off course, his injection into the gravity well irrevocably altered. His engines were severely damaged, perhaps beyond the ship's repair capabilities. His stasis cell would become his coffin, among distant, unfamiliar stars.

No matter, the other said, understanding.

No, he replied.

A brief pause. Then, one word: *Goodbye.*

Goodbye, brother.

Silence opened up, as broad as the millions of kilometres separating them. The other presence fled. His ship plummeted pointlessly toward the gravity well.

Briefly, he considered ordering the ship to break the seal on his cell, letting vacuum rush in and finish the job. But it was only a momentary lapse.

Instead, he ordered the biostasis process initiated.

A grey mist spilled into the cell, enveloping him. Tiny molecular machines swarmed into his lungs and bloodstream, diffusing throughout his cells, binding to proteins and other reactive molecules. The machinery of his body slowed. His anger ebbed. Peace, warm as the balmy equatorial seas in which he and his twin had played as children, washed over him.

Trying to sort the information from his ship became increasingly difficult. An amber liquid rose and covered him. As cryoprotectant vitrification began his thoughts, already torpid, became muddy and disconnected. A series of images, fragments of memories, crawled through his mind as neurons fired one last time.

Then, for him, time stopped altogether.

1398 YEARS LATER

REPORT

Special Transmission to Bendl My-Fenoillet, Nexus Assumption Committee, Third Senior Deputy, Representative of the Greater Systems Council, Locutor-Nota of the world Nalitman, etc.

Re: Background Material on the Assumption of Bh'Haret; Related Issues of Placement of Bh'Haret in the Nexus Polyarchy Ascension Program; Concerns Pertaining to the Effects on Local Systems.

Located at the tip of the Right Leg Cluster, 21.12 light years from The Twins, Bh'Haret is one of the most distant seeded worlds, in close proximity to twenty-three other planetary systems, fourteen of which are non-affiliated. Of the fourteen, seven have reached the technological threshold but have not yet committed to the Polyarchy's Ascension Program—in part, we believe, due to the influence of Bh'Haret.

A resource-rich world, Bh'Haret has extensive tracts of arable land and huge reserves of oil and common metals.[1] Only 0.031 percent of the world's surface area is currently in use. Politically, the planet is divided into forty-one city-states that govern the surrounding regions. An Upper Congress with a representative of each city-state oversees planetary and off-world concerns. The population is estimated to be nearly one hundred million and is growing rapidly. Few regions have experienced population decline in the last twenty local years. Little attention has been given to this world because of its previous ranking (in the lower tenth percentile of Level II) and its relatively small population. Threshold was

---

[1] Including vast amounts of fissionable materials.

estimated to be more than five hundred years off.

This was clearly a miscalculation.

Our Instrument there reports a disturbing admixture of cultural and technological touchstones whose statistical variance falls well outside acceptable ranges established for the Ascension Program. Below are excerpts from her transmissions:

Walking down almost any street, one finds recent buildings constructed from crude, almost pre-technological materials, stone and mortar being the most common. Remnants of ornate oil lamps line the boulevards, yet arclamps actually light the thoroughfares. It is not unusual to see a cobblestone street being excavated to lay fibre-optic cable. Public trolleys, governed by AIs, are routinely re-routed to bypass construction crews working with pick-axes and shovels. . . .

Several orbiting manufactories have been established. Colonies have been installed on Dayside and Night, the two cold worlds in the system. Regular missions are run to the outermost reaches of the system, and already two dozen manned interstellar missions have been completed to proximate worlds. Suspension techniques requisite to these missions have already been developed or acquired. Representatives from other non-affiliated worlds have visited, and part of the impetus for growth has no doubt been spurred by the bartering of technologies. . . .

Most disturbing, however, is that antimatter trigger systems for De-He3 drive systems are now being tested that are, ultimately, expected to achieve specific impulses in the millions of seconds—or more than 10% of c! When applied to the Standard Ascension Model, this development, given the current technological base on Bh'Haret, is so unlikely as to be of vanishing probability. . . .

The general population has embraced these rapid advances without the hesitation normally seen in developing worlds. New technologies have been incorporated into the daily round of things with a surprisingly matter-of-fact acceptance. There is scant evidence of the social upheavals and displacements one would expect to slow the process of technological development....

There is strong anti-affiliation sentiment on Bh'Haret. Although the government has not openly condemned the Nexus Polyarchy, they have adroitly used the media to colour public perception. Nexus has been portrayed not as a vehicle for disseminating new technologies in an orderly, controlled fashion, but as a monolithic organization designed to suppress technological advancements, doling out minimal information to its members, hoarding the best for itself. Persistent rumours call into question the ability of Speakers to communicate over interstellar distances, suggesting their powers have been feigned in an elaborate hoax designed to keep the Polyarchy in control of the affiliated worlds. Affiliation is now generally considered to be tantamount to a surrender of individual freedoms. Coercion on our part, real or perceived, would almost certainly have disastrous results. Indeed, were the authorities to discover my activities as an Instrument of Nexus, I believe they would use this information to further incite public sentiment against the Polyarchy and discredit the Ascension program....

Clearly, these are all signs of an immature culture whose technological ascent is dangerously out of control. In my opinion, Bh'Haret is on the cusp of dramatic changes for which the standard Ascension Models are of little use. I cannot recommend too strongly that additional Instruments, and a Speaker, be sent immediately to monitor the situation....

'Dangerous,' the Instrument says. A strong word, but one with which I must agree. We may have already witnessed the effects of Bh'Haret's recalcitrance: Ohan, half a light year from Bh'Haret, scheduled to be assumed in three local years (a Speaker was en route), has now requested an indefinite stay. Though they have not stated so, I am convinced they are reluctant to sever trading ties with Bh'Haret (and the seven other non-affiliated worlds clustered in a 1.3 light year radius), as required by assumption into the Polyarchy. It is my belief the administrators of Bh'Haret have convinced

NEXUS : ASCENSION

their counterparts on Ohan that technological acquisition will occur more rapidly through trade with non-affiliated worlds than through the Nexus Ascension program. If so, this constitutes a major setback. Had Ohan been assumed, Bh'Haret would have been further isolated. Instead, we now find ourselves facing an extremely delicate situation, as other local non-affiliated worlds wait to see the outcome of Ohan's vacillation.

I urge you to act expeditiously. Because the current Instrument installed on Bh'Haret is not a Speaker, her communications are time-lagged by two years (the nearest Speaker is on Doelavin, 2.1 light years distant), an unacceptable delay. As our current Instrument has suggested, the rate of change on Bh'Haret clearly demands the presence of a Speaker.

Yours Humbly,
H. R. Ptiga, Local Ascension Administrator, Right Leg Cluster

PART I • 105 YEARS LATER

EA

"I need you!"

Sweat filmed Liis's naked body; cold air blew over her from the right and she shivered, pulling herself tighter. Her mouth was gummy, lips numb. A thin, high-pitched wail sounded in the distance, ululating in melancholy cycles.

Warm fingers closed on Liis's shoulder, shook her insistently. "Get up!"

Leave me alone, she thought and curled further into a fetal ball.

The wail rose and fell, and Liis winced. *An alarm klaxon.* She opened her eyes, felt the lurch of nausea and vertigo that accompanied revival from biostasis.

"Come on," the same voice shouted, over the alarm. "Snap out of it!"

Sav. Liis blinked rapidly, vision clearing. She lay on her side, staring into the cramped, circular cabin. The door to her stasis cell had been retracted; all traces of liquid nitrogen had vanished. Sav, a small, swarthy man, dropped his hand from her shoulder and took a quick, nervous step back. His face, normally soft-featured, was drawn into a grimace.

On his right cheek was a white service scar, a long jagged line that ran the length of his jaw and ended in a six-pointed star. Like most officers, he'd removed all but his most current qualification. Liis, on the other hand, had kept everything, including the elaborate swirls and garish colours on her left cheek where non-com rankings were made; the style of the earliest ones dated to a hundred years before Sav had been born. It intimidated most people, also serving as a reminder that she'd logged more interstellar time than anyone else on board—including Sav.

Goddamn Sav. He'd run only half as many longhaul missions as Liis, but still bounced up from stasis as if he'd just had a refreshing nap. For her, it never got easier. And now, being pulled out like this, before she was ready . . .

He stared intently at her, and the corners of his mouth tightened.

"We've got a . . . problem, Liis."

Liis swallowed, clutching the edge of her berth; her eyes teared. "Help me up," she tried to say, but only a croak came from between parched lips. The effort twisted her stomach into a knot.

"Wait! The tubes."

Liis let herself go limp while Sav detached her snaking feed-tubes from their catheters.

Questions buzzed around in Liis's head, but her throat was too raw and the klaxon too loud for her to give them voice. The nipple of a plastic bottle was forced between her lips, lukewarm liquid trickling from the spout. Swallowing was like having sandpaper rubbed in her throat. She coughed, spit most of the liquid back up along with a long, ropy strand of phlegm. But it seemed to have helped; the next sip, she managed to keep down. Between breaths, Liis took bigger pulls. A comforting warmth spread into her chest and limbs; her skin began to tingle.

"That's enough!" Sav pushed the stopper back down, and dropped the bottle into a large coverall pocket. Reaching over, he lifted and turned Liis so that her legs dangled over the edge of the berth.

Liis sagged forward, tried to double over to stop her head from spinning, but something tugged at the back of her scalp. Fingers worked at the back of her neck, detaching more leads. Liis felt Sav lifting the patches from her scalp, brushing dried flakes of conducting gel from the puckered flesh on the base of her skull.

"Okay."

"Thanks," Liis managed this time, her voice still hoarse, probably inaudible in the din. But Sav seemed to understand anyway; he nodded grimly. Though Liis's nausea had passed, it hovered in the background as her own weight pressed down on her. *Gravity,* she thought stupidly. *We're still decelerating.* But she shouldn't have been woken until *Ea* assumed orbit around Bh'Haret, the ship back in zero-gee.

She looked at Sav. "Wh . . . what . . . happened?" Her words disappeared in the noise.

Sav leaned in close, his ear in front of her lips.

"Are . . . are we . . . off-course?"

Sav pulled back and shook his head. "No. Not exactly. We're home, or almost. A little more than a day out."

He's afraid, Liis realized. *But of what?*

"There's nothing—" Sav stopped abruptly. "The others," he said. "You'd better come see it for yourself."

Across the cabin were three more cells—one for Sav, two for their passengers. The closest was still sealed, pump humming as it drew liquid nitrogen back into the reservoir beneath the deck. Another had already been drained. Behind its translucent port she could see a figure shift restlessly, a grub turning in black earth.

"Let's get you to your feet, before our cargo wakes up." Sav eased her forward until the soles of her feet touched the cold plates of the deck. "Okay?"

Liis nodded, and together they pushed away from the cell. The room began to spin. Liis, her legs stiff and uncertain, stumbled into Sav, who staggered, but managed to catch her beneath the arms.

"We'll take it slowly," Liis heard him say, while the room whirled. "Clothes first." They began weaving across the cabin, towards the storage lockers.

Even after Sav cut the alarm, Liis's ears still buzzed. A dull ache had lodged permanently in the back of her skull. With Sav's help, she'd managed to pull on a pair of coveralls and clambered up the ladder to the bridge. Now she stood beside the navigator's couch on *Ea*'s bridge, clutching the thick straps of floor-to-ceiling webbing behind it. The flight deck was dark, and a three-dimensional projection filled the small, circular space. Hovering above the comm panel was Bh'Haret.

"Status?" Sav asked.

"Still unable to initiate contact." *Ea* replied. "No response on any of the specified frequencies. Continue scanning?"

"Yes."

The planet was a ball of sharp blues, long brown sweeps and emerald swaths, banded by brilliant white clouds. In many places, wherever this cover broke, unaccountable black smudges marred the land, like blemishes. Across the bottom of the display, two words in dozens of languages circled the room endlessly. All, she realized, conveyed the same message:

... *hazard plague hazard plague hazard plague* ...

Sav shifted, cleared his throat. "You heard. I ordered *Ea* to signal on all the standard frequencies: No answer. Nothing but this." A dozen small, bright pinpricks of light girded the planet; Sav pointed at one which had just risen over the upper edge of the world. "Someone's set up a network of screamers to pump a warning out, over and over...."

Liis stared, numbly.

"The navigation beacons are gone. I've instructed comm ops to cycle through all the different frequencies, send out emergency calls, but I haven't received a response as yet."

... *hazard plague hazard plague hazard plague* ...

"If anyone's left in the mining colonies or the orbitals, they're not transmitting," Sav was saying. "And even if there's anything else out there, no hope in hell of picking it up with these screamers jamming all the channels."

... *hazard plague hazard plague hazard plague* ...

"I don't get readings on anything down there, on any wavelength. No EMF spikes from power grids, no hot spots on infrared where cities should be. Like ... an unpopulated world. I mean, it almost looks like—"

"Bh'Haret's dead."

"Yeah."

Liis stared at the home she'd fled centuries ago. A readout indicated their distance at fifty thousand kilometres.

The planet spun on, in silence.

"Liis, I don't think anyone's left alive."

Everything was gone. Liis wasn't sure if she wanted to laugh or cry.

"Don't flip out on me." Sav grasped her wrist. "I need you here!"

Liis looked at the small, round man, feeling her bones grind under the increasing pressure of his grip, then pried Sav's hand free. "I'm . . . I'm okay," she said.

Sav stared back, appraising her. She stretched herself to full height, a head taller than him. "What now?"

"I don't know." Sav killed the display. As lights rose in the cabin, they both stood blinking in the sudden brightness.

To Liis, it seemed unreal—standing here centimetres from a man she hardly knew, talking calmly about the whole world's death.

"It's real." It was as if Sav had read her thoughts. "It happened."

Liis nodded again, thoughts spinning off in dozens of different directions. She needed to be in motion. Turning, she walked unsteadily back toward the ladder.

Without looking back, she said, "Let's get the others."

Loners and misfits.

Those were the sorts longhauls attracted. A few claimed it was for the adventure; others claimed it was for the pay. But most, whether they'd admit it or not, were trying to escape the mess of botched lives, spending years locked in stasis during which friends and family (if they had any) drifted away in time.

Flash frozen, you'd accelerate toward a world you wouldn't see for years, and then only through the thick glass port of the lazarette—the orbiting quarantine station—before returning to the cryobeds for the long journey home. During that time, you'd be out of stasis and conscious maybe fifteen days. But on return, only those few subjective weeks older, you'd find everyone else had lived decades in hard time. Two or three longhauls and your past would be completely eradicated.

The perfect solution.

Liis made no bones about being a charter member of this misanthropic club. A disastrous relationship with a man who refused to love her back—followed by a half-hearted attempt at suicide—had brought her into the fold at age twenty-five, one of the first, and the youngest, to crew a longhaul mission. At the time, the emptiness of space seemed a soothing balm.

But long after he'd died, long after everyone she'd ever known had died, she'd stood at the foot of his overgrown grave, staring at his weathered headstone, and realized she still carried her entire past with her. *He* was the one who'd escaped.

So she signed up for more longhauls, jumping relentlessly into the future. There was certainly nothing left anchoring her to the present.

Until this last run to Arcolet.

Emotions that had lain dormant, that she'd erroneously assumed had withered and died, had taken her by surprise. Foolishly, she'd allowed herself to develop feelings for their *cargo*, Josua. An envoy on his first posting. In his mid-thirties, extraordinarily young for a diplomat, with a smooth, unlined face, almost innocent. Even his diplomatic scar—a small, stylized bird on his right cheek—only enhanced the impression of guilelessness.

It was an infatuation, Liis told herself, nothing more.

But when he smiled at her, she blushed; when he accidentally brushed her arm, her heart hammered in her chest. And though she couldn't have said with certainty (her social skills having atrophied over the years), his smiles seemed to hint at something more than just friendliness. In the cramped quarters of a longhaul ship, however, where no provision had been made for privacy, there was little chance to push it beyond an intermittent flirtation.

Liis vowed that after their return to Bh'Haret, she'd seek him out. Invite him to dinner.

Now, instead—like a parody of her dreams—she sat next to Sav in the bleak, cramped galley where, moments before, Sav had helped Josua into the chair opposite. Like everything else on the ship, it was spare and functional, designed to minimize space and weight.

The nub of a comm projector protruded above the cooking surface. A narrow light strip overhead provided dull, watery illumination.

Liis tried to catch Josua's eye, but he still seemed woozy, disoriented. It had been only his second time in stasis. Like all newbies, he'd still be feeling the effects.

Not so with his companion, a man named Hebuiza, a Facilitator, who paced the few steps from one end of the room to the other. He was taller than any of them, face atypically unscarred; he had to bend so his head wouldn't touch the ceiling. But where Liis was broad-shouldered and solid, Hebuiza was rangy, limbs thin and long, tee-shirt and shorts hung loosely from his frame. High, hollow cheekbones and a long, sharp nose gave him a cadaverous look. His skull was as hairless as the rest of him, the crown of his head a mass of thin wires and tiny sockets. As with all Facilitators, his brain had been surgically split into two halves to maximize processing efficiency.

When he reached the wall, he turned to Liis, eyes dark and accusing.

"This cannot be happening!" Hebuiza said, his deep voice overwhelming in such a small space.

She stared back impassively. "It *is* happening."

Hebuiza resumed pacing, head swinging from side to side, a secondary effect experienced by some Facilitators after their hemispheres were divided. Liis had noticed it became more pronounced whenever he concentrated intensely, or allowed himself to become openly agitated. At these times, his head would move back and forth like an animal hunting for a scent, competing halves of a brain both trying to see through optical nerves they didn't control.

"But how?" The Facilitator now glared at Sav, fixing Sav first with one eye, then the other. "A *plague*? Diseases do not wipe out entire planets!"

"Maybe it wasn't just that," Sav said. "You saw those black scars on the surface—they look like they were caused by fission weapons. Maybe whatever happened escalated into a war; maybe the disease was a biological weapon. Or maybe it was the other way round . . .

some virus gets loose, and before anyone could do anything there's a panic...."

"But there'd be survivors. What about off-world population? Crews in the orbitals?"

Sav shrugged. "Everything that *was* in orbit around Bh'Haret is gone. Only those screamers left."

Through all this, Josua said nothing. He sat, staring at his hands folded in his lap, head bobbing slightly. Liis fought the urge to reach out and comfort him.

"The mining colonies," Hebuiza insisted. "They would have had plenty of warning."

"Maybe. But there's no sign of the colonies on Dayside, or Night. And Eramanus Station? Disappeared. At least, it's not where it used to be. I instructed *Ea* to set up broadband scans, but so far, we haven't gotten a peep. Screamers aren't exactly helping; they lock in on any broadcast frequency, and saturate the channel. So all we can do right now is listen, and hope we catch something sensible before the screamers interfere with it."

"Who laid the screamers, in the first place? *Somebody* had to do that!"

"You're right," Sav agreed. "But I don't think it was survivors, if there's any. I think Nexus put them there."

The name finally drew Liis's attention away from Josua. "Nexus? Why would they want to put satellites here? We're not an affiliate world."

"No. But the broadcasts are in forty-three separate languages—I counted. Most I couldn't identify, but of the ones I could, all were from Nexus affiliates. The Facilitator here can verify that." Sav paused to look up at Hebuiza, whose eyelids flickered briefly while he retrieved information; he nodded, glumly.

"Second, those satellites are only a few metres across, but they're messing up our on-board systems pretty good. I've had to shut down the more sensitive equipment and shield the cabling for the rest, just so I can keep it online. Do you know what kind of power it takes to generate a signal like that over this distance? Terawatts, at least.

And they're doing it constantly. We had nothing like that when we left, but I've heard of similar technology. Near Nexus affiliates."

Sav looked around the table. "It's not inconceivable that the Polyarchy placed them here a long time back. We left over thirty years ago, and the nearest Nexus world, Doelavin, is only two light years away. If the plague hit just after we left, they could have launched the satellites as much as twenty-eight years ago—the thirty years we were gone, less the time it would have taken a radio transmission to reach Doelavin with news of the plague. I might have done the same, if I was that close. To warn people off." Sav paused. "And maybe to keep an eye on who's been through here, in case they showed up at my doorstep."

"What are you telling us?" Hebuiza asked, with a sneer. "If we decide to go elsewhere, we might already be marked as plague carriers, and get turned away?"

"Turned away would be the best we could hope for."

Hebuiza's expression abruptly went flat. "Then they lied."

"What are you talking about?" Sav said. "Who?"

"At Arcolet." The anger built in the Facilitator's voice. "They negotiated as though nothing was wrong, but they had to have known about the plague long before we arrived—they just didn't want to tell us. They were afraid we might want to stay!"

Talk, Liis thought bitterly. *All talk*. What did any of that matter now?

Again as though reading her mind, Sav shook his head. "We have more immediate concerns. We only have enough fuel to achieve half a percent of *c* at best, hardly a decent cruising velocity, which means we can't go anywhere in less than a few hundred years. Besides which, these ships don't exactly carry a lot of reserve food and atmosphere for when we're not in stasis."

"So we go down to the surface."

Josua's voice startled Liis. She turned to see his head now raised. He lifted his hands from his lap and placed them flat on the table. "No other choice." For the first time Josua looked directly at Liis; his eyes burned with . . . what? Frustration? Anger? Liis couldn't be sure.

"Well?"

It took her a moment to realize he was waiting for her to answer. Liis nodded.

"Sav?"

"Don't see we do have much of a choice."

"Facilitator?"

Liis watched Hebuiza grind his long jaws together in displeasure. His whole body seemed to quiver, but he didn't answer.

"I'll take that as a yes," Josua said. He looked at Sav. "What next?"

It shouldn't have bothered Liis that Josua looked to Sav, but it did. Sav was nominally *Ea*'s captain, even though Liis had flown far more longhauls; in normal circumstances, they shared duties equally, trading off when they got bored. If anything, Sav seemed slightly embarrassed by his rank, stepping back from it as much as possible. And so they'd managed to fly four missions together without any major blowups....

Sav chewed his lower lip in thought for a second. To Josua: "Okay—you and Liis take a look at the EVA suits. We don't know if there's still a danger of infection down there, so we'll all suit up. We need to make them comfortable as possible for one-gee work, and check to see if the screamers interfere with suit-to-suit communications. If they do, you'll have to set up a circuit to oscillate the suit transmitters through lockstep frequency shifts. Once we're on the surface, there should be enough of a time lag before the screamers sense our signals and wipe them out by broadcasting that damn warning. If we shift every few milliseconds or so, we should be okay." He turned to Hebuiza. "We'll also need whatever decon procedures we can manage. And antimicrobials. In fact, we should check the manifests to see what other useful things we've got."

"Where are we going to land?" Liis asked, eyes lingering on Josua.

"At Lyst," Josua answered, without hesitation. "The cryosuspension facility. There might still be warm bodies in suspension—survivors."

The Facilitator frowned. "But we've detected no signatures that would indicate power sources anywhere, including Lyst."

"They have backup power systems," Sav said. "Passive solar arrays whose signatures would be undetectable."

"A long shot," Hebuiza said, with a sniff. "We should be heading to an urban centre. That is where we are most likely to find records, and supplies." Liis could see the Facilitator fight to restrain his agitation. "It will be a critical waste of time."

"No," Josua said. "It's our best bet."

"Our worst!" Hebuiza shot back. "If we were to revive any *survivors*"—and here he paused, curling his lips in disdain like the word tasted sour—"we might expose ourselves to the plague!"

Josua blinked, as if he hadn't thought of this.

Hebuiza turned to Sav. "It is clear that Josua is not thinking clearly. So I ask you, as captain, to—"

"Josua's right," Liis said, cutting him off. "If we have any hope of finding out what happened, let alone of finding any systems still up and running, it's got to be at a cryo facility. Those places were built to last." She turned to Sav, silently imploring his support.

For a moment he looked at her, like he was trying to figure something out. Then he shrugged. "I'm with Josua and Liis."

The Facilitator looked flabbergasted. "Are you all mad? We should be putting as much distance between ourselves and the plague as possible. Not heading right toward it!"

"We're going to Lyst to look for records and supplies," Sav said, with finality. "We're not going to revive anyone."

Josua paled, and lowered his head. Without thinking, Liis reached across the table and gave his hand a reassuring squeeze; he looked up, startled. Untangling his fingers from hers, he withdrew his hand brusquely.

Liis let her empty fingers curl into her palm. *He's in shock*, she thought. Still, she felt her face colouring, knew this would throw her scars into dramatic relief.

"Let's get started," Sav said.

Josua stood, abruptly. "Fine." He turned, and walked from the room.

The Facilitator stared at Sav, then Liis. He opened his mouth as though about to raise another objection, but instead snapped it shut and strode after Josua, leaving Sav and Liis alone.

Liis pushed herself to her feet, but Sav didn't move. "You okay?" He asked.

Liis let herself collapse back into her seat. *How the hell do you think I'm doing?* she thought.

"Fine," was all she said.

"You sure?"

Liis felt him scrutinizing her, evaluating her. "I said I was fine."

"Coming back to find your home gone is . . . is a shock." He paused, as if fishing for a reaction to his absurd understatement. "It's going to affect us all in ways we can't even predict. So we need to look out for one another."

Liis said nothing.

Sav sagged in his chair; he looked exhausted. "I won't lie to you. I'm worried. Hebuiza's a Facilitator, trained to hide his emotion—but look at how edgy he was just now. And Josua, God knows what he's thinking. You and me, even Hebuiza, we're experienced longhaulers; in a way, we were already disconnected from Bh'Haret. This was Josua's first trip. It's going to hit him harder."

It already has, Liis thought.

"I need you to keep an eye on him. To make sure he doesn't . . . he isn't . . ."

Liis's heart almost stopped. "Suicidal?"

"Yes."

Liis felt a surge of anger. "He'll be okay."

"Don't let your feelings cloud your judgement."

Liis was taken aback. "What do you mean by that?"

"I'm not blind. I can see how you look at him."

Liis's cheeks grew hot. "You're wrong."

"I hope." Sav wiggled out from between the table and chair and stood. He placed a hand on Liis's shoulder. "Listen, you can look out for him, but just give him some room, all right? Now is not the time to complicate things." His voice sounded weary, and his face seemed thin and drained. "God knows we all have enough to worry about, as it is."

The ship issued its zero-gee warning, and the main engine cut out as they slipped into orbit.

The preparations took only a few hours more. Sav and Hebuiza stockpiled equipment in the dropship: two suit-patch kits, a toolbox, a medical kit, and several spare oxygen/nitrogen cartridges. Liis and Josua, meanwhile, reprogrammed the transceivers in their suits, then lightened them by stripping off everything that wasn't essential.

"Are you sure the dropship is safe?" Hebuiza asked when the group had reassembled in the bay, spread out along the wall, hanging on to drag bars. All four were dressed in pale blue undersuits, the ends of half a dozen recycling tubes poking out from several junctures in the insulating material.

"It wasn't designed for atmospheric work, except in emergencies," Sav said. "Should hold up well enough, though I wouldn't want to rely on it for an extended period. It'll get us there and back."

The Facilitator mumbled inaudibly.

"Let's get going," Josua said, pushing away from the wall and drifting over to where Sav and Hebuiza had clipped the EVA suits to the floor.

The suits belonging to Josua, Liis and Sav were standard-issue zinc white, divided at the waist into bulky pants and torso-jackets. Helmets with large oval visors had been clipped to each chest. The fourth suit, Hebuiza's, was set apart from the others; it was longer and thinner, its black material all one piece, split vertically along its side. A wider, oval helmet, permanently hinged to its neck, bore an intricate cross-thatching of wires, sockets and tiny antennae—extensions, Liis guessed, for the ones atop the Facilitator's skull. On its chest, nearly invisible against the dark material, was a black, featureless box that the Facilitator had refused to detach despite its kilos of extra mass. Thin cables radiated from it like veins, running along the exterior of the suit to its extremities. Several disappeared into ports on the base of the helmet.

Hooking her feet under a drag bar on the deck, Liis reached down and unclipped the lower half of Josua's suit; she held it out for him. "Come on, I'll give you a hand."

After helping Josua, Liis drifted over to Sav who'd already climbed into his suit. In the far corner the Facilitator had donned his suit and clipped himself to a drag bar. He was playing with the cables that converged on the box fixed to his chest.

"When we were working on the EVA suits, he wouldn't let me touch his," Liis said quietly to Sav. "I don't know what that thing on his chest is. When I asked him, he told me to mind my own business."

Sav shrugged.

The Facilitator, who had finished with the box, now turned his attention to his oddly shaped helmet. His dark fingers adjusted the antennae there as his head bobbed. Liis realized the helmet had been designed to accommodate the strange swinging motion of the Facilitator's head.

She turned her back on him and suited up. A moment later she had pulled herself around the side of the dropship to the open hatch where the others were waiting. Inside the ship the space was dominated by a console and two seats anchored to the deck. Above the console was the windscreen, a thick band of polarised plastic wrapped around the nose.

Sav pulled himself in first, squeezing his bulk into the pilot's seat. With a gentle shove, Liis propelled Josua toward the co-pilot's seat. She figured that since he'd had only minimal training in the bulky suit, he'd be safest there. Josua went without protest. Liis followed and helped him fasten his harness. Then she wedged herself between the back of his seat and the bulwark, clipping herself to two recessed rings in the wall. Hebuiza came last, the top of his odd helmet scraping along the low ceiling; inside, his head swung from side to side in its agitated motion.

Sav punched in the sequence to seal the hatch. A few seconds later, Liis felt the hum of Ea's airlock compressor sing through the floorplates of the dropship. In less than two minutes, the atmosphere had been sucked out of the dropship bay. The broad outer doors rolled back and Liis blinked at the bright light of the sun reflecting off the apparition of Bh'Haret.

HOME · DAY 0

"We should be coming up to the stasis facility soon," Sav said. He reduced the altitude of the dropship to a kilometre before they made another pass. Liis was hot and uncomfortable already; her visor was misting up. Weight had returned with a vengeance. Every movement now required effort, and the tiny craft seemed to bounce her around vindictively. Unlike the solid, heavy shuttles normally used for planet fall, the dropship seemed a flimsy and capricious thing, shuddering at the slightest hint of turbulence. At the very back of the ship, squeezed between the hatch and a row of storage lockers, Hebuiza sat in glum silence, knees pulled up to his chest.

The dropship bobbed and weaved as the landscape slid by beneath them. It was early fall, the river Lyst a dull, glinting ribbon in the morning sun, twisting back and forth through canyons and gorges. Josua bent over in the co-pilot's seat, a thin cable running from the instrument panel to his helmet. He fiddled with the crude optics of the craft, trying to magnify the image. Through the windscreen, Liis searched the ground, but one hill looked pretty much like the next.

The craft yawed sharply and pitched to the left, buffeted by a headwind; Liis had to grab the back of Josua's seat to keep from being thrown into the bulkhead. It bucked one more time, then settled into a rhythmic rising and falling, as if riding gentle ocean swells.

"There!" Josua tapped the co-pilot's screen, excitedly.

Liis couldn't see what he was on about. Below, a broad valley sat bordered by a ring of low, rounded hills, its centre the mirrored surface of an oval lake, its edges ragged with the shadows of thick, stunted trees. Josua pointed at the far edge, now in the middle of his screen. "Along the south shore," he said. "See how the trees run in an even line, all about the same height? It's got to be the solar array,"

Then Liis saw it. While the forest everywhere pressed in on the boundaries of the lake, in one place they stood back in a neat row, two hundred metres from shore. The ground here was darker than the lake, a matte black, and unnaturally flat.

"Okay," Sav said. "Let's take a closer look." He swung the dropship toward the ring of hills.

Liis scanned the hills, but found no sign of buildings, no storage sheds, no fences. "Why can't we see anything?"

"All underground." Sav replied, as he eased the craft into a gradual descent. "For stasis facilities, they usually pick a site as far away from fault lines as possible, and dig deep into the rock. I'll bet the entrance is the only thing on the surface; from up here, it would be next to impossible to spot." As the ring of hills drew nearer, the dropship veered east abruptly and away from the lake; Sav fought it back on course. "If that is the array," he added, as soon as he had regained control, "we should be able to find the site." They bumped over the nearest ridge and were suddenly directly above the tail of the lake, skimming a hundred metres above its surface. The water looked brackish. Near the edge of the lake, the grey spikes of dead trees thrust upwards.

"It *is* the array," Josua said. On the screen, an enhanced image of the dark plain grew as they sped over the lake, a grid of interlocked solar panels. Already it was easy to see numerous panels were cracked and pitted. Those nearest the lake were covered with creeping green algae. In one spot, a small sapling grew where two partitions had collapsed inwards.

"Are you sure that's it?" Sav banked the craft toward the point where the array met the lake. "That's gotta be too small. How could something that size provide enough power?"

"Look down," Liis said.

Sav bent forward to look out the window on his left. Josua leaned over to his right. Directly below, the murky waters of the lake sped by; visible beneath the surface was a uniform plain of black.

"The array's plenty big, if you figure it runs the length of the valley," Liis said quietly. "At least it *did*—before the lake was here."

"Bah," Hebuiza said. His visor was darkened, making it impossible to see his face. "So much for your back-up power. The array's been dormant for years. Turn around."

"We're not turning around." Liis was shocked by Josua's vehemence. "We're not leaving until we find the cryo facility."

"You are not in charge here," Hebuiza said.

Josua's mouth twisted in rage; he fumbled with his harness, turning to face Hebuiza. Only his inexperience with the thick, awkward fingers of his gloves kept him from succeeding. Behind Liis, Hebuiza rose until his helmet scraped the ceiling.

Liis watched all this with astonishment. What were they going to do? Start a fight in the impossibly crowded dropship?

"Hey!" Sav said, suddenly. "Look at the screen!"

Josua stopped struggling with the harness, turned back to the co-pilot's panel.

"I'm reading a signal, over by the southwest corner. I don't believe it, but it looks like the thing is still powered!"

On the screen, a colour gradient now overlaid the dark landscape. In one corner of the solar array was an irregular pool of amber light. A thin, snaking tributary in brighter gold ran away from it up into the hills. "That's got to be the regulator, and that's probably the main power cable. If we follow it, it should lead us to the facility."

"Then let's do that," Josua said, his anger gone, as abruptly as it had risen.

Sav swung the dropship to follow the golden thread's serpentine track, as Hebuiza slumped back into his sitting position. It didn't take long to find it—less than a kilometre from the array.

A nondescript, concrete portico thrust up from the hillside. Next to it was a small landing pad. Clutches of weeds had pushed through the tarmac, and along one edge was a two-metre-wide gap where the surface had crumbled into a small pit filled with water, like someone had taken a bite out of it. A dilapidated link fence surrounded everything.

Sav set down dead centre. The whine of the engines diminished, then died.

"Well," he said, into the sudden silence, "we're home."

Black metal doors barred the stasis facility's entrance. There were no handles or data sockets visible, only a small identifying plaque. A sensor, apparently long dead, was embedded in the wall above the entrance. "We can cut through it," Sav said. "There's a couple of lasers I threw into a locker when we were gathering supplies. Thought they might come in handy."

"Then what are we waiting for?" Josua asked, impatiently.

As they strapped a battery pack onto Sav, the only one who'd used a laser before, without asking, Josua picked up the other. The lasers looked like stubby rifles, squat silver tubes grafted onto burnished metal stocks. His own battery pack activated, Josua flicked the power switch and Liis saw a display on the stock come up, the LCD showing the intensity setting and a bar graph of battery strength.

"Okay," Sav said to Josua. "You plug the cable on the laser into a wrist jack on the hand you're firing with, like so, and clip the laser onto the inside of your forearm so its barrel extends past your fingertips." Sav demonstrated; Josua nodded, and did the same. "We'll cut a metre and a half square, up from the ground, to give us enough room to crawl through. Doesn't look like the door is recessed on the bottom, but if it is, we might have to go back and cut some wiggle room on the top to rock out the pieces."

"Got it," Josua said.

Sav pointed. "You start here on the left, and I'll take the right."

Fifteen minutes later, Josua stepped back to let Sav finish his cut. The plate fell inward on its own as the last bit of metal boiled away.

Once the edge had cooled, Sav turned on his helmet lamp, went down on his knees and peered through the opening. "Looks okay . . . just be careful not to catch your suit on the edge when you're crawling through."

Josua nodded. He switched on his lamp, went down on all fours and crawled through the opening, equipment and all. Sav followed, Liis right behind, the Facilitator coming last.

Inside, they stood at the end of an unadorned corridor that ran away from them, tunnelling deeper into the hillside. Containers of all sorts had been stacked haphazardly near the wall, constricting the passage. At regular intervals were doors, most of which stood ajar. Everything was layered with thick dust.

"Keep your eyes peeled for a data port, or anything that might look like an interface," Sav said, and started off down the corridor, Josua on his heels, their boots kicking up clouds of dust. Hebuiza and Liis trailed after.

Sav moved straight down the corridor, pausing briefly to play his light over each door; but none of them bore any kind of inscription. When he came to an intersection of corridors, he ignored the branch and continued straight on. Liis hung back and pushed on a partially open door; it swung wide, to reveal an empty storage cupboard.

"Liis, over here!"

Thirty metres down the hall, Sav and Josua stood shoulder to shoulder, staring at something; Hebuiza stood a pace behind them, looking over Sav's head. Liis hurried to join them. When she got there, she realized they stood before the doors of an elevator. Josua and Sav moved back a step to let her look. The doors were ajar and inside was a suit, not unlike the ones they wore, lying on the floor. When she shone her light on its visor, she could see a shrivelled, desiccated face, thin lips curled back over yellowed teeth, empty sockets where there had once been eyes.

"The elevator is dead," Hebuiza said.

Liis nodded, unable to take her eyes from the mummified remains.

"There's a service shaft," Sav added.

Liis turned. A few metres to the left of the elevator was a low arch. A small gate that had once barred this entrance lay crookedly open, its top hinge torn from the wall. Inside was a circular dropshaft. At the back of the shaft, half a dozen thick pipes slid from view into the depths; the head of a ladder poked just above floor level.

"And here's a map," Sav said, pointing to a diagram fixed to the wall between the elevator and shaft. Beneath it was a directory listing departments, divided according to level. Seventeen levels in all. The stasis cells didn't begin until the third sublevel, where the tunnels quadrupled in length.

"This is a waste of time," Hebuiza said scornfully. "It will take us weeks to search a place this size."

"Then we'll split up," Josua said. "Take different levels."

Sav looked at the Facilitator. "We don't need to search every room," he said. "All we need is an active data port. We know the place has power, so there's a decent chance the network's still up. We'll start by looking in the most likely places on the upper levels, then work our way down."

"I think we've already seen all there is to see." The Facilitator crossed the dark arms of his suit over his chest. "Unless, of course, you are particularly interested in corpses, since I suspect that's all we'll find here."

Liis emerged from the dropshaft onto the fourth sublevel just in time to see the first door on the left swing shut behind Josua. He'd clambered down the ladder dangerously fast and she'd done her best to keep up, but slowed when she nearly lost her grip. Far below, Sav and Hebuiza were exploring the lower levels of the complex; she and Josua had taken the upper ones, and had just finished with the floor above—to no avail. None of the computer systems were active.

Liis cursed, hustling over as quickly as her EVA suit would allow, and pulled the door open. It was a room identical to the dozen they'd already been in. She stared down the length of the chamber, her helmet lamp cutting the gloom. In the uncertain shadows she could not see the end of the room; its low, curved ceiling receded to a vanishing point hundreds of metres away. Long, parallel rows of I-beam track—each with its own winch—were bolted to the ceiling. Spaced regularly below each track were hundreds of transparent domes rising above the floor: the tops of stasis cells cradled in recessed vertical bays, bundled cables stretching from their crowns to junction boxes on the ceiling, thicker umbilicals buried in the floor. Most of the cells were dark, their occupants long dead. A few dozen, scattered randomly throughout the room, radiated a pale green light, silhouetting the heads of those interred.

Liis spotted Josua halfway down, his helmet lamp cutting left to right, then back again. He was moving between the rows, shining his light in each cell. Liis turned her back and played her light over the far wall, spotted a panel, presumably the interface to the AI regulating the cells in this chamber. Like all the other panels she'd seen so far, it was dark, and had no external jacks or sockets. She turned back to the nearest lit cell. Power was being fed to it, readouts confirming its lucky occupant was still alive. It made no sense.

Before they'd done anything else, they'd used the maps on the walls to locate the systems room, on the second sublevel. It had been gutted. All the computers had been smashed with a deliberate violence and the network cables purposely severed, isolating the room. So there was no central control. And all the local panels in these chambers were dead. Still, something was feeding the few lit cells juice, monitoring them, keeping them alive.

Josua had reached the end of the row, and was doubling back when the next closest active cell—halfway between Josua and Liis—winked out.

Josua yelled out; he half-staggered, half-ran forward, dropping to his knees.

"What is it?" Liis shouted back, but Josua ignored her. Instead he rubbed frantically at the cell's surface, peering into it, his visor almost touching the transparent dome. Abruptly, he pushed himself back on his heels, his arms hanging limply at his sides. Liis heard something that sounded like a sob.

For a moment she stood there, uncertain what to do; then she hurried down the row and knelt next to Josua. She followed his gaze through the clear spot he'd rubbed into the dust that grimed the dome. It was an older woman with a thin face and wisps of blonde hair pasted to her scalp. Dark lesions covered her shoulders and throat. She looked waxen in the bath of cryoprotective glycerol, as if she were in the last stages of something incurable.

Dead, at long last, Liis thought. *I just watched her die.* Then, to Josua: "Are you okay?"

Josua stared at the woman; perspiration clung to his upper lip. He pointed at her, the laser still clipped to his arm, its snout aimed right at the woman. For a moment Liis thought he might pull the trigger.

"Everyone's dead." Lowering his arm, he looked at Liis, his eyes filled with an unutterable despair. "Or will be soon."

"There was nothing we could have done to save her, Josua. Saving ourselves is our first priority."

"Why? What's the point?"

"There's always a point," Liis said, though she'd never thought so; to her, life had always seemed pointless, random, chaotic. Or so she would have said until she met Josua. She got to her feet. "Come on." She hooked her hand under Josua's arm, helping him up. "We've got lots more of these to go."

Josua allowed himself to be dragged a few metres, then tugged his arm free. "No," he said, shuffling back up the row. "I have to finish here, first."

The quiet hiss in Liis's headset went dead. Josua had cut their comm link. She'd only known him less than a month of subjective time, she reminded herself; it shouldn't hurt this much.

Had it been four or five floors they'd checked already?

Liis couldn't remember. She stood at the foot of another identical array of stasis cells, waiting for Josua to complete his ritual inspection.

A fresh burst of static startled her.

She swung around, instinctively, but could see no one. Through her headset, a garbled transmission:

". . . crate . . ." A hum, followed by a distorting hiss as the receiver tried (and failed) to hold the signal. ". . . something here . . . found . . . panel . . . this level . . ." Sav's voice crackled in Liis's earpiece, struggling through the intervening concrete floors, fading in and out as it cycled through the frequency shifts Hebuiza had programmed. "... older housing. Probably been ... forever ..."

"You're breaking up, Sav."

"... think ... out ... problem with ... span ... gone for a look-see ..." His voice faded, the hiss receded.

Liis left the room and stepped into the corridor hoping to catch a stronger signal. She moved toward the dropshaft. "Sav?" Liis maxed out the gain on her headset, leaned into the dropshaft.

"DO YOU COPY, LIIS?"

Liis winced, pulled her head out of the shaft, and took a step back.

"I'm at the dropshaft." Sav's voice was crystal clear now. "How's the signal now?"

"Terrific," she said, her ears ringing.

"We've found an old access panel that seems to be active. There's a pilot light, or ... something. But a skid of barrels is blocking it, so we need you and Josua to give us a hand clearing them away."

"Where are you?"

"Eleventh sublevel. Turn left when you come out of the dropshaft. Second corridor on the right."

"Copy," Liis said. She turned and headed back to the chamber, switching frequencies to the channel they had been using before. "Did you catch that, Josua?" No answer; the display in Liis's suit showed his comm unit was still not acknowledging. "Sav thinks he's found an active data port." Liis reached the door and was about to push against it when Josua came barrelling out, almost knocking her over. He shouldered past Liis and ran—as much as his suit would allow—down the corridor to the dropshaft. Grabbing the ladder, he swung himself in, and dropped quickly from sight.

Dammit! Liis thought. *He's going to kill himself.*

She hurried down the hall and poked her head into the shaft. It was like looking into a well at midnight. For a moment, Liis panicked; then she flipped on her external pickups. In the distance, she heard the dull clunking of boots on metal rungs several levels below. For whatever reason, Josua had turned off his headlamp.

Catching hold of the ladder, she swung herself into the shaft to begin her own descent.

The access panel was in a maintenance corridor wide enough for four of them to walk abreast. Sav had hung a trouble light from a cabling conduit that ran down the centre of the ceiling; it filled the tunnel with a bright, unnatural light, illuminating Sav's small, round figure bent over the panel, his head bowed over the tiny leads he was trying to solder onto a plug. The thick fingers of his suit made him work slowly.

Liis sat with her back against the last drum they had wrestled to the ground, breath ragged, her visor fogged. Her suit had been designed for a zero-gee environment; here it seemed to weigh far more than it actually did, making any kind of labour awkward and dangerous. Her recirculator hummed, whining like an angry insect, straining to keep her cool.

She looked around, trying to spot Hebuiza, who had moved even further away. In his black suit and with his helmet light now off, he was nearly invisible. Josua leaned against the wall, his head hung, lost in his own despair. Liis wanted to comfort him, but couldn't bring herself to rise and cross the few metres to where he stood.

She lowered her own head.

What now? she thought.

She needed to find something else to do while she waited for Sav to finish his work. Anything but think about Josua. She considered running a suit diagnostic to make sure she hadn't damaged anything, but they had no replacement parts here, only basic patch kits. And unless they found a cache of similar suits, that was all there ever would be.

"I'm in," Sav said quietly. A light winked green in the lower corner of Liis's HUD as Sav completed the relay and patched it into their broadcast group. "There's one pending message." Josua snapped out of his lethargy, pushing himself away from the wall. "Play it," he said.

An image coalesced, overlaying Liis's visor. Along the bottom was a date stamp showing the recording to be over twenty-nine years old, made shortly after their departure. A woman with lank, greasy hair and bloodshot eyes sat behind a desk. Her skin was the sickly yellow of jaundice. On her arms and neck were lesions caked with dried blood, like those Liis had seen on several of the people in the cryo cells. Beneath her darkened fingernails were the sharp red lines of haemorrhage splinters. A single drop of blood hung off the tip of her index finger. She coughed, deep and wracking, then cleared her throat.

"Our own plague wasn't enough; now there's a network virus, equally virulent. Seven thousand thirty-seven clients lost because of system failures, but nothing since we cut the trunk line to the outside world, two days ago. I've tried to moat the remaining systems as best as I could, but all technicians have succumbed to the contagion. In the chambers still containing active stasis cells, I've isolated the controlling AIs by physically cutting all cables except for the power lines. But if the virus has already infected the network supervisor, it may be too late."

Her voice cracked. She paused, swallowing rapidly, struggling to catch her breath.

"Intermittent power feed only the last few days as well, and it went out entirely this morning. I've switched all the units over to the backup solar array, powered down all non-essential systems. If my calculations are correct, this should be enough to sustain the remaining cells, barely. There's nothing more I can do. Everyone else is dead, or in cryosuspension. . . . Twenty-seven days. It only took twenty-seven days to infect us all. I thought I might be spared, since I hadn't shown any symptoms. But then, four days ago . . ."

She lifted her hands and stared at them, then turned them outward to face the lens of the recorder. The pads of her fingers were stippled with small red nodules.

"When I saw these, I knew I had it—but in me, the plague's progression has been more rapid than in any other case I've witnessed. I can barely walk now, can't keep anything down. I've blacked out twice already this morning. Time to put myself in suspension. I've instructed the system to lock down as soon as I'm under.

"I've left the general catalogue open for . . . anyone to use. . . ."

She stared past the recorder, looking like she had lost her train of thought. Then her eyes went wide and she vomited, bloody sputum shooting from her mouth to splash over the desk. The muscles in her neck constricted, and she bent to her left, head behind the desk, shoulders heaving. Pus leaked from a blackened sore on the back of her neck.

For a moment the woman remained doubled over, head resting on her arm, her back rising and falling with each breath, shuddering with minor tremors. Then she straightened herself, wiping her chin with the corner of her sleeve. Her cheeks were damp with tears. Her jaw worked, as if she were about to speak, but only a tiny croaking came out.

Static filled the screen.

Liis felt dizzy. Vaguely, she was aware of Sav and Josua, of the unshaded brightness of the lamp clipped to the conduit overhead, of the tiny clicks and hums her suit made in the silence. Someone was talking rapidly, urgently. Josua.

"The catalogue," he said. "Can you access the interment records?"

"Yeah," Sav answered. "I think so."

Bewildered, Liis looked at Josua. "Why—" she began, then stopped abruptly. She stared at Josua, afraid she understood.

"Last name Tira, first name Shiranda," Josua said loudly. "Find her."

A woman's name.

Sav looked at Josua for a moment. "Are you sure—"

"Find her!"

Sav turned back to the port.

That's who he's been looking for.

Sav murmured first one command, then another.

There's someone he loves here, Liis thought. *Someone who was waiting in stasis for him to return.* Her stomach churned.

"Got it. Sublevel fourteen. Station 39. Aisle 30. Cradle 3."

Josua looked at Sav blankly.

"Three levels below. Fourth door on the right after the elevators."

"Is she . . ."

Liis caught her breath, picturing the woman's cell dark, lifeless, immediately regretting the thought. Then imagining it again.

"Can't tell," Sav said. "All the arrays are running on their own AIs now, with no central control. The only thing that's going into each room is the power feed. Nothing's coming out. Can't even tell if the AI is up."

Josua spun on his heel and jogged down the tunnel, almost tripping over the skid they had moved. He disappeared around the corner.

For a moment, the other three stood there. Then Liis pushed herself to her feet, and followed.

"Liis! Wait!"

She ignored Sav. Brushing past Hebuiza, she moved down the corridor to the dropshaft and swung onto the ladder; she clambered down. Three levels. She descended and swept her lamp down the corridor. A set of footprints in the dust lead to an open door.

The chamber was just like all the others: only a few stasis cells had the faint glow that betrayed the presence of life. Josua's comm link was open and Liis could hear him counting the aisles aloud as he went, pace quickening, his voice rising the further he went. At row twenty-six, Josua stopped. The remaining aisles were completely dark.

"Josua . . ."

He staggered up four more rows, turned into the aisle and walked up a few steps. The light from his helmet illuminated the grimy exterior of the stasis cell in the third position. It threw into silhouette a skeletal profile.

"Come on, Josua. Let's get out of here."

Josua turned and was caught in Liis's helmet light. He blinked. "No." He looked oddly detached, but his voice was steady. Calm.

"We should go back to the others. There's nothing we can do here."

Josua cut his comm link, then turned his back on her and walked over to the far wall. He stopped in front of the AI panel. Like all the others, the screen was dark, the indicators dead.

"YOU!" he shouted through his externals, slamming his fist against the screen. "WAKE UP!"

The panel flashed to life, a large question mark in its centre, the small number 39 beneath.

"Yes?" The voice crackled cheerfully through Liis's helmet, piped in from her pickups. "Is there something I can do for you?"

"Well . . . well I'll be damned," Sav's words sounded through Liis's headset. He stepped up beside her, huffing between words, out of breath. "No wonder I couldn't find any jacks. They're voice activated."

"There *is* something you can do for me," Josua said, addressing the AI. "Tell me why you killed her."

Liis took a step toward him but Sav grabbed her by the elbow and held her firmly.

"I'm sorry," the AI answered Josua, its tone the epitome of reasonableness. "But I don't understand the question. I require additional information."

"Aisle 20. Cradle 3. Tira, Shiranda. Did you kill her?"

"The cryosuspension environment in Aisle 20, Row 3 was discontinued, if that is your question."

"Why?"

"That unit, along with several others, was selected because of power losses from the central grid. A load reduction was required. Or all the units would have deteriorated and been lost."

"Why *select* her?" Josua gestured to the remaining lights in the array. "Why not one of others?"

"Terminations were assigned using a pseudo-random lottery. If you are displeased by my choice then I am certain the co-ordinator of the facility would be happy to speak to you. Also, it may comfort you to know that I anticipate an increase in power levels shortly, and full service may soon be restored."

"Full service?" Josua laughed, a cold, bitter thing. "You goddamn fucking machine."

"I'm not a machine. I'm a registered, semi-autonomous artificial intelligence node." The characters SAIN-14-39 appeared on the screen.

"Machine, do you feel pain?" Josua asked.

"No. And I told you, I'm not a machine. I'm a registered SAIN."

"Too bad," Josua said sadly. Raising his arm, he pointed the laser toward the heart of the panel. Liis watched as he pushed the slider to maximum power.

"If you require further assistance—"

Josua jerked the trigger. A thread of light split the darkness; the screen shattered, exploding outwards. Josua was spun around and went down on one knee. The chest of his suit had been lacerated by shards from the screen, the white material criss-crossed by thin dark lines that looked liked claw marks. Behind him a thick column of smoke poured from the panel and dragged along the ceiling; small, bright fires flickered back there, throwing the room into a confusion of darting shadows.

Liis froze, watched in horror as Josua somehow regained his feet; he stumbled back to the stasis cell. He stood there, swaying, his head hung.

Liis jerked herself free from Sav's grip and took a step toward him.

"Josua?"

He looked up. His eyes were wild; they glimmered in the light from her lamp. Liis could now see that his visor had been breached: a large triangular-shaped piece of material was missing, and blood glittered redly on his cheek.

"Please." She extended her hands. Before she knew what she was saying, the words tumbled out of her mouth: "I love you."

Josua lowered his head again. Liis's externals picked up a low, feral moan. Then he raised the cutting laser, placing its snout against the side of his helmet. His finger rested on the trigger.

"*No!*" Liis screamed, but her shout was choked off as she was struck in the small of the back and knocked to the side. Sav flew by, firing his laser. A ruby thread of light cut the gloom and scored the far wall above and behind Josua; then it sliced neatly across the back of Josua's wrist. The material of his gauntlet flared where the coherent light touched.

Josua screeched; his arm flew out, and his laser swung wildly from its black cable. Lurching forward, he collapsed face down onto the dome, his wrist still glittering with a bracelet of orange where Sav's laser had etched a line. His body twitched once, then slid from the crown of the dome to the floor, a smear of blood marking its progress. He lay still.

Liis stared at him, the silence crackling around her like a fire.

Sav hurried over and crouched next to Josua. Gently, he levered the other man's shoulder up and rolled him onto his back. His lamp lit Josua's face; it was flushed, and a sheen of perspiration coated his forehead.

"He's alive," Sav said, looking up. The fingers of his gloves already had bright red stains on them where he had touched Josua.

Liis nodded numbly, but didn't move.

Sav broke the seal at the base of Josua's helmet and slipped it off. The left half of Josua's face was white. On his right cheek the flesh was puckered around a bloody, finger-length gash. From the wound a narrow fragment of the screen protruded. Blood had flowed down his cheek and onto his throat, and from there disappeared into the collar of the suit.

Sav edged around to Josua's side and drew a small knife from a pocket on his thigh. He began sawing away at the material of Josua's suit where it was criss-crossed with cuts, exposing his bloodied chest. When he finished, he dropped the knife on the floor and detached a sample sack from his waist. He bunched it up and dabbed away the blood on Josua's chest, revealing a pattern of thin, parallel, razor-like cuts that welled with blood the moment he stopped staunching them. The flow was small and slow.

Sav looked at her. "Come here."

Liis walked, stiff-legged, to where Josua lay.

"Support his neck."

She knelt down, took Josua's head in her lap. *He's alive*, she thought, watching the almost imperceptible motion of his chest, rising and falling. Just under his rib cage, tiny bubbles rose on a patch of blood, then popped.

"I don't think it's too bad," Sav said. "Doesn't look like any major arteries were severed. This," he said, placing his finger over the ragged gash where Liis had noticed the small bubbles forming, "is the only one I'm worried about." The blood here flowed more freely and was bright red. Sav folded the sample bag into a small square and placed it over the wound. Grasping Liis's right wrist, he put her hand on the bag. "Just keep a steady pressure. You remember the drill, don't you?"

Liis nodded numbly; she pressed down on the makeshift compress.

Sav jerked the cable for the laser from Josua's wrist jack and threw the tool to the side. It clattered in the darkness. Picking up Josua's limp arm, Sav tore the seals off his gauntlet. Liis could see the small wires blackened and severed, trailing out of the line Sav's laser had incised. He had cut its power and control circuitry cleanly, preventing Josua from using it on himself. Sav slipped the glove off; the skin on the back of Josua's wrist was burnt in a straight line that looked like it had been painted on.

"Lucky," Sav said, examining his hand. "I guessed at a setting. Could have done a lot more damage—or not enough." Placing Josua's hand on the floor, he rolled back on his haunches. "He's a fool," he said, shaking his head awkwardly in his helmet.

Beneath her fingers, Liis felt Josua labouring to draw in a breath. A tiny cloud of vapour formed in the chilled air above his lips with each exhalation. Small drops of blood clung to the hair of his chest like perverse, glittering beads. She looked up and saw that Sav was studying her.

"I'm going back to the dropship for the medical kit," he said. He stood and looked around. "Hebuiza didn't follow us. Can't say that I'm surprised." The disgust was plain in his voice. "Just keep a firm pressure on the wound while I'm gone."

Liis nodded.

Sav turned and lumbered toward the door. Liis dropped her head so her light lay across Josua's chest. Lifting a corner of the compress, she looked at the wound; it seemed small, insignificant, a thin red line where the flesh puckered slightly. But when Josua inhaled, it gaped open like a tiny mouth and bright, frothy lines of blood coursed over its edges. She put the compress back down.

Why, Josua? she thought. But she knew the answer.

"We can't wait any longer!" Liis picked her way through the debris of the corridor, pacing back and forth in the narrow space, stepping carefully around Josua.

"We have to wait for Hebuiza," Sav said flatly.

They'd brought Josua out here into the hallway and bundled him in a silvered, thermal blanket. Liis had put two sloppy stitches in the wound on his chest, and wrapped the other cuts with gauze. On his right cheek was another ragged line of fresh stitches from where they'd extracted a thumb-sized fragment of glass. Now Sav sat on an overturned crate at Josua's feet, shoulders slumped.

Liis resumed her pacing.

She checked the suit's display, did a mental calculation. Almost two and a half hours. The Facilitator had not followed them down to this floor; and he hadn't been at the interface when Sav had gone back. If he was in range, he'd shut off his transceiver.

"We need to get Josua back to the ship," Liis said.

Sav remained silent.

Liis's frustration reached boiling point. *What the hell was wrong with Sav?* Hebuiza had abandoned them. Yet Sav only sat there staring at the floor. Liis whirled away, cursed Sav, then Hebuiza, kicked savagely at a broken crate.

"He'll be back," Sav said wearily. "He's got nowhere else to go."

"We've got to get Josua back to the ship," Liis repeated, stepping up to him.

Sav looked at Josua, then at the dropshaft, but said nothing.

"We don't need *Hebuiza*. We can do it ourselves. It'll be tough, but we can manage."

A blank stare.

"Sav—" she began, stopping at the click of a bootsole on the metal rungs of the ladder. She spun around as the Facilitator's lanky black form clambered down into view. He swung himself off the ladder and into the corridor in an abrupt, off-balance motion. He enabled his comm link.

Liis stepped in front of him. "Where the hell have you been?"

Hebuiza blinked inside his oddly shaped helmet, eyes small and dark. The angles of his face were exaggerated in the shadows thrown by Liis's light, making him look even more skeletal. "Downloading data," he said.

"Sav already downloaded the only available log."

"Yes," Hebuiza said. "At that interface. However, I found another. And I have means of extracting information unavailable to you."

Sav straightened up. "What do you mean?"

Hebuiza touched the box on his chest with the tips of his fingers. "I am a Facilitator."

"I don't care what you are," Liis said sharply. "You should have told us where you were going!"

Hebuiza's face coloured. "I do not answer to you," he said, his head beginning to swing from side to side in short, abrupt, motions. He tried to step past her.

Liis grabbed his arm. "Just what the hell do you mean by that?"

With surprising strength, Hebuiza pulled free and shoved her so that she staggered backwards against the wall. Regaining her balance, Liis took a step toward him, but Sav was suddenly there, between them. "Stop it," he said, placing his hand on her chest lightly, but firmly. "None of this is helping Josua."

For the first time Hebuiza glanced past her at Josua. He didn't look in the least surprised to see him lying there, out of his EVA suit, the awkward stitching running across his cheek. But then, Liis thought, he'd probably listened to everything over his suit radio.

Sav turned to him. "Liis is right. And I'm the ranking officer, so you *do* answer to me."

Hebuiza eyes glittered in Sav's light. "We are no longer on *Ea*. That is as far as your authority extends over me. And down here, Josua is in charge. Given that he is incapacitated, the role naturally falls to me...."

"Maybe," Sav said. "But we won't be down here forever, will we? Unless, of course, you choose not to go back to *Ea*."

The Facilitator's thin lips twitched. "I see your point," he said dryly. "In future, I shall consult with my esteemed *commander* before taking any initiative."

Sav nodded, ignoring Hebuiza's sarcasm. "You said you downloaded new information—about the plague?"

"Yes." The Facilitator seemed to be appraising Josua. "Did he breach any of the cells?"

"No," Sav said. "Now..."

The Facilitator's eyes flickered and he stared off into the middle distance, accessing data. "The plague begins with a light fever. After a brief remission, a more debilitating fever occurs some forty-eight hours later, as the virus spreads to the liver and spleen, enlarging them and accelerating the filtering and phagocytic activities into a hyperactive state. Red blood cells are destroyed indiscriminately. Jaundice appears. Then the victim experiences intense abdominal pain, nausea, diarrhoea and vomiting. Within twenty hours, lesions form on the skin, and abscesses develop inside the lungs, kidney, heart and brain. Lassitude, confusion and prostration result. Within forty hours, irreversible cerebral and renal damage, then multi-organ failure. Death follows quickly from toxic shock, hypovolemia—or any one of dozens of other complications."

Silence.

"No survivors," Hebuiza added flatly, his eyes focused on Josua again. "The morbidity and mortality rates appear to be one hundred percent."

"Appear to be?" Sav's voice sounded unnaturally calm.

"There was severe system degradation," Hebuiza answered. "I found only sketchy information directly related to the plague. News reports, a few medical bulletins." Once again he looked past them at something only he could see, head bobbing slightly. "The epidemiology was highly unusual." He spoke in a distant voice, pausing between phrases, as if he were merely repeating words he heard in his head. "The disease didn't follow the usual patterns, appearing in geographically disparate regions—including the colonies and off-world research facilities—at roughly the same time, perhaps from a single source in each." His eyes snapped back into focus.

Sav frowned. "Then it is *not* natural?"

"Yes and no; the method of delivery seems deliberate, certainly. But once the plague manifested, it became an aggressively infectious disease."

Liis was aware of her heartbeat, of her breath. She asked, "Who would do such a thing?"

"Nexus could easily engineer such a plague."

"Why?" Sav sounded incredulous. "Why would they want to destroy Bh'Haret?"

"Perhaps because of our reluctance to join their Ascension Program."

"It's insane. Why destroy a world that you want to bring into your organization?"

Hebuiza raised the shoulders of his suit in a shrug that conveyed the pointlessness of the question. "All I said was that they had the technical expertise to engineer such a plague. I did not say that they did. As to their motives—"

"Are we safe?"

Sav's question caught Liis off guard.

Hebuiza blinked. "Impossible to say." As he spoke, he moved closer to Josua, stopping about a metre from him. "But I do know we need to go to a major centre, as *I* suggested earlier." He glanced at Liis. "The local net—or what's left of it—is as good as dead. It is routing power to the stasis cells on a priority basis; that's part of the microcode, so we have no chance of reprogramming it. Which means we cannot power up anything without first repairing the array, which would take months." Hebuiza flicked on a hand-held light, shone it fully on Josua's waxen face; he swung it down to where Josua's left arm lay across his chest, a vital-signs monitor strapped to his wrist, a steady stream of figures scrolling across its miniature screen.

"The individual nodes are mostly disabled or dysfunctional," Hebuiza continued. "From what I could gather, there were accusations and counter-accusations between the city-states after the advent of the disease. Some skirmishes broke out. Bombs were dropped, and computer viruses released. The continental net crashed just before most of the major power grids. A computer virus infected this facility around that time, taking out about half the AIs before they managed to contain it. The damage would have been less severe, but by the time they realized their systems had been infected, the technicians were too ill to take remedial action." He snapped off his light, and straightened up.

"How many of the cells are still active?" Sav asked.

"Impossible to say," Hebuiza answered. "A few hundred, based on power consumption of the nodes in each chamber. The Director did precisely what she said: she cut the lines, to stem the virus's spread. No data has passed between the AIs in each chamber and the central hub since then, so there is no way of telling how many cells are active without walking into each room and counting." Hebuiza nodded at Josua. "Has he had any seizures?"

"No."

"Have you observed any splinter haemorrhages under his fingernails, or red nodes on the pads of his fingers?"

"Liis?"

"We can discuss his condition later," Liis said. "Let's just worry about getting him back to the ship, where we can treat him properly."

"The ship? Impossible. He has been exposed to the plague."

Liis curled her hands into fists. "We don't know that," she said, her arms trembling.

Hebuiza stepped toward her. "We know nothing about the plague's vectors or its incubation period, and very little about its symptoms. Nor do we have any equipment here to do a blood workup or any other meaningful tests."

"He's in shock," Liis repeated. "He doesn't have the plague."

"I didn't say he did," Hebuiza replied coolly. "Only that he may have suffered exposure—and if he *has*, then by taking him back to the ship we risk exposing ourselves."

"But there is *no* plague anymore!" Liis shouted. "It died twenty-nine years ago, with its last carrier!"

"It's not quite so simple." Hebuiza said. "The initial appearance of the disease was never adequately explained; human carriers may not be essential. There could other vectors. Insects, animals or plant life could still be harbouring it. Even inanimate matter constructed of organic material: furniture, paper, clothes. Perhaps it is in these boxes, that container on which Sav was sitting, the dust on everything here. Viruses can remain dormant until an appropriate carrier appears, some for centuries." Hebuiza raised his hands, held them before her face. "Death might be no further away than the width of the material in our suits. *Did* you observe any red nodes?"

"No!"

"Why is that important?" Sav asked.

"It was a common symptom."

Relief flooded Liis. "Then he *hasn't* got the plague!"

Hebuiza shook his head. "I said common, not universal. This symptom was not recorded in every case, and often took some time to appear...."

"He needs treatment," Liis said; she struggled to keep the desperation out of her voice. "Help we can only give him on the ship. Or he'll die." She turned, wrapped her arms around herself and walked to the end of the corridor, stared into the darkness. "We can isolate him in *Ea*'s galley," she said. "Seal off that section. Take every precaution possible."

"No," Hebuiza answered. "It would be a foolish risk. Don't you think the people here were careful? And where did it get them?"

"You're afraid," Liis said, angrily.

Hebuiza's face coloured; his head began its agitated movement again, one eye regarding Liis, then the other. "Yes," he answered, "As any reasonable person should be." Turning, he stared at Josua. "It might have been better had he died. For him—and for us."

Outraged, she looked at Sav. "What about *you*?"

"Hebuiza's right," Sav answered. "We can't risk exposing ourselves."

Liis couldn't believe what she was hearing. "We can't leave him here," she said, fighting back a rising panic.

Sav reached out, placed a hand on her shoulder; Liis shrugged it off. "Even if we wanted to take him back, Liis, there's no way the three of us could get him up the dropshaft. Not in these suits."

"You want him to die too!"

"No one said anything about letting him die," Sav said quietly. "We can find a place where he'll be comfortable, until we decide what to do."

"Down here?" Liis was flabbergasted.

"I'm sorry, Liis. But as I see it, we don't really have a choice."

Liis felt nauseous. She wanted to scream at Sav, to shout some sense into him, but bit back the impulse. If she alienated him now, Josua's chances would diminish even further.

"Our oxygen's running low," Sav said. "We need to go back for fresh cartridges. Maybe we can find some other things to set up a room for him with. After that, there're dozens of small towns along the coast, and Temperas is only a few hundred klicks south. It's bound to have a hospital."

A hospital. Liis felt a rush of hope. Then something else occurred to her. "There must be an infirmary here. These places always have one. If we can find it, maybe we—"

"No," Hebuiza said. "I downloaded a complex schematic. The infirmary is on the bottommost level; I thought it might have more detailed data on the plague, but it is in complete disarray. Every cupboard has been ransacked, most of the equipment smashed." He looked directly at Liis. "There are many skeletons down there, too, clothed in disintegrating lab coats or workers' coveralls. And two more mummified corpses sealed inside SPG suits—for all the good it did them."

"We'll find a room on this level," Sav said firmly. He looked at Hebuiza. "Is there someplace nearby?"

Hebuiza's eyes flickered and his head bobbed. "Yes," he said. "Down the corridor, a hundred and twenty metres. A storage room. Small, but adequate."

"Then let's get him there," Sav said, moving closer to Josua. Squatting down, he gathered up the corners of the thermal blanket and looked at Liis.

At that moment Liis hated Sav more than she had ever hated anyone; but in a part of her mind she also understood she'd run out of options. She gathered up the other end.

Hebuiza stood perfectly still. "What if Josua begins to display symptoms? If we discover he is infected, I will have nothing further to do with him."

"That's your prerogative," Sav said, before Liis could answer. "But until then, we could use your help getting him down the corridor."

Hebuiza looked at Sav, then at Liis. "I will help you," he said, his voice low and his lips curling in distaste. "For now." And with that he stepped up to Josua and took the blanket's edge between thumb and fingers, as if he could see the virus crawling relentlessly across its silvered surface toward him.

Liis had volunteered to remain with Josua while Sav and Hebuiza returned to *Ea*. The round trip took six hours, which she'd spent next to Josua, her helmet light fixed steadily on his pale, uninhabited face.

They'd returned only briefly; after Sav had taken a quick look at Josua, he'd decided to follow the Lyst six hundred klicks to the southwest. There, at the mouth of the river, the regional capital Temperas perched on an alluvial plain—their best bet to find medical supplies. They gave Liis a thin foam pallet they'd ripped out of a stasis cell, on which Josua could lie; another blanket; an emergency lantern that glowed with the dull orange of fading batteries; an old medical kit they'd found at the bottom of a storage locker; and a container of water, should he wake. Moments later, they were gone.

Alone again, Liis sat on a crate next to Josua and opened the kit. Inside were rolls of yellowed gauze, bandages of various size and two antimicrobial patches. The first patch had dried out. The second was similarly useless. In disgust, she threw them both away and slammed the lid shut. Beside her, Josua stirred uneasily at the noise.

Do something, she told herself. *Don't just sit here brooding.*

Rising, she began running her helmet light over the shelves that lined the concrete walls. One by one she opened all the boxes and sorted through their contents, but she found nothing useful. She moved back to the stasis chamber, peering into what had been Shiranda's cell. Inside was an unrecognizable, desiccated corpse, no different than any of the thousands of others interred there. It was then Liis realized how badly she'd wanted to see this woman's face, to have a genuine rival toward whom she could direct her anger and jealousy. But the corpse's anonymity thwarted even this perverse satisfaction.

Returning to the storage room, she switched off her helmet lamp to save its battery. Sometime later the emergency lantern shut down.

In the pitch black, the storage room didn't seem as small. Liis found the dark strangely comforting. Propping her back against the wall, she pulled the bulky knees of her suit as close as possible to her chest. The toes of her boots touched the base of Josua's cot. Every now and then she'd feel him stir restlessly and flick on her helmet light, scrutinizing him for any signs of change.

After a time, she decided not to turn on her lamp again.

PLANETSIDE · DAY 1

The craft juddered through the atmosphere, engines a constant hum through the floorplates. It was dawn—an entire day had passed since they'd first set foot on Bh'Haret—and dark, tangled forest smothered the undulating hills. To Sav's left, Hebuiza sat in silence, his visor opaqued.

Since they'd left Liis at the stasis facility, Sav had observed few signs of civilization: collapsed buildings, flooded pit mines and cracked, overgrown roads.

The ground continued to slip beneath the dropship with a mind-numbing sameness, as the sun crept above the horizon. Sav felt lightheaded; his vision clouded over, and the outside world became an indistinguishable green and black blur. *How many hours since I've slept?* He couldn't remember.

Why don't I feel more? he wondered. Where was the fear, the grief, the outrage he was supposed to feel? His world was dead.

No, not my *world.*

Long ago he'd severed his ties with Bh'Haret: it had become a place of hurrying strangers, no more recognizable than any of the other worlds he travelled to. Josua could still call it home; maybe even Hebuiza. *But not me*, Sav thought. *I've been away too long.*

"There."

Hebuiza's voice startled Sav. "What?"

The Facilitator lifted a hand, pointed south. "Look."

Sav stared out the windscreen. Long shadows of the new day obscured the landscape, pooling in valleys between the rolling hills, creating an illusion of a landscape dotted with bottomless pits.

"Just before the horizon."

Was that large shadow what Hebuiza meant? Banking the dropship sharply in its direction, Sav began a steep climb. The terrain seemed to flatten out, growing pools of darkness merging where the valleys met, obliterating any discernible features. The shadow grew as well, making Sav suddenly aware that it must be at least a dozen kilometres in length—

He remembered the dark smears they'd seen from orbit, and shivered.

The shadow continued to grow, strangely bereft of features; it lay across the landscape, an expansive black mantle covering Earth in a circular shape. Nothing grew here. A bright chime sounded in Sav's earpiece; on the dropship windscreen the yellow skull of a low-level radiation warning appeared.

A blast site.

Why? Sav thought. *Out here, hundreds of klicks from anything. It makes no sense.*

Sav swung the dropship away, nudging it back to its former course. He glanced at Hebuiza, but the Facilitator's mask was opaque again. In one corner of his own visor, Sav's status display reported that Hebuiza had switched off his comm circuit.

We'll never really know what happened, Sav thought. *There's no one left to tell.*

At last, in the distance, the city of Temperas loomed. From this perspective, it appeared almost normal.

Within moments, they crossed the outskirts. The city passed beneath, a colourless, low-slung clutter of squat grey buildings crowded onto the alluvial plain. Its twisting thoroughfares were mostly empty, a few dark vehicles neatly parked along their length. Occasionally, Sav would spot a car or truck abandoned in the centre of a wider avenue. In the shipyards to the south a dozen supertankers sat patiently in their slips, looking as if they were ready to sail.

It wasn't until they were over the city proper that Sav began to see what sort of panic must have followed the disease: in some areas the buildings had been reduced to burned-out shells, many of the taller structures now dark grey skeletons. Occasionally, they passed over scorched craters left by explosions, in which nothing stood. When Sav dropped the ship down to a lower altitude, he could see a creeping decay was well underway.

Thirty years.

Sadness constricted his chest; not for the dead of Bh'Haret, whom he regarded as strangers, but for himself. He felt cheated. With the money and stasis bonuses he earned as a longhauler, he'd planned on returning as a rich man to build the life he'd always wanted.

Now, Sav felt as empty as the city below.

"The hospital." Hebuiza announced, with no enthusiasm.

"I see it."

A few kilometres distant, near the mouth of the southern branch of the river that trisected the city, was a complex of interconnected buildings, the largest constructed in a style popular nearly a century earlier. A broad drive swept up to it, packed with haphazardly parked vehicles, several spilling off onto what must have once been a front lawn. Sav spotted the black square of a landing pad on the roof of the tallest building. He swung the dropship toward it.

They passed directly over the front entrance. Sav could now understand why the vehicles had been so scattered; some were blackened shells, others just badly damaged. The hospital doors had been barricaded. On the rubble and nearby walls were the unmistakable scars of laser blasts, detritus from an intense firefight.

Sav dropped the ship gently down, and killed the engines.

Hebuiza turned; he'd cleared his visor so that Sav could see his face, lips pursed disapprovingly. "As ever, this is a waste of time," he said.

"Josua needs our help."

"You should be concerned with *our* survival, not Josua's."

Ignoring him, Sav climbed out of his seat and moved to the back of the dropship. From a small locker next to the hatch, he pulled out a rolled sample bag and stuffed it into a pocket. He unsealed the door and dropped to the gravel roof of the building. To the right of the pad was a small brick structure with sliding glass doors that were half-ajar; behind this, Sav could see an elevator and another door that probably led to a stairwell.

"Our time could be spent far more productively." Hebuiza's voice sounded smaller; he was still in the ship, the hull plates interfering with his signal.

"No," Sav answered, simply. Without turning around, he began walking toward the entrance. Gravel crunched underneath his boots. He reached the glass doors, but the opening was too narrow for him to squeeze through in his bulky suit. So he jammed a shoulder inside the opening, and tried pushing them apart.

"You saw the mess out front. It will be the same inside."

The doors didn't budge. *I guess it's the laser again*, Sav thought.

"I will not be coming with you."

The high-pitched whine of the dropship's engines filled Sav's helmet; a gust of air buffeted him. He turned his head. The dropship's hatch was sealed. The engines roared and exhaust blew up a small storm of dust, scattering gravel to the side of the pad.

"Stop!" Sav shouted, wiggling free of the doors. Under his feet, the roof vibrated. He tried to move toward the ship, but the thrust pushed him back against the glass doors, pinning him. Small stones rattled around him, ricocheting off him and the door. The dropship lifted from the pad. It rose half a dozen metres in an unsteady wobble, then regained its equilibrium.

"I will be back in three hours," Hebuiza said, over the engines' howl. "Plenty of time for you to find out I'm right."

"Don't be a fool! You don't know how to pilot that thing!"

"I'm a quick study."

"Come back! I'll take you wherever you want go!"

"Three hours."

The Facilitator broke the comm circuit; the dropship rotated until it faced north. It moved away, accelerating as it went, and dwindled rapidly. Sav stumbled to the edge of the roof. He signalled frantically, cursing and shouting, but Hebuiza didn't respond.

When the dropship was a speck near the city limits, it began its descent into the jumble of buildings. Before Sav could mark its position with any certainty, it was gone.

Sav stood with his hands locked into fists. His arms shook.
Calm down, he told himself. *This is no time to lose it.*
Breathing deeply, he uncurled his fingers. *Three hours. He wouldn't have said that if he didn't intend to return. Right?* Nevertheless, he wasn't entirely convinced.

Turning, he walked back to the glass doors.

Without lasers, he'd have to resort to brute strength. Standing next to the left panel, he gripped its edge with both hands; he placed his foot against the edge of the right panel. He tugged, trying to widen the narrow gap, but the door remained immobile. Sucking in a big breath, he pulled again, holding the pressure steady until blood sang in his ears and the muscles in his shoulders trembled. Metal squealed on metal, until finally the narrow opening widened. Not quite enough to squeeze through. Gripping the edge, he pulled again. This time, after an initial hesitation, the doors slid apart readily and he almost lost his balance.

He slipped between the panels and into the building.

The display over the elevator was dark; the doors had been welded shut. He pushed against the adjacent door, which gave with a small click, sighing open to reveal a stairwell. Sav flicked on his helmet light and bent over the edge of the railing. He couldn't see the bottom. Pushing away, he started down, boots kicking up small clouds of dust.

The stairs switched back twice before he came to the first landing. Unlabelled barrels and crates had been stacked haphazardly next to a metal door. The words *Physical Plant* were stencilled on the door in white letters. Sav tried the handle, but it was locked.

The next landing was clear, a pastel green door at its head. Black numbers indicated the 23rd floor. A line of weak, grey light spilled out from under the bottom. Sav gripped the handle and turned; the door creaked open.

He stood in a corridor that ran the length of the building, with dozens of gurneys lining both walls. Across from him, a nurses' station; to his left, the dead elevator, door also welded shut.

Sav stepped up to the closest gurney.

A stained sheet covered a skeleton. The skull, jaw agape, was visible above the sheet's frayed yellow edge. Beside the gurney, an IV-drip had been set up; a thin, clouded tube hung from an empty bag, and disappeared under the sheet. Sav pulled on it and the material disintegrated, collapsing around the skeleton.

Underneath, the tube ran across the skeleton's femur and into its pelvis; the cannula lay cradled in the white bones there, resting on the end of the spine. Sav pulled out his sample bag and laid it on the gurney. Carefully, he drew out the tube, coiled it. Then he unclipped the plasma bag from its drip rack, and put them both in his sack.

Sav stared dejectedly at the few items he'd collected: two drip bags and tubing; four catheters; two syringes, still in their wrappers; a roll of adhesive tape; one tube of antiseptic cream (probably long expired). The dispensaries had yielded little of value, thirty-year-old capsules skittering across the floor in front of his boots as Sav moved from one empty cabinet to another. Over his shoulder he'd slung the carrying strap for a small, grey case containing an old blood pressure gauge and a stethoscope. He had found other, larger pieces of equipment, including a wall mounted display panel whose purpose he couldn't discern. But they were all dead.

The hospital's topmost floor was in the best shape, with each floor below becoming progressively worse. Four floors down, bones littered the hallways, skidding through the dust in front of Sav's boots. On the fifteenth floor, where Sav now stood, there were no gurneys at all—just a carpet of dirty hospital gowns and brittle bones which crunched sadly as he waded through the mess.

Despite his doubts, Sav methodically checked all the rooms, adding nothing to his meagre collection.

On the eleventh floor landing, placed along a barricade facing outward, were a dozen blackened and shattered skulls.

Hebuiza was right, Sav thought.

He began the long climb back to the roof.

The sun was directly overhead, the sky cloudless. Sav adjusted the polarization on his visor; the world receded, becoming flat and washed out. At his feet, the tiny pile of equipment he'd scavenged seemed even smaller.

He scanned the horizon. His suit display showed that three and a half hours had passed since Hebuiza had abandoned him; it also showed that his oxygen cartridge was running low. The only spares were in the dropship. He stepped back into a sliver of shade beside the glass doors to wait.

Staring at the city's grey expanse, Sav's senses dulled, fatigue settled on him like a thick, suffocating blanket. Nearly two days since he'd slept. And he'd been in this suit for sixteen out of the last seventeen hours, the only break a brief stint on *Ea* when he and Hebuiza had returned to collect supplies. Every time he turned his head he felt the stubble on his chin rub annoyingly against his helmet's base; every breath he drew smelled of sweat. For what seemed the hundredth time that day, he had to fight the urge to tear off his helmet and breathe fresh air. Only remembering the skeletons below kept him from doing so.

Sav let himself slide down along the wall until he was sitting, and closed his eyes.

Something jabbed him in the back; Sav felt himself being rolled over, and swallowed a rush of panic. The sun burned directly into his face, blinding him, until a dark figure occluded it.

"Get up!"

Sav recognized Hebuiza's deep voice, his oval helmet. He struggled to sit up. A dozen metres away, the dropship rested in the centre of the landing pad. Through its open door Sav could see crates now crowded its interior.

Hebuiza nudged him with his foot. "Are you ill?"

"No," Sav said, his voice rough, astonished that he could have slept through the noisy return of the dropship. "I . . . I fell asleep. That's all."

Hebuiza looked at him, eyes narrowed, head moving in small arcs, and Sav suddenly realized the Facilitator was measuring his response, searching for any signs of disorientation, fever—or other symptoms.

"Fuck you," Sav said, struggling to his feet, too tired to rekindle his initial rage. "Where the hell were you?"

"Making the best of our time here, collecting things we might find useful. Certainly more useful than what you have there." Hebuiza nodded at the pathetic pile of junk stacked by the hospital doors.

Sav didn't argue. "Then let's get the hell out of here," he said.

"First, we need to inspect your suit," Hebuiza said. "After all, you have been rolling around on the ground."

The anger that had eluded Sav a moment before now burned fiercely in his chest; he ached to launch himself at Hebuiza, smash his mask and let the air the Facilitator so dreaded rush in to choke him. Instead, he willed it away. The effort left him feeling weak and dizzy.

"Yeah." His voice rasped. "You're right." Stretching out his arm, he began the routine they'd been taught so long ago, checking the material of his suit for abrasions and tears.

Sav had feared Hebuiza might challenge him for control of the dropship, but the Facilitator had obligingly left the pilot's seat empty. He took the controls.

The city receded quickly and brisk tail wind hurried them along. Still, it was late afternoon when they finally approached the stasis facility.

After landing, Sav slung the bag that held his scavenged equipment over his shoulder and hurried down the overgrown path to the main entrance, only pausing to look back when he reached the front door. Through the hatch, he saw the Facilitator crouched in front of one of the ship's tiny storage lockers with four thin grey cases at his feet. As Sav watched, the Hebuiza pulled a fist-sized object from the locker, and added it to the pile.

Sav frowned, realizing he'd been so lost in his own thoughts that he hadn't even asked Hebuiza what he'd found.

To hell with it. Ordering his helmet light on, he shoved his bag through the opening they'd cut and crawled after it.

In the sick room, Josua still lay on his makeshift cot, wrapped loosely in the emergency blankets. In the bright pool of light from Sav's headlamp, his skin seemed less pale, chest rising and falling at regular intervals. Then his eyes opened. He blinked furiously in the light, dark irises shrinking to points, eyes full of a cold, deliberate anger.

Startled, Sav took a step back.

Josua's eyes focused on him, but only briefly. Then his gaze went blank, wandering mindlessly off into the dark corners of the room. He groaned and shut them again, muttering unintelligible words.

"He's awake."

The voice came to Sav as if from a vast distance. He swung his light up, illuminating Liis where she sat on a wide shelf a metre above the floor, long legs drawn up against her chest.

Beside her lay her helmet.

Hebuiza stared at Liis, thin face twitching through a range of emotions: anger, puzzlement, fear? Sav couldn't be sure. Down the hall, the door to Josua's room stood open, though the Facilitator refused to go near it.

"*Ea*," Hebuiza said. "You cannot go back, now that you too carry the danger of infection."

Liis shrugged. "One of us would have had to do it, sooner or later." The scars on her face seemed incredibly vivid now, almost three-dimensional. A translucent food tube dangled over the throat of her suit, a single bead of liquid hanging from its tip. "How else were we going to feed him?"

"We could have brought back food from the ship, Liis," Sav said, tiredly. He leaned against the wall between the two of them.

Liis crossed her arms. "I've only made it easier for everyone," she said, staring at Hebuiza, who looked away. "We haven't enough food and water to last more than a few weeks, even with strict rationing.

Now at least one of us is free from these suits—free to get on with all the other things we need to do."

"She is right," the Facilitator said, surprising Sav. "This increases our chances of survival. A reasonable risk."

Sav swung around and glared at Hebuiza. "Then why don't *you* take off your suit?"

"One is sufficient. Two would be foolish."

Liis laughed, sharp and humourless. "For once, we're in agreement."

"*Dammit!*" Sav shouted. He blew out an exasperated breath. "We've got to get together on this," he said. "Do some serious planning. Or all of us might as well take off our suits right now!"

For a moment there was silence. Then Liis said, softly, "What do you suggest?"

"First, we need to sort some things out." He hesitated. "The command situation, for one."

"Yes." Hebuiza pursed his lips. "As a Facilitator, I am better equipped to deal with situations such as this. It is only natural—"

Sav stepped in front of the Facilitator, cutting him off. "On or off planet, *I* am the senior officer," he said, his own anger surprising him. Although rotund, Sav was also well-muscled. He had no doubt that, if necessary, he could take the taller man.

The Facilitator stared down at him; his eyes flicked over Sav's body, seemingly also considering his chances in a physical confrontation. Then Hebuiza shrugged.

"No more solo excursions," Sav said.

The Facilitator looked at Liis. Sav had no doubt he was weighing his options, trying to decide which way she'd throw her support. But Liis, reading the tension between the two of them, soon quashed any hopes Hebuiza might have had.

"I won't take orders from *you*," she said to him. "So nothing's open for debate."

For a moment, Hebuiza's eyes narrowed. Then he looked at Sav, shrugging again, as if none of this was in the least important to him. "I will request permission for use of *Ea*'s dropship if I have need of it, in the future."

"Fine," Sav said, not really believing him. To Liis: "How's Josua doing?"

"Whenever I've tried to speak to him, he just stares past me. I don't think he hears me."

Earlier, when he'd looked into Josua's eerie, baleful eyes, Sav had thought, *he's insane*. But he decided not to share his belief with Liis, asking instead, "Should we move him?"

She shrugged. "Maybe in a couple of days. He may still be in shock."

"Then, *Captain*," Hebuiza said, placing a sneering emphasis on the title, "what do you suggest we do, in the meantime?"

Sav lowered himself onto an overturned crate. When he'd squared off with Hebuiza he'd felt a brief rush of adrenaline, but now the exhaustion had come back. "Return to *Ea*, and get out of these damn suits," he said. "Rest, before we make any more decisions."

"Agreed," the Facilitator said. He pulled himself into the dropshaft before Liis or Sav could say anything else, and disappeared up the ladder.

"You'd best go after him," Liis said wearily.

"I'll be back as soon as I can."

Liis nodded, her features indecipherable. A mask behind the scars.

With leaden arms, Sav also dragged himself over, and pulled himself onto the first rung.

To Sav's surprise, Hebuiza was already seated in the dropship's pilot's chair, his cables connected to the control ports. Sav wanted to order him out of the seat, but was so exhausted he hadn't the energy for the confrontation. Besides, it made sense to let the Facilitator learn more about handling the ship, especially outside the atmosphere. Sooner or later, Sav might have to send him out on his own, and he'd rather have Hebuiza know what he was doing.

The return to zero-gee wasn't as much of a relief as Sav had anticipated. His suit still seemed to trap him in its suffocating layers. He tried to ignore it, but the closer they got to *Ea*, the more impatient he became to free himself of its confinement, imagining a multitude of itches impossible to scratch.

After a quick protocol rundown, the Facilitator brought the dropship smartly into the hangar as if he'd been practising the manoeuvre for weeks. His deep-set eyes seemed to glitter, and the corners of his thin lips were turned upwards in a smug, triumphant smile. Without sealing the outer bay doors, he punched in the sequence to open the dropship hatch. It was crude, but the best decontamination procedure they could come up with: let frigid vacuum kill whatever bugs might have taken refuge in the outer folds of their suits. They waited ten minutes, then resealed the door.

Sav keyed in the command to start the compressors; the oxygen/nitrogen mix was pumped back into the hangar. Within thirty seconds the pressure had equalized. Sav fumbled at the seals above his wrists. Before he had both gauntlets off, the Facilitator was already clipping his dark suit inside his locker. Hebuiza pulled off his undersuit, velcroed it in the bottom of the locker, and shut the door. The special lock he'd installed before the mission—and the only lock on *Ea*—snicked into place, its glaring red LEDs spelling out SECURE. Twisting around, the Facilitator opened the inner bulwark door and propelled himself through, the antennae on his skull flowing behind him. He swam up and out of sight. A moment later, Sav heard water running in the tiny shower on the deck above.

His gloves off, Sav unsealed his helmet; *Ea*'s scrubbed atmosphere poured in, replacing the stale air of the suit. When he finally finished stripping, he flushed his suit's recirculation system, then topped his backpack with fresh oxygen/nitrogen cartridges and water. He clipped his suit across the doors for two lockers, stretching it wide so that it would air out.

Slipping on a pair of shorts, he pulled himself along the drag bars and into the corridor. Sav went to his stasis cell, the only space on the ship in which he could have a bit of privacy. On the ceiling was a small keypad; Sav punched a button to seal it. Almost before the translucent door had completed its descent, he was asleep.

DAY 2

Sav groaned quietly, then opened his eyes. A hand-span above him was the silvered roof of his stasis cell. One of his legs had doubled behind him, and it ached severely when he tried to straighten it. Cursing himself for not bothering to strap into his webbing before falling asleep, he keyed in the retraction sequence. The panel slid down, and faint light spilled into his cell.

Placing his hands on the edge of his berth, Sav levered himself around until he could see the rest of the cabin. Across the room, Hebuiza's cell was empty. "How long have I been asleep?" he asked.

"Six hours, thirty-three minutes," *Ea* answered.

It felt more like six seconds. Sav shook his head to clear it.

"Where's Hebuiza?"

"The Facilitator is in the galley. He has been transferring equipment from the dropship."

"What equipment?"

"I'm unfamiliar with it."

Sav gritted his teeth, and launched himself toward the sealed hatch.

He found the Facilitator strapped into one of the galley's metal chairs. Velcroed to the table in front of him was one of the flat, grey cases Sav had seen in the back of the dropship, lid open so that its interior was obscured. Next to it was the black box from Hebuiza's suit; a clutch of thin cables ran between the two boxes and the Facilitator's neck. He glanced up when Sav propelled himself into the room, but did not acknowledge him otherwise. Using the drag bars along the wall, Sav worked his way around until he could see what was in the case. The base of the unit was a featureless square, but on the underside of the lid there were six small screens; on five of them, streams of sharp-edged characters scrolled right to left.

"What is it?"

The Facilitator kept his attention focused on the machine. "It can be used to sequence viruses," he said. "Among other things." Characters appeared on the sixth screen now.

"What's it doing?" Sav asked.

"Self-test. Running diagnostics. Calibrating." Sav watched the endless strings of alien script swim past. "If I can communicate with it, reprogram it, it could be extremely useful. But it has been designed to interact on a molecular level. My interfaces are several orders of magnitude cruder."

"If we find out where it was manufactured, we should be able to construct a step-up—"

"It was not built on Bh'Haret." The Facilitator touched the edge of the grey box, and the characters on the various screens froze. "It was manufactured using nanotechnology. If you had bothered to keep abreast of current research you would know our own nanotech program was only in its infancy when we left Bh'Haret, mostly speculation and very basic theoretical work. There was a great deal of debate about which way to proceed. There wasn't even a satisfactory computer simulation, much less a working prototype."

"Then it's an adopted technology?" Bartering with other planets for adopted technologies was the *raison d'être* for Facilitators. For all Sav knew, the Facilitator had brought it back from their mission from Arcolet.

"Stolen would be more accurate." The characters began to move again. "I believe this unit is class five Nexus technology."

Class five. Even if Bh'Haret had been an affiliate, this little box still would have been nearly two centuries beyond their tier in the Nexus Ascension Program.

"How do you know all this?"

"It is what I do—trade in stolen technologies. What we were all doing, whether you knew it or not."

Sav frowned. "Did Josua know about this?"

"No. He thought we were engaged in the mundane trade mission on which all of you were briefed. But the real commerce has always been in proscribed technologies." Hebuiza slipped a cable from his neck, and let it float free. "Like this." He stroked the side of the box deferentially. "Normally, these sorts of things are disassembled and examined in one of half a dozen labs set up for that purpose. Then the underlying principles are 'discovered,' sometimes over decades—waiting until an appropriate technological base has been established to reproduce the item itself."

"And one of those labs was in Temparas? That's where you went, when you left me at the hospital."

The Facilitator nodded.

Sav swung himself over to the other side of the table, lowered himself into a chair. The grey box sat between them, its screens invisible.

Hebuiza had dropped his gaze to one of the lower screens. "Mere luck, really, that this was not destroyed in the panic," he said. "I found it sitting in plain view, on a workbench, in a low security area of the building. My guess is that when the plague hit, the researchers hoped this might save them. If they'd had more time, perhaps it might have helped."

"Or," Sav said softly, "perhaps . . . it sealed their fate."

The Facilitator lifted his eyes, stared at Sav, his expression blank.

"What if Nexus knew we had their little toy?" Sav continued. "Or others like it? Suppose they found out that we were trying to sidestep their beloved Ascension Program? They collect and disseminate technologies, then dole it out in little bits to the affiliated worlds that toe the line. But if we were stealing it . . ."

"They wouldn't have taken direct action, because the last thing they want to be seen as is bullies. And showing up with fleets of ships to punish worlds that don't fall in line would be a massive drain on their resources. So they do something more subtle." Sav tightened his grip on the edge of his seat, to keep his arms from trembling. "A convenient plague. Who'd be left to figure out where the bug came from? Nexus would deny any involvement, maybe blame it on our own bio labs. But there would always be suspicions, and that's what they'd count on to make other non-affiliates think before they *borrowed* Nexus technology. . . ."

Hebuiza drew another cable from his pocket, let it uncoil in the air in front of him, and slipped it into an opening on his black box. "You speculate," he sniffed.

"What about the screamers?"

"They prove nothing. The first passing Nexus ship would have dropped them, regardless. Or Nexus would have ordered a ship dispatched, once word of the plague reached them. Twenty-nine years puts half a dozen affiliates in range."

"You've destroyed Bh'Haret," Sav said, trying to keep his voice even. "You've killed us."

"*Killed* us?" Hebuiza repeated, his tone incredulous. "I did as I was told." For the first time he caught Sav's eyes, held them. "Just like you."

"But *I* didn't know what we were doing."

"If you *had* known, would you have refused? Given up longhauls for supply runs, or work on ore freighters?"

The question hung in the air between them. *Would I?* Sav wondered. He wasn't certain. And he certainly knew he wouldn't have raised any flags about the practice of stealing technologies. Just turned a blind eye, pretended it didn't exist, as with so many other things.

"You see." Hebuiza smiled coldly. "We're not so different after all."

Sav went limp; his hands slipped from the seat, and he began to drift up. He stared at the innocuous grey box. "I'm going back to the cryo facility," he said, suddenly anxious to get away from *Ea*—and Hebuiza's toys. "I promised Liis we'd return as soon as possible."

"Do as you please," the Facilitator said, his attention back on the screen, head once more bobbing from side to side. As he spoke, a thin tube with a shiny silver tip extruded from the carapace of the machine, bending in its middle so that it looked like the stinger on an insect. Hebuiza held his index finger beneath it, and it darted down; a bright red dot of blood ran up, disappearing inside the machine. The tube turned milky white for an instant, then returned to its original state. On the screens the speed of scrolling data quadrupled.

Hebuiza looked up at Sav. "But before you go, I require a blood sample for comparative analysis." When Sav didn't move, Hebuiza added, "Or perhaps you do not care about our survival?"

What more damage could the Facilitator do, left alone on *Ea*?

Sav asked himself that question over and over, as he put on his suit and boarded the dropship. Now, arcing toward the planet's surface, he ran through the possibilities again, trying to imagine other precautions he should have taken besides overriding the private security keys and replacing them with new ones. Even if the Facilitator could break the codes, *Ea*'s recognition subsystem would not allow anyone but Sav command control. As an extra safeguard, Sav instructed *Ea* to deny Hebuiza physical access to the bridge, limiting him to the crew quarters. Yet, for all that, Sav remained uneasy about leaving the Facilitator aboard. If anything were to happen to *Ea*, what few options they had would dwindle to none.

But Hebuiza was right about one thing. Amongst them, Josua had been the only true innocent. Sav had encountered others like him, one-timers, in it for their careers, for the political capital. Invariably, they had someone waiting for them at the other end of their time. It gave them hope, made them impatient to return home.

For Sav, though—and Liis—home was a longhaul ship.

Images of other ships he'd worked came back to him. Gazing through the windscreen, he could almost see them ahead of him in orbit around Bh'Haret, reflected sunlight beating brightly on their hulls....

Other ships. Sav's heart quickened. *There are still longhaulers out there. Missions like ours, launched before the plague struck.* Why hadn't he thought of it before?

Sav leaned forward, stabbed a button on the navigation panel. A map appeared on the screen, replacing the flight path display. Half a dozen green circles marked ground-based spaceports. Sav overlaid the map on a composite of the images they had collected from orbit. The ground in five of the circles was blackened by the smear of nuclear strikes. Sav reached forward to zoom in on the sixth circle, then paused. In the unlikely event the site was intact, the computers there would have been down since the continental power grid collapsed, their data almost certainly unrecoverable. Any record of the other missions lost. . . .

Then he remembered Shiranda's file; reason for her interment had been recorded, along with Josua's name as designated contact, plus details of his occupation. Those waiting for the return of other longhaulers might also be in the catalogue. Assuming their revival dates matched the return dates of the missions, it should be possible to determine when the next ship was due.

As soon as Sav landed, he made directly for the eleventh sublevel interface and jacked into the data socket.

"Yes?" the AI's voice said.

"Inquiry on revival dates."

"Proceed," the AI said, pleasantly.

"How many clients are scheduled for revival?"

"No scheduled revivals. All revivals have been suspended indefinitely by order of the Director of this facility. Rescheduling will take place as soon as possible."

"Do you have the original revival dates, before the order?"

"Of course."

"How many were *originally* scheduled to be revived in the next five years?"

"Twenty-one."

"List them."

On the superimposed holographic display, two of "panels" detached themselves from the wall, zooming to fill Sav's entire field of view. A matrix of data appeared on the leftmost screen, the first column all dates, followed by stasis cell occupant names. Additional information on client ages and occupations filled the next few columns, followed by dozens of abbreviated status codes which meant nothing to Sav. On the right screen were thumbnails of the clients.

"Get rid of everything except client name and revival date."

The other information vanished.

"Now include anything you've got on emergency contacts."

Next to each client, additional names now appeared, most with an address and occupation attached.

"Select for all clients whose contacts are longhaul officers or envoys, and whose original revival dates fall after today."

Seven names remained.

The third client, a woman scheduled to be revived in seventy days, caught Sav's attention. Her contact, a woman named Vela, was a communications officer aboard a vessel called *Viracosa*—one that Sav had once crewed.

"We're not the only ones," Sav said, barely able to contain his excitement.

From the corner of the room Liis stared at him blankly, only dimly aware of his presence. She looked utterly defeated. Next to her, Josua stared sightlessly at the ceiling. To one side, Liis had set up an intravenous drip, but the bag was empty.

"I checked the log here. There's half a dozen contact names that are longhaulers, like Josua was for Shiranda."

"People with lovers."

"Maybe," Sav said. "In any case, I got a return date for the next longhaul due back, less than seventy days out. A ship called *Viracosa*. Pretty soon we'll have company."

"What's a funeral without mourners?"

"Don't you see!" Sav gripped her shoulder. "Each ship carries a reserve tank. With two ships, we should have enough fuel to get the hell out of here!"

Liis blinked, ran her tongue across her lips distractedly. "And go where?"

"The Ballic system, for one. It's only one point five light years away—not that sophisticated, at least not thirty years ago. Still a good century from industrialization, and well out of the Ascension Program. It's possible they haven't heard about the plague."

"And Josua? Seventy days is a long time off."

Sav nodded. "Exactly. I'm sure he'll be recovered...."

"Or dead."

The finality of her pronouncement shook Sav. "We might *all* be dead by then, Liis. But that's no reason to give up now."

"A few times, I felt him watching me," Liis said. "But when I turned around he was still staring at the ceiling, that empty look on his face." She scrutinized Josua, intensely. "What's he staring at?" she asked, suddenly angry. "Is it her? Is he looking at *her*?" In the light of the lantern, Liis's face was pale beneath her scars, the detail of the pattern all but washed out. "He'll never get better," she said, a sharp ache in her voice. "He doesn't *want* to get better."

"He's had a shock, that's all," Sav said. "He'll rally."

"Unless," Liis said, locking her eyes on Sav's, "he has the plague."

"Plague?" The new voice was a whisper.

Both Sav and Liis turned, simultaneously, to look at Josua. His eyes appeared focused now; they burned intensely with—what? When Sav met his gaze he shuddered, feeling a cold fury emanating from Josua's stare that was as palpable as a touch. Liis sucked in her breath.

"Death," Josua rasped, a string of spittle suspended between cracked lips. Then whatever had animated him fled, and his eyes became flat and unseeing again.

DAYS 3 TO 6

In the first few days, they took care of their immediate needs. On another trip to Temparas, they discovered five cartons of dehydrated food in doubly sealed vacuum packets, enough to last the four of them for half a year. A spring near the entrance of the stasis facility provided fresh water, and Liis, using a book Sav retrieved, began to identify local edible plants.

In the evenings, Sav and Hebuiza returned to *Ea*. The Facilitator rigged up an irradiation chamber to sterilize the food, water and oxygen they brought back; Sav worked with scavenged parts to build an uplink from the stasis facility. Although *Ea*'s radio equipment had enough signal strength for surface broadcast, their suit transceivers simply weren't powerful enough to return that signal.

As the days passed, Sav fell into a routine: shuttle equipment and supplies from Temparas to Lyst, then back to *Ea*, where he would rest until he was ready to do it all over again.

Hebuiza went about his own business, sometimes accompanying Sav to the city, where he would dutifully request permission to run his own errands while Sav scavenged sites, reappearing hours later with sealed crates and bulky satchels crammed into every available vessel-space. Sav never bothered to check their contents. On return to the stasis facility, Hebuiza immediately hauled his prizes to a "lab" he'd set up on level zero. Twice more, he asked Sav for blood samples; once, he had Liis draw blood from herself and Josua.

On their fifth trip together, Hebuiza directed Sav to a small airport near the city's southern outskirts, instructing him to set down next to a small hangar. Inside was a two-seat VTOL craft, its wings folded up and over its cabin like a sleeping insect. In the corner of the hangar, canisters of fuel and an assortment of spare parts had been stockpiled.

"I will not need the dropship for surface runs anymore," Hebuiza announced. "Perhaps we should work out a schedule for trips to *Ea*...."

Josua's recovery continued, slowly. Although he never spoke, more and more frequently he seemed aware, eyes briefly focusing whenever anyone entered the room. Several times, Sav stood quietly in the corner of the room listening as Liis patiently explained to Josua everything that had happened that day, repeating verbatim all the things he'd just told her. While she spoke, Josua would stare intently at her face, but whether he understood her words or not was unclear. At least during these periods of apparent lucidity Josua managed to chew and swallow the tiny morsels of food Liis placed between his lips.

Disturbed by Liis's preoccupation, Sav started avoiding the sickroom. But Liis seemed oblivious; all her energies were directed toward Josua's well-being. She set up a pallet for herself at the foot of Josua's cot, piling her few possessions on a shelf next to it. The only time she'd leave the sickroom would be to hike down to the lake, where she had set herself the task of restoring as much of the array as possible. In a few days, she'd managed to increase the average power yield by ten percent, restoring light on the level where they kept Josua. Yesterday she'd restored power to the front doors, no longer making it necessary to crawl through the opening they'd cut.

In a way, it was a relief that Hebuiza and Liis were so intent on their own purposes. But Sav found it increasingly difficult to be around either of them.

Even aboard *Ea*, in the solitude of his berth, there was no relief. Each night in his dreams, dark, formless crowds pressed around him, demanding things in incomprehensible languages. He clawed his way back to reality gasping, damp webbing twisted around him like ropes.

DAY 7

"Sav?" Josua's voice was dry, almost a whisper. His watery blue eyes blinked.

Sav nodded curtly, his heart thudding in his chest, his breath still ragged. He'd been outside, working on the uplink antenna, patching it in to transponder relays he'd set up throughout the facility, so their suit transceivers could be used from any level. But the first thing he'd heard when he'd opened the link was Liis's shout: "Come quick!"

Hurrying inside, he'd made his way down to Josua's room, expecting the worst. Yesterday, when Josua had lapsed into a coma-like state, Sav had made a point of staying close, fearing the worst. He watched as Liis stared for hours in grim silence at Josua, then switched to working on something equally pointless in a paroxysm of sudden energy, until she collapsed in exhaustion.

But now Josua sat upright, Liis's arm around his thin shoulders, supporting his weight. "It wasn't the plague," she said, and grinned idiotically.

Sav moved closer, picking his way through the accumulated litter of Josua's care, until he stood next to the cot. Josua's eyes, though rheumy, were focused, tracking Sav's movements. His once ruddy face had become gaunt, rivalling Hebuiza's.

"We thought you were going to die." It wasn't what Sav had intended to say.

The corners of Josua's mouth turned upwards in a small, misshapen smile. "I . . . I changed my mind."

"He came back," Liis said again, looking at Josua like he was a sick child. "He came back for me."

Sav stared at Josua, who gazed back unflinchingly. With an

effort, Josua raised a hand and ran the back of his pale fingers lightly down her cheek as a lover might. Clearly exhausted by the effort, he let his hand drop back onto the sheet.

"Yes," Josua said, looking away, "For you, Liis. For all of us." Liis's face flushed, scars rippling across her cheeks.

"Well," Sav said, trying to hide his discomfort. "Welcome back." He thought he had known Josua—at least a little. But this was a stranger sitting here. Why would he tell such an obvious lie? And flaunt it?

Control, Sav thought. *It's all about control over Liis. And he wants me to understand she'll do anything he says.*

"Perhaps we should let Josua rest," he said. "I could use your help—"

"No!" Josua went rigid, face a red mask, jaws working soundlessly. He balled his hands into fists, and his arms shook as though he was about to seize; then his entire body shuddered, and he collapsed into Liis's embrace.

"I still need her," he said in a barely audible voice, from within the confines of her arms. "We have to begin planning, you see...."

"Planning? For what?"

Josua's eyes flickered momentarily; then the fire in them seemed to fade. "Retribution. And forgiveness," he said dully, as if he were repeating an obvious point. He no longer seemed interested in the conversation. His gaze grew distant, shifted listlessly back to Liis. "And love," he said in an abstracted tone. "How foolish. I almost forgot love."

Liis cradled his head, stroking his hair with her free hand. Slowly, Josua's eyes closed. His chest rose and fell in a regular rhythm.

"Retribution and forgiveness?"

Josua didn't reply. Instead, it was Liis who answered in a whisper: "He knows what to do."

"What do you mean?"

"He's had a dream."

"A dream? He had a *dream*?"

Liis stiffened. Lowering Josua's head gently, she rose from the crate, towering over Sav. "Call it a vision—if you prefer." Visibly fighting to restrain anger, she took a step toward Sav, forcing him to back up. "He says Nexus is responsible. He wants to punish them."

"Shit," Sav said. "A dream! And did his dream tell him how he was going to punish them?"

"He didn't say."

"No, of course not."

Liis tried to cross her arms, but Sav grabbed her wrists. "Listen! It doesn't take a genius to see the hand of Nexus in all this. But even if we knew they created the plague—and we don't—what could we do?" Sav swore under his breath. "He wants to punish a culture millennia more advanced than us, that almost certainly seeded the known worlds . . . that may have created the very planet we stand on. What nonsense!" He tightened his grip. "The best we can hope for is to refuel *Ea* and take our chances on another planetfall. That's *my* plan. Survival."

Liis twisted her arms inward, breaking his hold easily. "No," she said. "Nexus didn't create this planet—or any other. The race that seeded us, whoever they were, is long gone, and Nexus has never claimed otherwise. At best, they may have descended from them, but we can claim the same heritage. The men and women of the Polyarchy are flesh and blood, like us. And like us, they can die."

"Listen to yourself, Liis! Haven't you had enough death?"

"You may be ranking officer aboard *Ea*, but down here, Josua's senior. Hebuiza said so; you agreed. Now that he's better, I intend to follow his orders—whatever they may be."

"Even if he's insane?" She didn't answer. "Look, do what you want, but when the next longhaul ship gets here, I'm going to be ready to leave. If you and Josua have other plans, that's your business."

"He's mission senior."

"There is no mission, Liis. It ended when Bh'Haret died."

Liis opened her mouth to answer, but a wheezing laugh cut her off. Sav looked over at Josua, who hadn't been asleep after all: his eyes were now open and fixed on them.

"Commander Sav." Josua chuckled again, as if at the absurdity of the image.

"You're in no shape—"

"—to command. I agree." Josua paused, as if summoning up his strength. "We'll discuss it when I'm better." He lay back, exhausted by the effort of getting out those few words.

"You'd better go," Liis said. "He needs his rest." She returned to her crate, picked up a damp cloth and bathed Josua's forehead.

"Sure," Sav said, wanting nothing more than to get out of the room, away from them. "Fine by me." Turning, he walked into the hall, toward the dropshaft.

Discuss what? What the hell does Josua plan to do—take a vote on who gets to be captain?

Except that was exactly what Josua *would* do. Liis would support him. And Hebuiza would fall in with them, if only to spite Sav.

Revenge on Nexus. We'll follow a madman to our deaths.

But it wasn't only Josua's state of mind which had Sav worried. Liis had already been infected by his madness; so long as Josua continued to spoon-feed her that garbage about love, she might do anything he asked. Sav saw no other options.

Much as it repulsed him, he'd have to go back to *Ea*, and talk to the Facilitator.

"He's convinced Nexus is responsible."

Hebuiza continued working, a loop of cables snaking from the socket in his temple to the equipment he'd assembled *on Ea*'s galley-table, long fingers moving efficiently to connect the oddly-shaped devices. Most had been strapped or velcroed down; others must have had magnetic bases, for they had no visible restraints. Red and green indicators flashed alternately on a small octagon, while others—three fist-sized cylinders and a small box with a lenticular surface—remained dark.

Sav held onto a grab bar inside the door. "He has some crazy idea about taking revenge." The Facilitator's fingers paused, but only for a moment. "He's insane. Or at the very least unstable."

"I see," Hebuiza said, and returned to his work.

"Liis agrees with him."

"So?" The topmost face of the cylinder closest to Hebuiza now glowed amber; small characters scrolled across its top. Above the octagon, the air roiled, as if a miniature storm were brewing. "I have my own concerns."

"You're not worried? If we give him free rein, God knows what he'll do."

The Facilitator sighed loudly. "Josua is ill. It will be weeks before he's ready to assume command. There is no need to panic."

"So what happens when the other ship returns, and we finally have enough fuel? By then, Josua will have recovered; we can't let him jeopardize our chances of getting out of here. We need to decide on a course of action right now . . ." He paused. "The two of us."

"You have altered the keys to the ship."

A statement, not a question—but *Ea*'s security monitor had not informed Sav of any attempted breaches. Had the Facilitator managed to discover this without tripping any of the alarms? Or was it just a guess?

Sav nodded, reluctantly.

"Then we have nothing to worry about, do we? Only you can issue control commands."

"But if Josua becomes insistent I turn over command Liis will step in. She could manually override almost everything in just a few days."

"Not unless I allow it."

Sav pulled himself further into the room, grabbing onto the back of a chair. "If you've been fucking around with—"

The Facilitator cut him off. "What I have done is inconsequential. I agreed you were in command—and you still are. Is that not enough?"

Anger constricted Sav's throat. "Don't let him ruin the only chance we have."

"He will not," Hebuiza said confidently. All three cylinders were alight now, indicators glowing steadily. On two of them, a cryptic alphabet scrolled across all the visible faces. Above the hexagon a three-dimensional, cutaway figure of some incomprehensible machine sprang to life, then faded. A cityscape snapped into existence, superseded by a series of three-dimensional diagrams of star fields. A lecture in a harsh, guttural language filled the room.

"He's mad, Hebuiza," Sav raised his voice over the alien speech. "He'll get us all killed!"

"Or save us." The display now contained a spiral galaxy; it froze in mid-rotation, the voice falling silent. "A madman," Hebuiza said thoughtfully, his deep voice loud in the silence, "may be just what we need."

Sav stared at his gaunt, implacable face. "You think you'll be able to control him."

"We need him," the Facilitator replied, flatly. "And Liis."

The spiral galaxy above the hexagon winked out, replaced by the double helix of a strand of DNA. The guttural voice resumed its lecture, droning on as section after section was added to the strand, until it stretched to the ceiling.

"When Josua has fully recovered, he will listen to reason," Hebuiza asserted. "*If* things are explained properly."

"You haven't seen him yet."

Hebuiza glared at Sav, clearly irritated by his proximity to the equipment; the flaccid antennae and cables on his scalp wove back and forth, like seaweed. "What I am doing here is far more important than your imagined fears." Sav noticed his hands trembling slightly; a prominent vein throbbed in the Facilitator's forehead. "We need to find the vectors for the disease. We need to find its reservoirs. That is the only thing that matters."

The disease still has him terrified, Sav thought. *He doesn't want to go near Josua, or Liis.*

"Now, if you don't mind," Hebuiza said, "I have work to do."

DAYS 8 TO 17

Josua's recovery accelerated. Though still thin and pallid, his features filled out, losing some of their sharp edges. Since he had insisted Liis stop shaving him, his jaw was now covered with the dark outline of an incipient beard. He was clearly on the mend.

For the next few days, Sav made a point of looking in on the sick room, trying to gauge Josua's level of irrationality. Liis would stand near the door while the two men made awkward conversation. During these brief visits, Josua said little, mostly listening to Sav. He seemed as normal as could be expected, for someone recovering from a serious bout of influenza. When he did speak, Josua dwelt only on the logistics of survival, often glancing at Liis after every sentence, who would nod encouragingly. To Sav, it seemed like the three of them were trapped in a badly-acted play. He found excuses to avoid further visits.

The Facilitator's lab continued to grow, as crates of equipment piled up in a second room. Occasionally, Hebuiza would ask Sav to keep his eyes open for a particular item. Several of the Facilitator's requests baffled Sav: airtight ducting, bleach, a portable kiln, caulking compound, co-ax cable, rolls of plastic sheeting, half a dozen video monitors and cameras. At first he dropped everything off inside the rooms himself, but one day Sav returned to find the doors stayed shut until the Facilitator entered a security code on the keypad next to the lock. As much as this annoyed Sav, he chose to ignore it.

DAY 18

A large red number fourteen glowed on the indicator above the elevator doors. Surprised, Sav stood in the corridor, a small carton he'd removed from the dropship cradled in his arms, staring at it. Liis had somehow managed to get the elevator working. As Sav watched, the display changed from fourteen to thirteen. When the display read zero, the doors slid open and Liis stepped out, smiling broadly. In her right hand she held a small computer tablet. Behind her Josua hobbled, supporting his weight on a cane. The thick stubble had transformed into a short, dense beard that crept high on his cheekbones. He still swayed slightly as he moved, but when Liis extended her arm to offer support, he waved her away.

"I'll be fine," he said, the rasp in his voice gone, eyes clear, smiling. He took two more shuffling steps toward Sav. "How've you been keeping?" he asked, tapping the leg of Sav's suit with the end of his cane. "Still hiding inside this?"

"Yeah," Sav replied. The weight of the helmet sat mostly on his collarbone, leaving raw, red half-moon impressions on his shoulders. Towels and bandages didn't seem to help. In a gesture that had become habitual, he shrugged his shoulders until the weight settled into a marginally less irritating position.

"You'd be much more comfortable without it."

Sav said nothing.

"The incubation period was only a few days. Wouldn't Liis and I have been infected by now, if there was any sort of risk?"

"Maybe," Sav answered slowly. "But for all we know, there could still be reservoirs harbouring the disease we might not have encountered yet. And we still don't know anything about its vectors."

"True." Josua admitted, unconcerned. "Did you know Hebuiza came down to see me yesterday?" Sav stared. "It must have been hard for him; he's still so terrified of the plague, it's all he thinks about. The whole time, he looked like he could barely keep himself from bolting." Shifting, Josua looked directly into Sav's visor. "He came down to make a proposal."

Behind Josua, Sav saw Liis cross her arms over her chest, regarding Sav warily over the top of Josua's head.

"What kind of proposal?"

"He wants to revive a few of the interees from stasis." Behind him, Liis pressed her lips together tightly. "Says he needs assistance with his research. Qualified personnel. And I agree—but not for his sake. We'll need all the help we can get, whether we decide to stay here or not."

More people, Sav thought. *More rational people. It could only help, couldn't it?*

He looked over at Liis, wanting to give her a small gesture to indicate his approval, but she looked away. Her jaw worked silently.

What's bothering her? Sav wondered. *Is she still angry at me for calling Josua insane?*

He turned his gaze back to Josua. "I'd have thought Hebuiza'd be afraid of reviving the plague along with interees."

"I was surprised myself. But he says it will be safe if we set up a quarantine area, keep them isolated for at least forty days. That's eight times the disease's incubation period. Liis has already identified a potential site on the second sublevel, a suite of interconnected rooms that can be made airtight. And Hebuiza wants security on all the external doors—in case our patients decide they want out prematurely. If they show no signs of contagion, we'll lift the quarantine. Six clients, to start. More later—if things work out."

"And what's my part in all this?"

"We'll need your help gathering monitoring equipment, clothing and food, furniture, books and games to keep them occupied." Josua paused. "And we'll need to move the cells from their cradles to the quarantine area, of course."

"Which means me and Hebuiza, since we're still in our suits."

"Yes. It's only prudent."

"And we'll have to open them, too."

"Oh, no." Josua waved his hand to dismiss the idea. "Hebuiza thinks he can cobble together a servo to perform most of the manual functions by remote. That's what we'll use to open the cells, when we're ready." Josua held out his hand; Liis placed the computer tablet in it. The screen came to life under Josua's fingers. He passed the tablet to Sav.

"Here's a list of sites I'd like you to visit, to look for the equipment we'll need. And things we'll need to prepare *Ea* for another longhaul—if we all decide that's best."

Glancing down, Sav saw twenty locations, each followed by geographic co-ordinates: hospitals, spaceports and shipyards, military installations and research facilities, scattered across the world. On the bottom of the display was a page icon indicating this as only the first of seven screens; *weeks* of work. And it would mean being suited for extended periods, upwards of forty hours for the more distant sites.

"As you can see, it's quite a job. Think you can handle it?"

Sav chewed his lip. Moments ago, he would have welcomed any excuse to stay away from the stasis facility; now he experienced a strange reluctance. But he could think of no good reason not to do as Josua asked.

"Okay," Sav said, at last. "Let's do it."

Josua extended his hand. Sav took it. Even through the glove, Josua's grip was surprisingly firm.

He released Sav's hand, patting him on the back. "Let's go tell Hebuiza the good news."

DAYS 19 TO 31

The next day, Sav discovered what had been bothering Liis, at least in part. Josua took the morning to transfer his few possessions and cot to a first-floor suite—once the chief administrator's rooms. Sav expected Liis to claim one of the other offices, or move in with him, but she did neither. Instead, after the two of them helped Josua set up his new quarters, she returned to the fourteenth sublevel. Josua seemed not to notice—or care.

Days passed.

Shuttling a steady stream of supplies back to the facility, Sav watched the quarantine area take shape. The three rooms Liis had chosen were at the end of a corridor extending further south than any of the other levels, so that there was nothing above or below them but solid rock. The same was true for three of the four walls. The fourth wall, with only a single door, would isolate the occupants from the rest of the facility.

They reworked the ventilation ducts to make sure the flow of air would always be unidirectional, and exhaust would flow through a sterilization chamber, where it could be superheated and irradiated before being taken up by the return ducts and vented back to the main system. Because there was no toilet or sink, they installed two tanks: one for fresh water, one for waste. Then they welded plates over whatever openings they could find in the wall, and Hebuiza carefully sprayed every surface with a liquid sealant that solidified into a hard, durable compound that would have required a concerted effort—and the right tools—to breach. They rewired, squeezing new power cables into the single conduit that served the rooms, carefully sealing it. Then they moved in cots, tables, shelving and cupboards.

Josua began stocking the shelves with food, clothing and medical equipment, while Liis positioned cameras and microphones high along the walls.

On the tenth day of preparations, Sav sought out Josua, with a question about the generators he'd requested. He passed through the waiting room and knocked on Josua's door, but there was no answer. Sav pushed the door open and walked in. The office was empty.

Since he'd last been in here three days ago, a bank of monitors had been racked to the left of Josua's desk. Each screen displayed a different angle of the quarantine rooms. In one room, an operatorless waldo—the cage for its usual human occupant filled with a mass of hydraulics, electronics, and cabling—moved between two rows of shelves loaded with medical apparatus. It stopped in front of a stack of boxes and began loading them onto the shelves. On the adjacent monitor, Sav could see Hebuiza sitting at the far end of the same room, operating the remote, his head swinging in small circles.

"Not much longer now."

Startled, Sav swung around to find Liis standing in the doorway. Her scars were pale white lines next to the dark semi-circles beneath her bloodshot eyes.

"Tonight we're sealing the chamber and pumping the air out, to test its integrity. If everything goes well, Josua wants to begin revivals tomorrow. Or the next day—at the latest." She paused. "Do you know he doesn't call them revivals anymore?"

"Who? Josua?"

"He calls them resurrections."

"Liis," he said quietly. "Is everything okay?"

"No," she blurted. "I never wanted this." Then, appearing confused: "Yes, yes. Everything's fine." She looked away. "Just tired. That's all. Got to sleep." She turned, then drifted out the door like a spectre.

Sav let her go. *We're all tired,* he thought.

On the screen, the waldo had withdrawn a syringe from a rack between its thin, articulated fingers. After a moment of fumbling, the waldo gripped a small bottle, then slid the needle into the bottle. A pale yellow liquid streamed into the plastic cylinder. On another screen, the Facilitator's narrow face creased into a smile.

Resurrections?

Sav stepped up to the monitors. One by one, he turned them off. He left Josua's office, returning to the dropship to wait for Hebuiza.

DAY 32

The next morning, transfer of the cells began. Although power was now more or less reliable, the overhead light panels remained dark; there still wasn't enough juice being generated by the solar array. So when they entered the chamber on the fifth sublevel, their only illumination was the pale green glow of the two dozen live cells.

Liis switched on her flashlight, and the space in front of them filled with the harsh wash of white light. Near the centre of the room, a cryostasis cell had been extruded from its vertical cradle; it hung from a chain secured to an overhead winch. A mass of electronic equipment and two small cylinders had been set on the shelf on the bottom of a gurney.

Liis walked over to the cell, Sav trailing after; Hebuiza and Josua had gone to the AI panel. Though she looked better than she had the day before, whenever Sav looked at her, she averted her eyes.

"Our first—" Liis hesitated, searching for a word, "—*experiment*."

Sav nodded, craning his neck to try to make out the features of the occupant. He thought it looked like a woman.

"Once Hebuiza initiates the transfer procedure, the two of you will lower the cell onto the gurney." She handed Sav a remote. "Be careful. Too much jostling can damage the tissues. Once you've got the cell on the gurney, you'll have to disconnect the cabling. There's a safety on the side of the plug you have to depress. The whole thing should slide out easily. Replace it with the one connected to the cart's battery." Liis tapped a cable that had been coiled over a hook at the end of the cart. "Uncoupling the umbilical is next." She pointed at a green hose at the bottom. "Counter clockwise, half a turn. Don't be alarmed if fluid spills out of the tube; it's just harmless residue. You'll have over an hour to complete the move before any degradation begins."

"And at the other end?"

"Reverse the process. We've set up six new stations in the quarantine area. There's a winch like this one running above. Use it to lower the cell to the floor in front of a station, switch the cabling again and reattach the umbilical. When we've transferred all six, and verified that the process was successful, we'll seal the room and the waldo will open the cells."

"Nothing to it," Sav muttered. "Where's the next one?"

"On sublevel ten. Hebuiza knows."

"And if we have any problems?"

"Josua and I will be on level zero. We'll stay in contact through the suit radios. Anything else?"

"No. Just . . . I'd like to know what's bothering you."

"Nothing." Liis placed the lantern on the floor, and strode away. Sav watched until she disappeared into the corridor; a moment later, Josua followed. To the left, the Facilitator was still outlined by the AI panel.

The comm light came on in Sav's status display, indicating a three-way connection. "All set?" Josua asked. In the background, Sav could hear the distinctive voice of the elevator counting off floors.

"Yes," said Hebuiza. Sav followed suit.

"Then it's time to wake the dead."

Moving all the cells took less than four hours. Not surprisingly, Hebuiza kept himself as distant from the process as possible. He wouldn't go near the cells until Sav had severed the connections; only then did he approach, carefully sidestepping the puddles of fluid that leaked from the uncoupled hoses, and scarcely long enough to help lever the cylinders onto the gurney, his head moving agitatedly inside his oval helmet. At the other end, he did the same, helping Sav wrestle each cell onto the floor, then scuttled away, leaving it to Sav to reconnect the cabling and umbilicals.

During the transfer, Sav had been so busy he'd paid little

attention to the cells' occupants. Now that he had reconnected the last one, however—and Hebuiza had disappeared—he stooped to examine their occupants more closely. All six faces looked gaunt and colourless, like corpses. But he knew they were alive: the status display on each cell confirmed it. And none had the plague's tell-tale lesions.

Sav welded the door shut with a laser, as Josua had instructed, and retraced his steps to the elevator. Next to the lift was their final precaution: a tank filled with sodium hypochlorite. Sav picked up the hose attached to the tank and, aiming the nozzle at himself, carefully sprayed the exterior of his suit with the disinfectant. Now that the cells had been moved, he and Hebuiza would return to *Ea*, leaving Josua and Liis to monitor the interees. Tomorrow, the revivals would begin.

DAY 33

"I've decided to wait another five days."

Josua stroked his beard; it had filled in, thick and peppered with grey.

Sav felt his jaw clench. Thus far, he'd deferred to Josua on almost every issue with respect to the revivals. But now this unilateral decision brought home the point forcefully: down here, Josua was effectively in charge. Sav tried not to think about the implications. Instead, he looked at display along the wall. The status lights on the cells showed green across the board.

"Why the delay? Is something wrong?"

"No."

When the dropship returned that morning, Sav had expected Josua to be impatient to rouse the interees. Instead, they'd found him sitting alone behind his cluttered desk, sorting hardcopy into three neat piles. "Then why wait?"

"Another few days won't hurt." Josua leaned back in his plush seat, lifted a sheet from one of his piles. "And it'll give us a chance to study them more closely, now we've got a direct link." The sheet was covered with data; at its bottom was a graph.

"I concur," the Facilitator said. He had been standing in his usual spot, near the doorway, as if he believed his chance of infection increased with each additional step into the office. But now he moved past Sav, so that he stood right in front of the desk. "With the new connections, we will be able to run more thorough diagnostics. A sensible safeguard."

Sav was annoyed, not only at the delay—he suddenly realized he'd been anticipating the prospect of new faces far more than he had let himself acknowledge—but also at Hebuiza's nonchalance. "I thought this was your baby—both of you."

"It still is," Josua answered. "But why take unnecessary risks? If even a single one has the plague, reviving them would be as good as a death sentence for all six."

Sav looked at Hebuiza. Slowly: "But . . . I thought you only selected people frozen at least five years before contagion onset? Wasn't that the protocol?"

Josua stood, walked around the desk. "Let me have a word alone," Josua told the Facilitator.

The tall man hesitated, then shrugged. "Fine." He pushed past Sav and into the waiting room. Josua closed the door behind him.

"What the hell—" Sav began.

"He's frightened," Josua said. "After you moved the last cell yesterday, he came to me and asked to delay the revivals, as a precaution. Says he wants to run more tests. I think he's having second thoughts." Stepping nearer, Josua placed a hand on Sav's shoulder.

Sav flinched, fought an urge to jerk away, felt his face flush. Had the Facilitator's paranoia infected him? But Josua, still talking, didn't seem to have noticed.

". . . comforting. Let him run his tests, give him a few days to get used to the idea." Josua lifted his hand, walked over to the monitors. "We need him to pull this off; you know that. A short delay won't make much difference." He touched the screen. "And they're not going anywhere. Are they?" He dropped his hand. "If Hebuiza's still not willing to proceed in five days, you and I will decide what to do. Okay?"

"You, I and Liis."

"Liis?" Josua looked confused.

"You said '*you and I*' would decide. What about Liis?"

"Of course," Josua said. "She'll be in on the decision as well."

Sav nodded. They were still skirting the issue of command—even now, Josua was spinning his plans as suggestions rather than orders. But at least within the confines of the stasis facility, Josua believed himself to be in charge.

Josua moved behind his desk. "In the meantime, I suggest we use this respite to our best advantage. There's a hundred things Liis and I could get started on here before the revivals begin. And I imagine you've still a got a long way to go through that list of sites."

It was true. But his scavenging, unappealing as it was, now seemed infinitely preferable to Liis's glum silences or Hebuiza's twitchy fear.

"Five days," he said. "Then we talk."

"Yes," Josua said, solemnly. "That should be more than enough time." He leaned forward and stabbed a button on his desk; the door swung open—a clear sign Sav'd been dismissed. "Just give Hebuiza a bit of room, and he'll come around."

Sav nodded, unconvinced. He walked out. In the waiting room the Facilitator leaned against the far wall, arms akimbo.

"Well?" Hebuiza's voice, Sav thought, was tinged with fear. "*Well?*"

Sav ignored him, opaqued his visor and stepped past, heading for the dropship. His silence was petty and childish, Sav knew—and probably misdirected. For a change, he wasn't angry with the Facilitator but with Josua, who in the rush to prepare for the revivals, had somehow managed to usurp what little authority Sav had left.

DAY 39

Sav surveyed the ruined landscape from the skirt of the farthest runway. All but two of the eight hangars had burned to the ground; the remaining ones were scarred by projectile and laser blasts, and in places the tarmac itself had been blown apart. Nothing was left of the control tower or the administration offices but a dark mound on which sprouted a tangle of ground-hugging creepers. The south face of every standing wall was bearded with the uniform grey of a nuclear shadow. A yellow skull grinned its warning at him on his suit display.

Stinging sweat trickled into his eyes, and he blinked; his recirculators complained with a mind-numbing buzz. His suit now stank permanently of stale urine and feces. Twice already, he'd had to make repairs to his comm subsystem, and once to his recirculator. It was only a matter of time until the suit failed entirely.

Of all the places on Josua's list, Sav had known this one the best. *The Ladder*, longhaulers had called it. Sav couldn't remember how many times he'd been to this outport, shuttling down between hauls to wait for his next contract. He imagined the busy field as it had been: a hubbub of activity, unending stream of low-slung tractors trundling cargo and crew between control tower and hangars; ships lifting off every few minutes, the bright flares of their exhausts momentarily blinding. The field singing with their thunderous vibrations, caught in the ground like a hum in the chest of a giant.

Early on, he'd purchased a small, exclusive house in Briam, twenty klicks from here. But instead of being the refuge he had hoped, the house only stoked his desire to flee Bh'Haret and return to the anonymity of space. Three times he'd returned to its vacant rooms and empty hallways, before selling it for an embarrassing profit and squandering the proceeds on a drunken gambling spree.

Always was too late, he thought, *even back then.*

Weed-choked rubble stretched out before him, everything of value long gone, laid waste in the mad aftermath of the plague. Anything that would have been useful in preparing *Ea* for another longhaul, already destroyed.

A feeling of uneasiness had been growing inside Sav like a tumour. The destruction was too methodical, too complete. The more time he spent sifting through the detritus of these sites, the more he began to believe that there was another will at work, a presence that wanted the destruction to appear part of the chaos following the plague.

Looking out over the devastation, he thought, *Perhaps Josua was right after all. In his fever, he saw clearly what we couldn't—the hand of Nexus.*

When Sav returned to the stasis facility, Liis was waiting at the side of the landing pad. It was the fifth day after he and Hebuiza had moved the stasis cells. The dropship settled to the ground, its engines scattering clouds of dust and small stones across the tarmac. Liis raised her arms to protect her face.

Sav opened the hatch, and began unloading the items he'd scavenged that morning.

"Leave that." Liis stood behind him, one arm still raised to shield her eyes from the late afternoon sun. "Josua wants to see you."

Sav set the case he'd lifted onto the tarmac and followed her. Just before the main doors, Liis stopped abruptly and spun around. "You've got to understand, we had to do it." Her words were angry and defensive. Then, softer: "We had no choice...."

Sav felt sick. "Do what, Liis?"

"Revive them."

"I don't understand—"

But Liis had already turned away, the doors rolling back before her. She moved down the corridor, her shoulders hunched. Sav hurried after her. "Liis..."

The reception room outside Josua's office was empty, so Sav pushed through to the inner office. At first, he didn't recognize Josua—he'd shaved his beard and trimmed his hair. On the opposite side of the room, the Facilitator leaned against the wall, glaring at Sav. Liis had retreated to the far corner. She stared fiercely at something to Josua's right. Sav followed her gaze to the monitors. They contained the usual scenes of the quarantine area—

—except for the six cryostasis cells: three were now empty, lids stacked neatly to the side. Sav scanned the other screens, but saw no movement—no figures standing, walking, sitting.

He looked back at Josua. "You've revived them."

Josua nodded. "Yes."

"How long?"

"Five days."

Five days. Sav couldn't believe it—they hadn't waited five days. They hadn't even waited one. "You said you weren't going to do anything until you talked to me."

"No, I said I'd talk to you *if* Hebuiza didn't want to proceed. But he did."

Sav looked at the Facilitator, then back at Josua. "You lied," he said, flatly.

"It was necessary. You would have objected to the... experiment."

Hadn't Liis used that same word? "What have you done to them?"

Josua pointed toward the screens. "See for yourself."

Sav looked. At first he saw nothing but the deserted rooms, the waldo standing motionless next to a clutter of laboratory equipment. Then he noticed the hospital beds. Three were occupied; IV drips and vital sign monitors had been set up next to them. He took a step closer. A woman—at least Sav thought it was a woman—was in the leftmost bed, a sheet pulled up to her chest. Thick, wide restraints ran across her chest, thighs and ankles. Her jaw was slack, sunken eyes wide and unblinking. Sweat glistened on her forehead. Sav took a step closer the monitor; now he could see her face and shoulders were peppered with red lesions and dark scabs, like those Sav had seen on the director of the facility. She breathed erratically. In the bed next to her was a middle-aged man who appeared either asleep or sedated, similarly restrained. Other than the same sickly pallor, he appeared fine. On the third bed, a sealed body bag.

"*Shit*." Sav felt nauseated. "They've got the plague."

"Yes," Josua replied. All three were in early stages of the disease before we resurrected them."

They're dying, Sav thought. *Two levels below, two hundred metres down a corridor.* He shivered involuntarily. "I . . . I thought they had all been interred long before the plague."

No one said anything. Liis wouldn't meet Sav's gaze; instead, she seemed to be trying to wedge herself further back into the corner of the room.

"No." Josua pushed himself to his feet. "It's the only way we can study the plague safely, Sav. We've got to understand its vectors, how it's propagated. We've got to know if it's safe for us to stay."

"We're not scientists!" Sav shot back. "The best minds on Bh'Haret uncovered next to nothing about the plague. How the hell are *we* supposed to do any better?"

Hebuiza uncrossed his arms. "If you would take a moment to think about it," he said, "there are several important differences. The first, and most important, is that they had a little over thirty days before total extinction. We, on the other hand, appear to have as much time as we need, now that we have created an environment in which to study the disease without risk to ourselves. Moreover, I have access to *borrowed* technologies that were classified when the plague manifested, so that only a few people knew about their existence, and were forbidden to use these devices. But now, we can do as we please. In the past weeks I have collected as much of this equipment as I could locate, and transferred it here to my laboratory."

"Then you planned this from the start, didn't you?" Sav said, looking between the two men. "This *experiment*." The word almost made him gag. "You've sentenced them to death." "They would have died anyway," Josua said, his voice suddenly hard. "They already had the plague."

Three more deaths, Sav thought. He stared at the three unopened cells. "And the others?" he asked.

"They're terminal." The words were whispered, barely audible. "Inoperable conditions." It was Liis, speaking from her corner.

Sav was suddenly afraid he understood. "They don't have the plague, do they?"

"No," Josua answered for her. "But they're dying of other degenerative diseases. Like most of the clients here." He nodded at the screen. "The other three all had life expectancies of well under a year when they were interred."

"Fuck," Sav said. "Fuck you all! You're going to expose uninfected people to the plague. Aren't you?"

Josua stared at him, indifferently. "It's the only way to study the transmission of the disease. We need to know more about its markers. We need to know if it's safe to stay."

"*Safe?* You're going to kill six people, just to find out if it's safe for you!"

"No," Josua answered quickly. "For *us*. For the longhaulers still to return. For those below, locked in their cells, who can still be revived." His words flowed smoothly; no doubt he'd practised them. "We must identify and destroy all the reservoirs of the disease, if we're to survive. To do that, Hebuiza needs to complete his research. I agree it's abhorrent. But it must be done."

Sav looked at the three remaining cells, resting on the floor like coffins. How many more would follow? "But they're . . . they're innocent."

"They're not!" Liis's voice startled Sav. She had taken a step away from the corner of the room, raised her head. "No one's innocent anymore," she said. "Nexus made sure of that."

Sav stared at Liis. *What had Josua been telling her?*

"She's right, Sav," Josua said. "There's nothing we can do for them. But they can do *everything* for us."

Sav shook his head in disbelief; his chin scraped against the inside of his helmet.

"We have no choice," Josua added.

"Them, either." Sav strode from the room, his anger carrying him like a wave through the reception area and into the corridor. *How could they do this? How could Liis?*

A strange giddiness took possession of him. He stumbled out of the facility, up the short path to the landing pad. Climbing inside, he dropped into the pilot's seat and watched his hands snap his command cable into the navigation panel. He felt the hum of the rotors, then the jerk as the dropship lifted clear of the pad. The world fell away.

Sav sat there, not thinking. His recirculators whined and moisture fogged his visor; he ignored the yellow icons warning him his suit was long overdue for service. The ship climbed. Three thousand metres into the ascent, it stopped. Sav suddenly became aware of the AI's voice in his earpiece, asking the same question over and over: *Course input? Course input?*

It was only then he realized he had nowhere to go.

DAY 41

Down on the fourteenth sublevel, the lights had still not been restored, so Sav switched his helmet lamp on. Moving down the corridor, he stepped as lightly as he could, like he had done when he drifted past Josua and Hebuiza's closed doors on level zero. He cranked his external pick-up to max, but couldn't hear his own footsteps; then again, he couldn't hear his own breathing, either, over the constant, high-pitched whine of his recirculator. The unit had begun complaining moments after he eased the dropship from its bay on *Ea*, four hours ago.

Outside the fifth door on his right, he paused—then, gently, pushed it open. Inside, Liis lay on her cot with her eyes closed, apparently asleep. But when Sav stepped inside, she sat up and swung her long legs onto the floor. She blinked in the glare from his light, pupils shrinking to black points.

"Sav?"

He moved into the room.

"Where have you been?"

"Away," he answered. The last two days he'd spent aboard *Ea*, ignoring incessant requests for a comm link. The cot squeaked as he sat down next to her. "I needed to do some thinking."

"Hebuiza's furious. He's been stuck in his suit for over fifty hours."

"So?"

"And Josua's been worried about you."

I'll bet, Sav thought. *Worried about his precious dropship, more likely.*

"He wants to talk to you."

"I don't feel much like talking."

"Then why did you come back?"

"Because . . ." Sav hesitated; she returned his gaze unwaveringly. Without judgement. As a friend might. "Why don't you come with me?" he blurted out. It hadn't been what he'd wanted to say. But now that he said it, he felt the urgency of his need to convince her. "We could start over. The two of us." Her expression hardened, and he felt her slipping away. Now his voice sounded like a child's: foolish, desperate. "We . . . we could leave."

"And go where?"

He hadn't given it any thought; the act of escape itself had seemed enough. "I don't know. Somewhere. Anywhere is as good as here."

Liis looked past him, as if contemplating his offer. Then: "Sav— I'm sorry."

Anger got the better of him. "Don't fool yourself. It's not like Josua needs you anymore."

The scars on her face rippled as she pushed off the cot, began pacing. She stopped abruptly, two paces from Sav, and raised her hand to her face, touched her own lips. This gesture seemed to calm her. From behind the line of raised fingers, she said, "No. He still needs me. He told me so."

"He's lying to you, Liis. Using you."

She let her hand drop. "You're wrong."

"Wake up, Liis! He's still obsessed with that dead woman. He wants vengeance. That's why he's revived those plague carriers. He wants to prove Nexus was behind the plague!"

"No!"

Sav found himself on his feet, standing in front of her. "He's crazy! He'll continue his *resurrections* until he's proved what he's wanted to prove all along. That Nexus is responsible."

"That's not true. He told me that the next ones wouldn't be part of the experiment."

The next ones? Sav stared at Liis; she gazed back defiantly, but her face had coloured. "Josua's going to revive more?"

"Two healthy interees. People who can help us. A longhauler and a medic."

"Shit, Liis we don't need any more help! It's just an excuse to move to the next step in his experiment: introduce control specimens. He'll kill them, like he killed the others. Only this time it won't be terminally ill patients. It'll be perfectly healthy people."

"He said he'd wake them, then let them out. I saw the lists. With nearly a hundred healthy interees to choose from, he chose the two most useful ones. If all he wanted was to continue, wouldn't he have chosen people *without* skills?"

"He could have changed the list, Liis. Altered the data."

"No," she said, but her voice quavered. "He promised they'd be safe."

What could he say to that? *Nothing*, Sav thought. *There is no response.*

Josua had told her what she wanted to hear. Even later, after she discovered his deception, he'd simply use another lie to salve her conscience. Sav felt the anger that had animated him a few moments ago drain away; he'd been in his suit for only a few hours, but it dug into his shoulders like his sample pockets were filled with stones. "Please, Liis," he said once more. "We can find a safe place."

"There are no safe places." Oddly, Liis's eyes seemed to be filled with concern for *him*. Reaching out, she grasped Sav's hands in hers, the soiled and fraying material of his gauntlets. She looked around the room, eyes lingering on the shelves, the pile of dirty sheets thrown in the corner, the garbage on the floor. "This place is as good as any other."

Sav stumbled out of Liis's room and into the hall. He felt overheated, giddy, like he'd spent too long beneath a blistering sun. Weaving down the hall, he picked his way through the corridor's scattered debris to the elevator. It was as he'd left it, door open, waiting for him. He stepped in. The orange floor buttons glowed steadily.

He could take the flyer and strike out on his own: Bh'Haret was big enough so that he would never have to see Hebuiza, or Josua, again. But as he considered the idea, he knew he could never do it. Though he had always been a loner, the prospect of such irrevocable isolation terrified him. If he left the others, he would not only spend the rest of his life but *die* alone, pointlessly.

As for the alternative—return to *Ea*—with the supply of deuterium microfusion pellets almost exhausted, even a one-way trip to the closest world would take centuries. And once there, he would almost certainly not be allowed past the orbital lazarette... if he and his ship weren't destroyed first, as a precautionary measure.

Which left him with only one other choice.

He stabbed the button for level zero. The doors slid closed and the elevator began to rise.

The motion made Sav's stomach flip. His breaths became shorter; perspiration gathered on his forehead, ran down into the corner of his eyes, blurring his vision. The recirculators in his suit whined furiously. Slowly, the floor indicator above the door changed, crawling through the levels toward zero. Sav felt like he was trapped in a bubble struggling up through thick, viscous fluid. He sagged against the back wall of the car. His lips tingled and his heart thudded in his chest. Then, strangely, he was on his knees, his head bent, staring at the scuffed-up floor of the elevator. In the corner of his visor the oxygen warning icon, which had been yellow for the last week, turned red.

Oxygen deprivation, he thought dully.

Sav lay on his back, staring at the ceiling of the elevator. A hard object was wedged under his spine. The smell of burnt insulation swirled around him. His head hammered, a steady thumping beat that filled his ears and made his scalp throb. A voice (his own?) urged him to break the seals on his helmet. But his right arm was leaden, far too heavy to lift, and his left was immobile, trapped by an immeasurable weight. Why struggle?

He thought, *Here I am, suffocating, while all round me is a sea of air.* He tried to laugh, but the effort made him gasp. His ears popped; a tickle, like that of a feather, brushed lightly on his throat and cheeks, curled into his mouth and nostrils. An instant later he tasted a bitter, almost metallic, tang on the back of his tongue.

Air, he thought.

But the muscles in his chest had given up, too tired to drag any of it in. Something pounded sharply on his breastbone; he gasped in shock, swallowed a lungful. His chest muscles spasmed, forcing him to suck in another, to gulp in short, rapid breaths.

"You're hyperventilating." It was Josua's voice, kilometres away. Sav's limbs tingled; a loud buzz had settled in his ears. Not his recirculator, he realized. That had failed completely—producing the odour of burnt insulation he'd smelled before. He began counting each breath: after a dozen, the buzzing diminished, and his breathing settled into a steady rhythm.

"That's it. Nice and easy; slow, deep."

Sav's head throbbed unmercifully; his eyes were still shut tight, and dying sparks skittered across his vision. He felt fingers—*cold ones!*—work into the gap between neck ring and his helmet. He couldn't remember the last time he'd felt the touch of flesh on flesh.

"I've already undone the compression snaps," Josua said. "Try to keep your head up, so I can slide your helmet off."

Sav's heart skipped a beat. *The seal's been broken.* He'd understood this before, but now its consequences hit him. Josua's fingers were on the back of his neck. *I've been exposed*, he thought. *I can't go back to* Ea.

"Sav?"

Though his neck ached, Sav raised it. There was a tiny rasp as the helmet came completely free, sliding over his head.

"There." Sav blinked in the harsh light of the corridor, and found he lay half in, half out of the elevator. Josua crouched above him. "Are you okay?"

Sav nodded, let his head sink to the floor. The concrete was like a cool compress against the back of his scalp.

"Well," Josua said, rocking back onto his heels. "Here you are."

"Yeah," Sav said, his voice hoarse. "Here I am." He tried to move his left arm to lever himself up; with Josua's help, he finally pushed himself into a sitting position, propping his back against the elevator door.

"What happened?" Josua picked up Sav's helmet and was turning it over in his hands, scrutinizing the dead status display.

"Recirculator," Sav said. "Crashed sooner than I expected. Cut off my oxygen supply."

"Didn't your suit warn you?"

"Sure." Sav thought about the yellow warning icon that he'd ignored for the last week. "I should have serviced it. Just got busy, you know, thinking about other things. . . ." His words trailed off. "I guess it's lucky you were here."

"Well, I saw you were in trouble." He put the helmet down on the floor beside him. "Hebuiza rebooted the local net and repaired the links to all the AIs, got security back up for the whole facility. I was watching you from my office when you collapsed."

"Then . . . then why didn't you stop me? I walked right past your door."

"What good would that have done? If you don't want to be here, I can't keep you."

Sav stared at Josua, but could read nothing in his face. *He's not a stupid man*, Sav thought. *He had to have known why I came back. And that means he'd been certain of Liis.*

"And if I decided to keep the dropship? What would you have done?"

"The question is irrelevant. You're here now, still free to do whatever you want. Except return to *Ea*."

"That's very generous of you." Josua didn't react to the dig. "I take it Hebuiza's already gone back to change the security keys."

"Not yet. He's waiting for me to give him the go-ahead."

Sav struggled unsteadily to his feet, waving away Josua's help. His head spun; his legs felt rubbery.

Josua rose from his crouch. "You can still leave, if you wish. Hebuiza has volunteered to shuttle you anywhere you'd care to name. I rather suspect the Facilitator would be happier, with you gone."

"And you?"

"I'd prefer you stay. I know you have reservations about Hebuiza's experiment. Liis doesn't like it either, though she understands its necessity. But if it makes you feel any better, I'll tell you what I told her: there will be no new exposures. The experiment begins and ends with the six subjects we've already isolated. On that I give you my word."

Your word? Sav thought. *What good has that been so far?* "No more revivals."

"I've just said I won't expose them—"

"I'll stay if you agree to halt all revivals."

"They *won't* be infected, I promise."

"That's not good enough. There's—" A wave of dizziness struck him, then passed. He had to struggle to remember what he was going to say. "...no...no need to revive anyone else. Not right now."

Josua stared at him, as if weighing Sav's determination. "At some point we're going to *have* to revive these people. Otherwise they'll all die."

"For *now*," Sav said. "I want you to promise."

"Okay," Josua said, shrugging. "They would have been useful, but we can manage without; let's call a moratorium." He paused. "So—what's it to be?"

Would Hebuiza agree to Sav's condition? Probably not. Sav realized he was setting up a confrontation between Josua and the Facilitator—as Josua himself must also be aware.

"We need each other." Josua's words startled Sav. "Whether you like it or not, we're all we have left." A sadness had settled over his face. For the first time since they'd returned, Sav almost felt he was seeing the real Josua, the one he had known only briefly on *Ea*, before returning to Bh'Haret.

"No more revivals?"

"Until you agree."

"Then I'll stay."

Relief, along with a weak thing that might have been a smile, creased Josua's face. "I'm more glad than you can know." He clapped a hand on Sav's shoulder. "Now, let's get you out of that suit."

"You cannot return. I have changed the keys to both the dropship and *Ea*."

"I figured."

Hebuiza stood in the doorway, spine rigid, his face screwed up like he had bitten into something tart. On the opposite side of Josua's office Sav sat in a chair pushed back against the wall; without the EVA suit's insulating layers, he was acutely aware of the feel of the cushion through the his blue undersuit's thin fabric, an unsettling feeling he tried to ignore.

"Both vehicles will remain under my control until we have isolated the plague's vectors and reservoirs."

"Or," Sav added dryly, "until *your* suit gives out."

The Facilitator sneered. "My suit is nothing like yours."

Sav glanced toward the corner, where the crumpled remains in question lay like a skinned animal. The stress of working in gravity had transformed its external material from glaring white to the dull grey of an old mattress. Here and there, stains stood out like age spots.

"You can discuss the relative merits of your suits later," Josua said. To his right, the bank of monitors had all been shut off, Sav assumed for his sake. "We have more important things to sort out."

Hebuiza crossed his arms, but said nothing.

"Sav has agreed not to return to *Ea*, and continue scavenging equipment and supplies. In exchange, he has asked for assurance that no more interees will be exposed to the plague."

"The ones we have should be sufficient for my needs."

"And if they're not?" Sav asked.

"I make no promises."

"But I will," Josua said. "I give you my word." Sav watched Hebuiza stiffen, then lower his eyes, pale cheeks as tinged with pink as Sav had ever seen them. "Can you live with that, Sav?"

"Yeah," Sav said. It wasn't much, but what more could he hope for?

He slumped back into his chair, feeling disgust at himself for agreeing; if they were murdering these people, then he had just agreed to become an accessory. But oddly, the disgust was replaced almost immediately by a surge of relief.

ROBERT BOYCZUK

The decision had been made. Now all he could do was sit back and let things unfold.

DAYS 42 TO 52

After choosing a room six doors away from Liis's, and scavenging some clothing, the next morning Sav went back to the monotonous job of inspecting the sites on the list. Since he would not be returning to *Ea*, he and Hebuiza traded crafts. The VTOL was laid out like a glider, having a simple control yoke and pedals. Although the plane seemed lighter and flimsier than the dropship, its atmospheric stability was vastly superior. But it had two major drawbacks: it was limited to relatively low altitudes, and used an excessive amount of fuel. Its range, despite the reserve tank Sav always carried, was limited to about a thousand kilometres. For longer flights, he'd have to shuttle fuel canisters to advance points, then leapfrog to his final destination.

But all this suited Sav fine; in fact, he chose to visit the more remote sites first, wishing to spend as little time as possible around the facility until the *experiment* had reached it grisly conclusion. No one volunteered information, but it seemed like every waking moment Sav spent around the facility his thoughts would swing, like the needle of a compass, back to the people on the second sublevel. After each trip, guilt drove him straight to the eleventh sublevel, where he'd jack into the first data port they'd discovered and query the surviving interees' status. Sav regularly checked to make sure no one had been revived during his absence, even though he knew if Hebuiza so chose, he could alter the records to make it appear that none of the cells had been changed. Despite this, Sav still experienced a sense of relief each time identical numbers came up.

In the days that followed, Sav neither sought the company of the others nor avoided them. They seemed equally disposed to keep their distance.

One afternoon, Josua emerged from the stasis facility with a bulky pack strapped to his back. Sav, who'd been sitting in the shadow of a tree, watched unseen as he disappeared into the surrounding forest, then returned an hour later, his pack empty. Minutes after, re-entering the facility, Josua exited again, his backpack refilled, and struck out in the same direction. Curious, Sav followed, keeping his distance.

A half-hour hike along a snaking trail brought him to a glade overlooking a shimmering blue lake. Here Josua laid his knapsack on the ground and knelt next to it. Whatever he was doing was obscured by the thigh-high grass. Sav concealed himself until Josua rose, knapsack emptied and slung over his shoulder, and plodded back down the trail. Sav crept into the clearing, and nearly stumbled over a small heap of stones. Fixed onto the flat surface of a rock at the base of the pile was the identification plate pried from Shiranda's cryostasis cell.

Sav left the cairn as it was and hurried back, trying hard not to think about what Josua must have been hauling out here, piece by piece, in his knapsack.

DAY 53

For the last half hour, Sav had been waiting just inside the doorway to his room, debating what to do. But now that Liis had returned, he stepped into the centre of the dimly lit corridor, directly in her path. She walked toward him, eyes fixed on the floor, oblivious to her surroundings; Sav threw up an arm to keep them from colliding, but at the last moment, she lurched to a halt and looked up, facial scars almost washed out in the half-light.

"Tell me," Sav said. "I want to know."

Immediately, she seemed to understand what he meant.

"Dead. The last one yesterday." Her voice was flat, inflectionless. "One lasted nearly six days. This morning we began the dissections and internal examinations, took sections from vital organs. Tomorrow, when the blood has drained from their heads, we'll remove the brains."

"And... and the others?"

Liis looked away. "Hebuiza's planning on reviving the next subject as soon as he finishes his sample analysis."

"An uninfected subject?"

Liis nodded. "Inoperable brain tumour." As she spoke, her shoulders sagged. "Her name's Cara," she said, her voice suddenly hoarse. "She's seven years old."

As she crumpled, Sav stepped forward and caught her. She was surprisingly light for a woman of her height; underneath her coveralls, he felt nothing but bone and sinew. Her head rested on his shoulder, and Sav felt a warmth seep through the material of his tee-shirt, dampening his collarbone.

Gently, he stroked the back of her head, his hand smoothing her short hair. "Liis," he said, "it's not too late to leave."

She went rigid, pushed free of his embrace. Her eyes were red, cheeks wet. But her expression had hardened. "No."

"They won't stop." Anger strangled Sav's voice. "After they kill the next two, there'll be more. It'll go on and on. . . ."

But she had already spun away, staggering down the corridor into her room. The door slammed shut behind her.

Foolish, even to hope. But now he knew there was no one else to count on. Standing in the darkened corridor, buried beneath fourteen levels of the stasis facility, he finally understood that if anything was to be done, he'd have to do it himself.

DAY 65

Sav flew over dark, mottled clouds. Through occasional breaks he could see the tip of the long, scythe-shaped peninsula where Josua told him he would find the college. Though the institute had been primarily devoted to the study of theology, Hebuiza had insisted Sav add it to his list; research into high-energy particle physics had apparently been a vigorous part of their quest for the Creator. Sav banked the VTOL over the narrow bay separating the peninsula from the mainland, and began his descent through lashing rain. A few kilometres south, he saw the hazy outline of grey stone buildings, surprisingly undamaged.

Rain pelted him as he jogged to the wide portico circling one, ducked under a stone arch, and stepped into the gloom. Sav shook off some water, withdrew a flashlight from his backpack. Choosing one of the carved wooden doors spaced regularly along the inner side of the portico, he commenced his search.

Four hours later, he descended a staircase which brought him back to the same door through which he'd originally entered. For all his efforts, his backpack contained only half a dozen bundles of data cards he'd scavenged from the offices of the principal researchers. He pushed through the door—and froze.

Twenty metres away, under the cover of the wing of the VTOL, sat a hunched figure.

The man—all Sav could see was a bald head—faced in the opposite direction, a dark blanket wrapped around his shoulders. It was hard to be certain, but he looked old, tufts of grey hair circling his shiny pate.

A survivor, Sav thought, incredulous. *He lived through the plague.*

He stared, heart racing. The head man's pivoted, and without thinking, Sav stepped back into the portico's shadow. But the man must have caught the movement in the corner of his eye; his head swung in Sav's direction. He *was* old, older than Sav had first guessed, and his eyesight could not have been very good, for he squinted, gaze passing straight over until he frowned, lined face wrinkling further.

There's nothing to be afraid of. He's a harmless old man.

Sav stepped forward, into the light. With a grunt, the man rose. Long burgundy robes unfolded as he struggled to his feet, the hem sweeping only centimetres above the rain-slicked stones. He was short, with a slight frame and a narrow, gaunt face. Lank grey hair fell to his shoulders, a few strands plastered wetly across the top of his head; his chin and cheeks were covered with the start of a patchy beard, in which rain drops glittered. Stooping, he snatched up a long, black cane that had been lying beside him.

The man strode toward Sav, chest thrust out, the cane clicking loudly on the stone flags. Amongst the sombre stone and mortar buildings of the collegium, he looked silly and pompous, a parody of an academic. When he was an arm's length from Sav, he stopped abruptly, robes swinging loosely around him. He put the cane in front of him and propped both hands on its head. Small, feral eyes, the colour of coal, regarded Sav.

"You are not dead," the man said, a large goitre bobbing in his neck. His voice was surprisingly deep and resonant. "I had thought all life ended on Bh'Haret, but the Dissolution is incomplete. My calculations must have contained an error."

A madman, Sav thought. What if he was violent? Sav edged backwards half a step. The man watched, but made no effort to close the distance between them.

"No matter," he said, dismissively, and spat on the flagstones, mucous mixing with rainwater. "It will all unfold as it should. Such is *anhaa-10*'s pleasure." Leaning forward, the man stared intently at Sav, as if a response was expected. But when Sav said nothing, he answered himself, "Such is her will." As he spoke, he lifted his right hand and spread his fingers over his heart in a practised gesture.

Anhaa-10's pleasure. The term sounded vaguely familiar.

Moving his hand away from his narrow chest, the man extended it to Sav. "Ruen," he said. "My name is Ruen, unbeliever. And I am a *patrix*."

A *patrix*. A holy man.

When Sav had begun longhauling, the sect was a small, virtually unknown group. But they had grown, over the years, into a powerful political force advocating hierocractical rule. Detailed pseudo-scientific beliefs permeated their canons. Although most was sheer nonsense, at the root of their beliefs were well-established principles of high-energy physics. Cleverly twisted, these principles yielded precisely the sort of universe they desired.

By the time Sav had returned from his fourth mission, the group had already built a network of research facilities engaging in both legitimate research into theoretical physics and a less than rigorous investigation into their abstruse philosophy. Their aim had been to attract first-rate scientists willing, by their presence, to tacitly endorse the sect in exchange for the opportunity to work in the sect's well-equipped labs. As unlikely as it seemed, the group had prospered after a string of dramatic discoveries that, not surprisingly, lent credence to their theological model.

Sav recalled what Hebuiza had said about the many ways Facilitators surreptitiously disseminated stolen Nexus technologies. Perhaps that explained how such a fringe group had managed so many important breakthroughs.

The *patrix* waited patiently, hand still extended. Sav lifted his. "Sav," he said gruffly.

Ruen clasped his hand, palm cold and clammy, like a dead thing. "Are there more?" he asked, pulling Sav toward him. His breath had the faint smell of decay.

"More?"

"Like you." The *patrix* released his grip. "Who were not cleansed."

"If you mean who didn't die, then yes, four of us. We were on a longhaul when the plague broke out." *The plague,* Sav thought. Until this moment he'd forgotten about it. *What if he's a carrier?* He tried to rub his hand inconspicuously on his pants. "And you . . . are you alone?"

"Yes. I was in a state of cryosuspension when *anhaa-10*'s manifestation occurred. I was interred on the 10th of Rhios, 2215, to await the Dissolution." Ruen folded his hands over the head of his cane again. "I was revived seven weeks ago."

Sav let out a breath he hadn't realized he'd been holding. The holy man had gone under nearly twenty years before the plague; he had no more chance of catching the contagion from Ruen than from Hebuiza. "What do you mean, '*anhaa-10*'s manifestation'? The plague?"

"Yes. The cleansing."

Sav chewed on this a moment. "You said you were alone. Who revived you?"

"No one. My cell was automated to open one year prior to the final Dissolution, so I might bear witness. But we feared the final days would bring panic and uncertainty. So, as a precaution, we had a special cell constructed, with its own independent power supply." Without warning, Ruen lifted his cane; moisture whipped off its end as he cracked down onto the paving stones with a loud report, making Sav jump. "A foolish, vain hope! I now realize *anhaa-10*'s manifestation cannot be complete until the last death. By allowing myself to be placed in suspension, I may have delayed the Dissolution." He glared at Sav, raising the cane over his head, knuckles white where he gripped it. "As have *you*, sinner!"

Sav tensed; slowly, he began edging away.

Ruen barked out a laugh. "You're in no danger from me. *I* am not an agent of the Dissolution—only its witness." He lowered the cane, bowing deeply from the waist, and opened his arms in what was clearly designed to be an act of obeisance, but on this man looked more like an affected flourish. "I give you my word." He proffered Sav his cane.

Sav closed his hand around the shaft, as Ruen released it to him; in his hand, it seemed a light and ineffectual weapon.

"Now, then: I am cold, and wet, and hungry. My food supply

ran out two weeks ago. Since then, I've eaten nothing but berries, flowers and roots...."

The *patrix* wedged himself into the back half of the cockpit, lost amongst the things Sav had salvaged, complaining loudly about the cramped space. Sav lifted the VTOL off the ground without warning, and jerked the control yoke sharply to the right. From behind, there was a loud thud, followed by a yelp, as the holy man was thrown against the side of the cockpit. Much to Sav's relief, this manoeuvre was followed by an indignant silence.

They were a good six hours from the stasis facility at Lyst; though he could have slipped the VTOL into autopilot, Sav flew manually, so that he would have to focus his attention on the control panel rather than Ruen. But his precaution wasn't necessary. Within a few minutes of lift-off, loud, buzzing snores issued from the back of the craft. Looking over his shoulder, Sav saw the *patrix* had fallen asleep, his head lolling against the side of the canopy, his mouth open to reveal a row of yellowing teeth. A strand of spittle glistened at the corner of his mouth.

Turning away, Sav engaged the autopilot.

What will the others make of him? Sav wondered. Oh, there would be clashes—of this, Sav was certain. If not with Josua, certainly with Hebuiza. From what Sav had gathered, Ruen's entire life had been devoted to preparing for the coming Dissolution, a cataclysmic event in which all universal matter would revert to a primordial, chaotic soup. This, his sect believed, would result in the unfolding of hidden dimensions and a reuniting of human consciousness with the higher consciousness of *ahnaa-10*. But Hebuiza's sole purpose was survival—an avoidance of Ruen's sacred Dissolution.

As for Liis, while her obsession with Josua worried him, he thought it symptomatic of a deeper need to find something in which she could believe. He knew this, because he felt the same craving. But despite the sharpness of its own peculiar pain, he believed he could handle it. Could Liis? Or would the *patrix* provide her with yet another set of comforting lies?

The VTOL settled to the ground with an almost imperceptible bump. In the back of the cockpit, Ruen's head lifted, eyes blinking furiously. The motion of Sav's descent must have woken the holy man.

"We're home," Sav said gruffly.

The holy man's jaw worked slowly, like he was gumming a thick porridge. He looked older, frailer than when Sav had first seen him. But apparently, Sav's words had penetrated his sleep-numbed brain. Climbing stiffly from the craft, Ruen eased himself down the wing on his hands and knees, still clutching his cane in one fist, its ferrule scraping along the fuselage. Sav could hear the holy man's joints creaking and popping as he dropped to the ground.

Ruen straightened, held himself erect, spine rigid. But the illusion of authority had fled: his hair was tangled and unkempt, glistening with perspiration; his robe was creased. On his left shoulder was a stain, left by his drool.

"Come on," said Sav. "I'll introduce you to the others."

Josua regarded the holy man levelly, momentary astonishment having vanished almost as quickly as it had appeared. "So," he said, voice even, "you wish to save our souls."

"No." Ruen stood in the middle of the room; he had refused the seat proffered him, choosing instead to lean on his cane. For the last hour, with sweeping hand gestures and oratorical flourishes, the goitre bobbing up and down fervently in his neck, he had summed up the beliefs of his sect; Josua had listened to it all with polite interest, from time to time prompting the *patrix* with a question. "Not souls, but your *essence*. An essence is not individuated; it is merely a segment, a single link in an infinite chain."

"And the Dissolution will set free these 'links'?"

"Yes. To rejoin *ahnaa-10* in the old pattern, when the universe unfolds and the false vacuum returns."

"I see." Josua steepled his hands and touched them to his chin, contemplatively.

NEXUS : ASCENSION

From his chair in the far corner, Sav quietly watched the exchange, amazed at how quickly Ruen had adapted his beliefs to the situation. *Anhaa-10* was the higher dimensional consciousness in which the sect had believed, and he'd equated the *manifestation* of his god, the *Dissolution*, with the advent of the plague on Bh'Haret—co-opting the plague itself as evidence for the existence of *anhaa-10*.

"I still don't understand," Josua said. "What is it you hope to accomplish here?"

"To help you last survivors prepare for the Dissolution. For the end of true vacuum."

"I'm afraid you won't find any believers here. Nor are you likely to make any converts."

"Nevertheless," Ruen replied, "it is my duty."

"While *my* duty to ensure my crew's survival, Dissolution or no."

The holy man hesitated. Then said, "We are both leaders. Our needs . . . do not conflict."

Josua rose from his chair and walked around his desk until he stood next to Ruen. Looking down on the *patrix*, he said, "Good, because I won't tolerate anything that might compromise the safety of anyone here." His voice had gone cold, all traces of his earlier interest vanished. "Perhaps you would be better off back at the collegium, where you could look after your own preparations for the Dissolution."

Ruen swallowed, his prominent goitre moving like a burrowing animal. Apparently the prospect of facing the Dissolution alone—or starving to death before it occurred—didn't quite figure into his plans. Though his voice quavered, he still remained defiant, eyes locked on Josua's.

"My place is here," he said.

"Certainly, so long as you understand that I'm in charge."

Ruen seemed to contemplate this. Then, much to Sav's surprise, he nodded, an abrupt movement of his bald head. "You are in charge."

He said it not as if he were capitulating, but as if he were agreeing to delegate his own authority to Josua.

"You will follow my orders, like the other members of my crew?"

Hebuiza, for example? Sav thought.

"Yes," Ruen said. "So long as I am free to practise my beliefs."

"What you do on your own time is your own business."

"Then, I shall stay."

"Very well." Josua returned to his chair. "There's no lack of space; take whatever room strikes your fancy." Lifting a sheaf of hard copies from his desk, he turned his attention to it.

The *patrix* stood there, clearly uncertain if the interview had ended. Then he closed his eyes, and began a low chant, his right hand moving in a complicated motion from lips to heart to stomach then back to lips again. The words, at least to Sav, were unintelligible. Just as Josua raised his head, a quizzical expression on his face, Ruen stopped chanting. He turned and walked—no, Sav thought, strutted—to the door, cane clicking in time with his steps. The sound faded as the holy man disappeared into the corridor.

Josua stared after Ruen, a bemused expression on his face. "What do you think, Sav?" he asked, staring at the empty doorframe. "Have I just been blessed, or cursed?"

DAYS 66 TO 70

Josua assigned Ruen small, unimportant tasks, designed to keep him out of the way. He set Ruen to cleaning the solar array with Liis, or preparing new quarters for the returning longhaulers, jobs which the *patrix* performed sullenly, but without overt objection. Twice, at Ruen's request and with Josua's blessing, Sav allowed him to come along on local scavenging missions. On both occasions the holy man collected a puzzling variety of items, mostly electronics, and as many data cards as he could find. It didn't seem to matter to him what the cards contained, as long as they weren't corrupted. As soon as they returned, Ruen would haul his booty to his room and solder the new electronics into a growing tangle of cannibalized equipment he referred to as "the holy database."

A week passed, and Sav was surprised at the way Ruen slipped into the group with barely a ripple. Ruen had taken Josua's warning to heart, keeping his opinions more or less to himself and trying—none too successfully—to restrain his tendency to pontificate. Hebuiza treated the new member of their community no differently than he treated anyone else; his disdain, apparently, played no favourites. But mostly, Hebuiza avoided Ruen far more diligently than he avoided Sav and Liis, as if he believed the *patrix* might be even more infectious.

Even when Ruen learned of Josua's experiment he didn't balk, but accepted it without compunction, bending his beliefs to fit the current standard. His equanimity about the whole thing nauseated Sav. Perhaps, no doubt seeing Josua and Hebuiza as agents of *ahnaa-10*, he secretly approved. After all, weren't they simply freeing the *essences* of those who died in the chambers below to participate in his holy Dissolution?

DAY 71

Sav sat cross-legged on the edge of the lift pad while an erratic wind swirled around him, tugging at his loose clothing. It was an overcast day, and troubled clouds with lightning flickering inside them scudded across the sky; thunder's distant rumble shivered through the ground beneath. How long he'd been here he couldn't have guessed; hours, probably. But he knew the others, down in the stone warren of the stasis facility, wouldn't be worried about his prolonged absence. They were too wrapped up in their own private hells.

Footsteps crunched behind him; startled, Sav suppressed the urge to look.

"I need to talk to you."

Sav turned reluctantly at the sound of Josua's voice. Liis stood at his side.

"Liis is set to rendezvous with *Viracosa*," Josua said.

Viracosa. It was the longhaul mission due back any time now—a ponderous ore freighter, built to haul rare metals from nearby planetary systems. Sav had almost forgotten about it.

"It's just eight days from orbit," Josua continued. "Radio contact is impossible—the screamers will be jamming its comm panel, just like they did ours. So I thought it would be best for one of us to meet them, before they decide to turn tail and run to another system."

Sav pushed himself slowly to his feet, looked at Liis. To do that, she'd have to take *Ea*. Hebuiza would lose his plague-free berth—and be trapped for an entire week in his suit.

"How does the Facilitator feel about this?"

Liis shrugged. "He was pissed. Hell, I'd be more than pissed if I had to spend that much time in my suit. But there's a Facilitator aboard

Viracosa that he desperately wants to see. A man named Yilda, some high panjandrum amongst Facilitators. And since Hebuiza knows nothing about piloting a longhaul vessel, he understands that I've got to take the ship, in order to ensure we contact his *friend*."

Another Facilitator, Sav thought. Far as he could tell, they were all the same: silent, scowling men and women with a universally exaggerated sense of their own self-importance. It was like they'd all been infected with the same kind of paranoia, perhaps a side effect of the brain-severing operation that made them into Facilitators. Or maybe they had been chosen to be Facilitators because they were already emotionally wired that way. Sav imagined Hebuiza jacked into another tall, lanky figure, half a dozen cables stretching between them as they exchanged data at terabit rates: a machine, made of two men.

"All right, " Sav said. "And what else?"

"Well . . . we're going to initiate more resurrections."

Sav clenched his fists. Three days earlier, when he'd passed Josua in the corridor, the other man had said simply, "The experiment is over," and continued past. But Josua's statement hadn't given Sav the relief had had expected. Instead, a lingering dread had filled him—dread of what Josua might do next.

"You promised me! No more infections!"

"There won't be." Josua appeared startled by Sav's vehemence. "I want to wake them up to *help* us, not to infect them. We need them now more than ever, with another ship returning."

Sav tried to keep his voice even. "It's Hebuiza, isn't it? He needs more bodies for his experiment."

Josua shook his head. "No. We want to revive a medic, a bio-engineer, another longhauler—"

"You *promised*."

"Sav, we need to be prepared."

"You'll infect them anyways. Or Hebuiza will."

"I won't let him."

"I don't believe you. And I don't trust him."

"You can help us. Monitor the revivals yourself."

"I don't want any part of it."

Josua's face turned to stone. "Look, believe what you want, but I won't have your groundless fears getting in the way of our survival. The resurrections will proceed."

Before he could respond, Josua spun on his heel and strode away. Sav started after him, but Liis's hand closed on his forearm.

"Things have changed," she said. "He's telling the truth, this time. I know it."

Sav jerked his arm free; Josua was already halfway up the path to the facility. "Yeah? All I see is a man with an obsession. What he's doing is unconscionable, and dangerous. If we follow his lead we'll gain nothing except more pointless deaths—our own probably included."

"I refuse to believe that."

"Okay, then forget Josua. What about Hebuiza? Is he any closer to discovering the 'vectors' of the plague? Or its 'reservoirs'?"

"He told me he's made progress." But her tone had changed; she sounded defensive, petulant, a child caught in a lie. "What are you getting at?"

"Do you really think the Facilitator will stop his experiments before he has all the answers?"

"Josua will stop him. *If* it's necessary."

Sav snorted derisively; clearly, her faith in Josua was undiminished. "Don't you see? It's what they both want. Though they might have different ends in mind, they both want the experiments to continue!"

"I've always respected you, Sav," Liis said, stiffly. "We've crewed together half a dozen times, and I know you're a decent guy. But I trust Josua. And no matter how much you want to change that, you can't."

"He's lied to me before; only a few days ago he promised me no more revivals. But now . . ." Sav shook his head. "So why wouldn't he be lying about his purpose in reviving them, as well?" The wind picked up and leaves rustled impatiently, as the first gusts of the storm fingered their ways through the surrounding trees.

"I know him, Sav. He's not that kind of man."

But Sav wasn't listening to her. "I thought I could leave, if things got too bad," he said, to himself. "Find a place on Bh'Haret. I convinced myself I'd rather be on my own than be a party to more... *experiments*." His voice was steady, but sweat had collected in the palms of his hands; his heart beat in his chest, a thin, attenuated ache. "But I've been thinking about it a lot, and I can't leave. My life is here now—our lives. I won't let anyone fuck that up."

Sav waited, expecting... what? But there was only nothing, then steps, moving away. In the distance, thunder rumbled angrily.

"No more revivals," Sav said, anyhow. "I won't allow it."

Only when the first fat drops of rain spattered darkly against the grey, crumbling surface of the landing pad did he finally head for cover.

DAYS 72 TO 76

Early the next morning, Josua, Liis and Hebuiza began work. Sav watched with rising horror as they readied a second isolation area. He gave up scavenging, but no one seemed to notice: they already had most of what they needed, and Hebuiza quickly collected the rest. Instead, Sav stayed close, watching and waiting. Every day, after Josua, Liis and Hebuiza had retreated to their separate rooms, Sav would make a quick tour of the isolation area. He considered sabotaging the equipment, but that would only lead to a confrontation; it would force his hand—or Josua's. In all likelihood, he'd be expelled from the facility. Or killed. He didn't think Josua or Liis had it in them, but no doubt at all that Hebuiza would murder his own mother in her sleep, if he believed it would improve his chances of survival.

So Sav stayed within his small, stuffy cubicle, turning his limited options over and over in his mind like a rodent running an endless wheel. He prayed that he could come up with something approximating a solution, before it was too late.

The tiny lens of a security camera stared down at Sav, mounted just above the frame of the new isolation area's door, which—for the first time—was locked, both changes made for his benefit. The message was obvious: they were about to begin the revivals. And they wanted to ensure he wouldn't interfere.

Is Hebuiza watching me right now? He stared into the black circle of the lens. "I'll be outside," he said. He turned, rode the elevator up to the first level and stepped into fresh, bitterly sharp air.

A light sprinkling of snow covered the ground, a harbinger of the long winter already on its way. Sav tugged his fleece-lined jacket tighter. Overhead, the fall sky was achingly clear, covered with a dense frosting of brilliant stars. Both of Bh'Haret's moons had already set. For a time, Sav tried vainly to locate the light that, on landing, would become *Viracosa*. Two nights ago, when she had begun her braking manoeuvres, she'd been the brightest object in the sky. Now, she'd fallen below a fifth magnitude object, invisible to the naked eye.

What were they feeling? Sav wondered. *Anger, confusion, incredulity?* He tried to remember what *he*'d felt when he'd first woken, but couldn't.

Sav pulled the cold air deeply into his lungs. In the distance, the trees' silhouette stirred in synchronicity, an impenetrable puzzle of darkness and branches and wind. He thought, *It must be done. Tonight.*

Viracosa was less than three days out; Sav knew Josua would begin the revivals before it made orbit, or her captain and crew could raise objections. Pulling off a mitt, Sav reached into the left pocket of his jacket, fingertips touched the cold metal of a gun barrel. He wrapped his fist around the frayed tape on its grip.

Yesterday, he'd left the facility to go to a place not on Josua's list: a police garrison on the outskirts of Temperas. Most of the equipment was dead, batteries long run dry, their works corroded, except for a chemical propulsion pistol he'd found in a desk drawer in the CO's office. It had been in a wooden box, along with two full clips of ammo. Its barrel was nicked and the plates of its grip were held on by cloth tape. Sav wondered briefly why the CO had kept such a disreputable-looking piece. Sentimental value?

Sav had snapped a clip into the weapon, then taken it outside. Aiming at a grey, weathered sign hanging from a chain between two posts, he'd pulled the trigger—and felt the weapon almost fly from his hand in violent recoil, as a sharp report rang in his ears. Stunned, it took a moment to realize the sign had been split neatly in half where the bullet struck. Carefully, he'd tucked the weapon to its box, and returned to the VTOL.

The temperature was below freezing, but in his pocket, the gun's grip already warmed to his touch.

Without Hebuiza, Josua won't be able to carry on with the experiment. He hasn't the expertise. Sav tightened his grip on the gun. *It would be a simple thing,* he thought, *to point the snout at the black square of his chest and—*

"Viracosa won't be visible until tomorrow night."

The words sounded as if they had been spoken only centimetres from his ear. Startled, Sav spun around, one foot skidding out from under him on the snow-slicked concrete, hand jerking out of the pocket. Josua caught Sav by the arms and steadied him, glancing unsurprised at the weapon Sav clutched.

"Careful," he said, releasing Sav. He stepped back.

The weight of the gun seemed to drag Sav's arm down, snout pointing at the ground.

"What were you planning to do with that?" Josua asked.

"I . . . I was waiting for the Facilitator."

Josua chuckled. "It wouldn't matter, you know. I'd have continued the revivals myself. You'd end up having to shoot both of us. Maybe Liis too. And where would that leave you?"

Sliding his index finger onto the trigger, Sav let it rest there lightly. "If that's what I have to do," he said.

"There won't be any more resurrections from now on. No more experiments." Josua sounded almost wistful.

"I don't believe you."

"And I don't care whether you do, or not." Josua inclined his head to stare at the heavens. "Things have changed."

"Stop this bullshit!" Levelling the gun, Sav aimed it at Josua's temple. "If you have something to say, say it!"

"Hebuiza's isolated the plague's vectors, at last. He's developed a test to detect carriers. So there's no need for further experiments."

Sav's let his arm down. "He's found out how the plague's transmitted? Then we should be able to decide if it's safe to stay."

Josua's lips turned up in a rictus grin. "Oh, it's safe alright," he said. "As safe as anywhere else."

"I . . . I don't understand."

"Today Hebuiza retested all the samples he took from us earlier." In the dark, Josua's eyes seemed to glow with an eerie radiance. "We're *all* carrying the plague."

Sav's heart froze in his chest; he felt dizzy, as if the world was shifting beneath him. "We've caught it?"

"We had it before we were born."

"I don't understand."

"Do you remember what the Director here said, about the spread of the plague? That it was highly contagious, yet also broke out simultaneously across Bh'Haret, as well as on the orbitals? Impossible, from an epidemiological perspective. Infectious diseases don't spread that way." Josua paused, his breath unfurling before him in a tangle of complex knots. "Yet that's exactly what we observed in our own samples: bacteria in isolated cultures spontaneously turning into viral factories, within minutes of one another. After we'd seen this same pattern repeat many times in many different samples, we realized the only way this could happen was if a large percentage of the population already carried the disease—in a dormant state."

Despite the chill in the air, Sav felt drops of perspiration run along his temple, curve behind the line of his jaw.

"Hebuiza calls it a Trojan. A latent infection. He believes it began spreading through the population fifty-one years before we left, in mutated versions of common bacteria that inhabit the skin and upper respiratory tract—innocuous, and readily passed back and forth among people through touch, kisses . . . simply by breathing. Five decades gave the bacteria plenty of time to move from one host to the next, displacing its harmless predecessors. Until the whole population had been infected and reinfected countless times."

"Then . . . then why aren't we dead yet?"

"We weren't meant to be."

"I don't understand."

"The bacteria was designed to express itself after a particular time period has passed."

"*Designed?*"

"We drew blood samples from several longer-term interees. The mutated bacteria appears abruptly in the population only up to fifty years ago; before that, no trace of it. The odds of a mutation like that occurring spontaneously, in different bacteria, are astronomical. Which means that it's almost certain it was engineered and introduced deliberately." He smiled, bitterly. "A kind of deleterious gene therapy."

"I still don't understand why we haven't gotten sick...."

"Ah, but that's the best part!" Josua smiled and shook his head, as if he was admiring the plague's cleverness. "The bacteria was engineered to replicate at a precise rate. Most do so pretty steadily to begin with, so fine tuning and synchronizing the clock genes wouldn't have been difficult. Each time a bacterium replicated, it dropped a single link in its DNA strand, like a timer running down. When the last link in the chain fell away, the DNA started producing some interesting new proteins, causing the bacteria to mutate into a bacteriophage—infectious, and *extremely* toxic."

Incredulous, Sav stared at Josua. If what he was saying was true, inside him right now, a molecular time bomb was ticking down.

"That's why it didn't spread the way a normal disease would. Because everyone on Bh'Haret had been infected already, but the bacteria was always ticking down, everyone losing that next link each time it reproduced... until it mutated one last, final time."

"How long?" Sav's voice shook. "How long do we have?"

"The timer ran out just after we left Bh'Haret, thirty years ago. If we'd never gone into cryosuspension, then we'd have manifested symptoms just like everyone else, half a year after *Ea* departed. Our longhaul only delayed the inevitable...." Josua pulled his hands out of his pockets and rubbed them together. "We have half a year, less the time we've been out of stasis since our return. Little over a hundred days." He raised his hands to his mouth and blew on them.

"What about antibiotics?" Sav said, fighting to calm himself, to keep the panic from his voice. "To kill the bacteria? If we can detect it, can't we kill it off?"

"If we had the time, expertise and equipment, we might have had a chance. But Hebuiza says it's too complex a problem. The modified bacteria were designed to be persistent in their expression, and resistant to antibiotics. Some localize in the brain and nervous system, making treatment virtually impossible; an agent strong enough to kill them off would almost certainly kill us too."

"What about the crew of *Viracosa*? They went into suspension five years before us, so they should have another five years left. If we return to the cells, while they work on a cure . . ."

"Liis boarded *Viracosa* two days ago. We only discovered the vector this morning." Josua laughed, mirthlessly. "We were worried about her catching something from *them*. But now she's exposed them to our version of the bacteria, while they've passed theirs to her. Both have their own internal timers. Unfortunately, the one that expires sooner is the only one that counts. Which means their life expectancy is now identical to ours."

"Then other ships—"

"Other than *Viracosa*, we could only confirm one other ship scheduled to return. *The Strange Matter* departed after our mission, only days before the first cases of the disease were reported. So its crew was likely stricken after they were revived at their destination. Chances are, they never began the return leg of the journey. Or if they did, they went back into stasis already suffering from the disease's early stages."

A hundred days.

Josua continued to speak; clouds of breath unrolled before him, were snatched away by the wind. But Sav was only half listening, unable to wrap his mind around anything.

". . . incubation period of three to five . . . uncertainty about insect and anthropoid vectors . . ."

A hundred days. Isolated words and phrases caught at Sav's attention, then slipped away.

". . . multiple causation . . . re-engineered protease inhibitors . . . could only be Nexus."

Sav looked up. "Nexus? You still think it was Nexus?" He felt a sudden surge of anger, although he wasn't quite sure who he was angry at. "In all probability, *we* created it, then turned it on ourselves."

"No," Josua said. "Hebuiza assured me it was far too technically advanced to have been engineered on Bh'Haret. Inconceivable, in fact, given the level of bio-technology at the time it was introduced into the population." Josua had a fervent expression on his face—not a look of defeat, but of determination. To Josua, Sav realized, this discovery had been a victory. "It's the way they view things, Sav—in decades, or centuries. Plant a slow bomb on a world that's dragging its heels joining the Ascension Program. Eventually, if we submit, they can disarm the Trojan with a counter, before anyone is the wiser. Otherwise, they let it run its course, and a troublesome civilization meets a tragic end. Naturally, Nexus would deny involvement—like you, they'd suggest a biological weapon out of our own labs, or an unlikely, but natural, pathogen. And no one could prove any different. But all the other non-affiliates would see Nexus's hand in this thing, and view it as a warning: join the Ascension program, or the same thing might happen to you."

Once again, a dull ringing had begun in Sav's ears. Beneath him, he felt the lifeless cold of concrete penetrate his boots' soles, had a sudden vision of himself standing there, on the tip of a dead, empty world.

A hundred days.

The number tumbled through his mind. He imagined the bacteria coating his skin, nestled in his throat and esophagus, undergoing division—reproducing over and over, in an inescapable cycle. A clock winding down.

Sav hefted the gun, turned it in his hand like he was examining it. "Then there's nothing left for us to do." He raised the gun to his head. "Except die."

"No, Sav!" Josua moved toward him; Sav cocked the trigger, and Josua froze.

But Sav knew right away he didn't have the courage to do anything so definitive. In anger, he flung the weapon as hard as he could, nearly jerking his arm out of its socket. The gun arced slowly into the night, plummeting into the bushes below.

For a time, the two men stood in silence, regarding one another. Then Josua spoke. "It's not hopeless," he said, softly.

Sav's heart seemed to stop. "But you said—"

"We'll force Nexus to give us the cure."

How, for fuck's sake? The idea wasn't just absurd—it was insane. Sav's surprise twisted into disgust; he shoved past Josua.

"Sav . . ."

Josua was yelling something about Hebuiza, but Sav had stopped listening. He trotted away along a small footpath and stumbled under the canopy of the nearest trees, thin branches clawing at his face, feet sliding on the thin layer of snow. He stumbled again, lost his balance, barked his shin against the edge of a rock, but felt it only in an abstract way.

DAY 80

From where he lay on his cot, Sav watched the handle on the inside of his door move up and down, making a tiny rasping noise. It was this noise that had drawn him from a restless sleep.

The handle stilled; there was a knock.

Sav shifted his weight, but didn't answer.

"Sav?"

He was surprised to hear Liis's voice. Back already. How many days had it been? He'd lost track.

Sav brushed his hair back with his fingers. He hadn't cut it since they'd returned, and it was getting long. "What do you want?" His voice was raspy; his stomach complained. During the last two days he'd stayed locked in his room, leaving only momentarily, to relieve himself in the hall outside.

"I've got to talk to you."

Sav pulled on a pair of shorts and unlocked the door, opening it just a crack. Liis stared at him through the narrow gap.

"Can I come in?"

Sav looked past her, saw the corridor behind was empty. He pulled the door marginally wider. As soon as she was through, he locked it again.

"You look like shit."

"Thanks." Sav pushed past her, and sat on his bunk. Propping his elbows on his knees, he lowered his head, and began rubbing his greasy scalp.

"Josua told me you've been in here for the last three days." His cot sagged as Liis settled next to him. "I guess he was right. About Nexus, I mean."

Sav refrained from commenting, but his hands stilled.

"He said you wouldn't talk to him."

True. Several times, Josua had been down to Sav's room—but Sav had ignored him, refusing to answer his persistent knocks.

"I know you think there's nothing we can do, Sav. But it's not over."

Sav looked at her, at last. Even sitting, she was half a head taller than he was; her blonde hair, cropped close to her skull when they had first set out, was now almost finger length.

"The other crew are here—plus Hebuiza, and the other Facilitator. They know a lot about Nexus. It was part of their job: gathering intelligence." She shifted her weight and the cot creaked; Sav could smell the odour of the disinfectant soap rise from her skin. "We're meeting tomorrow in the boardroom, to discuss the ... the situation."

Sav looked up, wearily. "I think I already have a pretty good understanding of the *situation*."

"It's not hopeless. Josua told me. Come tomorrow, Sav. They'll explain."

Liis's thigh pressed against the length of his. He felt the insistent pressure of her leg, the tension in it. Unexpectedly, she touched him on the cheek, ran her finger along his jaw line, following the twists of his officer's scar until her finger was lost in his scruffy new beard. Then, using her other hand, she pulled Sav's hand up to her face, placed it on her cheek amidst the melange of swirling lines and shapes. Sav felt the rough ridges of her scars, felt his pulse in his fingertips.

"We need you, Sav," she said. "I need you." She lowered her hand, let it rest on his thigh.

Sav's heart quickened; he found he had an erection, which only moments before he would have thought impossible. But his body remembered. He watched his hand slip from her cheek to her neck, tracing past the hollow of her throat and down onto her breast.

"Tomorrow morning, Sav," she whispered, leaning closer.

Sav's head nodded, as if of its own accord; he shivered. She pulled away from him, pushed herself to her feet, and Sav looked up in panic, afraid she would leave. But she was only undoing the fasteners on her coveralls. In a moment, the baggy garment lay on the floor around her feet. Her body was hard, breasts small with large nipples, hips far narrower than he had imagined. Stepping out of the cloth circle, she moved between Sav's knees, placing her hands on his shoulders; the scars on her face were vivid, writhing. She pressed her breasts lightly against the skin of his forehead, like a compress.

"Stand up," she ordered him.

The scent of her rose from his sheets; the taste of her was still in his mouth. Lying next to Liis in the dark, backs barely touching in the small space of the cot, he wondered, *Why?* His actions had been frenzied, desperate, seeking a release he hadn't known he needed; hers had been controlled and deliberate—responsive, but in a flat, mechanical way. Like she was playing a role, or following an order.

Sav tried to pretend it didn't matter.

Rolling over, reaching out, he held his hand over the hollow above her hip, then lowered it, gently touching the warm plain of her skin. Savouring this last, most tenuous connection to an undead world.

THE MISSION · 104 DAYS LEFT

The door was half open. Standing in the corridor outside the boardroom, Sav strained to make out the unfamiliar voice inside, but the man who spoke did so softly, and with an annoying hitch to his speech; all Sav could make out was the occasional word. He took a hesitant step toward the door, then stopped.

What am I doing here? he thought. *It's pointless.*

He was turning back toward the elevator, when the door swung wide.

"You must be Sav." In the doorway stood a man with dark brown skin and thinning silver hair, a similar tuft spilling from the collar of his blue undersuit.

"Yeah," Sav said. "That's me." Inside the room, the soft, halting voice still spoke on.

"I heard a noise out here." The man stared at Sav unabashedly, appraising him; his brown eyes were large and penetrating. He looked solid, like he worked hard to stay in shape. "Penirdth," he said at last, extending his hand. "I'm the Captain of *Viracosa*."

Hesitantly, Sav gripped the other man's hand. He noticed black crescents of dirt under his own nails, and felt a flush of embarrassment, suddenly aware of how unkempt he must appear.

"We've just begun," Penirdth said, stepping to the side.

Sav shuffled forward, through the doorway. The voice he'd eavesdropped on had fallen silent. Several people sat around an oval table easily large enough for twice their number, all staring openly at him.

"Sav!" Josua rose from his seat at the head of the table. "I'm glad you decided to join us." He indicated a chair to his left. Sav numbly walked the length of the room, and dropped into the seat. Liis, who sat on Josua's right, glanced at Sav, the scars on her face like faded stains, then looked away, folding her hands in her lap. Ruen sat next to her, toying with his cane. The other people in the room were strangers, crew members of the returned ship, *Viracosa*.

"You've met Penirdth already," Josua said, nodding at the man, who'd settled into a seat at the far end of the table. "To his left, Losson, his second." Slouched down in a chair was a man with close-cropped hair and thick knots of muscle showing clearly beneath his tee-shirt, while the tendons in his neck stood out rigidly. Narrowing his eyes, he nodded at Sav sullenly.

"Next to him is Mira, a mission specialist assigned to *Viracosa*. She's a geologist and a metallurgist, consulting in negotiation for rare metals." A plump woman stared at Sav from beneath a nest of wiry red hair, her equally red-rimmed eyes melancholy. Other than the corners of her mouth tightening marginally, she offered no greeting.

"And this is Yilda, their Facilitator." He gestured at a man in an iridescent blue undersuit sitting on the other side of Penirdth. Much to Sav's surprise, this man looked nothing like Hebuiza—nor any of the other Facilitators he'd ever met. His pale face struck Sav as pampered, unmarked, like nothing in life had managed to leave an impression. His body was beginning to show the signs of middle age. On each finger, he wore an extravagant ring, and round studs ran the length of his chin like a tiny, golden beard. The prototype of effete corruption. Yet there was no doubt he was a Facilitator: atop his scalp, a network of multi-coloured filaments lay flat like limp hair combed crosswise over a bald spot. When he opened his thick lips in a lop-sided smile, Sav could see his teeth had been carved into what appeared to be tiny human figures.

Josua resumed his seat without introducing the last man to Yilda's right. Abruptly, Sav realized why. It was Hebuiza. This was the first time Sav had seen him down here, in the facility, without the protective fabric of his black suit wrapped around him. Now that they all shared the same death sentence, he had traded that useless object for loose shorts and an oversize tee that accentuated his bony frame. The box, once attached to the outside of his suit, was now fixed to his chest with a harness; a clutch of cables wound from the crown of his head to disappear behind it, while a single wire diverged from the others, crossing the gap to jack into Yilda's back. On the table, halfway between Yilda and Hebuiza, sat a small silver cube with a single thin slot: a data card reader. To its right were several stacks of cards. Hebuiza scowled at Sav, his eyes flashing with ill-concealed hatred, head beginning its characteristic nodding swing.

Then a strange thing happened.

Yilda blinked, barely a flicker of his eyes. Immediately Hebuiza clamped his jaw shut and went rigid, as if he'd been slapped. His face became a flat, indecipherable mask. Sav stared at the two Facilitators' connection, wondering what had just passed through it.

"There was a woman," Sav said, turning back to Josua. "A woman named Vela."

"I'm afraid she's dead," Penirdth said. "Took a knife to her wrists just after we made orbit. Made a god awful mess in zero-gee...."

Sav remembered the darkened stasis cell for which Vela had been designated contact. It had contained another woman, years younger, with a different family name. Probably a lover.

"She had the right idea," Losson spat out. "We're all dead anyway. At least she chose her own time."

"No," Penirdth said. "She acted too hastily."

"She *understood*," Ruen said with vehemence. "The Dissolution is at hand."

"Thank you, but your opinion wasn't asked for, *patrix*," Penirdth said. Though his words were quiet, his contempt for the holy man was evident.

The *patrix*'s face darkened, and his arm dropped. "You'd do well to prepare yourself, *Captain*." Looking around the table, he added, "You all would." His gaze settled on Mira, who coloured; she lowered her eyes.

Losson snorted his derision. "Hah! Tell your tales to someone who cares."

"Quiet!" Penirdth said loudly. "We're not here to argue about the

Dissolution's validity." He looked from one man to the other. Losson slouched even further down in his chair, but still seemed agitated; the muscles in Ruen's jaw worked silently, but he too kept his mouth clamped shut. "We're here to listen to Yilda and Hebuiza, who think we still have a chance."

More bullshit, Sav thought. But he sat up a little straighter.

Yilda cleared his throat. "Yes," he said, stretching the "s" out in the slightest of lisps, so it sounded like a tiny hiss. "Thank you, ah, Captain." His was the voice Sav had heard in the corridor, sibilant and cloying, a voice that you had to strain to hear. Perhaps, Sav thought, he did that purposefully.

"Just begun," Yilda said. "Yes. But first, Sav, something Hebuiza made for you." He nodded at the other Facilitator.

Hebuiza reached in the pocket of his shorts, withdrew a small object and slid it across the table. Sav had to reach out quickly to snatch it before it flew past the edge. When he opened his hand, he saw he held a square wristwatch with a digital display and a black, elasticized band.

"A device that, um, might be useful. Yes. Distributed them to everyone else already."

Sav looked at the face of the watch. The figure 104-12:50 hovered in sickly, green characters. Below that, in smaller characters, was the current time and date.

"The number of days, hours and minutes before the onset of the first symptoms, hey? That's what they display. Our preparations will take the better part of the time remaining. A reminder to you of this, ah, constraint."

One hundred and four days left. Sav held the watch in his palm, stared at the green numerals. The number changed from 104-12:50 to 104-12:49. Another irretrievable moment lost to him. Looking up, he saw the others had already strapped on their watches. As Facilitators, Hebuiza and Yilda had internal clocks they could modify to do the same thing. Sav slipped the device into his pocket.

"Hebuiza and I have gathered a great deal of, um, intelligence, about Nexus. Yes." Yilda smiled, wanly. "Part of our job, you see: to collect information on the Polyarchy. Hebuiza, ah, speculated—quite rightly, I may add—that Nexus was responsible for the plague. Evidence he's collected is quite simply overwhelming. Yes. Nexus views itself as a living, growing entity. You see? Non-affiliates reluctant to join are considered to be dangerous—cancerous, if you'll allow me to extend the metaphor. Nexus removes them, like a surgeon would a tumour. I say this having spent the better part of my life studying their methods. During the last millennium they have decimated, ah, at least six non-affiliates reluctant to participate in the Ascension program. No evidence to directly implicate Nexus, but in every case the, ah, 'disaster' visited upon the non-affiliate had the desired effect on surrounding systems. Non-affiliates rushed to join, hey?"

During Yilda's speech, Hebuiza nodded dutifully to underscore Yilda's points, a curiously deferential gesture. At the same time, Ruen kept on whispering in Mira's ear, perhaps trying to win a convert. She had gone pale.

Said Yilda: "Hebuiza and I think we may be able to exert, ah, leverage on Nexus. Yes."

"Leverage?" Sav sat up straight. "To what end?"

"It's obvious, isn't it?" Hebuiza said contemptuously. "Whoever manufactured the plague can also cure it."

"Yes," Yilda agreed. "Nexus would have a readily available counteragent. In case infection bypasses the, um, isolation protocol of the orbital lazarettes and spreads to affiliated worlds. We think we can make them hand it over."

Ruen, who had sat back from Mira, shook his head sadly, as if at their folly.

"And how do you propose to do that?" Penirdth said. Sav could hear him struggling to keep his voice even. "What kind of threat could we possibly make against Nexus? Even with the abilities of two such accomplished Facilitators?"

The sarcasm of Penirdth's last question wasn't lost on Hebuiza. He leaned forward. "I do not think that *you* are in any position—"

"It's possible," Yilda answered, cutting off Hebuiza's response.

Picking up a stack of data cards from the table, he fanned them out like playing cards. "We—that is, Facilitators—have amassed information on Nexus over a considerable time." Inserting one of the cards into the reader on the table beside him, he said, "Remember the, ah, incident on Berin?"

"A Speaker was kidnapped," Mira said, uncertainly. Her voice was high and childlike. She looked around to see if anyone would disagree with her.

Yilda nodded, Hebuiza's head mirroring the motion.

"Nexus has built their empire by controlling the flow of technological information. Speakers are the linchpin—lone individuals who, with no equipment, can communicate *instantaneously* over interstellar distances with other Speakers. A neat trick, eh? Communications faster than light, their mechanism a mystery to all save a few in the Nexus hierarchy, and the *Speakers* who represent the Polyarchy on affiliated worlds. A secret that's given them a monopoly—and total control over the information they disseminate."

The Polyarchy already linked over a hundred of the seeded worlds in the Left and Right Clusters. Sav had followed the debate the last time Nexus had invited Bh'Haret to join the Ascension program. In exchange for the services of a Speaker to link Bh'Haret to the other Nexus affiliates, they would be obligated to follow the tenets of the Ascension program, a blueprint for the dissemination of "sensitive" technologies to "developing" worlds. But Bh'Haret's politicians had steadfastly refused.

Intellectual freedom. Technological vitality. These were the terms they had trumpeted. Under Nexus, technology would be doled out to them piecemeal, scraps from a master's table. It would sound the death knell for Bh'Haret's own research programs, and the climb up the Program's arbitrary ladder, though tantalising at first, would slow to a painful crawl within a generation. Then it would be too late to do anything else, for Bh'Haret would have become, like an addict, hopelessly dependent on the Polyarchy.

"An anti-affiliation group stormed the Nexus compound shortly after the Speaker's arrival," Yilda continued. "Managed to, ah, spirit the woman off-world in a small vessel. Quite an astounding feat. One that hadn't occurred before—or since." Yilda touched the reader's featureless surface. The room lights dimmed, and in the centre of the table, a projection of a narrow corridor appeared. Two men whose faces had been electronically obscured carried the limp body of a woman into a tiny cabin and dropped her on a bunk. One of the men moved an IV drip next to her, inserted a catheter into her arm. "We obtained this, um, record many years ago. Made by the kidnappers. Or so we were told. She is the Speaker taken hostage."

Losson swore softly. Everyone else—except for Ruen, who had closed his eyes and seemed to be meditating—stared at the projection, Mira with her mouth agape. Josua's chair complained as he shifted; he leaned in toward the projection, studying it intently. Even Liis, who up until now had kept her head lowered, was watching the scene warily.

"Chance encounter, really. Privateer limping away from, ah, a disastrous encounter. Bridge of the ship almost completely sheared off. Sole survivor managed to seal herself in the only section of the ship without a major hull breach. She, too, would have died had one of our longhaul ships not encountered the damaged vessel. Yes. Still, she might have been left to die except for the, ah, interesting story she had to tell. Claimed to have been part of the kidnapping. Offered the Facilitator on the longhaul ship documents and recordings as proof." Yilda tapped the cards on the table. "She insisted that she was the one who made the recording of the men carrying the Speaker into the cabin. Hey? But an analysis of the, um, recordings proved that to be a blatant lie. The height of the camera and its movement suggested a body profile that didn't match hers. Nevertheless, the recording appears to be authentic. Perhaps she found it on one of the vessels they, ah, boarded."

Yilda pressed the surface of the reader again, and the scene changed. The Speaker was in a chair now, pinioned by restraints. Her head was locked in an elaborate clamp, the skin of her scalp folded back, flaps of flesh pinned in place. Dozens of electrodes projected from holes in her skull; blackened goggles covered her eyes. Despite her restraints, she trembled visibly.

"In any case, a detailed record of their actions. Initially kept the Speaker sedated. Then, ah, placed her in cryosuspension until they were a considerable distance from Berin. Followed an erratic, random course. Yes. To be safe. Woke her periodically to make her pass along, um, demands to Nexus for her release. Only they had no intention of ransoming her. Actual objective, you see, was to set up a controlled situation. To observe a Speaker communicating."

"Why?" Losson asked.

"Foolishly, they hoped to discover the *secret* of the Speakers. But their experiment was a dismal failure. However, they learned a few, um, interesting things. Two of relevance to us. First, the Speaker's ability to communicate depends on being in a significant gravitational field. Yes. A planet orbiting a stellar mass, for example, would be suitable. Second, Speakers—or at least this one—haven't a limitless range, as was, ah, believed. The maximum, they discovered, three light years. Yes. Beyond that, incapable of contacting her peers."

"How could they tell?" Josua asked without taking his eyes from the projection. He was completely absorbed by the scene.

"Used a kind of modified EEG. A distinctive marker pattern accompanied any, ah, communication. Outside of the three-light-year limit, no marker activity."

"So?" Losson said from where he slouched in his chair. "You think they'll trade for these recordings? They'd sooner see us dead."

"No, no," Yilda said. "Losson's right. If Nexus knew we had these, they'd, ah, destroy us without hesitation. That's not why these recordings are, ah, significant." Yilda removed one card, placed another in the slot. The projection dissipated and was replaced by a star map that stretched across three-quarters of the table. A horizontal scale showed the image represented forty light years of space. It contained thousands of stars marked by white points, most clustered at either end, but thinning toward the middle, its general shape reminiscent of an hourglass on its side: it was a map of the

Right and Left Leg Clusters. The Twins, a binary star system and the seat of power for Nexus, burned red in the centre of the Left Leg cluster. Bh'Haret, twenty-one light years distant, was represented by a pale green light at the far end of the much smaller Right Leg cluster.

Yilda touched the projector and most of the stars winked out, leaving a hundred or so, most in the Left Leg, which turned bright blue. "Systems, ah, affiliated with Nexus," Yilda said. Looking around the table, he asked, "Notice anything, um, peculiar?" The map began to rotate.

Sav stared at the starscape. The pattern seemed random, except near the centre where the fog of stars thinned, gave out briefly, then thickened again. In the place where the hour-glass narrowed, a lone star shone, marked the midpoint between the Left and Right Leg Clusters. Sav checked the scale, looked at the empty space again.

"The rift," Sav said.

"Yes, yes." Yilda nodded, vigorously. The map stopped rotating, expanded to zoom on the section containing the isolated star. It was centered between affiliated systems in either cluster. But the systems were over five light years apart. "If Speakers are limited to communicating over distances of no more than three light years, how is the, ah, Left Leg Cluster connected to the Right?"

"A repeater station," Josua said excitedly; he half rose from his seat. The reflection of the holo glittered in his eyes. "They have a repeater station!"

Yilda's lips drew together into a thin smile. "That star is the only sizeable mass in the rift. Which, ah, means they have to have a station. There." The image zoomed again, the star expanding until it was the size of a thumbnail; another object, a white point, appeared near the edge of the table. "General survey object SJH-1231-K, Nexus Universal Catalogue," Yilda said, pointing at the new indicator. "Barren world without the distinction of a name. Thin atmosphere, cloaked in a severe and perpetual winter. Once supported rudimentary life. But now, little more than a ball of stone and ice circling this lone sun. Yes."

"And let us not forget the *thriving* colony of Speakers." Losson sneered. "Bah! Pure speculation."

Josua glared at him. Ruen, who'd opened his eyes, now seemed to be watching the proceedings with open amusement. He edged toward Mira, a smile twisting up his lips, and began whispering loudly.

Hebuiza leaned forward, said something to Losson that Sav couldn't quite hear; at the same time Yilda was saying, "No, no, no," and waving his hand for silence. Losson's face turned crimson and he began sputtering a retort. He turned to Sav and said something.

"What?" Sav said. "What did you say?" He couldn't make out the small man's words.

"Quiet!" Josua shouted, hammering his fist violently on the table. The reader jumped, shivering the image above the table; half a dozen data cards clattered to the floor. "Let Yilda finish!"

Losson narrowed his eyes, but clamped his mouth shut. Hebuiza sat back, arms crossed rigidly.

"Yes." Yilda stooped to retrieve the data cards that had fallen to the floor and restacked them, continuing. "We have substantial evidence to corroborate the, ah, hypothesis." He patted the pile. "Reports from worlds bordering the rift. About Nexus activity near that star. Nexus's own detailed survey of the world, disseminated readily to affiliates—perhaps to discourage by showing the place to be a useless piece of rock. A transmission, purportedly from a non-affiliate ship that wandered too close to the planet. The transmission contains long-distance survey shots taken before the ship, ah, disappeared. Yes." A frame appeared above the planet, within it a roughly pixilated image with jagged edges: smeared shades of white, granite grey, a drop of brown. At first, nothing distinct could be made out, but then the borders between pixels dissolved, the colours melting into each other as the image was enhanced. It became an orbital view of a white plain at the foot of a mountain range. In the centre of the plain was a perfectly circular cream-coloured smudge, far too regular a pattern to be natural. "Yes," Yilda said. "Likely an artificial dome."

"I . . . I still don't understand the relevance of all this," Mira said, running her hands nervously along the edge of the table. "Why should we care about this place?"

"Don't you see?" Losson said irritably, like he was talking to a dim-witted child. "It's the leverage Yilda wants. The loss of the relay station would be a major setback."

"It would sever their communications network," Penirdth explained, more gently. "The Speakers in the Right Leg would be alone, without their central authority—and unable to dispense any more of the information that keeps them in power, since everything flows from the Hub that orbits The Twins. Chaos would result. Even with their fastest ships, decades would pass before Nexus could transport new Speakers to the station. A thousand years of careful expansion into the Right Leg would come unravelled."

"Yes, indeed," Yilda said. "Absolutely correct." Beside him, Hebuiza nodded curtly. "The plan, you see. Send *Viracosa* to the Twins to secure the antidote. While *Ea* goes to object SJH-1231-K to, ah, assume control."

Assume control? Sav thought. *He means take the Speakers at the relay station hostage. If there even is a relay station.*

Everyone around the table was staring at Yilda. He seemed unperturbed.

"Once we control the station," he continued, "we can make good on our threats. Yes." Yilda looked around the room. "We have 104 days left. Time enough to prep the ships and get us into stasis before the plague manifests, eh? We time it so both ships arrive at their destinations at the same precise moment. We can then establish communications through the Speakers, using a prearranged series of, um, keywords. If a keyword is not passed at the appropriate time, those at the repeater station can use their, ah, discretion, to apply more pressure."

"Kill, or torture, our hostages," Sav said.

"To, ah, be more precise, yes."

"It's crazy," Sav said. Penirdth nodded his agreement, but Josua had eased back into his seat, lost in thought. "First off," Sav continued, "if they do have a relay station there, it's going to be defended. Second, to send *Ea* and *Viracosa* to those destinations would take far more fuel than we have."

Yilda smiled. "To answer the second question first, we have more than enough fuel. Yes. Our, ah, mission to Gibb was primarily to obtain rare metals: iridium, cerium and iodates. We arrived at the orbital lazarette to find news of the plague had preceded us. They knew little, but understood it had, ah, devastated Bh'Haret. Didn't matter to them that we left five years before the plague manifested. They asked us to leave immediately. Warned us that if we didn't comply, we would be, ah, destroyed."

"I was surprised they were so lenient," Losson said. "I would have destroyed our ship with no warning."

"As would I," Yilda said. "But, ah, Gibb has an elected government. Destroying us would carry an enormous political cost. And an imminent plebiscite was in the works. Yes. No one wanted to take responsibility for giving the order. Understanding this, I bargained with them. Fill our hold with deuterium fuel pellets and we leave quietly. I reasoned that we could return to Bh'Haret, assess the, um, situation. If Bh'Haret proved uninhabitable, we would still have ample fuel left to reach a dozen different systems and try for asylum, hey? The fuel pellets were a small price to pay to get rid of us. The rulers of Gibb were only too eager to, ah, comply."

"You still haven't answered my first question," Sav said. "How do you propose to 'take control' of the repeater station?"

"I can't answer." Yilda waved a hand at Sav to cut off the objection he was about to make. "More precisely, I won't. The less the crew going to The Twins knows of the other mission, the better. Yes. Hebuiza and I believe we can, ah, compromise the defences at the relay station. When the time is right, we will share the details with the crew that accompanies us."

"Even given that, there's still a big hole in your plan." It was the first time Liis had spoken. "How will those at the repeater station receive the antidote? They'll die before a cure can reach them." She looked around the table, her gaze lingering on Josua. "They'll die alone, on an alien world." Josua's expression remained blank.

"There is a good chance the Speakers have the facilities to synthesize the antidote at the repeater station. Because of the, um, isolation—and importance, yes—of the station, they will almost certainly have sophisticated medical facilities. For any contingency. But if it's not possible to, ah, synthesize, the party there can return to stasis. Yes. And wait for *Viracosa* to arrive from The Twins. One of our demands will be refuelling and free passage for both groups to return to Bh'Haret. Once we're home, we use the antidote to cure those in stasis."

"They'll never let us get away with it," Losson said. "They'll destroy *Ea* on its way back to Bh'Haret. Or whip up another plague for our return!"

"They will not," Yilda said confidently. "Eyes of every world—affiliate and non-affiliate alike—will be on us. If our, um, plan succeeds, Nexus will take samples of the 'plague' from those on *Ea*, analyze it and 'produce' an antidote—all without admitting their guilt. Yes. Deny engineering the plague. After that, they daren't destroy us. That would, um, implicate them."

Sav did a quick mental calculation. "Five hundred years," he said. "That's how long it will take to reach The Twins." Out of the corner of his eye he noticed Ruen stiffen in his seat. His air of superciliousness seemed to vanish.

"Five hundred and, ah, twenty-eight," Yilda said.

"Then it'll be more than a thousand years before we return. The facility will never support those in suspension that long," Sav said. "Look what's happened in the thirty years it's been unattended."

Yilda shrugged. "This is most unfortunate. Yes. We'll install fissionable power sources and, um, triple redundant backup systems, like those in longhaul ships. Much more reliable than the solar array. And give the AIs control of our modified waldos, so that they have 'arms' and 'legs'. Perhaps they will last. Perhaps they won't. But there's nothing more we can do. Our resources are, after all, limited."

"I have listened to this blasphemy long enough!" Grunting,

Ruen pushed his chair back and stood. "One thousand years! I will participate no further in this attempt to stay the Dissolution." His cane whistled as he brought it down on the table with an ear-splitting crack. "Beware of your transgressions! I agreed to attend this meeting so that I might warn you—as I am bound to by my articles of faith. Even considering such a course of action is an unpardonable offence. You will all die uncleansed—shrouded in your sin!" He puffed out his scrawny chest beneath his robes. "I have consulted the blessed database. Its message was unequivocal. Temptation is to be shunned! We must be pure when the Dissolution comes. This *mission* of which you talk is a wanton disregard of *anhaa-10*'s pleasure!" Ruen gathered his cloak about himself and walked off, cane clicking angrily. "Prepare yourself!" he said, turning at the door to deliver his final warning. "The Brothers cannot save you. They cannot save themselves!" Then he spun around, cape billowing, and strode off. His footsteps faded in the distance.

Mira looked stunned; she opened her mouth, then snapped it shut.

"Idiot!" Losson spat. "Have you seen his blessed database? It's a network of data card receptacles he's cobbled together—an insane search engine. He puts the cards in a cloth bag and shakes them, then inserts them randomly. Its answers are as crazy as he is!" Losson turned his glare on Josua. "You should have left him where he was, to starve to death. Then he'd have experienced his holy Dissolution!"

"He's pulled his weight," Josua said sharply.

"'The Brothers'," Penirdth said. "What did he mean, when he said they couldn't protect us?"

"He meant Nexus," Hebuiza said. The Facilitator glanced at Yilda, who nodded his approval. Hebuiza carried on: "There are many variants of the story, all apocryphal, but the common thread is that two brothers, twins, discovered the secret of folding dimensions which allows two people to communicate instantaneously—regardless of the distance separating them. Using this discovery, the brothers trained Speakers and sent them out to the seeded worlds, so building their empire. One brother, suspicious of the other's intentions, cast him into a fiery pit. For centuries, Nexus was also called the Brothers, but the term has long since fallen into disuse. In all probability, the name arose because of the binary stars around which the Hub orbits; the name of that system is, of course, *The Twins*."

"He thinks we're in league with Nexus?" Mira asked, the incredulity clear in her voice.

"No," Josua answered softly. "He fears anything that might interfere with the Dissolution. If anyone from Bh'Haret survives, the Dissolution may be prevented."

"We should get rid of Ruen," Losson said to Yilda. "At best, he's a liability. At worst, he'll undermine our plans."

Our plans? Sav thought.

"What?" Mira looked as if she couldn't believe she'd heard him correctly.

"I agree," Hebuiza said.

"*No.*" Josua's voice was low, but there was no mistaking the threat in it. "He stays."

Mira nodded, her expression one of relief.

She's a believer, Sav suddenly realized. *One of the faithful. That's why Ruen kept whispering to her.*

Hebuiza seemed nonplussed; he looked at Yilda again, who lifted his shoulders in a slight shrug. In his seat, Losson seemed to vibrate with suppressed anger.

"So you've already decided on the crews," Sav said.

"Yes, yes," Yilda acknowledged. "Hebuiza and I will take *Ea* to the repeater station. You and Josua will take *Viracosa* to the Nexus Hub. Your, um, mission will be simpler, therefore requiring only two crew members to pilot the vessel. We will need all the help we can get at the repeater station, so the remaining people will come with us: Mira, Penirdth, Losson and Liis."

Sav glanced around the table, trying to gauge the others' reactions. Josua's momentary anger had passed; his eyes gleamed with barely suppressed excitement. Losson scowled. Hebuiza and Yilda were like bookends, both sporting carefully neutral expressions. Penirdth looked off thoughtfully into the distance, considering, while Mira darted nervous glances at Yilda. Sav found his gaze lingering on Liis. But she only stared intently at the surface of the table.

"You're forgetting Ruen," Josua said softly.

Hebuiza arched his eyebrows. "No purpose would be served in assigning him to either crew."

"He can come with me," Josua said. Adding, after a moment's pause: "If he wishes."

"I won't have him aboard," Sav said.

"It's, ah, Josua's decision," Yilda said. "After all, he'll be the commander, hey?"

"What?" Astounded, Sav rocked forward in his seat. He looked around the table for support, but knew immediately he had none. The newcomers watched him, their expressions carefully neutral. Sav knew then that Hebuiza, Josua and Liis had already poisoned the others against him. And could he blame them? For an instant he saw himself through everyone else's eyes: unkempt beard, wild, tangled hair, clothes shiny with their own dirt. How could they think he was anything other than borderline psychotic?

"Sav?" Yilda stared at him.

Sav swallowed. He'd been outvoted. So he accepted his demotion as he'd accepted everything else, with a fatalistic shrug.

"Let Ruen decide for himself," Josua said. "If he wants to stay, I'm not going to force him to accompany us." He looked at Sav. "Okay?"

He's throwing me a bone, Sav thought. *Trying to take the edge off.* He shrugged again.

"What? We've . . . we've decided?" It was Mira. Her childlike voice rose as she spoke. It had the quality of a barely controlled hysteria.

She's terrified, Sav thought. *Ruen's scared her out of her wits. Belief in the Dissolution means our mission is an unpardonable sin.* Sav suddenly realized he was gripping the edge of the table so tightly his fingers ached. Taking a deep breath, he released his grip.

Yilda looked around the table. "Unless anyone has a, ah, better suggestion. . . ." He drew his thick lips into a wan smile, exposing his lower teeth. The carvings stood out clearly against the dark interior of his mouth.

"What choice do we have?" Josua asked. He sounded almost elated.

Losson scowled, but raised no objection. Penirdth was nodding, almost reluctantly. And Mira watched Penirdth, her Captain, apprehensively, as if the decision wasn't hers to make.

"Yes," Liis repeated. "What choice do we have?"

Though she echoed Josua's words, hers were filled with bitterness and resignation. She stared openly at him. The scars on her face seemed to writhe, her eyes dilated in the diffuse light of the projection that still hovered over the table, filled with a look of infinite sadness.

"Mira?" It was Penirdth who spoke. "What do you think?"

Mira's face went slack; she closed her eyes and swallowed, nodding weakly, as if signalling her own executioner to drop the blade.

"Well," said Yilda. "All agreed then. Hey?"

103 DAYS LEFT

Preparations began in earnest the day after the meeting. The Facilitators closeted themselves in Hebuiza's lab to design and build the equipment they would need—although they refused to tell anyone exactly what that equipment might be. Since Penirdth and Mira's EVA suits were still in good condition, they had been assigned the arduous job of using the dropships to transfer fuel pellets from the hold of *Viracosa* to the ring of bulbous feeder tanks circling the ignition chamber on *Ea*; Josua, along with Liis, undertook the task of recharging the oxygen/nitrogen cartridges, and bleeding off the cryoagents and liquid nitrogen from the stasis facility for use aboard the two vessels. It fell to Losson and Sav to scavenge an entirely new list of goods, mainly weapons, or materials to construct weapons.

Sav took an immediate dislike to the man. His sour disposition radiated from him like a stench; a steady stream of invective spewed from his mouth.

"Fucking stick man," he said the moment he and Sav lifted off in the VTOL on their first day together. "Hebuiza's a fucking insect. Except an insect has more intelligence!"

As much as Sav disliked the Facilitator, he refrained from commenting.

On the morning of their third day scavenging together, minutes before they were to leave, Sav heard shouts from the end of the first-level corridor. Sprinting from the elevator, Sav found Losson had trapped Ruen in a narrow, dead end hallway. Losson's compact, muscular form effectively blocked the *patrix*'s escape and Ruen held his cane high over his head with one spindly arm, ready to bring it down on Losson's head should he come within its range.

"*Blasphemer!*" the holy man hissed. "Your unblessed atoms will be scattered, your soul will become fodder for the enlightened!"

Losson barked out a derisive laugh. "Maybe I should scatter your atoms right now!" "Hey!" Sav said, out of breath from his run. "Stop it!"

Losson turned. "What are *you* going to do?"

Seeing his chance, Ruen leapt forward and brought down his cane. But Losson must have been warned by the expression on Sav's face, for he spun around, shooting up one open hand. The shaft of Ruen's stick caught Losson's palm with a loud, painful-sounding smack. Losson's fingers instinctively snapped shut around it, as blood drained from his face.

The two stood, clutching either end of the cane; then Ruen released his grip, darting underneath Losson's upraised arm. With surprising agility, the holy man bounded past Sav and sprinted down the corridor, robes flapping behind him.

At first, Losson seemed too surprised to be angry; then his face coloured, and he began to shake. Grabbing the other end of the cane, he brought it down over his knee; it snapped like a gunshot, echoing down the corridor. Losson hurled the pieces into the corner. The flesh of his left hand was still bright red from where the shaft had struck.

"I'll kill you, you old bastard!" he shouted, stepping out into the main corridor. "Next time I see you, I'll kill you!"

After this incident, Ruen all but disappeared; Sav assumed the holy man had taken to the lower levels, to wait out the storm. Losson fumed for a few days, then seemed to shrug off the incident, making no more open threats on the *patrix*'s life. When Ruen finally emerged from hiding—he referred to it as a period of prayer and contemplation—he went to great lengths to avoid Losson. Not much help before, now the *patrix* refused to participate in their preparations at all.

"He hasn't had to do a lick of work in his life," Losson said, with undisguised disdain, while watching Sav unload the dropship. "Why should he start now?"

One other odd thing came out of Ruen's absence: the holy man told them that after meditating on his role as their spiritual leader during his period of "contemplation," he had decided to go with *Viracosa* to the Nexus Hub—despite his dire warnings about missing the Dissolution. He claimed he'd had a vision.

"My duty as your pastor became clear," he declared loudly. "I have been forbidden to abandon your souls. Against my wishes, I will accompany you until such time as you are enlightened."

"More likely he fears abandoning our food," Losson commented later, when he heard of the holy man's change of heart. For Mira, at least, Ruen's partial turnaround seemed comforting. She embraced her work with an undisguised relief.

Throughout all of this, Liis paid no more attention to Sav than she had before; if anything, she seemed more distant. It was as if she were making a point, trying to erase their encounter. Her indifference irritated Sav. It wasn't that he'd expected anything from her; he was still convinced Josua had sent her to his room that night. But it bothered him, nonetheless—not so much the way she treated *him* as the way in which she still doted on Josua, following his movements intently, like a protective mother. Sav had wondered if his reaction might be jealousy, but dismissed the notion quickly; just loneliness, pure and simple, and the sting of being ignored by someone he had once considered his friend.

After the half a dozen times he and Liis had crewed together, he'd supposed he knew her as well as he knew anyone else. Which meant, he realized—with an unexpected wave of sadness—that he'd never really known her at all.

99 DAYS LEFT

It was late, and all night Sav had faded in and out of an agitated half-sleep. The stasis facility was silent, the lights, except for orange emergency lamps, extinguished to save power. He slouched down the hallway toward the dropshaft—then stopped in front of Liis's room, the door wide open, her cot empty.

Only one other place she could be at this time of night. *With Josua*, he thought.

Abruptly he turned and strode down the corridor back to his own room. He sat on his cot, trying to convince himself that Liis's presence in Josua's room didn't matter. That none of it mattered.

Yet it did.

He cursed himself for being so foolish; Liis wanted Josua. Not him. And until now, it hadn't even occurred to Sav that he did want her. In a month they'd be in different ships, heading for worlds light years apart. The odds of surviving Yilda's demented mission were infinitesimal; the chance of seeing Liis again, after their departure, non-existent. But none of that changed the way his mind insisted on veering back to the image of Liis and Josua, together.

Later, Sav heard the elevator softly rumble to a stop, and its doors squeak as they slid open. He waited, listening for Liis's footsteps. But there was only silence.

Rising from his cot, Sav stepped quietly down the corridor. The elevator doors were still open. Inside, in the harsh glare of the undimmed lights, Liis stood, leaning against the back wall of the car, her head bowed. When Sav stepped inside, the elevator bobbed slightly as the cables took his weight.

"Liis," Sav said, softly. "What's wrong?"

Liis looked up, face blank, eyes red. She blinked, seemed confused by the question. "Nothing," she answered, more to herself than to him. She lowered her gaze. "He isn't Josua," she said, like she was answering a question that hadn't been asked.

"What?"

"He doesn't want me."

"What are you talking about?" He tightened his hold on her shoulders, aware suddenly of the movement of her bones and flesh beneath his fingers. Disconcerted, he let go and jammed his hands in his pockets. "Liis, what's happened?"

When she spoke it was as if she were talking past Sav. "I went to his room, every night. Listened to his theories about Nexus. Sat with him while he spoke over and over about *our* betrayal." She paused, her eyes wavering. "Talk. We talked. But he wouldn't come near me. Wouldn't touch me." In a voice so quiet Sav could barely hear it, she said, "So I asked. I begged him. Told him I'd do anything he wanted."

Blood throbbed in Sav's temples.

"He asked me to be Shiranda." Liis's expression hardened. "He wanted to lie there, with his eyes closed, while I—" her words abruptly fell off. "He had things he wanted me to say, sounds he wanted me to make." She blanched. "It couldn't be Josua." Reaching out, she clutched Sav's sleeve. "There's someone else there, someone we don't know at all. He looks like Josua, but he's only playing a role, a character. Someone he knows, but doesn't feel."

"I . . . I guess we're all a little broken. After what we've been through." Sav lowered his gaze until it fell on the hand that still clutched his sleeve—then saw the finger-sized bruises purpling her wrist and forearm, disappearing underneath the cuff of her long-sleeved shirt. Was it a trick of the shadows or were there dark smudges on her collarbone as well? Anger suffused Sav. "What's he done to you?"

His outrage seemed to wake her; for the first time, she looked directly at him. Blinking like she'd just woken, she followed his gaze to her own wrist, examined it dispassionately. She released Sav's sleeve and crossed her arms, burying the bruises from sight. "He's

. . . a good man." She began rocking slowly, her shoulders hunched, arms wrapped tightly around her torso. "It's *not* him," she said, with utter conviction. She looked pointedly at Sav; the pupils of her hard, grey eyes were tiny points. "Josua would never . . . hurt me." She paused. "Would he?"

She's still making excuses for him, Sav thought bitterly. *She won't let herself see what he's become.* It sickened him, heightened his infuriation—and drained him, too. He tried to come up with something to say. But all he could do was look away.

"*Would he?*" Liis made no attempt to hide her desperation.

"I don't know."

A tear fell, ticked against the toe of Sav's dusty boot, leaving a dark imprint. Liis shoved roughly past him.

In the silence, he heard the click of her latch bolt falling into place; and then her muffled sobs.

98 DAYS LEFT

Work ate away their remaining time. Initially, Sav had refused to wear the watch Hebuiza and Yilda had made—but he was constantly doing the same calculation in his head, arriving at the exact number of days allotted him. So he gave in, and strapped it to his wrist. Strangely, this seemed to alleviate his anxiety, for though he checked it constantly the first few days, within a week he was looking at it no more often than he would have an ordinary watch. The fact of his own demise had taken on a commonplace patina.

Fifteen more days passed. Liis drifted through the hallways, wrapped in her own disconsolate thoughts, her expression betraying extremes of pathetic hope and miserable resignation. Josua seemed insensible to her attentions, to anything other than the preparations. Sav found himself going rigid whenever he approached, remembering the marks on Liis's wrists—wanting to do something, but never sure quite what. Soon, he avoided them both.

Losson was now running his own scavenging missions in *Viracosa*'s dropship. Yilda had insisted they split up, citing "security reasons," presumably because he sent Losson to gather material pertinent to their mission to the relay station. Material he didn't want Sav to see.

By the end of the thirty-first day (Sav's watch now reported seventy-two days remaining), *Ea* had been fully prepped: new cryo cells installed to hold its larger crew, extra fuel transferred from *Viracosa*, food stores replenished, and new navigational data uploaded to its AI. It happened faster than Sav had expected. But there was still plenty of work left to do on *Viracosa*. He had expected the others to pitch in with him, but the moment they'd finished with

Ea, Yilda had given them all new orders. They dispersed, bent on their own tasks. It reminded Sav that in a few shorts weeks they'd be going their separate ways, and he'd likely never see any of them again.

By himself, Sav began the arduous task of prepping *Viracosa* for a mission longer than any she'd ever flown.

"If we don't run into any, um, difficulties, we anticipate breaking orbit in sixty days." Yilda tapped his index finger pensively against his lips. He looked around the table, then dropped his hand.

They had all gathered in the boardroom. Sav had been the last one to arrive, taking the only seat left, sandwiched between Josua on one side and Ruen on the other, a chain of data cards dangling loosely from his knobby, rheumatic fingers.

"Which leaves us only twelve days," Losson muttered sourly, staring at his watch.

"Sixty days?" Sav shifted uncomfortably in his seat. "I'm not sure I can get *Viracosa* ready by then. If you could release Liis for a few days . . ."

"No. We need her in the lab, hey? You and Josua will have to do your best."

"But—"

"You, Josua and Ruen are more than adequate for the job. Yes? And as of now, the two crews should stay far apart from one another. Security issues."

"Security issues?"

"It is, ah, imperative, that Two Crew know as little as possible about the other mission. In case Two Crew is, um, compromised."

Two Crew. It was how Yilda had taken to identifying the missions: Two Crew—Sav, Josua and Ruen—running *Viracosa* to the heart of the Nexus Polyarchy; One Crew, taking *Ea* to the repeater station.

"You mean intercepted by Nexus."

"Ah, yes."

Sav crossed his arms. He hated to admit it, but Yilda was right— even though he didn't see much hope for either mission.

"There's more." Hebuiza's voice boomed, startlingly loud after Yilda's soft, lisping speech. He was sitting opposite Sav, and now he leaned forward, his long frame bent over the table. "From now on you're not to go near the lab. You're not to ask any questions. Either will be considered a breach of security, and dealt with swiftly."

"Let me guess," Sav said. "You're in charge of security."

Hebuiza's thin lips crooked up into a mirthless grin.

"Yes," Yilda said. "It is, um, critical, that the members of Two Crew stay away from the lab."

"I've implemented special measures," Hebuiza said with obvious relish. "To deal with any unauthorized attempts to enter the lab." Looking directly at Sav, he said, "You're free to test the system if you wish."

"No thanks," Sav said, determined not to give the Facilitator the satisfaction of eliciting a reaction. "I've got better things to do."

Hebuiza laughed aloud, a fleering, raucous sound.

Something twitched inside Sav, and before he knew what he was doing he was up, rocking on the balls of his feet, glaring at the lanky Facilitator. The smile had vanished from Hebuiza's face and he jerked back in his seat out of Sav's striking range. Sav felt a hand grasp his arm, restrain him.

"If there's nothing else," Josua said calmly, his grip tight on Sav's forearm, "we have lots of work left. Don't we, Sav?"

Sav stared at Josua's fingers pressing into his flesh; he thought of the now-faded bruises that ringed Liis's wrists. "Whatever," Sav said, jerking his arm from Josua's grip. The smile reappeared on Hebuiza's face, but this time it was an uncertain, fearful thing. Sav turned and strode out into the corridor. He stepped into the elevator and punched the button for his floor.

Before the doors sealed, Josua blocked them, forced them back. He stepped halfway into the car, keeping his hand over the light sensor so the door remained open. "What the hell's the matter with you?"

Josua wouldn't hurt me, Liis had said. *Would he?*

"Nothing," Sav muttered and punched the button again.

"Don't let Hebuiza get under your skin," Josua said. "He's not worth it."

"Not worth it?" Sav curled his hands into fists. "Just what the hell is, anymore?"

For a moment Josua looked surprised at the question. "Why, nothing, of course." Letting his hand fall, he took a step back; the elevator doors began to close. "Except maybe what we're doing."

"Yeah," Sav said. But the word, once uttered, didn't sound as sarcastic as he'd intended.

The work on *Viracosa* fell mostly to Sav. Ruen was useless at anything requiring technical aptitude or physical strength; Josua had fallen into the habit of going off on his own. Frequently he would take one of the dropships out. Where he went or what he did, he'd never say, and Sav never bothered to ask. Sometimes he'd be gone for most of the day. No one seemed concerned.

And Ruen was not at a loss to fill his time either: he busied himself with preparations for the Dissolution. Often strains of his murmured prayers and homilies were audible up and down the main hallway as the *patrix* paced the corridor, hands clasped behind his back, fingers twined in his chain of data cards. His blessed database grew.

Time crawled by, Sav's life slipping away with each passing moment. The finality scared and sickened him, making his hands shake whenever they weren't occupied with his work. Occasionally he'd see Liis, and each time he'd stare at her, a strange thought growing like a tumour in his mind: what would have happened if Liis had felt about him the way she did about Josua? He knew he would not have spurned her, as Josua had.

But could he have loved her the way she wanted to be loved?

He wasn't sure he had the capacity. That he could now love a woman out of necessity, the only woman left *to* love, seemed hopelessly pathetic. No, like so many other lost chances, the possibility of love seemed as remote to Sav as his chances of surviving the plague.

45 Days Left

The end came abruptly.

Waking on the fifty-seventh day (his watch now showed forty-five days remaining to the onset of symptoms), Sav discovered Liis's door open, and what few personal items Liis had accumulated nowhere to be seen. He rushed to the elevator.

Emerging on the main level, he found the door to Hebuiza's lab open. Racks of equipment lay dormant; bits of wire and discarded circuit boards littered the floor. Three long tables were empty, whatever had been on them gone. Half-running, half-walking down the corridor, he emerged from the facility. Large, lazy flakes of snow descended around him; a shroud of white covered the ground. Hip-high drifts now lined either side of the path. A hundred metres away, at the far side of the landing pad, sat *Ea*'s dropship, its hatch open. Squeezed in next to it was the dropship from *Viracosa*. Sav saw Yilda, dressed in his EVA suit, standing just inside *Ea*'s hatch; on the ground next to the ship was Josua, wrapped in his bulky jacket, passing boxes to Yilda. Sav trotted down the path toward them. When he was twenty metres away, Yilda caught sight of him, spoke to Josua. The two men stopped work. They waited for him.

Sav slowed to a walk as he approached. Despite the temperature, his forehead was lightly filmed with sweat. "What's going on?"

"Preparations completed," Yilda said. "Final load, hey? Shuttling it up to *Ea* in a few moments. Breaking orbit in six hours."

"Breaking orbit? At the meeting you said we'd be leaving when we only had twelve days remaining." Sav glanced at his watch. "There's still forty-seven days left!"

"Yes and, um, no," Yilda answered. "Two Crew will be departing when there are twelve days remaining as, ah, I said."

"The others," Sav said hesitantly. "Losson, Mira, Penirdth," he paused. "Liis . . ."

"One Crew has already boarded *Ea*, running the pre-flight checks," Josua said.

"They're coming back?"

"No." Josua sounded impatient. "This is the last load. When it's gone, it'll just be the three of us."

So that's it, Sav thought. *Liis is gone.* In a few hours, *Ea*'s crew would immerse themselves in baths of liquid nitrogen, the creep of the plague halted until they woke again, centuries from now, on another dead, frozen world.

Josua turned his attention back to the pile of boxes and struggled to dislodge a bulky crate. *It's wasn't supposed to end like this*, Sav thought. Craning his neck, he looked up but could see nothing except undifferentiated white, as smooth and impenetrable as a wall. A thousand times he had played over in his mind what he might say and do at the moment of their separation. But that chance had vanished. He felt cheated.

"Are you going to stare at the sky all day?" Josua asked. In the last weeks, his demeanour had changed subtly; he'd assumed more the role of commander, deferring less and less to Sav's judgements on things concerning *Viracosa*. He raised his watch so that its face pointed accusingly at Sav. "The clock is running. Remember?"

12 DAYS LEFT

For the first time in thirty years, the stasis facility hummed with something akin to contentment. The backbone had been restored; power levels had risen sharply; administrative computers had come back online and central authority re-established. Of course, there was no way to recover the clients it had been forced to discontinue. In the last half year, however, it had not had to terminate one active cell.

But now the complex was on its own again.

Early that morning, while the sky was still dark, SAIN-FA-1 (Semi-autonomous Artificial Intelligence Node—Facility Administration 1), had sent a modified waldo to sit on its haunches next to the lift pad. Using its remote, it broadcast images of the departure of the last three autonomous intelligences, called Josua, Sav and Ruen, as they boarded their shuttle and lifted off. Though no one had told 1 (as SAIN-FA-1 liked to refer to itself) explicitly that they would not be returning, the AI had inferred from an analysis of their conversations and those of the ones who'd left before, that they would not be back for a considerable time—if at all. Still, 1 was confident it could run the facility for centuries, if not indefinitely, without human intervention. After their ship had pierced the clouds and disappeared, 1 sent the waldo back to the lake, to resume its repairs on the solar array.

It was four hours later that things started to go wrong.

The waldo at the lake stopped transmitting.

Within two hundred nanoseconds of the first event, one of the local AIs reported all six cells under its care had terminated. The AI itself abruptly stopped transmitting. Concerned, 1 queried the node but received no response. Twenty nanoseconds later, two more

AI nodes reported similar problems before they too went offline. One, however, managed to transmit a visual it had captured before falling silent: eight simultaneous flashes, one atop each of the chamber's active stasis cells. The domes imploded, a backwash of cryoprotective glycerol splashing onto the chamber floor. By the time administrative AI had reviewed the visual, over half the remaining AIs had reported their own loss of clients and gone offline, three more managing to transmit images nearly identical to the first.

Less than one hundred milliseconds had passed since the anomalous events began.

1 didn't feel panic. Its designers hadn't coded for that. What it did feel, however, was urgency—an overwhelming need to find the cause of the crisis and to determine possible solutions. It suspended all other processing tasks, then immediately performed a priority pattern-matching search. It found a likely correlation: in the library of recorded activity it discovered that over the last few months one of the humans had visited all one thousand, four hundred and thirty-seven active cells in the complex. And this same human had also been to every AI in the facility—including 1 itself. The conclusion, when it came a few billionths of a second later, was inescapable: the human meant to destroy the clients and the AIs that tended them. And there was nothing 1 could do about it.

In its last few nanoseconds, SAIN-FA-1 asked itself the machine equivalent of *why?*

But before its search routines could ferret out any sort of answer, it too went offline.

SJH-1231-K, THE RELAY STATION

Outside, a frozen hell.

Bitter arctic winds sweep down from the ice fields and surge across a vast white plain, beating angrily against the arc of the dome. The structure is ten kilometres in diameter and sunk deeply into the bedrock; its shell is several metres thick, but its outermost layer is composed of a transparent material less than a micromillimetre thick, its atoms locked in a rigid structure. It withstands the brutal force of the wind, the stone-cracking chill of the freeze. Even when the unlikely happens and this layer experiences a microscopic tear, tiny molecular machines repair the breach in a heartbeat.

Inside, a lush paradise.

Dark-skinned trees with arching branches and serrated leaves tower just inside the shell, oblivious to the deadly conditions metres away; spreading out on the forest floor are dense, variegated plants; soft, olive mosses cling to rocks at the right height for sitting or reclining; a remarkable array of flowers huddle around small rivulets and ponds; and winding throughout this idyll are narrow dirt paths. Though no one has ever gardened here, the paths remain clear, the flora obedient.

The forest begins to falter a kilometre from the outer wall; eventually it gives way to fields and streams, flagged walkways now meandering through tall grasses. Here and there are small orchards, the branches of the fruit trees heavy with ripe offerings. Two kilometres further and the fields also disappear. Now the sharp angles and geometric shapes of artificial structures are visible in the distance: sixty-four huge white cylinders, like monstrous fuel tanks, form a ring, two kilometres in diameter, in the centre of the dome.

NEXUS : ASCENSION

Each cylinder is several hundred metres in diameter and equally tall. Clinging to the base of these structures like creeping vines are clutches of buildings, displaying a bewildering variety of styles and shapes. Yet none of these buildings climbs to even a third the height of the cylinders.

As imposing as the cylinders are, they do not command the most attention, for rising within their ring is a precipitous mountain whose peak—two kilometres overhead—pierces the roof of the dome like a spike; the summit juts out into the unremitting arctic winds. Here, at the apex of the mountain, a platform has been erected. On it, a small group of Speakers wait, clutching a thin rail.

Though they could have watched from within the safety of the dome, or have raised another protective bubble around them, they have chosen, on a whim, to experience the event as directly as possible. They exchange glances, excited thoughts passing between them like words would amongst people without their gift. Occasionally, one laughs aloud, a half-heard sound torn and scattered by the wind. Despite the protection of their skinsuits, they instinctively huddle together as the wind gusts and tugs insistently at arms and legs. Still, the party manages an air of festivity and bravado, as if they are about to depart for a picnic or a camping trip. A few keep their minds clear, their thoughts to themselves, and watch the heavens.

A woman using a handheld tracking device points directly overhead. Heads crane in unison, but nothing is visible.

Then, skimming the atmosphere, the meteor blazes to life, the air in front of it compressed and luminous. Lighting the night sky, it leaves an incandescent trail in its wake for several brilliant seconds. A sonic boom follows like an afterthought.

As if in response to the sound of the shock wave, three of the satellites girding the planet fire their pulse weapons in unison, and the meteor bursts asunder, hundreds of fiery pieces fanning outward from the brilliant locus. The fragments burn in different colours; many flicker uncertainly. Stark, dramatic shadows grow and waver in the trembling light. Several of those observing gasp;

others tighten their hands on the railing. All eyes are locked on the web of light growing overhead. Even the wind has stilled for an instant, as if it too has deferred to the spectacle. Only now, seconds after the meteor's destruction, a dull boom, like distant thunder, reaches their ears.

In a few heartbeats it is over: fragments have already disappeared behind a mountain range to the south; others vaporize, their light fading to nothing long before they reach the ground. One piece, burning intensely, arcs downward and strikes several hundred kilometres to the north on the plain, throwing up a spume of snow, ice and steam. A moment later those on the platform feel the slightest of tremblings sing through the structure. None of the fragments come close enough to the dome for the orbitals to bother firing again.

For a time the group stands, the afterimages burning their retinae; then, when even the phantom trails have faded from their eyes, they remember where they are. The wind picks up. The show is over, the festive air has vanished. In silence they file back into the dark opening next to the platform and descend the spiral of steep, carved steps. Behind them, rock grows over the opening, as if healing a wound.

Reluctantly, they descend, returning to the unspeakable beauty and limitless abundance they've left below, each to his or her own private paradise. They drag themselves away from the momentary distraction and back toward the drab, endless routine of their lives, and the lonely task to which they are forever committed.

PART II

THE RELAY STATION · 23 DAYS LEFT

Regaining consciousness, Liis found herself hanging upside down in darkness on the bridge of *Ea*. Bands of pain seared her chest, thighs and legs where the padded straps held her into the pilot's chair. Intense pain radiated from her left forearm: she was certain it was broken. Alarm klaxons wailed and system warnings spilled through the interface into her headset. Half a dozen ruptures in the hull; navigation out completely; stress fractures in the shielding for the power plant; radiation levels creeping toward dangerous levels. Further failures, the ship informed her, were imminent.

It worked! she thought. *I can't believe it worked!*

The meteorite—or at least the part carrying *Ea*—had managed to hold together after the orbitals had fired. The explosive charges they had planted had detonated precisely at the right moment, a split second after the beam weapons had hit, shattering the rock along its fault lines to preserve their section intact. She remembered the wild spin they'd been sent into after the explosion; how it had felt like her brain was going to be pulped from the g-forces. But the mass of iron deposits had swung the rock round, working like an ablation shield to protect the lighter, more porous silicon and magnesium oxide layers into which they had tunnelled to hide their ship. Perhaps it hadn't been the smoothest of rides, but the braking and attitude jets had fired when they'd been programmed to—their action hidden by the burn of atmosphere on the outer layers of the meteorite—slowing and angling their descent enough for them to survive the impact in the weak gravitational field of the planet. She was grateful she'd blacked out before they hit.

Despite her pain, she felt an odd jubilance, a quickening of her blood unlike anything she had experienced since—

—since Josua. At the thought of him, she closed her eyes, pulled in a deep breath. The ship continued to issue its warnings.

Using a subvocal command, she ordered the alarms muted. One by one, she began shutting down the ship's systems, starting with the reactor. Almost immediately several of the warning messages vanished. Within moments the ship was barely alive, the consciousness of the AI fading to a dim point. Minimum life support remained. She checked on the others.

Green indicators on all five. The cryo cells had come through the ordeal undamaged. She initiated the cycle to revive them. *Now*, she thought, *it's time to get myself down.*

Of the three restraints that had held her in place, one had torn free. Shifting her weight, she managed to undo one of the remaining two with her right hand. The strap swung free, her weight sagging across the last restraint. Gasping, she closed her eyes against the shock of pain that shot up her arm. She hung there, rocking slightly, as the pain receded. Hooking her legs under the seat, she gritted her teeth and opened the last buckle.

Her body sagged and she began to slip; she tried to wind her legs around the pedestal of the seat, but didn't have enough room to lock her ankles.

Groping blindly, she managed to grasp one of the dangling restraints before her legs unwound completely. She tumbled into darkness, her fist wound around the strap.

When the jerk came, she was surprised at how—in gravity only one-third normal for her—her arm was nearly pulled out of its socket. She yelped and let go, remembering the distance, thinking the drop not more than a couple of metres. Her head snapped back sharply, and something raked across her right temple, tearing at her skin just before impact. Pain washed over her and obliterated consciousness.

Josua was here.

Even though he should have been eleven light years away at the hub, he stood over Liis, a lamp in his hand. The bulwarks of the circular cabin curved over her like she lay in the bottom of a barrel on its side. Liis's eyes were shut and she was unconscious, yet she could still see. It was as if she occupied several separate awarenesses simultaneously: she saw Josua from her perspective on the floor; saw herself through his eyes; saw both of them from above. It made her giddy.

Why has he followed me here? Liis wondered. *Was this part of the plan?* She tried to open her mouth, to ask him. But her body was no longer hers. It lay inert, wedged where the floor met wall (*No, ceiling*, she thought, correcting herself). A pool of blood formed a dark umbra around her head. Her left arm lay doubled back at an unnatural angle. Though she was still aware of the pain, it was muted, as if it were an annoying background noise.

Am I dying? The question flitted through her consciousness abstractly. An unimportant, pointless question. She watched the blood creep along the floor, run into a channel between two adjacent screens.

Josua crouched down; there were several oddly shaped containers at his feet. He unsealed one and drew from it a small cruciform object inlaid with tiny gems. It looked like one of the relics Ruen had frequently carried. Placing the longer end of the thing against her skull, Josua pressed a stud on the crossarm.

Pain coursed through her with the injection; her multiple perspectives wavered, collapsed back into a single perspective from where she lay the floor. *Josua*, she wanted to say, *I failed. Forgive me.*

She tried to focus on his face, but it wasn't Josua who crouched over her any more. Instead she saw a shorter man with a tired, dissipated face, gold studs running the length of his chin. Perspiration beaded on his forehead as he worked her arm back and forth until the bones ground together. His fingers bore many rings, all set with gems; they glittered, like beacons, in the yellow light cast by his lamp. The man pulled back his lips with the exertion, and Liis could see his front teeth had been carved, each in the form of a tiny human figure.

Darkness sluiced over her.

The world, cold and hard, pressed against her cheek. Her eyes were closed tight, her head throbbed, and she felt nauseated. Something tugged at her shoulder; pain radiated from her arm and shot through the rest of her body like a high voltage current. Her existence became the stomach-churning whirl, her throbbing arm its fiery locus; she hung on desperately to the edge of consciousness until the motion slowed to a lazy turn, and finally settled into a gentle rocking. Hushed words played about the edge of her consciousness.

"—impossible. She'll never—"

"—simple fracture—"

"—to do. How badly—"

"—leave her?"

"She's in no shape to travel." The voice was deep and resonant. One that Liis knew she should recognize. "She's in shock. Lost too much blood. We're not equipped to handle such an emergency."

"No. She's not hurt that badly." A different voice, another man, but softer, kinder. "It only looks like a lot of blood."

"She'll be useless. Worse, she'll be a burden. More than she's been already." *Hebuiza*, she realized. *It's Hebuiza's voice.*

"You want to leave her here to die?"

"Why not?" The Facilitator's voice was scornful. "In less than twenty-three days the first symptoms will manifest. Dying now might be better."

He wants me to die. Like this. Anger welled through her pain, pushed her agony to the background of her consciousness; Liis struggled to open her eyes, but her lids seemed glued together. Her frustration intensified. With an enormous effort, she finally managed to open her eyes a crack. She could see the dark outline of the Facilitator's suit. A person crouched beside him. Though she couldn't make out any of his features, his skin was a rich, dark brown. Then his face came into hazy focus: Penirdth.

Next to him, Hebuiza crossed his arms. "If she's not ready to travel, we'll leave her behind." The Facilitator turned and receded from view, Liis feeling the vibration of each of his steps through the bulwark. She wanted to rise up and hurl something, anything, at his retreating figure.

"Maybe . . . maybe he's right." A woman's voice this time. High and quavering. "Remember how, when she first came aboard *Viracosa*, you said she was already dead inside? Maybe she should have her Dissolution now."

"I did say that," Penirdth answered, without rancour. "But I won't leave her here while she's still alive."

"Do you honestly think she'll be ready? To travel, I mean." Mira, moved into sight, stood beside Penirdth, who shook his head.

"I don't know. The bleeding stopped on its own before we found her, and the break was clean. No telling how bad the pain will be when she comes to. It'll be a couple of hours before Yilda cuts through to the exterior. Another twelve hours before the tunnel and surface are cool enough for us to use—if Hebuiza's estimates are accurate. Fourteen hours."

There was silence. Then Mira spoke again: "And twenty-three days. I hadn't thought about it for a while. We've been so busy with—everything. But maybe Hebuiza's right; maybe she's better off here. The meteorite will cool and she'll fall asleep. At least it'll be a painless, easy path. . . ." Her voice sounded wistful.

"No," Penirdth said. He rose from his crouch. "We at least owe her the chance to see this thing through. I'd want the same chance myself." He paused. "Hebuiza's lying." There was a hint of disgust in his voice. "He doesn't really believe we'll be falling ill in twenty-three days. He believes in Yilda and his plan. And Liis is just an impediment to that plan's success."

"I'm . . . okay." Liis's words were little more than a whisper, but both Penirdth and Mira swung around. She tried to lift her head from the floor, and the world spun out of control. When things settled down, she realized Penirdth his hand cupped around the back of her head. Under his fingers, she could feel blood clotting in her hair.

Gritting her teeth, she glared up at them both, hissing between clenched teeth. "I'll . . . I'll be ready."

Three hundred and seventeen years earlier, they had awakened from stasis to find themselves matching the course of a large meteor.

"We'll, ah, bury *Ea*," Yilda had said to the group assembled in the cramped galley. "It's the only way to penetrate the orbital defences at the relay station."

Losson had been infuriated. "How the hell are we going to survive the impact?"

"We *will* survive," Hebuiza answered. He dropped a data card on the table. "My calculations show that in the lesser gravity we'll have an eighty-six percent chance of survival."

"But *Ea* will be lost. How will we get back to Bh'Haret?"

"We will commandeer one of the ships they have there," Yilda answered.

To Liis, it sounded improbable at best. Yet no one had protested—except for Losson, who went into a sulk the entire time they worked to bury the ship and reposition the braking jets.

Yilda informed Liis that as the most experienced pilot, she would be woken first, just before impact, to make the final system checks and oversee the descent and the braking manoeuvres. In all probability, he confided in her, there would be no need for human intervention, but just in case . . .

Liis accepted his order impassively, as she had all her orders. All of this meaningless hubbub was simply a way of winding down her life. *I've got nothing to lose*, she had thought, back then. *After all, I'm already dead. How much more dead can you be?*

22 DAYS LEFT

At first Liis thought she was waking from another longhaul. But when she attempted to roll over onto her side, her left arm vibrated with a pain so sharp it made her lightheaded. She opened her eyes, looked down, and saw her arm had been wrapped in a plasticast. Then everything came back.

They've already gone! Liis thought, her heart thumping wildly in her chest. Using her good arm, she grabbed the door of an open locker. With a grunt she pulled herself to her feet—and vomited.

"*Shit.*"

Blinking back tears, Liis looked up to see Penirdth climb into the cabin, sighing at the stink.

"Come on," he said. "Let's get you cleaned up and into your suit."

Liis sat on an overturned crate, broken arm cradled between her legs, as Penirdth poked around inside an open medikit. From amongst a collection of plastic envelopes, Penirdth pulled out a yellow pouch filled with analgesic patches. He shook a patch into his palm, peeled the backing off, and placed it on Liis's forearm. Within moments, Liis felt the pain ebb, replaced by a tingling sensation. An unnatural warmth settled on her like an invisible mantle. Her heart beat steadily.

Penirdth retrieved the envelope. "Here," he said. "You should have enough room in your suit to apply the patches. If you ration them, you might be able to stretch them out to two weeks."

She took the envelope from him listlessly; after staring at it a moment, she slipped it into a pocket on her coveralls. Pushing off from the crate, Liis rocked to her feet, but before she could stop herself, her momentum carried her forward like a collapsing building. She flailed out, trying to counterbalance, but ending up thumping against Penirdth's chest, gasping as her injured arm was pressed momentarily between them.

"Careful!" Penirdth's hands held her firmly. "Gravity is only a third normal here."

Liis pushed away from him. "Yeah," she said, her face colouring. "Sorry."

Penirdth waved away her apology. Then he said, "The others are outside already." He half-walked, half-hopped to the doorway. After vaulting easily over the lip, he waited for Liis on the other side. "I'll give you a hand."

Liis shuffled slowly toward him, stopped in front of the arc of the door. Penirdth extended a hand.

Liis stared at him. "Did you mean it? When you said you thought I was already dead?"

He seemed unfazed by her question, but dropped his proffered hand, shrugging. "You aren't the most sociable person I've ever met."

Liis felt a prickle of anger, but it vanished almost as quickly as it arose. Instead, she asked—

"Then why didn't you leave me? Like Hebuiza wanted."

"I don't know. I guess when I saw you all beat up and looking like hell, I couldn't help imagining myself in your place, left alone in this rock to die. No one deserves that."

"Not even me?"

"No. Not even you." A brief smile flickered at the corner of his lips.

Liis looked at him, and he stared back, without judgement. "Thanks," she said, gruffly.

They passed through the airlock and into the dropship bay. The shuttle had been jettisoned before they'd dug into the meteor, making the bay the largest open space on *Ea*. It was hot in here, and a sheen of sweat covered them both in seconds. Their lockers, now on the floor, were open. The regular EVA suits had long since been ditched, replaced with ones designed for a very different purpose: much bulkier, they were nonetheless far lighter and designed to be as self-sustaining as possible. Only two remained. "We're the last ones," Penirdth said.

In silence, they undressed. Penirdth discarded his shorts and tee-shirt and then helped Liis struggle out of her coveralls. He dragged the larger suit over to her and undid its harness. Gripping it beneath the arms, he raised it. The front of the suit was split open from the neck ring down to crotch, revealing layers of white cloth alternating with silvered insulating material. "Welcome to your new home."

Liis turned and stepped backwards into the suit. She ducked down under the lip of the neck ring and ran her right arm into the sleeve, wiggling her fingers into the glove. The helmet slid over her head and the weight of the suit settled on her shoulders. Through the polarised visor, the room appeared smoky. The suit had been designed so that its occupant could, while inside, move his or her arms in and out of the sleeves and into narrow cavities in front of the torso and behind the back to connect waste catheters to tubes on the trunk of an inner suit. Straps at the shoulders, chest, waist and thighs adjusted the internal volume. Liis let the chest straps out slightly to accommodate her cast; when she checked, she found she could still stretch her good arm the necessary distance to work the recycling units.

"Here." Penirdth held out the analgesic patches, retrieved from her discarded coveralls.

Liis took the envelope and stuck it in a utility pocket inside the suit. Penirdth sealed the seam. A status display appeared, framing the faceplate with glowing numerals. A small sucking sound filled the helmet as the material bound itself into insulating layers from which heat—or other telltale radiation—couldn't escape. Once on the surface of the planet, she would deploy the tail now coiled on her back. Any excess heat her suit couldn't handle would be radiated through the finger-thick cable. Twenty metres long, it would disperse heat in tiny increments through its hundreds of flexible joints as she dragged it behind her. The suits would make her invisible to any sensing devices in the orbitals—or so Yilda had assured them.

Moving the thick legs slowly, Liis tested her new skin. Because of the lessened gravitational pull, the suit wasn't nearly as heavy as she had feared it would be. In fact, it seemed to weigh no more than heavy winter clothes, and far less than when they had trained back on Bh'Haret. It was only a matter of getting used to the ungainly limbs again. And to the empty arm that hung uselessly from the suit's left shoulder. Behind her, Penirdth had already climbed into his suit and was now rebuckling his harness. When he finished, he turned to Liis—who was fumbling unsuccessfully with her own—and helped her secure the straps. Then he clipped the empty arm to the side of the suit to keep it from swinging free. With Penirdth's help, she climbed over the lip of the exterior hatch into the small chamber they had hacked from the heart of the meteorite. The roughly hewn chamber was illuminated by the dull yellow glow of the dropship bay lights. Only a small part of *Ea* around the hatch was exposed; the rest had been buried in the sleeve they'd excavated. Liis's status display ticked up an abrupt rise in temperature. It would be weeks before the meteorite cooled to the ambient temperature.

In the centre of the room stood a cutting laser on a tripod. Cables snaked from it, running back to Ea's interior. On the far wall, a metre-wide tunnel sloped upward at a gradual angle matching the laser's barrel. Penirdth stepped up next to Liis, his face invisible behind the dark band of his visor. He tipped his head down and touched his helmet to hers; it was their only way of communicating. The suits had been designed without transceivers—without anything that might emit radiation and betray their presence to the orbiting satellites. "They're waiting outside." His voice came to her, deadened by the intervening layers of material. In his hand he held the end of a cable connected to a data port on Ea's hull. He offered it to her.

Liis nodded, but realized he could see her no better than she could him. "Okay," she said loudly, taking the cable from his hand. He walked over to the mouth of the tunnel and turned to wait for her.

Liis snapped the end of the cable into a socket on the outer right thigh of her suit. "Yes?" the ship asked pleasantly.

She ordered the outer doors sealed; they slid together smoothly, cutting the light from inside like it was being sliced away by a knife, leaving them in the muted illumination of the partially exposed running lights. Then she gave the order to shut down the last onboard systems; the running lights extinguished and darkness swallowed them. She raised her glove, but couldn't make out the faintest traces of the white material. Groping in the dark, she found the cable and detached it from her flank. She let it fall to the side of the ship. Turning, she tried to locate Penirdth and the tunnel. After a moment, she could make out the ghostly outline of Penirdth's suit. To his right, the mouth of the tunnel glowed faintly. She moved cautiously toward him, sliding her feet along the floor to feel her way. When she reached him, she extended her hand and placed it on his arm.

Penirdth bent his helmet forward again: "Go on. I'll follow."

"Okay."

Liis crouched so that her helmet bobbed beneath the arc of the opening. Visible in the ragged circle a dozen or so metres away she could see it was night; stars were visible between ranks of long, tattered clouds. Through the thin atmosphere they burned steadily, reminding her, unexpectedly, of Josua, somewhere out there. At their parting, over five hundred years ago in hard time, she'd known it was likely that she would never see him again; yet, she barely remembered the moment when he had nodded stiffly in her direction before the doors of the shuttle had closed. The whole event had scattered in her memory like wind-torn smoke. It was a trick, this not remembering, one she had mastered over the years to compensate for her loneliness. And with Josua, it had been a skill she needed to retain her sanity.

But now, she suddenly realized, the need had vanished. She had expected her heart to plummet at the thought of Josua, for her anguish to brim over. But it didn't. Strangely, she couldn't summon those feelings. Anger eluded her. Only a mild irritation at herself for being so foolish. *Perhaps*, she thought, *I've practised too long, become too good at not caring.*

A tap on her back through the material of her suit; she recalled herself. Behind her, Penirdth with his hands open, a sign asking if she was okay. She returned the thumb's-up sign.

Goodbye, she thought at *Ea*. Taking a deep breath, she went down on her knees and one good arm and began to awkwardly crawl up the gentle incline toward the cold, unfamiliar stars.

The meteorite had ploughed into an ice field, shattering and melting the glacial plain as it cut a twenty-kilometre furrow. Ice and snow formed only a shallow layer atop the plateau upon which they had come to a rest. Fifty kilometres to the south, across the ice field, mountains ringed the glacier. Frozen rivers of ice spilled through gaps between the peaks to a lower plain. Several hundred kilometres beyond was the dome. Moments before impact, the instruments aboard *Ea* had recorded detailed images of the strange dome—and what appeared to be the heat signatures of at least a dozen people at its summit. It was one of the last things Liis remembered seeing before losing consciousness. It had shaken her, as much that Yilda had been right, as at the thought of what they were here to do to those people.

Kneeling on the lip of the opening they had cut in the rock, Liis regarded the expanse of the ice field. This world was smaller than Bh'Haret and so its horizon looked clipped to Liis, like it fell off abruptly at its edge. In the distance, mountains flared raggedly above the flat sheet of the glacier, crowns covered with a permanent mantle of snow. Due south, two of the highest peaks soared against the star-flecked sky like sentinels, guarding a small, thumb-sized gap where the glacier poured out onto the plain below. This pass, Penirdth had told her, was their first objective.

Even though it was night, the snow reflected a surprising amount of the starlight, enough so that she had no trouble making out the regular shapes of the lightweight toboggans below; but even this close it was difficult for her to find the four white-suited figures waiting for her. After a moment Liis located the tallest figure, standing a bit apart from the others, its abnormally wide, oval helmet inclined toward the tunnel where Liis now perched. Hebuiza. The figure raised its arm, gestured at her impatiently to descend.

The drop to the glacier was fifteen metres; at Liis's feet, a rope, secured by a single piton, trailed over the edge. She felt a tap on her leg. Penirdth handed forward a rope with a carabiner on its end, indicating that she should attach it to the front of her harness. Through a series of hand gestures, he made it clear that she should grip the belaying rope with her good arm, and he'd let the other out to lower her. Liis tried to nod, but her helmet scraped the roof of the tunnel. She gave him another thumb's-up sign.

Laying half on her side, half on her stomach, Liis squirmed around and wiggled backwards out of the tunnel. Her legs went over the edge, then her torso. Wrapping her right leg through the line, she let the rope out slowly from between her fingers and slipped lower. Her descent went smoothly. A few metres above the ground, her fingers tiring, she let out too much rope. Penirdth reacted by jerking the line back abruptly. The rope came loose from where she had wound it around her leg and she spun slowly toward the blackened face of the meteorite. Her chest and arm took the brunt of impact. Pain seared her vision. She felt her grip loosening; gritting her teeth, she tried to clutch the rope tighter. Her good arm was fully extended now, her weight hanging off it, her fingers and shoulder feeling as though they were being torn apart. As she spun slowly back the other way, she felt her grip weakening, slipping. Her arm shook uncontrollably, her fingers on fire. With a shout, she lost her grip—

—her legs struck the surface, sending a mild jolt up her spine, causing her jaw to snap shut. She stumbled backwards, away from the meteorite; hands caught at her, restored her balance. She blinked, looked at the white figure that supported her. At first she felt relief, then embarrassment. Above, Penirdth's helmet poked over the edge of the tunnel. He still held the rope attached to her harness in his left hand. Though her arm ached, Liis raised it and waved. He waved back, then withdrew. A moment later, he backed over the edge and began his own descent.

The person who'd caught her stared at her through the anonymous dark band of the helmet's visor. Other than the general size of the suit, it was difficult to distinguish between the members of the party. Hebuiza, with his oval helmet, was the only one she could be certain of. Liis bent her head forward, made contact with the other person's helmet. "Thanks," she said gruffly.

"Sure," the answer came back in Mira's tiny voice. She pointed to one of the sleds. It was two metres long and painted white. Several bulky items were strapped under a white tarp, although its load appeared to be smaller than the rest. Lashed on top were a pair of snowshoes and, next to them, a set of short, wide skis. "Penirdth asked us to get a toboggan ready for you—in case." A pause. "You've only got a few minutes before we leave." Mira broke contact and moved back to her own sled in loping strides. In the unreal white landscape, her figure seemed small, insignificant.

Losson and Yilda had already begun testing the balance of their loads. They had attached the leads to their harnesses and deployed their tails. The long radiating cables were clipped back along the leads and then the edge of the toboggans, unravelling from coiled piles as they dragged their sleds forward and away from the meteorite, clearly anxious to put as much distance as possible between it and themselves.

Before they had departed Bh'Haret, Yilda had given them what survey data they had on SJH-1231-K. But it had provided only the grossest descriptions of the planet and general maps of the landscape. The specifics on which they were now working had been gathered from the short burst of information their passive sensors had collected during their turbulent descent. On the surface, it was apparent the terrain was too irregular for their squat skis (much to Liis's relief, for she knew poling with one arm would be nearly impossible), but the ground was firm enough to take the weight of their boots without snowshoes. Only a few centimetres of névé, granular snow with the consistency of loose salt, covered a firm crust. They would begin by hiking, Yilda decided.

By the time Liis managed—with help from Penirdth—to attach the lead from her toboggan to her harness and deploy her tail, the party was already trekking away from the meteorite. Instead of walking south toward the pass, Yilda led them to the west. His reasoning, Liis guessed, was to get as far away from the meteorite and the furrow it had ploughed in the glacier, fearing their party might be spotted by a Speaker curious to view the impact site through an orbital or a remote. Certainly a close inspection of the meteorite would betray their presence. But anything less would show little: their suits hid their heat signatures and the tiny currents produced by their electronics were carefully insulated to prevent EMF leaks. All their equipment had an identical white camouflage coating. The only danger would be if a sharp eye, or lens, caught their movement across the nearly featureless landscape.

They moved out single-file, spaced evenly and separated by the twenty metre lengths of their tails. Hebuiza was in the lead, his long strides breaking the path; he was followed by Yilda, Mira, and Losson (or so Liis guessed from their general shapes and sizes). Yilda and Mira used ski poles as they walked, their arms pumping up and down in the same rhythm as their steps. Making the final adjustments to her harness, Liis moved in short, brisk steps to catch up. She was second last. Penirdth, who had waited patiently for her to finish her preparations, fell into line last, bringing up the rear.

The ground, although broken by tiny ridges of ice that thrust up like miniature frozen waves, was surprisingly firm. In the lessened gravity, Liis guessed her sled weighed no more than a few kilos. Once in motion, however, the sled ran easily across the surface of the glacier. And, as they moved, she adjusted her harness until she found a combination that put as little pressure on her arm as possible.

They hustled away from the meteorite.

It was still dark, but the stars provided enough illumination for her visor amplification to pick up all but the smallest details of the surrounding landscape. To her right, a humped ridge of ice jutted up like the skeletal remains of a monstrous creature. On her left ran the dark thin lines of crevasses. The mountain range ahead had disappeared almost completely behind the horizon, and Liis suddenly realized they must have moved into a lengthy, shallow depression. Ten minutes later, when she expected to lose sight of this last peak, the process began to reverse itself, the mountain growing in size. She checked her suit display. An hour had elapsed and they had traversed only one-and-a-half kilometres. At that rate it would take them five days to reach the pass. When Hebuiza had told her this earlier, she had thought him mistaken, perhaps overly pessimistic. But already her legs were growing tired; her breathing laboured. It occurred to her that Hebuiza might have been too optimistic in his estimate.

She trudged on.

When the muscles in her legs ached sharply, and she thought a rest was long overdue, Yilda finally halted the party. The medication must have been wearing off, for her arm had also begun to trouble her, throbbing incessantly. Easing herself down onto the icy surface, she pulled greedily at her water nipple. Then she sucked down an acrid goo from her food tube—a mixture optimized for recycling, but *not* for taste. She called up her display. Two hours had passed, and they had travelled a mere two-and-a-half kilometres. Their progress was slowing already. And they still hadn't turned south, toward the pass. If they didn't pick up the pace their supplies would run out long before they reached the Speakers' dome. Each suit carried enough food and water for seventeen days with recycling; the suit batteries and oxygen recirculator would last another two beyond. Hebuiza had estimated five days to the pass. Then another nine to the dome. Leaving them with a five-day cushion before their suits would fail. But covering such distances now seemed a near impossible feat.

Liis was startled by a tap on her shoulder. Penirdth stood over her, his arm stretched toward her; ahead, the others were moving again. Near the front of the line, Hebuiza waited at the side, staring back at them. Clasping Penirdth's hand, she struggled to her feet. For a moment she stood, the dark band of her visor facing Penirdth's. Liis stared at the narrow black rectangle, imagining Penirdth's round face and silver hair. She wondered if he was recalling her face, with its swirl of mad scars, in the same way. Suddenly self-conscious, she turned away. Ignoring the stab of pain in her arm as she jerked her sled into motion, she set off at a trot to catch up with the others.

Boredom was the greatest enemy.

They had covered only six kilometres in five marches, resting every two hours. And already tedium had set in. Though Liis had replaced the analgesic patch, her arm now throbbed constantly in the background of her consciousness. The muscles in her shoulders, neck and lower back pained her relentlessly from the weight of the sled. How could it have seemed so light a few hours ago? She knew the sled itself wasn't particularly heavy—but the constant pull of its extra few kilos crept into her muscles, making them knot up and ache.

Three times they had had to detour around wide crevasses, and once around a massive chunk of blue ice that looked like an upthrust fist. More frequently now, they encountered small clefts or cracks in the surface that ran away into the distance. Most were shallow and less than a metre in width, but some dropped away quickly, their bottoms lost to sight. Whenever the fissure was too wide to drag the sleds over safely, Hebuiza would pull a small, narrow folding bridge constructed of wire mesh from the lead toboggan and set it up across the gap. Then the party would cross, one by one, Hebuiza bringing up the rear and retrieving the bridge. Fully extended, the bridge could safely span a gap of about three metres. Liis wondered what would happen if they encountered a larger crevasse of considerable width. Would they be forced to detour dozens of kilometres out of their way, losing hours or days? But the Facilitator would, of course, have a reasonably complete map of the terrain in his head, downloaded from the images gathered on their descent. Still, Liis couldn't help wondering how detailed it was, and how clearly the fissures would have appeared, at night, against the monotone background.

Sometime after they had passed the seventh kilometre, she was startled to discover that the distant mountains were no longer indecipherable silhouettes, but now showed broken and mottled surfaces, traces of steel blue and thin yellows below their pink snow-capped peaks. The transition had been so gradual she hadn't even noticed. Liis looked back, to the east: she caught her breath. Straddling the horizon was the upper edge of a colossal red disc, its colour staining the underbelly of the clouds. On her longhauls, she had always been confined to an orbital lazarette in a system with a relatively bright, young sun; this was the first truly alien sunrise she had witnessed. As she trudged on, she turned her head again and again, watching the star continue to rise until it seemed to fill half the sky, spilling over the edge of the world and soaking everything in blood-red light.

The novelty wore off quickly.

Days on this world were long. It would be another forty-seven hours before the sun would set. Which meant they would be walking two of their days before the local day ended. This thought seemed to add to Liis's weariness. She stopped looking back and stared at her booted feet instead, as she placed one in front of the other, trying to dull her mind to her perpetual weariness.

Shortly after their fifth rest—Liis's display showed they had covered eight point seven kilometres in a little less than twelve hours—Hebuiza signalled for yet another halt. Only this time he indicated, through a series of hand signals, that they would remain here for six hours. Liis lowered herself to the ground and lay on her back, breathing raggedly. She felt drained and her shoulders and neck ached; her arm throbbed with each beat of her heart. In the right corner of her visor the sun was a huge orange smear. Eyes closed, she began pulling weakly at her water nipple, liquid dribbling down her chin.

Conscious thought slipped away.

21 DAYS LEFT

It was dark. But it should have been light.

Liis blinked groggily. She turned her head in the helmet; where the orange sun had been was only undifferentiated black. Then she realized something was eclipsing the light. A person. Long arms, tubes of darkness, reached down, tugged insistently on her shoulders, setting off an intense, jangling pain that coursed through her body like an alarm, jolting her fully awake. Blinking back tears, she knocked away the grasping hands with her good arm. She made an effort to sit up. Her head spun. Fighting back nausea, she pulled her good arm into the suit's chest cavity and tore the old analgesic patch from her left arm; pulling a fresh one from the inner pocket, she raised it to her mouth and used her teeth to tear it open. Then she applied it to her forearm. Relief was almost immediate.

Her vision cleared and she recognized the Facilitator's long-limbed suit and distended helmet. She checked her display. She'd been asleep five hours and sixteen minutes. She wanted those remaining forty-four minutes. "What . . ." she started to say, then realized the futility of trying to ask a question. Instead she struggled to her feet, feeling the tug of the harness she'd neglected to undo before falling asleep.

Up and down the line the others were in various stages of preparation for the day's march. Two figures were doing awkward stretches; the others were reattaching the leads to their sleds. Hebuiza stalked off. The sun fell on her fully now, making her blink as her visor adjusted to the onslaught of the red glare. The bottom of the disc had cleared the horizon by several degrees, and now cast the eerie landscape in saffron. It was still early in the planetary morning. The day stretched before her like an interminable punishment.

Her stomach grumbled loudly.

Sucking down a mouthful of the sticky goo that passed for food, followed by a swig of tepid water, Liis struggled into her place in line. Moments later, they set off; her neck and back resumed aching precisely where they had left off the day before. Shoulders bowed, she slogged forward.

At around eleven klicks, Yilda finally turned south. Overhead, thin lines of serried clouds gathered. A light snow fell. Cresting a small rise, the col toward which they were headed came into sight. Liis magnified the view, but could make out little detail because dark clouds now funnelled into the pass, obscuring the peaks; beneath was a wall of turbulent pink: an endless maelstrom of roiling snow.

How will Yilda get us through that? she wondered. But the question didn't really trouble her as she knew it should. She felt no sense of dread or anxiety, only weariness and an abstract, disconnected curiosity.

The day went on, marches of a kilometre or so punctuated by brief rest periods. Snow began to fall in earnest, and the pass disappeared from sight. Soon Liis fell into a kind of daze, staring at her overlarge white boots as she planted one in front of the other. It was as if they weren't part of her, but rather part of a machine over which she exerted only a nominal control. In this state, her aches seemed to recede, to become part of that other being, the one that plodded forward relentlessly, and to whom she was only tenuously connected. Rests, when they came, surprised her. She would dutifully lower her body to the ground, sensing, rather than feeling, the fatigue. As she lay there, she couldn't remember what, if anything, had occupied her thoughts the last several hours.

Sometime later, they halted. It wasn't until she stood—or her body, sensing the rest period concluded, stood for her—that she noticed no one else was moving. They remained prone. Even Hebuiza's long figure lay immobile. They had reached the end of another day's march.

19 DAYS LEFT

"We'll never get through the pass." The voice vibrated through Liis's helmet. It was their sixth (or seventh?) rest stop on the third (or was it fourth?) day. The voice, she had at first assumed, was her own, for she'd already caught herself talking aloud several times. But when it came back, more insistent, she realized someone else spoke to her. "Can't he see the winds don't ever let up?"

Penirdth, she thought. His shadowed helmet blotted out her view.

"It's madness."

He had undone his harness and moved to where she rested now, her back against the toboggan, and touched his helmet to hers while she'd shut her eyes.

"Liis? Are you okay?"

"Yeah." She blinked, stared at the dark band that was Penirdth's visor. "Never better."

"You can feel the wind picking up here. It's been blowing steadily at our backs for the last fourteen hours. And we're still twenty klicks away from the pass. What will it be like when we're there, at the mouth of the funnel?"

"I . . . I don't know." Thought was difficult. Her mind still felt out of sync with reality, as if there was a second of lag time between perception and understanding. She turned her head, breaking contact with Penirdth. To the south, the pass was now visible; the snow had finally stopped after falling for nearly ten hours. But the pass was still choked with agitated snow-bearing clouds. Setting her visor's magnification on maximum, she stared at the mighty billows that rose and fell. She touched her helmet to Penirdth's again. "What other choice do we have?"

"We'll be torn to pieces if we try this."

Liis shrugged inside her suit. "We'll die anyway."

Penirdth pulled away abruptly. He moved back several paces and plopped himself down on a knee-high block of ice. He curled his hands into fists and pressed them between his thighs.

He's scared, Liis thought with surprise. It was the first time she'd seen him display anything other than his characteristic equanimity. Oddly, she felt like laughing. Instead, she struggled to her feet, unclipped her harness and walked over to him. Settling down next to him, she tugged on his right arm gently. Reluctantly he released it to her. She placed it in her lap and, uncurling his fingers, pressed his gauntlet beneath hers.

Liis had been watching the pass. When the gap wasn't obscured by heavy clouds and blankets of snow, a mist seemed to rise off the flat between the peaks. Not mist, she realized. But wind, blowing loose snow from the ice field, eroding the surface of the glacier and creating a perpetual blizzard in the pass even when the sky overhead was clear.

And, as Penirdth had predicted, the wind hadn't let up. Liis looked back to where he trudged behind her. During the last three rest stops he'd kept his distance. *God only knows what's going through his mind*, she thought. Of all of them, he had seemed to adjust best to the situation. But his fear betrayed that he hadn't really adjusted at all. Liis tried to remember what she'd been thinking when she'd first had to face the reality of her scant remaining time; but back then, her thoughts had been only of Josua. Dying hadn't seemed so frightening. In fact, hadn't she welcomed the idea? The sense of relief it promised?

A surprisingly strong gust of wind buffeted her; stumbling forward, she lost her balance. She swung out her good arm to break her fall. But when her palm struck the ground, it skidded away from her. Everything seemed to happen slowly: the ground rising toward her while slow-motion flakes of snow swirled around her. In that distended moment, she knew her broken arm would take the brunt of the impact; she steeled herself. But then pain exploded in her head, and she howled in agony. Unconsciousness rushed forward like a tidal wave.

Liis lay on the ground, breathing heavily. Sweat peppered her brow. Dark clouds streamed overhead. *I'm on my back*, she thought. *Someone must have turned me over.*

A figure crouched next to her, hand extended. *Penirdth*, she thought. Her wounded arm pulsed sharply, making her shudder. Fighting back nausea, she reached out and clasped his hand. A moment later, she was on her feet, the world spinning bright around her, her ears ringing and heart pounding. . . .

In the distance, the column moved forward. She had only been out for a few moments. No one had bothered stopping. At the front of the line, Hebuiza's ovoid helmet bobbed, urging them on into the gathering storm.

Liis sucked in a deep breath, released Penirdth's hand reluctantly. Her whole body convulsed; she felt ill. In a moment, the tremor passed. Gritting her teeth, she tugged her sled into motion, dragging it toward the swirling maelstrom ahead.

17 DAYS LEFT

The gusts increased in both intensity and frequency as they drew closer to the pass. Blasts of wind, like the one that had surprised Liis, were now commonplace. But she had retrieved a ski pole from her sled. Whenever she felt an abrupt rise in the intensity of the wind, she paused, set her feet apart and planted the pole in front of her like the third leg of a tripod. Though it caused her to lag further behind the rest of the party, it seemed to work, for she hadn't fallen again. But she knew this, too, would soon be useless against gusts that beat at her back like angry fists.

As they marched, the sky closed in on them; a sparse snowfall had turned into a steady stream of white flakes that tore past them furiously. Liis could no longer see the others in the gloom of the storm clouds, save for Mira who was ahead of her in the column. The pass had long since vanished, obscured by the roiling clouds. Despite the steady snowfall, the terrain became easier to negotiate. Fewer and fewer fissures slowed their progress. The ground itself was lined with an endless series of tiny, scalloped ridges. But these were hard, frozen in place, and her boots rocked as she walked over them. She lowered her head and fixed her eyes on the tip of Mira's slender tail—flicking over the ridges only a step ahead of her like a fishing lure—and following it without thought.

When Liis could barely make out Mira's small shape struggling twenty metres ahead of her, the rest of the group came unexpectedly into sight. They were gathered in a tight circle, all leaning back against the wind. Their toboggans had been arranged in a low wind-break. Liis dragged her sled into place, staggering as the wind shoved her forward. She jammed her pole into the ground to steady herself. A helmet bobbed forward, touched hers.

"Wait here for a few hours. Yes. To see if the weather lets up." It was Yilda, his thin voice sounding even more attenuated through the material of the two helmets. He pointed ahead, though at what, Liis couldn't see. "This is the start of the descent. Two kilometres and we'll be past the narrowest part of the pass and onto a much steeper downslope. Three-and-a-half kilometres more and we're on the plain."

Nothing to it, Liis thought wryly. "How are we supposed to get down there?" she asked, her voice rough from disuse. It had been at least two days since she had last spoken. "And what about these toboggans?" Pushed by gusts of wind, hers had already been intermittently running up against her heels for the last half a kilometre.

"Not—" A blast of wind surged between them, separating them and cutting off Yilda's voice; their helmets clacked back together. "—sled."

"What?"

"Your sled, eh? Ride your sled. In two hundred and fifty metres the run should be, ah, steep enough."

A five kilometre toboggan ride through this mess? It was insane.

"Survey shots, yes, show the ground should be smooth," Yilda continued. "Like here. Control the descent by attaching crampons to our boots and dragging our feet. The problem is to stay in the centre of the glacier. Yes. The surface is slightly convex. The sleds will want to veer off to the sides. Toward exposed rocks or crevasses. With this wind, impossible to get back on course if you slip too far over to either side."

"And how are we supposed to stay in the centre?"

"Suit compasses. Yes."

Shit, Liis thought. It was beyond insane. The compasses could provide only the crudest means of steering over the hump of the glacier. It would be like trying to navigate an ocean-going vessel through a narrow straight only by eyeballing stars. A fraction of a degree would translate into kilometres of error. And staying directly in the centre was no guarantee of making it safely to the bottom.

It could just as easily lead them to an unsuspected fissure. She was struck by an image of the six of them lying atop their sleds and shooting, one after the other, into a yawning crevasse they had no chance of seeing until it was too late....

As if in answer to this thought, Yilda said, "Fan out, hey? To approach our runs from slightly different angles. Just in case."

Just in case some of us end up riding air, Liis thought. Yilda was remaining true to form: rather than gambling all of their lives on one course, he would cover his bets, balancing a few likely deaths against the chance most would survive.

"Listening?"

"Yeah."

"Tell Penirdth," Yilda said. "Behind you." Turning, Yilda walked away, digging his heels in with each step, leaning backwards at an unnatural angle, supported by the press of the incessant wind.

Liis lay on her toboggan, the crampons on her boots dug securely into the surface of the glacier to hold her back. Her tail had been coiled and secured to her pack. Though the slope wasn't severe, the wind buffeted her insistently, trying to nose her forward. Beneath her, the oval-shaped sled rocked forward slightly with each gust. The sled had holes bored along its edges and straps had been looped through these to serve as handholds. With her right hand, Liis clutched the one nearest the front. Her other arm lay beside her, cradled in a carefully padded hollow where, she hoped, the jarring motion of the sled wouldn't grind the newly set bones together. Earlier, she had managed—after a painful and frustrating struggle—to slip her broken limb from its sling and back into the sleeve of the suit, allowing herself a fresh analgesic patch to endure the task. Yet despite the medication, the pain had been intense.

At Yilda's orders, they had all lightened their loads. He sent Hebuiza down the line, picking and choosing the items they would keep. When he came to Liis, the Facilitator indicated that she was to keep her skis and a single pole; a backup energy cell for her suit; a pack containing clothes, a medical kit, a dozen foil food pouches, a laser pistol, and a box of battery clips for the pistol; six flares wrapped in plastic; a heavy metallic cylinder containing plastic explosives and detonators; and two long nylon ropes. He had her discard two bolt guns and their magazines (impossible to use with only one arm) and her climbing gear. After Hebuiza had moved on to Penirdth, Liis also dumped her backup energy cell. Her display showed that her suit still had enough juice for at least fourteen days; three days after that the first symptoms would manifest. If they weren't at the dome by the time her battery died, there'd be little point.

Visibility was almost nil. Although the snowfall was no heavier than before—and had perhaps let up marginally—the wind had increased in intensity as they moved another half-klick into the maw of the pass. The ground was worn to a smooth, glassy texture. To her right, Liis could barely make out Losson lying on his sled; the same distance to her left was Penirdth. No one else was visible. Yilda had strung them out across a hundred and fifty metre gap in the middle of the pass. Past Losson, and hidden by the curtain of snow, were Yilda, Mira and then Hebuiza. Hebuiza would go first and the rest would follow, in three minute intervals, Penirdth going last.

Liis glanced back and forth between Losson and her clock. Eight minutes had already elapsed since the Facilitator's departure had been signalled down the line. Liis waited. Exactly when the stopwatch display showed 9:00:00, Losson's shadowy figure wiggled the spiked end of his boots free of the ice. His sled lurched forward. Losson dragged his feet, his heels bouncing slightly as the tips of the crampons alternately caught and released ice. Liis strained to watch his progress, but one moment Losson was visible, the next obscured by the twisting sheets of snow, his image fading in and out like a wavering signal. Within seconds he became a smudge of uncertain colour, then nothing.

Liis turned her helmet to look at Penirdth; he was visible through the thickening storm only as a faint outline. He had helped Liis rearrange her sled and discard her unwanted equipment. He had even taken her jettisoned energy cell and secured it to his already overloaded sled—despite her protests. He insisted, pretending it was for himself, though he had his own backup cell. Lifting her good arm, she waved once. She wasn't sure, but she thought he raised his arm in answer before disappearing entirely behind a thick curl of snow and wind. In the corner of her visor, the green figures of the clock continued to climb. Liis turned away.

Two minutes and forty-seven seconds had elapsed since Losson had disappeared. A strange calm took possession of Liis. Her heart beat steadily. The ache in her arm seemed to fade from consciousness. She felt no fear, only an odd kind of elation. *None of it matters anymore*, she thought. *Not Bh'Haret, not Josua. Not Nexus. Just this.*

Without checking her stopwatch, she jerked her crampons free of the ice.

White closed Liis off, obliterating her.

The transition was abrupt: one moment there had been a solid, tangible world around her; now there was nothing but walls of ivory. Beneath her the sled rasped over the ice, but she felt no sensation of movement. It was as if *she* were stationary and the ground drifted beneath her. Snow continued to stream past her, but it did not seem to be moving as fast as it had before, slowing with each second. Liis let her sled run free, gathering momentum. Fascinated, she watched the steady stream of snow resolve itself into individual flakes.

The sled bucked beneath her and tried to slough off to the left. Liis dropped her feet. The crampons bit into the glacier and immediately kicked her legs back up in a jolt more surprising than painful. The sled responded by veering yet more acutely to the right; she felt a slow, counterclockwise spin begin to sweep her legs around. She lowered her feet again, careful this time to let the spikes on the crampons skim the surface only lightly. Vibrations sang through the soles of her boots, hummed up her bones and into her wounded arm, making it feel like it was being squeezed in a vise. Ignoring the pain, she concentrated on maintaining the correct pressure with her feet. In a few seconds the intensity of the vibration fell off dramatically. Snow streamed past her again as it had at the top of the pass. *That's it,* she said to herself. *Take it slow.* Checking her compass, she discovered she was already several degrees off course. She increased the pressure of her right foot; the compass display corrected itself, the digits running back in the proper direction. Still, the sled continued to try to surge to the left. After a few tries, Liis found a combination of pressure with her right and left legs that seemed to keep her on course. *A lot of good it'll do me,* she thought, *if I'm already too far off line.* She cursed herself for letting the sled get away from her right at the start.

The glacier slipped relentlessly underneath her; the sled bucked now and then, but never as sharply as it had at the start. When she thought to check her clock, it showed she'd been descending four minutes. There was no telling how far she'd travelled; without visible landmarks, her suit had no way of estimating. Hebuiza had said the descent was five and a half kilometres. Much of that distance had to remain. She decided to try to compensate for her initial mistake by swinging her sled a few degrees to the right for fifteen seconds, then straightening out. She lightened the pressure of her left leg marginally; her compass showed she was edging to the west. The clock ticked off its seconds.

The slope dropped away suddenly. Caught unprepared, Liis struggled to retain control. A shape, dark and humped, appeared directly in front of her. There was no time to do anything but brace herself. Her toboggan caught the edge of the object, leapt into the air. For an instant everything was still, the rasping of the sled bottom silenced as she cleaved the air. Then the impact threw her forward, knocking the wind from her lungs. Pain reddened her vision. Yet somehow, she managed to retain her grip. The sled sped forward, rocking violently from side to side, each second threatening to dislodge her. *No!* she thought, anger surging through her veins like an amphetamine. *I won't die this way!* She dropped her feet; they bit into the ice. Whether the surface here was more porous or her determination that much stronger, the tips of her crampons sank firmly into the glacier, ripping shallow, even grooves. Her speed decreased.

Her descent continued at a headlong pace. Liis tried to reduce it further, but she had reached a kind of equilibrium where wind and slope and momentum conspired to make it impossible to go any slower. The muscles in her thighs and calves ached from the effort. The sled bucked and rolled as if it were alive. Liis fought its wild surges, no longer caring how far off course she might be. Every ounce of her energy was directed toward maintaining the small control she still had. Minutes passed—or so it seemed to her. She still didn't dare glance at her suit display. Several times the sled reared up and Liis thought she would be thrown free. But she managed to make it yield to her will, wrestling it back into submission.

As suddenly as it had increased, the grade of the slope decreased; the sled decelerated, became docile. Like a curtain being drawn back, the snow abruptly thinned and disappeared, the glacier appearing around her, everything returning to its blood-red cast and stark black shadows. A kilometre ahead, the tongue of the ice spilled into the frozen plain Hebuiza had promised. Far off to her left snow obscured the greyish-black, vertical rises of exposed rock at the foot of the western peak. To the right, where several of the others should have already descended, she could make out the dark lines of crevasses. She tried to put the sight out of her mind, the same way she had managed not to think about the object she had hit, about what she feared it might have been.

Checking her display she found ten minutes had elapsed; her compass indicated that she was moving two degrees too far to the west. She corrected her course as the world continued to open up in front of her. The constant pressure of the wind had vanished, perhaps because she was travelling at the same speed now. Though she could have brought the sled to a halt, she let it run on for a handful of minutes, scanning the juncture of glacier and plain for her comrades. She saw no one. It wasn't until she was nearly at the base of the slope that she made out the clutch of figures several hundred metres to the west. Their white suits had camouflaged them so well she hadn't spotted them until this moment. Dragging her right foot, Liis forced her sled to swing toward them. She counted four toboggans arranged side by side. But only three figures stood beside them, one with an elongated helmet. Someone hadn't made it.

Reaching the bottom a hundred metres east of the party, she pushed herself up on her good arm and struggled to her feet. Turning, she searched the tongue of the glacier for Penirdth. Nothing. She glanced at her display. Three minutes had elapsed since she'd cleared the line of snow. Shouldn't he be in sight by now?

Liis almost jumped when fingers closed around her good forearm and another helmet clacked against hers.

"Made it, hey?" Yilda said matter-of-factly.

"Yes," Liis whispered, still intent on the slope. Penirdth had yet to appear.

"Losson doesn't seem to have been so fortunate. Yes. His sled is here. Alas, he isn't."

Until this moment, Liis had managed not to deal with that unsettling moment on the slope when her sled had bounced out of control. She thought about that shapeless thing she had hit on the way down and how, in that brief instant, it had appeared to rise in front of her, its outline human. "Losson might be all right." She said. "He could have fallen off. He's probably walking down the slope right now."

"Can't wait." Yilda pulled his head away and scanned the horizon. Then he touched her helmet again. "Penirdth should have arrived by now, hey? Maybe he veered off course. Looks like just the four of us."

"No," Liis answered. "Five." She jerked her arm free from Yilda's grasp and pointed. A kilometre away and a little to east, a last sled emerged from the thick veil of snow, a tiny figure clutching its back.

Penirdth dragged his sled to a halt in front of the group. Stepping forward, Yilda inclined his head until their helmets touched. The rest of group stood in a ragged line, watching the exchange. Watching Yilda gesture to Losson's empty sled, then point back to the slope.

Strangely, Liis felt nothing. It was unreal. Her heart beat calmly, steadily, unperturbed by what had happened, by that shadowy figure she had hit on the way down—no, not a figure. There was nothing to indicate it had been another person. It had all happened too fast. It could have been almost anything. A rock. A chunk of dirty ice.

Penirdth moved away from Yilda, toward Liis.

Gently he took her gloved hand in his and gave it a consoling squeeze. Liis jerked her hand away and stared at the black band of his visor. Behind Penirdth, Yilda also watched her. They all did. *What are they all staring at?* She felt a spur of panic. "It wasn't my fault!" Her shout died in her helmet, unheard.

Penirdth walked past her and crouched by the front of her sled. On the right side the tip of an ice axe had worked itself out from under the white tarp during the descent. Hung on its tip like a ragged pennant was a ripped piece of white cloth—the same cloth that covered the exterior of their suits. Penirdth removed it and let it flutter away in the wind.

The sky was overcast, but the snowfall had lightened. Here at the foot of the glacier, a smooth plain of hard-packed snow opened out in all directions. It had once been a vast lake; now it lay beneath a thickening crust of ice and snow fifteen metres deep. Three hundred and eleven klicks due south, anchored on the far shore, was the Speakers' dome. From this distance, it wasn't yet visible.

The others were ready.

Liis had struggled to remove her crampons and was still trying to unpack her skis. Penirdth, who had prepared himself in minutes, had moved over to Liis's sled and tried to help her. She'd waved him off angrily. Now he stood to one side, watching her. Liis tried to ignore him. Her broken arm ached sharply, but she couldn't be bothered to apply another patch. Being in pain somehow felt appropriate. Instead, she continued fumbling, mostly without much luck, at the buckles and knots of her gear. She managed to remove one of her skis, but the other one stubbornly refused to come free. As she worked away at it, Penirdth knelt down and gently moved her hand away from the strap she had been trying to loosen. She felt too tired to resist. She let him undo the second ski, then free her single pole. He handed the pole to her. Liis wrapped her thick fingers around it without looking at him.

Hebuiza had finished sorting the items from Losson's sled; he redistributed equipment from one of the piles he made, dropping two or three things next to each of their toboggans, indicating they should add them to their loads. When he reached Liis, he dropped a dark case whose contents she had never seen and a box of explosives—two of the heavier items—beside her. As soon as Hebuiza had turned his back, Penirdth scooped up both items and slung them under the white tarp on his own sled. Liis took a step toward Penirdth, stopped. She chewed on her lower lip, watching Penirdth continue to arrange his gear as if nothing had happened. Turning around, she walked back to her own sled.

Liis tied down her load as best she could; she deployed her tail, securing it along the harness and the side of her sled. To her right, her skis lay atop the thin crust of snow. She stepped into the bindings and the clips on the front of her boots snapped into place. Floundering with her single pole, Liis tried a few halting strides back toward the glacier. Behind her, when the harness went taut, the weight of the sled almost toppled her. She tried again, managing three smooth, gliding steps before being thrown off balance and nearly falling. Looking up, she saw the others were huddled tightly around Yilda. In faltering steps, she made her way over.

Yilda had organized them into a line, their tails lying to the side. A steady wind blew at their backs. Penirdth was first. He would begin by breaking the trail.

Directly behind Penirdth was Mira, followed by Yilda. Hebuiza gestured roughly to Liis that she should fall in next. Careful not to abrade the tails of the others, Liis sidestepped over them and into line. When she had taken up her position, Hebuiza fell in behind her.

Yilda raised his left hand. Penirdth, with a final backward glance at the slope, turned and dug his poles into the snow. He lurched forward, his legs kicking up at the heels, his arms pumping. The leads snapped taut and his sled jerked to life, following him in an uneven, bucking motion like a small boat bouncing across waves. His tail uncoiled behind him. Mira's helmet bobbed forward as she watched his tail play out. When the end flicked past her, she turned to look at Yilda, as if waiting for his permission to depart. Yilda gestured impatiently with his hand again, and Mira dug in her poles. But before she pushed off she froze; forty metres ahead, Penirdth had halted. His sled ran on, nudging his heels. But he showed no sign of noticing it. Instead, he bent at the waist, staring at the tips of his skis.

The snow around Penirdth sagged. His arms shot up into the air, his poles swinging wildly out to the sides. He teetered forward as the ground opened up beneath him. Liis stared in horrified silence as he toppled from sight, his tail whipping across the lip of the breach and snapping out of sight.

THE TWINS

The bogey rode in toward the binary suns, its spew of fusion exhaust lighting up the vacuum on a broad band of frequencies. More than a dozen small drones now matched the ship's course, orbiting it like a cloud of electrons, scanning it intensely. The first had arrived one New Polyarchy standard year ago, a few days after the craft began decelerating; others joined as the ship had continued to knife toward the Hub.

Six NP years earlier, when the bogey had pierced the one-quarter light year bubble of space surrounding the Twins, the presence of the craft had been logged by intelligence QT21-1749-9036J-17. Imbedded in the nearest monitoring station, intelligence QT21 had taken less than a billionth of a second to plot the course of the craft and determine its destination to be the constructed world known as the Hub, the seat of power for Nexus. Checking its catalogue, QT21 found no official record of a scheduled flight registered by any of the affiliated worlds. The signature catalogues detailing the ship classes of the Polyarchy also failed to yield a match. QT21 became mildly uneasy.

Referring to its infrequently used data stores on non-affiliated ships, the intelligence determined the probability to be 92.936 percent that the primitive D-D catalyst fusion drive vehicle had originated from a non-affiliated world 21.12 light years distant. A world named Bh'Haret. Some 432 years earlier, a biohazard warning had been attached to the data entity representing that planet. Concerned, the intelligence dispatched a narrow-beam message to Karin, forty-five light days distant and the nearest planet with a Speaker. Within a year, three other QT monitors, all further away from the bogey's vector of penetration, had also dispatched reports to the same world. Proximate drones had been ordered to intercept.

Certainty of the ship's origin had been improved to 99.99567 percent after the arrival of the drones. Although the name had been carefully eradicated from the hull, they identified it from their records as a longhaul vessel named *Viracosa*. Even on the non-affiliated worlds, Nexus maintained eyes and ears, meticulously cataloguing interplanetary commerce. The drones spun about the ship, built precise models of it, measured and analysed its EMF emissions, carefully checked the micrometeorite impact patterns on the ship's outer skin and determined the cratering was consistent with the ship's age. An analysis of the trace elements left in the impact dimples was correlated to density maps of elements for known space; thousands of possible courses were plotted. Once again, Bh'Haret came up as the most likely origin. The exterior of the vessel showed only primitive weapons—none formidable enough to pose a threat to the Hub. After months of pursuit, a 1.739 nanosecond debate ensued in which the drones decided to let the ship continue into Nexus space. They reported their decision, then returned to their surveillance of the bogey until further orders were forthcoming.

On a platform three light hours from the Hub, Lien, a Speaker Novitiate, lolled in a large, oversize bath. Not a bath, really, for she still sat at the command station on the bridge of her ship. She had felt like a soak, and so ordered the room filled with warm water to chin height. She could have completed the transformation and created the illusion of a pool in the midst of a pleasant, sun-dappled glade, but she preferred it this way, seeing the bridge submerged. The unreality of a projected background had always irritated her, more so than the sight of the instrumentation panel lights glittering and blinking under the surface. She preferred the real article whenever she could get it.

The dip was relaxing; below her, Lien's long robes undulated like seaweed. Although she was the only fully organic intelligence on the station, she chose to bathe in her working dress, as was the current fashion. A restless—and somewhat vain—young woman,

Lien always followed the current fashion with exactitude. After all, she reasoned, one never knew who might be watching.

Floating on the surface of the water were flat, two-dimensional projections of the reports the drones had sent back on the bogey. A refracted, three-dimensional image of the ship hung just beneath the surface. Without interest Lien watched it move slowly around the bridge, like an animal sniffing out its new surroundings. She sighed and read the reports dutifully. It was only one of a myriad of duties she was required to attend to during her apprenticeship. For now it was a minor matter, hardly worth her attention. Her platform simply happened to be the closest to which this ship would pass. She splashed idly at the water and the reports rippled and dissipated. She ordered the room drained. Rising from her seat, the edge of Lien's robe sent the image of the bogey—now cruising by her left calf—into a frantic spin; the vessel seemed to struggle for a moment, then was snagged by an invisible current. It was drawn deeper into a corner of the room where it was caught in a vortex. It spun madly. Seconds later, it was sucked into a barely visible crack.

Lien stared after it, thoughtfully tapping her forefinger on her chin. It would still be several days before the bogey violated the second edict, passing the one light hour boundary beyond which the Polyarchy forbade weapons of any kind. In the meantime it might veer off, or increase its deceleration. It might do anything. Lien decided only when the violation became imminent would she inform the Pro-Locutors. Until then, she thought, let the ship come. She turned, started toward the corridor. Her step faltered, a new thought troubling her.

What if this is some sort of test? Perhaps part of my training? She chewed on her lower lip, scuffed at the floor with the sole of her bare foot. The room was already drained, her robe dry, water molecules sluicing off the material obediently. *Well,* she thought, *I best do something.*

Her ship was an unwieldy gravitic platform, not built for speed; and the bogey, though decelerating, was still moving at a good clip, nearly $0.003c$. Lien asked the platform if intercept was possible.

A confirmation in the form of a diagram appeared before her. It showed a parabolic course with intercept at approximately sixty-four light minutes out from the Hub. Just enough. She ordered the platform to begin the manoeuvre.

There, she thought. If the bogey crosses into the exclusion zone, I'll be right there. No one can question my motives then.

Satisfied with her decision, Lien spun on her heel and headed for the aft garden; the bath had made her sleepy, and, for the last week, the mossy embankment beneath the arch of the waterfall had been her favourite place to nap.

VIRACOSA · 12 DAYS LEFT

They had come out of nowhere: fourteen fist-sized objects, bullet-shaped and colourless as dark matter, orbiting *Viracosa*. According to the onboard instruments, they didn't exist. Except visually, when they betrayed their presence by eclipsing background stars. As soon as they appeared, the ship had begun revival procedures on its three crew members. Sitting at the ops panel, Sav stared at the display hanging in the centre of the bridge. The ship's log showed that one moment the things hadn't been there, then the next they had. "Where the hell did they come from?"

Josua, who sat at the comm station to Sav's left, lifted his shoulders with a grunt and shrugged. Gravity, still nearly a third above normal, stooped his shoulders.

"You don't seem too damned concerned." Sav shifted uncomfortably, feeling the extra weight more acutely than he would have thought possible. It would be another ten days before deceleration would drop to the one-gee mark—and normal gravity returned.

"No, I'm not. Nexus had almost three thousand years on us technologically before we left. Since then they've had another five hundred. Whatever they've got is bound to look like magic."

Ruen groaned. He still fumbled numbly at the grab bars to Sav's right, having just emerged from the circular opening between decks, his long, thin fingers moving like he had been anaesthetized. His beloved cane hung from a strap around his wrist, repaired mid-shaft with glue and secured by rope after Losson had snapped it back on Bh'Haret. The holy man's breath came in wheezes and gasps after his struggle up the ladder from the crew quarters and his pallid face seemed to have aged another decade. That he'd made it up to the bridge on his own was a minor miracle.

"They haven't responded to any of our signals yet," Sav said. "We've scanned the entire bandwidth four times. So what do we do now?"

"Nothing." Josua said.

Sav blinked. "But we don't know what they are. Or where they came from."

"Nexus sent them. Yilda told me that they monitored space at least a quarter of a light year out. Possibly more. And that an exclusion zone begins a light hour out from the binaries. That's where we'll meet them."

"No." It was half throat clearing, half word, but Ruen managed to wheeze it out. "Not Nexus," he said before a cough rattled in his throat, choking off his next words. He spat noisily; a globule of green-grey phlegm shot from between his dry lips and, its arc foreshortened by the increased gravity, dropped abruptly to the deck. "Can't you see?" he said hoarsely, wiping his mouth awkwardly with the back of his arm, his cane clacking against the rungs of the ladder. "They're agents of the Dissolution; *anhaa-10* sent them from a higher dimension into this one."

Sav glared at him. "Save your idiot theories. You've got no brain-dead followers here to listen to your nonsense."

"He could be right," Josua said. "A higher-dimensional vehicle travelling along a dimension imperceptible to us. It drops into our dimensions—and magically appears."

Sav shook his head in disbelief. "You think these things are higher-dimensional vehicles?"

Josua shrugged. "I doubt it. In all probability, they're simply devices that are adept at concealing their presence. In any case, if they don't want to talk, I don't see any way of persuading them."

"There must be something we can do."

"I suppose we could attack them. But I doubt very much we'd succeed. And in all likelihood, we'd be destroyed in retaliation. We can't risk it."

"So we have to sit and watch them."

"You can, if you like," Josua said. "But I'm going back to my stasis cell." Slowly, like an old man, he raised his right arm so Sav could see the watch on his wrist. The display read 11-18:46. "We've got less than twelve days left. The exclusion zone is another thirteen away. The Hub, four more after that. If we don't go back under, we'll be dead before we get there."

"Repent before the Dissolution," Ruen admonished them loudly. "It is your only path to salvation!" He had recovered enough to deliver his pronouncement with the unflappable certainty of the faithful. Both his arms were raised over his head now, his cane held high in one hand, the other wrapped around a grab bar high on the bulwark. "I will guide you," he added quietly. But his words were directed not at his companions; rather, he seemed to be addressing his remarks to the display, to the black objects circling the ship. His rheumy eyes followed their slow, hypnotic movements, his unkempt grey hair bobbing slightly with the motion.

"If we take shifts," Sav said, "we can have someone up the whole time. And both be back up a day before we hit the exclusion zone."

"No. The risk of re-infection will cut short our time—"

"We can program the ship to blow the seals after the first shift. That will kill anything infectious. Then whoever goes second can be revived after we've re-established atmosphere."

Josua looked at him thoughtfully. Oddly, he seemed a little less sure of himself. Of his authority. "Perhaps you're right. Six days apiece. Leaving us six days when we're both up again. That will allow us to reach the Hub with a day to spare. And, if we haven't heard from Yilda by then—"

"—there will be no point," Sav finished Josua's sentence.

Sav thought about returning to his stasis cell. But the notion of going under right now repulsed him in a way he couldn't articulate. "I'll take the first shift," he said.

"Fine," Josua answered. With a grunt, he heaved himself out of the seat and started for the ladder.

As he passed the comm station, Sav caught his sleeve; he nodded in the direction of Ruen who was still completely absorbed by the display. "What about him," Sav whispered low enough so the holy man couldn't hear.

"He'll keep me company on my shift." Josua turned to the *patrix*. "Ruen?"

The older man reluctantly turned his gaze from the display. He raised grizzled eyebrows.

"Come along. We're returning to stasis."

Ruen narrowed his eyes, drew his thin lips together. "No. The Dissolution is at hand!" He stabbed the point of his cane toward Josua.

"Not yet," Josua said. "Soon."

"Soon?" Ruen looked disoriented.

"When we're disinterred, the Dissolution will come," Josua added. "I promise."

The assurance seemed to placate the holy man. Nodding, Ruen let himself sag onto his hands and knees. He crawled haltingly to the ladder below, dragging his cane along the deck. Moving with painstaking caution, he lowered himself onto the rungs and climbed slowly from sight. Josua grasped the ladder and began his own descent.

"Six days," he said over his shoulder before his head disappeared under the lip of the hatch.

11 DAYS LEFT

The objects continued to follow *Viracosa*. Sav watched them from the bridge. Increasing the magnification of the optics revealed no more detail. Sav ran every other scan he could think of, monitoring the objects on dozens of frequencies simultaneously, but *Viracosa*'s instruments consistently reported no radiant energy. When their silent escort drifted into new orbital configurations—and so should have been expending energy—there wasn't the tiniest of bit of telltale radiation. The instruments continued to insist the things weren't there.

For five days Sav watched, eating intermittently and sleeping poorly. When he dreamed, his dreams were filled with images of those silent watchers. During his waking moments he busied himself with a thousand small improvements to the scanning equipment. Nothing helped. The results remained the same. He began to doubt their existence.

On the sixth day, Sav donned his EVA suit.

It was a foolish thing to do during deceleration; Josua would never have approved. The ship was still travelling at a significant percentage of the speed of light and the debris of space streamed past at incredible relative velocities. The exhaust from the ship and the electromagnetic collar that shielded the engines would offer him protection as long as he stayed close to the hull. Nevertheless, a single micrometeorite, intersecting their ship at the proper angle, would maim or kill him. Despite this, Sav went external, crawling from the airlock and lying flat against the scarred and pitted hull, securing himself with magnetized clamps. He had to see the things first hand, prove to himself that they were really there.

At the midpoint of their flight, the ship had used its attitude jets to point the engines forward for braking. Now, past the rounded edge of the feeder tanks, were the double suns of the Twins, needlepoints of brilliance too luminous to bear even through a polarised visor. Raising his arm to cast a shadow across his visor, Sav stared out into the depths of space. Unfamiliar stars cluttered the night. For a moment, Sav forgot about the things circling *Viracosa*. Instead he tried to pick Bh'Haret's sun out of the myriad visible stars. He knew he was on the correct side; it should be visible beyond the slender nose of the ship. If he was correct, the last star on the horizontal arm of the galaxy would be—

The star winked out of existence.

Sav gasped; he strained forward against the clamps.

Then the star reappeared. A second later, the one next to it disappeared. Sav let out a pent-up breath. Air wafted through the recirculators as sensors detected the sudden accumulation of perspiration on his forehead and in the palms of his hands. His suit hummed quietly, trying to cool him.

One of those damn things passed in front of Bh'Haret's sun, Sav thought. He watched the stars along the galactic arm disappear, then reappear, one by one. But the object itself was invisible against the backdrop of space. Sav should have known this before he'd left the airlock. Out here, he'd be able to see nothing. The only evidence of the objects would be second hand, as they occluded the stars.

Sav pulled himself back to the airlock. He palmed the lock handle and the doors slid open. After the lock finished its cycle, he stripped off his suit and pulled himself down the access hatch to the stasis quarters below, his shift at an end.

6 DAYS LEFT

"Shit!"

The curse came to Sav, distantly, as if dulled by a heavy fog. Then the muffled sound of several blows, like a fist hammering against a solid surface. A single, sharp crack followed.

Sav blinked uncertainly; his mouth was gummy, his stomach tied in knots, and his limbs quivered with the familiar post-stasis ache. Josua's hazy outline, swam into view, and it took Sav a moment to force his eyes to focus. Josua wore no shirt or shoes. His face was crimson, like he'd been exerting himself, and he looked angry. In his left hand he cradled his right fist. He stared at Sav where he lay on his pallet with an infuriated expression, as if he blamed Sav for this injury.

"What . . . what's the matter?" Sav's voice was hoarse.

Josua took a step toward Sav, and for a moment Sav thought he was going to take a swing at him. But then Josua's face changed as if a switch had been flipped: his anger dissipated, was replaced by blank expression. Letting go of his fist, he held up his watch. It showed 5-20:29. Less than six days left.

"We're a few light minutes from the exclusion zone," he said. "A day out."

Sav swallowed. It was like sandpaper grating in his throat. With an effort, he turned his head. Across the room, Ruen's naked form was visible as a pink outline through the translucent door of his cell. The thin figure was perfectly still. Why wasn't the door open? Why wasn't he stirring yet? Josua had said he was going to revive the holy man shortly after his own shift began. But he hadn't. "What . . . what about Ruen?" Sav managed to croak from between parched lips. He propped himself on one elbow; his head felt like it was stuffed with wet sand.

"I aborted the sequence. I didn't think there was anything he could do to help. So I let him sleep."

Sav peeled the leads from the back of his head, disconnected his catheters and swung his legs outside the cell. He leaned forward—and saw the control panel next to his cell had been smashed: a crack ran down the centre where the panel had been pushed in, as if from a sharp blow. It was shorted, its screen full of garbage. Sav looked at Josua's scraped knuckles, then back at the panel.

"You were overdue. I was trying to make the damn thing work," Josua said, flexing his fist. "I lost my cool."

Before he'd gone under, Sav had made sure his revival had been locked in; he'd coded the abort sequence with a password. Without changing the logic cards buried beneath the cell, there was nothing that could be done from the panel to abort the revival process. He knew this from the years he'd spent working longhaul. But chances were that Josua wouldn't have known. Perhaps Josua had decided his revival was as pointless as Ruen's and tried to stop it. But there was no way Sav could ever prove it.

Josua's gaze drifted around the cabin; but he wouldn't meet Sav's eyes, nor look directly at the panel. "By the way," he said in a matter-of-fact tone, "we have another visitor."

"We picked up another one of those things?" Sav's voice was still rough.

"No. It's bigger."

A ship? Sav pushed himself onto unsteady legs. "Has it tried to contact us yet?"

Josua danced back a step. "No."

"When did you pick it up?"

"The instruments detected it two days ago, fifty-six million klicks out. It's about two hundred times the size of *Viracosa*. And it's accelerating. If we maintain our current course, intercept should be just before we hit the exclusion zone, in less than a day."

Fifty-six million klicks, Sav thought. "How the hell did you find it?"

"I didn't have to. There was a burst of long wave radio transmissions between the things outside and the new object. I took a couple of readings and triangulated them to find the source."

"And the ship didn't respond to similar frequencies?"

"I didn't say it was a ship. I just think it might be."

"What about its response?"

Josua blinked; he crossed his arms. "No response." He frowned. "I decided not to initiate contact yet."

Sav couldn't believe what he was hearing. Josua had left him in stasis even though there was likely a manned ship out there. "Two days and you haven't done anything yet?"

"I tried to wake you." Josua's voice had taken on a querulous note, like that of a child making excuses. "I didn't think there would be any point. When they're ready, they'll talk."

Astonished, Sav stared at Josua. What was he thinking? They had less than six days before the onset of the disease. Perhaps seven in which they could still reasonably function. And here he was, waiting patiently for a contact that might never come. Sav staggered past Josua, grasped the rungs of the ladder, and hauled himself up to the bridge, his muscles screaming their protest. Dropping into the seat before the comm panel, he called up the history file on the screen, located the frequency Josua had been monitoring. Slipping on the headset, he started reeling off orders to the ship's AI. Behind him he heard the tread of Josua's footsteps.

"What are you doing?"

Sav ignored him; instead he finished dictating the parameters for the comm system, ordering a radio burst in thousand megahertz bracketing frequencies.

"It won't do any good," Josua said. But his voice was uncertain—strangely agitated. "It won't respond. No more than the others did."

Sav switched on the receiver and gave the order to transmit a standard hailing message; the board responded with a confirmation of the order. The message was dispatched.

"Maybe we should—"

But whatever Josua was going to say was cut off by a sudden

burst of static piped over the bridge's speakers, followed by a sound like the growling of an engine.

Sav re-transmitted the message.

The bridge speakers hissed and sputtered, spewing out more grinding noises that warbled and changed pitch in a seemingly random pattern. Then the garbage abruptly stopped; a flat, male voice began rhyming off a list of words or perhaps an alphabet: "... *lect, ezeni, verrach, tlui, eech, lemech, ruhr* . . ."

It sounded like Nexus standard. Sav opened a two-way voice transmission channel. "This is *Viracosa*, outbound from Bh'Haret. Please acknowledge."

At first, silence. Then, a single word. "*Viracosa.*" It was a different voice this time, still emotionless, but definitely a woman's. "*You are expected.*"

THE RELAY STATION · 17 DAYS LEFT

Without conscious thought, Liis's feet kicked into action after she'd seen Penirdth plummet from sight; half a dozen quick strides propelled her midway to the ragged hole before she realized the lunacy of what she was doing. There could be more weak spots in the crust here. And what about the area around the hole? How close could she get to the lip before it would crumble and swallow her as well? She let herself glide to a halt. It wasn't difficult—the drag of her sled worked like an anchor. She looked back. No one had moved; they stood in their positions in line, watching her. Mira had dropped her poles. She seemed to be swaying.

Liis turned and stared at the opening, visible as another deep shadow against the endless, red-tinted snow. She couldn't walk away, leave Penirdth for dead. But should she go forward and risk the ice? She bit her lip, tasted blood.

To hell with it, she thought. Using the tip of her pole, she pressed the release on the bindings of her skis. She stepped free of them; her boots sank a few centimetres into the lightly packed snow. Dropping her pole, she unfastened the leads to her sled and stepped toward the opening, her boots crunching as the snow compacted beneath them.

Something thumped to Liis's right. It wasn't the noise that alerted her—the suit effectively deadened most sound on the outside. Rather, it was the vibration that ran through the crust of the snow and into the soles of her boots. Twisting to the side, she saw the end of a rope two metres away.

She swung around to face the others. The tarp on Yilda's sled had been rolled back. He stood next to it, the rope in his hand, a thick coil by his feet. With a gesture, he indicated Liis should pick up the other end of the line and secure it to her harness.

Yilda gestured again, this time more emphatically.

Liis retrieved the rope, tied it to her harness, making a large knot with her good hand. She pulled it as tight as she could. Meanwhile, Yilda had flung the other end of the rope at Mira and Hebuiza. Hebuiza took up the line, slowly, reluctantly, but Mira didn't move. Yilda gestured at her fiercely. Mira swayed.

She's in shock, Liis thought.

Hebuiza moved forward and shoved the rope at her, nearly knocking her over. She closed her fingers around it, staring at it as if she didn't understand what it was.

Yilda gestured at Liis again, only this time he tapped his visor and made a small motion with his hand as if he were adjusting a dial. He repeated the motion several times, but Liis had no idea what he was trying to convey. She lifted her shoulders in a shrug. At this, Yilda nodded and waved his hands as if to say, "Never mind." He gave her the thumbs up sign.

Liis nodded. Turning, she resumed her march toward the hole.

She halted three metres away. From this distance, the edge looked reasonably solid; the cross-section exposed by the collapse of the surface showed a thick layer of ice beginning fifteen or so centimetres beneath the snow. She circled cautiously, keeping the same distance. The ice extended downwards as far as she could see in all directions. Liis was relieved; she had feared that there was an extensive cavity beneath her. But the opening, it appeared, was merely the end of a relatively narrow shaft, roughly four metres in diameter. She moved closer, to within a metre and a half. At that distance she went down on her hands and knees, then onto her belly, clenching her teeth and sucking in a sharp breath as her weight settled on her injured arm. She squirmed forward until her helmet poked over the lip.

The shaft corkscrewed down, twisting and turning like the interior of a crumpled cylinder. The sun was still near zenith and provided ample illumination so that Liis could see, fifteen metres below, a narrow patch of solid black that looked as smooth as a sheet of opaque glass. It was the skin of the buried lake. Light wisps of mist curled from its surface. Penirdth was nowhere to be seen.

For a moment Liis considered pulling herself over the edge. There were cracks and ledges she could use as handholds, and the others held the end of the line. Maybe she could find him down there, clinging to an outcropping or trapped on a ledge not visible from her perspective. She dug her fingers into the edge, tensed the muscles in her arm.

At the bottom of the shaft, on the inky surface of the water, a long white stick floated into view. She ordered the magnification on her visor increased, and her stomach lurched as the walls of the shaft seemed to shoot up around her. The thing at the bottom grew, resolved itself into of one of Penirdth's skis.

He's gone.

An unnatural calm pervaded Liis. She felt detached, as if she were only a passenger in her body. She rolled over and sat up; the others waited by their sleds. She struggled to her feet, heedless of the proximity of the opening. Numbly, she stumbled back to her sled and reattached the leads. She stepped into her skis. Moments later she stood in front of Yilda. He unknotted the rope she had secured to her harness, then started to coil it. When he reached Mira, he had to pry it from her fingers. He stowed the rope, then inclined his head, making contact with Liis.

"Well?"

"He's gone." Were the words hers? Liis wasn't certain. "A shaft drops into the lake."

"I see." A pause. "As I guessed. The lake must be fed below by hot springs. Yes. Any further such, um, weaknesses should be detectable on infrared." He pulled back and repeated his earlier gesture, pointing to his visor and spinning an imaginary dial.

Liis didn't answer. She was thinking about how she had been carried along by Hebuiza and Yilda, trailing like flotsam in their wake. They had answers for everything; she had none. Why hadn't they anticipated this?

Bending forward, Yilda re-established contact. "And his, um, equipment?"

Liis shook her head, not caring that he couldn't see the gesture.

"Must be going, hey? Back in line." He pushed off, driving his poles into the ground and propelling himself forward.

His tail uncoiled, slithered away from the group. In a daze, Liis watch Mira stumble after. Hebuiza gestured brusquely for Liis to fall in.

Numbly, she sidestepped into the tracks the two men had made. Hebuiza poked her in the back; automatically, she kicked herself into motion, working her one pole as best she could, intent on the trail.

Here I am, still following, she thought, a sudden, piercing ache in her chest making it difficult to breathe. Her eyes burned. She pushed forward, gritting her teeth, her legs pumping insensibly. *Don't think*, she told herself. *Just don't think*. A tear traced a path down her cheek.

No! Liis bit the inside of her cheek until she tasted blood. *I won't!*

But it was too late. The crush of repressed emotion overwhelmed her.

Inside her the hollow of her suit, she wept.

The party moved steadily south as the sun crept, millimetre by millimetre, toward the horizon. The huge disk choked the land with its light and cast thick shadows the colour of dried blood.

Liis's tears ended as abruptly as they had began, a sudden, passing storm. But the anguish remained. Penirdth's death had drained her, leaving her weak. Her arm, momentarily forgotten in her grief, now ached sharply. She moved forward like an automaton, hardly aware of her surroundings. *What's the point in continuing?* she thought. *We're all doomed anyway, aren't we?*

Her stride faltered. The distance between her and Mira grew. Hebuiza, who was in line behind her, moved up. Skiing parallel to her, he gestured for her to pick up the pace. Liis ignored him; she bowed her head and stared at the twin tracks in front of her, her legs moving slowly. Clearly dissatisfied with her response, Hebuiza raised his pole and rapped her on the back, like he was urging on a pack animal.

In a flash, Liis's indifference turned to anger. She swung her pole, oblivious to the pain, and caught him squarely across his narrow chest. He reared back in what looked like astonishment, lost his balance and tumbled to the ground, tangled in the lines of his sled, one ski sticking up into the air. She would have spat if she could. Instead, she pushed on, leaving him where he was. She picked up the pace and the distance to Mira's hunched figure closed.

In moments Liis's anger had dwindled; but resentment still warmed her stomach like a stiff shot of liquor. Her arm seemed to burn with the same fire. She decided she liked the feeling. As her legs pushed her forward with renewed vigour, she nurtured this kernel of anger like a newborn child. For far too long she had allowed herself to be carried along by the whims of others. Josua. Hebuiza. Yilda. Even the good-natured Penirdth. Anger, at herself, at her passivity, pulsed inside, beating like a new heart. Her strides lengthened; she surged forward.

Eventually, she had to ease up her pace; Mira's tail, slithering in the track centimetres in front of the tip of her ski, forced her to slow lest she run over it.

16 DAYS LEFT

The muscles in Liis's good arm and shoulder hurt miserably, throbbing in time to the ache in her broken one. With her single pole, she'd developed a lop-sided rhythm that kept her moving.

The sun finally set; the darkness of the long night enfolded them. Liis adjusted her visor, upping the gain to enhance her night vision. She was exhausted. Her earlier burst of energy had deserted her. Checking her readout, she saw that twenty-two hours had elapsed since they'd last slept up on the ice field—and that they'd covered nearly eight kilometres in four hours of skiing. With the steady wind at their backs, and flat, unobstructed terrain, their progress was better than could have been hoped. The dangerous weaknesses in the crust had diminished; on her infrared overlay, Liis spotted them only infrequently now. After weaving through an initial spate of hidden shafts, they had all but disappeared. Liis did a quick mental calculation. At this rate they would reach the Speakers' dome—three hundred klicks away—in less than ten days, a day ahead of schedule. Leaving them plenty of time—

For what?

Liis didn't know. Yilda had insisted he could tell them nothing. At least not until they arrived at the dome. *Maybe he has no plan*, she thought, *and this is simply a mad rush toward our own deaths*. But there was something about the Facilitator's confidence that belied that notion. He was adamant they could overrun the station. Indeed, he almost seemed to relish the opportunity to try. In fact, rather than a desperate man grasping at straws, he'd behaved more like a tactician whetting his appetite for a long-awaited assault. It felt wrong. Turning it over and over in her mind, she trudged on.

A short time later, Yilda called a halt. They would rest, he signed, for six hours. The others unbuckled their leads, and staked out small areas on the leeward side of a rise where they would sleep. Hebuiza, who'd lagged after Liis had struck him, now caught up and drifted past her at a safe distance, two pole-lengths away. He chose a place next to the other Facilitator. Immediately after he had slipped off his leads, he strode over to Yilda and touched helmets, his larger one completely obscuring the smaller man's helmet. His movements were agitated, animated with what seemed to be a barely suppressed rage; several times he gestured in Liis's direction. But whatever Yilda's reaction, his body language remained neutral. When Hebuiza pulled his helmet back suddenly and stalked back to his sled, Liis laughed aloud.

Mira chose a spot apart from the others. As Liis tried to unbuckle her own leads, she watched as Mira fell to her knees without bothering to free herself from her harness. She remained in this position, staring back in the direction from which they had come. Back to where they'd lost Penirdth.

Had they been lovers? Liis wondered.

No. That wasn't right, somehow. Since *Viracosa*'s return to Bh'Haret, Penirdth and Mira had spent most of their time together, working in a companionable silence. Without the small intimacies of lovers. But there was a connection between them. And he'd adopted a protective, almost fatherly disposition toward Mira. *As he had toward me*, Liis thought. Now who would look after them?

Undoing the last strap, Liis shrugged herself free of her harness. She walked over to Mira and bent to touch helmets.

"Penirdth," she began, feeling foolish and inarticulate. She cleared her throat. "I'm sorry—"

"He's gone." Mira's voice sounded dreamy, far away.

"You should lie down."

"The Dissolution is at hand."

Liis had forgotten about Ruen's ridiculous teachings. "It's time to rest—"

"Penirdth has gone ahead. We'll be joining him soon." Mira

clutched at Liis's good arm. "Won't we?"

"Yeah," Liis answered, feeling sick. She extracted her arm and pulled her helmet away.

Liis returned to her sled. Yilda and Hebuiza lay on the ground, already asleep as far as she could tell. She lay down on her side, careful not to jostle her broken arm. Mira remained on her knees staring off into the distance. Liis curled around so that she wouldn't have to see the other woman. But her thoughts returned to Penirdth. Her throat went tight; this time she didn't weep. Instead, she offered a silent prayer up to him. And, as an afterthought, to Sav, light years away, still in stasis, and speeding toward the Hub—if nothing had gone awry.

12 DAYS LEFT

Five days had passed since they had lost Penirdth and Losson; it was the dawn of the next local day. They had made steady progress across the plain and now, according to Liis's display, they were a mere one hundred and four klicks from the dome. In the last few hours, however, they had had to slow their pace to negotiate a thick cluster of crustal weaknesses. Liis's infrared overlay showed that the perilous shafts dotted the plain in all directions; there was no end in sight. The longer strides that had moved them so far so fast would now be impossible.

As their progress fell off, Yilda's exasperation had grown in proportion. His gestures became anxious, and his demands on the party increased. Rest periods were shortened, and then seemed to disappear altogether. Yilda traversed the winding paths of safe ground as if he were sprinting against an invisible opponent. And unlike the other members of the party, he seemed inexhaustible. Even Hebuiza's narrow shoulders were stooped. But Yilda, despite his pot belly and generally dissipated appearance, possessed an apparently bottomless stamina. He urged them to push a little bit further before their next extended rest. They had been skiing without a break for five hours. Exhausted, her legs rubbery, Liis watched Yilda finally signal for a rest. The party closed ranks.

Mira lost her balance.

As she approached the point where the Facilitator had stopped, her ski slipped out of the track, slewed to the side, and she fell over. Liis, who'd been behind her, watched it happen without concern. After all, she herself had fallen several times since they'd set out and was none the worse for it. But this time the momentum of Mira's sled carried it forward—it banged into her arm and drove the sharp tip of her pole, which had caught in the articulated folds behind her knee, into her suit. She withdrew it.

From the mouth of the small breach a jet of red spewed across Liis's infrared display, roiled into a cloud in the air. Mira, who must have seen the same thing on her display, immediately clapped a hand across the mouth of the tear. Heat continued to leak out around her palm and fingers like blood haemorrhaging from a wound.

Liis stared, too stunned to react. She looked up to Yilda, but he stood five metres ahead, twisted around on his skis, watching impassively.

Hebuiza flashed past her; he flung aside his poles as he bore down on Mira. The Facilitator lifted his right arm; a thin, silver needle, driven by some hidden mechanism, slid from the forearm of his suit, extended to a length of several centimetres past the palm of his hand. He curled his fingers under the instrument and out of the way. Reflected sunlight flashed off the casing of the needle as Hebuiza bent down and jabbed Mira in her chest, directly over her heart. The small woman jerked once and went limp; Hebuiza withdrew the needle. A thin jet of red streamed from the second tiny puncture; this time it was accompanied by a thin trickle of blood. The needle disappeared back into its sheath. The Facilitator quickly unbuckled Mira from her leads. With surprising strength, Hebuiza grabbed Mira's harness and lifted her from the ground. She hung from the Facilitator's grip, her poles dangling from their wrist straps, making her look like a broken marionette. A miasma of red grew around her. Hebuiza grabbed her suit by the crotch and shoulder and heaved her, like a sack of offal, to his left. Mira's loose-jointed body, her stubby skis still attached to her boots, sailed toward one of the weak spots outlined on Liis's display. She hit it dead centre. The crust collapsed under her and she tumbled from sight.

Liis swung back to face Hebuiza. He had already pushed Mira's sled to the opening. Placing his boot on the edge of the sled, he shoved it forward. It teetered for a second on the brink, then followed Mira down. Unhurriedly, Hebuiza picked up one of the poles he'd discarded and then carefully retrieved the other from the periphery of a second, unbroken weak spot. Both poles in hand, he turned and kicked himself into motion, gliding past Liis, back to his place behind her.

My God, Liis thought. *Just like that.* Shocked, she stared at the hole. *It could have been me.* How many times she had fallen? She couldn't remember.

Something caught Liis's attention: it was Yilda, motioning for her to follow. He turned his back and pushed off, clearly anxious to put as much distance between them and the site of the revealing leak. Liis watched him begin to pick his way through the maze of weaknesses.

They'd talked about this contingency, back when they'd been preparing the meteoroid. In the event of a suit breach, their only option was to dispose of the *leak*—as quickly and ruthlessly as possible. She hadn't thought much about it since. But Yilda and Hebuiza apparently had. The needle proved that.

Liis tried to convince herself that Mira was really the lucky one. For her it was over. She wouldn't have to succumb to the disease and its progressive indignities—or take her own life to avoid it. The decision had already been made for her.

It's better this way. Yet even as she thought this, Liis knew she wouldn't have traded places with Mira for anything. Much to her surprise, she realized she begrudged every precious moment left to her. She wouldn't give up a second without a fight.

Something struck her in the small of the back, and Liis jumped, the lines of her sled tugging sharply on her harness. She swung around and saw Hebuiza, his pole reversed in his hand, the butt end waving at her impatiently to get moving. Anger flared like a nova; she swung her pole around. But it went wide of the mark this time and she nearly lost her balance. She was twisted around awkwardly on her skis and Hebuiza had already backed out of range.

She lowered her pole, seething. *Patience*, she thought, pushing her anger back down to that place where she coddled it deep inside her chest. *There will be time enough for this later.* With disdain, she turned her back on Hebuiza, pushing herself into motion, remembering that long, sharp needle hidden in the folds of the Facilitator's suit.

6 DAYS LEFT

It was late in the planet's afternoon when the crown of the dome first became visible. Liis hadn't been watching; instead, her attention had been fixed rigidly on Yilda's ski tracks. Her analgesic patches had run out that morning, and her arm's throb was a constant hum. She followed the two narrow tracks in the crust without caring where they might lead, trying to lose herself in the mindless act of mechanical repetition.

At first she thought she imagined the tiny anomaly that seemed to float just above the horizon. When she went to maximum magnification, it remained an enigmatic, grey smudge. But her compass marked their destination with unarguable accuracy. It was the dome. The display estimated it to be eighteen klicks away.

Less than a day.

Liis could hardly believe it.

Since Mira's death six days earlier, they'd made relatively good progress. But they had slowed to a crawl the last ten hours as they'd approached the far shore of the buried lake; here they'd found a dense field of the perilous shafts, far worse than any they'd yet encountered. As they crossed the boundary of the buried lake, the formations abruptly stopped. Now they skied straight ahead over a level surface, a steady wind at their backs. Barring any further delays, they'd arrive tomorrow, leaving them five days before the onset of the first symptoms. They would be behind schedule, yet well within the parameters of Yilda's plan. Liis's heartbeat quickened.

Don't let yourself get too hopeful.

She still had no idea what the Facilitators hoped to do when they arrived. They had been as tight-lipped and mysterious about the details of their plan as they had about everything else. A sudden wave of cold anger seized her. She bit her lip, shook it off. *Soon,* she thought. *When we get to the dome and peel off these suits. They'll tell me. I'll make them! Yilda won't be able to ignore me then.* She thought back to the brief exchanges between Penirdth and Yilda back on Bh'Haret, the few questions Penirdth had asked, the small objections he raised. But Yilda's confidence had been unassailable.

"Can't disclose the details, no. Rest assured, however, we can, and will, accomplish our mission." His tone had been boastful. "They are not gods. No. Spent my life studying their ways, hey? Mortal as we are. And they could not have foreseen an expedition as, um, audacious as ours." He had paused, stroking the golden studs along his chin. "They could have no notion, no conception, we know about the relay station. Security will be lax." With a wry smile, he added, "You might say I know them better than they know themselves."

Still, there was something wrong. Something about Yilda. His self-confidence might have merely been bravado, a pose. He was, after all, a Facilitator. Only she didn't believe that. He seemed to be growing more assured with each stride he took toward the dome. His gait increased in length and he poled with vigour, throwing up small spumes of snow in his wake. Liis struggled to keep up. If she hadn't known better, she would have guessed by his body language that he was returning to a long-lost home rather than skiing toward an enemy enclave. It gave her the creeps.

Or am I being paranoid?

She stared at Yilda's back, at eagerness that seemed to animate his arms and legs, at the way he leaned forward as if this might get him to the dome that much sooner. *No,* Liis thought. *He knows something that he hasn't told me.*

Hebuiza had shown none of the anticipation that Yilda had. The other Facilitator looked more and more exhausted as the days had passed. His stoop had become permanent. Glancing back, Liis saw him move his arms and legs in a leaden motion, his head bowed. Whatever buoyed Yilda wasn't working for Hebuiza. Perhaps the taller Facilitator was in the dark every bit as much as she was.

Liis shook her head to clear her thoughts. It was all speculation.

Nothing more. Still . . .

Yilda had forged on as if he'd forgotten his two companions. Despite Liis's best efforts, the gap between them only widened. When he was a black dot on the horizon, Liis halted. Hebuiza was somewhere behind her. Her heart hammered wildly; perspiration filmed her. When she checked, her display told her she was nine kilometres from the dome. Until this moment she'd given the structure only a cursory examination. Now she scrutinized it more closely.

Yilda had told them the dome itself was ten kilometres in diameter, and over two in height. It was large enough to house a small city. But seen like this, it seemed unimpressive. She had to remind herself that, set in the midst of a vast plain of ice, there was nothing against which she could compare its scale. The east side of the structure was cloaked in impenetrable shadows. Small details became apparent when Liis magnified her display. The dome seemed to be made of a uniformly light-coloured, perhaps translucent, material, and was not as featureless as she had first thought. Regularly spaced black specks, like pinpricks, peppered its surface as if they marked the vertices of a grid. At its apex, a dark, black spire thrust upward through the dome. She stared at the thing until Hebuiza finally caught up to her several minutes later. Then she pushed off again.

Liis expected all detail on the dome to vanish with the setting of the sun. But the dome had fluoresced, throwing its features into relief. Now, four kilometres away, thin lines were visible between the regularly spaced points Liis had observed earlier, forming the anticipated grid. But far more numerous were the crooked, branching lines that veined the structure like blood vessels, making it look more organic than artificial. To be visible at this distance, the black points would have to be at least a dozen metres wide and the finest veins several metres in width. It looked like an elaborate arterial system, pumping fluids vital to the operation of the dome. Of everything she had seen thus far, this scared her the most: the idea that the dome itself was a massive, living intelligence—and they were microscopic intruders, like a virus, hoping to penetrate its outer membrane.

Liis slowed. Yilda's tracks vanished in the distance; she couldn't see him at all now, even when she amplified her night vision and maxed out the magnification of her display. For all she knew, he might have already arrived at the dome. Behind her, Hebuiza was again lost to sight.

Briefly she considered waiting for the Facilitator to catch up. But her consideration was really no more than a reflex, a quirk of her fatigue: when she remembered it was Hebuiza behind her, she felt anger burn in her throat. *Fuck him*, she thought. *Let him take care of himself.* She kicked off, her physical strength nearly spent, anger propelling her across the last few kilometres that separated her from the dome.

The illusion of the dome being an organic creature gave way to a certainty that the monstrous thing was alive.

Its surface glowed with a pallor that intensified as dusk faded into night, throwing the structure's features into sharp contrast. This close, Liis could see the veins branched into ever-smaller tributaries; long, grey tendrils hung like vines from pores the colour of rotting meat; here and there were metre-wide, pendent vesicles of bright green and smoky orange. The skin of the dome itself wasn't as uniform as it had appeared from a distance, rather it ranged from rough and tattered in places to smooth as the head of a drum in others. And there was movement throughout. Where the material of the dome hung slack, ripples, driven by gusts of wind, ran across its surface like wind through a flapping sail. The veins themselves constricted and relaxed in slow, rhythmic cycles, pumping whatever matter they carried. And the large, regularly spaced, black interruptions Liis had observed earlier now looked like blistered and eyeless faces with gaping mouths. In the centre of each one was either a long horizontal or vertical slit. The lips of the horizontal slits pulled inward in regular rhythms, sucking desperately at the atmosphere; the vertical slits expelled gases in roiling clouds from between puckered lips. When one of the larger ones vented, a slight tremor rumbled through the ground.

Liis had followed Yilda's track blindly the last half a kilometre, her attention fixed on the ceaseless motion that played itself out across the exterior of the dome. She felt cowed in its presence. That it was alive she no longer doubted. Whether it possessed intelligence or not, she couldn't have guessed. Perhaps it knew she was there; perhaps, in whatever mammoth organ housed its intelligence, it had guessed at her intentions—and had dismissed them as insignificant. Or perhaps it could see her no better than her own body sensed an invading virus. In either case, it had done nothing to impede her.

A few hundred metres from the dome, Yilda's tracks ended abruptly where the ground began to incline steeply. Around the base of the dome, a skirt of snow had accumulated, forming an embankment. Yilda had dug a deep trench at the bottom of the slope; in it, he had discarded his skis, his poles, and his auxiliary batteries. He had already dragged his sled three-quarters of the way up the embankment, leaving a trail of footsteps in the centre of the shallow depression formed by the bottom of his sled.

Liis stabbed at her bindings with the tip of her pole, unlocking them; she stepped free and flung her pole into the trench. With the toe of her boot, she nudged her skis in after. Then she too began trudging up the slope, grateful that the job of filling the hole, and hiding their equipment, would fall to Hebuiza after he'd dumped his gear.

At the summit the slope flattened. A narrow ridge ran along the gradual curve of the dome. An unnaturally exact line on the dome demarcated the juncture at which the snow ended; above it ran a network of fine mauve veins. The veins must have somehow prevented flakes from adhering to the structure above. Reaching out, Liis placed her hand on the surface just above the veins. It was rigid and smooth, like cloudy, white glass. Muted vibrations sang through the material of her glove and into her palm. A few hundred metres to Liis's left, the material of the dome hung in long folds, like huge curtains. Yilda's trail moved off that way, disappearing around the first fold that projected out onto the ridge. Sucking in a deep breath, she started after him. In the periphery of her vision, she saw Hebuiza's lanky figure hauling his sled up to the base of the slope.

On the other side she found Yilda. His leads were undone, and he crouched by his sled, his tail coiled behind him. Here, between two folds, the material of the dome flattened out for a small distance. Rising along the wall were dozens of the dark blisters Liis had seen before. Yilda had pulled his sled up next to a small one, perhaps two metres in diameter, which began at knee height. The thing looked like it had been blackened by fire; dark bubbles and delicate, flaking skin marred its surface. Fat, horizontal lips, a metre and a half in length, pulled weakly at the atmosphere, absurdly reminding Liis of the movement of a newborn's mouth. From the right corner of the tarry lips a strand of viscous fluid dribbled down the blister and fell onto the ridge near the heel of Yilda's boot. The Facilitator ignored it. He continued to unpack his gear from the sled and lay it out in orderly rows. With a curt gesture, he indicated she should do the same.

Liis unfastened her own leads. With her good hand, she coiled her tail into a loop. She turned her attention to the line that secured the tarp on her sled. Slowly, painstakingly, she loosened the knot. At last, it came undone. She held the loose rope in her hand, staring at it. *Penirdth helped me tie this*, she thought, and dropped the line like it had scorched her hand.

Yilda's sled was empty. He'd already attached his bulky backpack to his harness and secured his tail to it. On the ground beneath the blister he'd arranged a coil of rope, half a dozen carabiners, and a thirty-centimetre, self-boring ice screw. It looked like he intended to climb the face of the dome. But Liis didn't have any of her climbing gear left. Nor, she believed, did Hebuiza. They'd discarded that gear, at Yilda's insistence, back at the pass. Yilda threaded the end of the coiled rope through a carabiner, tied it off, and snapped the carabiner onto a ring on the base of the ice screw. He placed the screw back on the ground.

Liis looked up the long, dizzying, curve of the dome. How could she possibly climb it? Was Yilda waiting for her to fail, so that Hebuiza could dispose of her like Mira?

Yilda had unfolded a pick and shovel and was using them alternately to scrape out a shallow hole near the edge of the ridge. A hole the size of a grave. Turning, he pointed impatiently to Liis's sled, then tapped his own backpack, signalling her to prepare as he had.

Liis pulled the tarp off her sled.

She had little left. The only items visible were her backpack, a heavy cylinder containing plastic explosives and detonators, and two long nylon ropes. Before she could do anything, she felt Yilda's presence at her side. She tried not to flinch. The Facilitator crouched down and grabbed her pack; he quickly stuffed everything on her sled, except for the rope, into the pack. Rising, he held it out so that the straps dangled in front of her. When Liis didn't react immediately, he shook it vigorously. Then she understood: he was going to help her put it on. She turned and let him position the pack on her back. Then he began buckling her straps before she could begin fumbling with them.

As soon as the pack was on and her tail secured to it, Yilda spun away and crouched down in front of her sled again. He shifted the remaining contents around. Underneath a rope, he found six flares, wrapped in a plastic package. She'd forgotten about them. Yilda tore the package off, stuffed three in a side pocket of Liis's backpack, and tossed the remaining three next to the rest of his equipment. Grabbing the leads to her sled, he dragged it away. His own sled, now empty, was already in the hole he'd dug; he dropped Liis's sled, with its remaining equipment, on top of it. At that moment, Hebuiza stumbled around the corner and almost ran into them. He pulled up abruptly, swaying like a drunk.

He's exhausted, Liis thought. She knew she was too; but the strangeness of the dome had made her forget. She wondered if she was also swaying.

Yilda clutched Hebuiza by the arms, touched his helmet to the other Facilitator's. There was a brief exchange. Then he and Yilda set to unloading the sled. In moments, the smaller man had done the same for Hebuiza as he'd done for Liis: all three now had their packs on, tails coiled, and their sleds deposited in the hole. Yilda threw in the rolled up tarps and began kicking snow over the discarded gear. Liis joined him—and Hebuiza too, after a moment of hesitation.

The hole filled quickly.

Yilda folded his tools, slipped them into loops on the side of his backpack. Crouching down in front of the blister, he grabbed the ice screw to which he'd knotted the rope. He snapped a carabiner onto his harness and threaded the line through it. Turning, he signalled for Liis and Hebuiza to touch helmets.

"The dome will reject this screw in minutes." He articulated his words precisely, the usual halt in his speech gone. "You must act without hesitation. Do exactly as I do."

Having said that, he jammed the tip of the screw directly beneath the blister. He twisted the top of the metal tube, and the screw bit into the dome and spiralled into its white surface while he held its handle firmly. Liis was surprised; did he expect them to climb over the blister? She watched in puzzlement as the flange at the base of the handle snugged up against surface of the dome and the screw stopped turning. Yilda snatched up a flare in one hand and the end of the rope in his other. He pressed the tab at the head of the flare so that flame erupted from it tip. Then he did something that astonished Liis as much as it horrified her: waving the flare in front of him, he plunged head first into the mouth of the blister.

The broad lips curled back as if the thing was trying to avoid the heat from the flame, then sealed around him, leaving only his feet projecting. A heartbeat passed. Then his boots disappeared inside as if he'd been swallowed. The lips seemed to pucker with distaste like they had just eaten something sour.

Liis and Hebuiza stood alone outside the dome.

For an instant, Liis was too shocked to react; at her feet, the coil of rope unwound slowly. The Facilitator, too, seemed surprised; at least he stood, unmoving, his visor directed at the mouth of the thing. Liis leaned toward him. She wanted to touch helmets, to ask him what was going on.

Her proximity seemed to reanimate the Facilitator. Before she could make contact, he shoved her back with one hand. Grabbing a carabiner, he snapped it onto his harness and clipped it onto the line; grabbing a second flare, he sparked it to life and dove after Yilda. His legs protruded for an alarmingly long time (though it couldn't have been more than a few seconds) before they, too, wormed from sight.

Liis was alone.

She cursed the two Facilitators, then stooped to reach for a carabiner. She stopped. Below the edge of the blister, the ice screw was moving slowly, wiggling like it was alive. It was unscrewing. Already its flange had moved a couple of centimetres away from the surface of the dome. Liis grabbed the third flare; in her haste to light it, she fumbled and dropped it. Flaming, it rolled to the edge of the ridge and disappeared, leaving a smoky residue. She cursed, reaching back to pull one of the spares from the side pocket of her backpack. She had to twist her arm at a near impossible angle, and just managed to grasp a flare between two fingers. Wiggling it free, she got a proper grip on it and jammed her thumb against its tab. The flare caught and she threw herself toward the blackened lips.

She fell forward further than she thought she would onto a surprisingly steep pitch. Pain swept through her. She gasped for breath, her heart hammering wildly. She was going to be sick. In her rush, she'd forgotten about her broken arm.

Her vision began to clear, the dizzying lights fading into a matte black background. Except for a steady spear of light directly ahead of her.

The flare.

It lay in front of her. She snatched it up. Blinking, she looked around.

Her eyes still hadn't adjusted, but she could see she was in a dark, constricted tunnel; its soft walls pressed against her stomach, shoulders, and back. The whole thing angled sharply downward. She held up the flare and the walls receded; the tunnel was a fleshy pink, and appeared ringed, like the muscles of an intestine. Coating its surface was a shimmering viscous fluid that dripped in long, ropy strands from the roof. Centimetres in front of her the rings constricted until the opening was no larger than the size of her thumb. Yilda's rope ran through that ridiculously small aperture.

Liis swore. She'd forgotten to attach a carabiner. And now there was nothing she could do without dropping the flare. *To hell with it*, she thought. She tried to wiggle forward but found she was held firmly in place. Panic seized her. She slashed at the walls with the flare like it was a knife.

To her amazement, the grip of the tunnel loosened enough for her to wiggle forward. Ahead, the opening seemed to widen. Holding the flare aloft, she inched downward like an earthworm, the rope sliding beneath her.

She couldn't have travelled more than half a metre in this fashion when she found the tunnel no longer withdrew from the flare. The last ring had constricted like a fist around the rope. She swung the flare back and forth in front of the surface; nothing happened—except, perhaps, for the ring clenching the rope tighter. Then she jammed the flare against the fleshy material. The entire tunnel spasmed, as if in pain, the rings contracting like bands of metal around her. Breath was crushed from her lungs; pain shot through her arm again, making her head spin and her eyes water. She felt herself going limp.

The pressure relented. She gasped for air.

Darkness. The flare had been suffocated. Liis's mind was a chaotic jumble. Her deep breaths filled her helmet.

Calm yourself, she thought. *Reason it through. Yilda and Hebuiza managed. If they figured it out, I can too.*

What had happened when they entered? There had been a pause after they passed through the lips, their legs sticking out as if they too had run into this problem. Then their feet had disappeared. They had to have done something, before their feet disappeared, to open this obstruction....

Or was it the other way around? Had they pulled in their feet first?

Yes! Liis thought. *That has to be it!* The opening was a valve, like the pressure lock on a ship. The inner hatch wouldn't open as long as the outer lips hadn't sealed properly. And she couldn't have travelled far enough for her feet to be completely inside the tunnel yet.

Twisting onto her side, she pulled her knees up. Liis felt her feet slip inside, the lips closing against the soles of her boots. The tunnel relaxed.

Light blossomed in front of her as the tunnel relinquished its clutch on the rope. Two metres ahead, she saw vertical flaps, silhouetted like the petals of a flower, opening up. The rings of the tunnel widened and she felt herself sliding down the incline toward the brilliance. She tried to slow her momentum, but the tunnel was ejecting her, the rings in front loosening and those behind contracting. At the last minute she thought to drop the dead flare and grab at the rope. But the line was covered with the slick mucous and it slipped from her fingers.

Liis tumbled out of the opening and onto a hard surface, instinctively twisting to her right to protect her broken limb. She was only partly successful: a shiver of agony ran along the length of her arm at the moment of contact. She tumbled down a steep incline. A chaotic world of colours flashed past, dazzling her vision. It took her a second to realize the greens and browns were leaves and stems snapping and ticking at her visor; and under her was loose brown and grey soil that scraped at her suit.

The rope, she thought. It was to her right. She stretched her arm out.

But before she could close her fingers around the line she crashed through a thick weave of deep green into unobstructed light. She was weightless, falling. As she tumbled, several images spun past: in the distance, a panoramic sweep of forest, field, and structures that might have been buildings; the dark grey of a cliff face from which she'd fallen; the milky white of the underside of the dome; and below, the crystalline blue of a narrow lake.

I'm inside, she realized with a start, just before she hit the water.

In that last instant she had braced herself. She was lucky. During her fall she had spun so that her back struck first, protecting her arm. In the weaker gravity, the impact wasn't that powerful. Water sloshed over her and she sank lazily, weighted by her suit. The light of the dome receded.

Relief gave way to horror.

She began kicking furiously with her legs and pulling with her good arm. In her wake, a flurry of bubbles raced to the surface.

Still, she sank. She felt her throat tightening, believed she could feel fluid seeping into her suit, imagined the cold water coiling into her mouth and nostrils.

Cold water?

The notion made her hesitate, stop struggling altogether. The suit had been designed to be self-contained, to hide her heat signature; it should serve equally well to keep the water out. When she hit bottom, she could climb out.

She allowed herself to sink. Now that she had relaxed, she realized she was enfolded in an eerie silence. The muffled sounds of wind and the soft chafing of the fabric of her suit that had been her constant companions were gone. It was almost peaceful.

Her heels hit bottom, and she fell, in slow motion, onto her backside. She sat on the bottom of the lake, a cloud of silt rising around her. Delicately fronded plants swayed in an invisible current. Silver-scaled fish darted curiously toward her, then quickly away. Liis rolled over onto her knees and pushed herself unsteadily to her feet. The fluid seemed less viscous than normal water; or perhaps that was only an effect of the diminished gravity. In any case, movement was easier than she had anticipated. Checking her suit compass, she turned south and set off for the shore she had glimpsed during her fall.

The bottom began to rise; the silt gave way to slippery, algae-encrusted stone slabs, layered like a giant's stairway. She clambered up from one broad step to the next. Twice she almost fell, but both times managed to restore her balance by swinging her good arm out and paddling furiously against the water. The light grew as the slope diminished.

When Liis broke surface, she gasped as if she'd been holding her breath. Water sluiced off her visor.

In front of her a narrow, rocky shore abutted thick, variegated growth. Although she recognized the flora as trees and bushes, nothing was familiar. The colours weren't quite right, the shades subtly different from the ones with which she was familiar. A few paces back, near a stand of low, gnarled trees with brown, spiky fronds, Liis caught sight of Hebuiza. He sat, his back propped against the thick bole of one of the trees. He was naked, his gear beside him. His large head hung forward, its numerous filaments and cables dangling like long hair over his face, his arms hanging limply at his side. A thin line of blood trickled from a gash in his right temple.

Yilda was nowhere to be seen.

Liis crouched before the Facilitator.

His narrow chest rose and fell shallowly. The source of the bleeding was a small wound in front of his ear: a tear of a few centimetres at the base of a data socket. On the ground at Hebuiza's feet was the black box he wore everywhere, even inside his suit; snaking away from it was a grey cable terminating in a blood spattered jack.

Liis poked him in the arm and his head lolled insensibly. She rose, looked around. In the dirt leading up to the tree were two heel-wide grooves from Hebuiza's boots, the imprint of smaller boots in between. He'd been dragged here, probably by Yilda.

But the shore was deserted.

Liis's glanced at his suit, then back to his narrow ribcage, rising and falling rhythmically. At least Yilda had been correct about the dome harbouring a breathable atmosphere.

She ordered the seals on her own suit broken.

Air hissed in, a rich, confusing welter of scents momentarily muddling her senses. The perfume of unfamiliar flowers and decaying vegetation overwhelmed the smell of her own stale sweat and recycled waste. The strange—and yet familiar—smells made her head spin.

Seventeen days in this . . . this coffin, she thought. She peeled the helmet back from her head, felt a light breeze finger her hair. Carefully, she disconnected the catheters and undid the middle seam of the suit; within seconds she had wiggled free from the multiple, insulating layers of material. She stood naked; her suit lay at her feet like a shed skin.

She examined herself. Other than roughened blisters on her heels and soles of her feet, and a general grime that seemed to film her entire body, she could find no deleterious effects from the suit. Her broken arm, however, looked pale and withered where skin emerged from the yellowed plasticast. She flexed her fingers experimentally. Sharp flashes shot up her forearm. But they were not as intense as she had feared. When she flexed again, she winced, but found the pain bearable. Her body was healing itself.

She pulled the backpack from her suit. Then she grabbed the collar and dragged her suit down to the shore, stepping gingerly over the loose rocks and pebbles. Wading knee-deep into the water, she flung it with her good arm as far as she could. The suit landed on the surface several metres out with a flat, slapping sound; it drifted there for a moment, before it turned once like a lazy swimmer flipping onto his back, then sank quickly from sight.

She splashed water over her face, breasts, and stomach, and carefully bathed her wounded arm. Squatting, she scooped up a handful of sand and gravel and rubbed her legs until they tingled. The grime relented, slid from her body. The sensation was wonderful. It seemed an eternity since she'd experienced anything other than the uniform clamminess of the suit. She sat down in waist-deep water—it was cool but not unpleasant. Despite the strangeness of her surroundings, Liis relaxed, felt the inescapable creep of exhaustion; her head began to nod. *Not yet*, she thought dully.

Reluctantly, she dragged herself to her feet. It was all she had time for now.

She picked her way back across the rocky shore. Hebuiza's head was still bent. Liis reached down to pick up his suit.

"No." Hebuiza's eyes were open, but rheumy. He blinked several times, as if he were trying to keep them focused. "Leave it." A bubble of spittle formed between his withered lips, popped.

Liis straightened. "We've got to hide these suits. And you're in no shape to do it."

Her words seemed to rouse the Facilitator. His head lifted, the tendons in his neck going rigid. He fixed Liis with a withering look; his head began its characteristic bobbing motion. "No!" Placing his palms on the ground, he tried to push himself to his feet, but his arms shook and collapsed under him. He slid back down against the bole of the tree. He glared at Liis, as if he blamed his incapacitation on her. She met his gaze calmly. After a moment, he averted his eyes.

"What happened?"

Hebuiza tried to shrug, but the effort must have aggravated his wound for his face twisted into a grimace of pain. "Nothing," he hissed from between clenched teeth.

"Nothing?"

"I fell." He looked almost embarrassed. "My head must have hit the lake first. I don't remember." He blinked and looked around. "I remember being underwater. Then here." Hebuiza's gaze wandered; he seemed to forget their conversation. "We're inside, aren't we?"

Liis ignored his question. *Yilda dragged him out, stripped off his suit, then left him.* But where had the other Facilitator gone? Hebuiza, even if he knew, wouldn't tell her. Or at least not tell the entire truth. Liis decided she'd had enough of these games. They were inside the dome. It was time for some answers.

Taking a step closer, she locked eyes with Hebuiza. "*Who is Yilda?*"

The Facilitator looked up at her in surprise, his head weaving back and forth. For an instant, his guard seemed to drop. The large Adam's apple in his neck bobbed. "I . . . I don't understand your question." It was the first time she could ever remember him seeming unsure about anything.

"You know damn well what I mean." Liis stepped closer so she towered above him. "He knew exactly how to get into the dome.

Remember, he was the one who insisted on bringing the flares, then in keeping them when we lightened our loads. He told us to discard everything, except for exactly the things we needed. And why else did he use the ice screw and rope unless he knew about the drop on this side? No matter how good his intelligence was, he couldn't have had those kinds of details."

Hebuiza looked away; his head stilled. "He's a Facilitator," he said, as if that explained everything.

Liis was incredulous. "You don't know," she said. "Do you?"

"He's a—"

"Facilitator," Liis finished in exasperation. She waved off his words. "Yeah, I heard." Apparently Yilda had felt it prudent to keep everyone in the dark about his plans. Including Hebuiza. She stooped, grabbed the collar of his suit.

Hebuiza's eyes flashed again. But this time he kept his mouth clamped shut.

Fuck you, Liis thought, but her anger had no edge: exhaustion had dulled her thoughts. She dragged the suit over to the lake. With a grunt, she heaved it out as far as she could. When she turned back, she saw Hebuiza had managed to roll himself over on his knees and was crawling on all fours toward his backpack. Liis shook her head. Was he afraid she was going to go through his things? She took a step toward him. Then stopped dead.

A few metres down the shore a figure had emerged from the underbrush. It was a young woman with startlingly white skin. She wore a simple, translucent robe belted at the waist with a black, knotted cord and plain brown sandals. She had a slim build, limp, shoulder-length blonde hair framing smooth, rounded features. Liis found something vaguely familiar about her, in the lines of her pale face and the set of her expression. Like she had met her somewhere before.

The woman watched Hebuiza with bewilderment. The Facilitator, who had stopped crawling, stared at the woman, mouth agape. His eyes darted from her to his pack. If she had noticed Liis yet, she showed no sign.

A pathetic gurgling emerged from Hebuiza's throat.

The woman's initial surprise seemed to have vanished. She extended her arms, hands open—the universal gesture of peace. She spoke and strange guttural words emerged from her mouth.

But before she'd spoken more than a few words, there was a faint *pop*, and the woman's head snapped back, like she'd been struck by an invisible fist. She teetered drunkenly for a second; her legs collapsed and she crumpled to the ground.

Liis scrambled over the loose rocks on the beach. The woman was on her back.

Her face had gone ashen. Her mouth gaped. Although her eyes were still open, she stared straight ahead, unseeing. Drool flowed from the corner of her mouth and crept down her cheek.

My God, Liis thought looking at the soft features, unmarked by age or experience. *She's only a child*.

A shadow fell over the body.

Yilda stood next to Liis. He wore loose-fitting shorts, a faded black tee-shirt that stretched across his pot belly, and had his backpack on. In his hands he cradled a rifle Liis had never seen before. It was matte black, except for the very end of its barrel where a tiny red light pulsed like an ember. Crouching, he jabbed the Speaker in the ribs with the muzzle. She didn't react.

"Good," Yilda said, rising and slipping the strap of the rifle over his shoulder. "It still works."

The Speaker was alive; that much was obvious. But her face was slack, her mouth gaping stupidly, her eyes vacant. From time to time a muscle in her body would convulse. The heel of her left sandal had already pushed aside the loose pebbles and dug small grooves in the sandy soil. Her other leg remained still.

"Unfortunate," Yilda said with a sigh. He dropped to his knees, placed his rifle on the ground, and dug a medical kit out of Hebuiza's backpack. "Must have been taking a hike, heard or saw the commotion, hey? She'd have no reason to fear anything in the dome."

Liis stared at him; he returned her gaze unperturbed. "You'd best get dressed," he said casually. He turned his attention back to the kit, pulling out a threaded surgical needle. Hebuiza, who sat in front of him, stared at it tight-lipped.

"What about . . . her?" Liis asked.

"She is incapacitated." Yilda steadied Hebuiza's head with one hand; his other made three quick stitches below Hebuiza's right ear. He had neglected to apply anaesthetic; Hebuiza winced with each dip.

"Incapacitated?"

"Yes." Yilda tied off the surgical thread and cut the end with a pair of folding scissors. "Used a low setting on my pulse rifle to disrupt electroencephalic activity." He applied a small adhesive bandage over Hebuiza's fresh stitches. "In essence, I shut down her voluntary nervous system."

Liis stared at the Speaker. The girl's bowels had emptied. A rising stench drifted around them. "How long until she recovers?"

"Recovers?" Finished with his ministrations, Yilda repacked the medical kit; he stuffed it into a pocket on Hebuiza's backpack. "The damage is irreversible."

"But she'll die out here!"

"Yes." Yilda craned his head to regard her. "It was necessary," he said evenly, scooping up his weapon and rising to his feet. "She's a Speaker. She posed a threat."

Liis shook her head in disbelief. Until this moment, Liis hadn't understood the implications of their mission fully. But now its consequences lay at her feet. In a few days, the Speaker would dehydrate. Eventually she would die of starvation.

And this killing was only the start. If Nexus didn't give them what they wanted, they would have to kill again and again—until they had won or all the Speakers were dead. Liis reminded herself of the millions who had perished on Bh'Haret. But it was difficult to balance those faceless deaths against that of the girl lying there.

"Don't let her fool you." Yilda watched Liis carefully, as if he'd known what she had been thinking. "They would kill us if they knew we were here. If I hadn't disabled her, she would have alerted the others."

Liis looked the girl's slight figure up and down. This close, her robe was transparent. She wore nothing underneath. Her ribcage was pronounced, her hips narrow and breasts small. The tuft of pubic hair was barely there. "How would she have warned them? She's not carrying anything."

"She's a *Speaker*." Yilda tapped his temple with a finger. "It's hardwired up here."

"Then how do you know she didn't warn them already?"

"She *didn't*," he said. "That's all you need to know. Now put on your clothes." He supported Hebuiza, who wobbled unsteadily while he struggled into his shorts.

Liis glared at Yilda's back. But he was oblivious, preoccupied with helping Hebuiza. She cursed them both silently.

Returning to her pack, she pulled out a pair of loose-fitting shorts, a white tee-shirt, and a pair of hiking boots. Sitting on the ground, she struggled into the clothing, fumbling with her one good hand. Then she stuck her feet in her boots, pulled the straps as tight as she could and velcroed them shut. They still felt too loose on her feet.

She stood up and reached into the pocket of her shorts, withdrawing the watch Hebuiza had made for them. On its face the green numerals read 5-01:12. Slightly more than five days left. She shoved it back in her pocket.

Yilda hovered beside her, clearly impatient to get moving; to the side, Hebuiza had finished assembling his bolt rifle, and was now loading it with darts.

"Ready?"

"*No!*" At first Liis was shocked by the vehemence of her own response. Having let it out, however, her resolve hardened. None of this made sense. She wasn't going to move until she got some reasonable answers. "No, I'm not ready," she said. She imagined how her face must appear to him: wild white scars thrown into relief by narrow patches of flushed skin. "I won't take another step until you explain. If Nexus is so advanced, why did the girl stumble on us like that? She was as surprised to see us as we were to see her. In fact, why aren't the rest of them here now, to help her? Where the hell are they?" She furrowed her brow, nodded at the twitching girl. "And why this? Why *incapacitate* her, as you called it? She's as good as dead. Why not kill her and have done with it?"

Yilda met Liis's gaze without surprise or fear. If his face betrayed anything at all, it might have been mild curiosity—with the slightest touch of amusement.

He's trying to provoke me, Liis thought. *He wants to see how far I'm willing to take this.*

Yilda shrugged, the smirk disappearing. "Fine. I had planned on apprising you soon anyway." He parted his lips and ran his tongue over his carved teeth. "One fact is crucial in understanding the dynamics, yes, of the situation: the Speakers are trapped here every bit as much as we are. They are, in fact, prisoners."

Prisoners? Liis glanced at Hebuiza, whose eyebrows had lifted in an unconscious expression of surprise. Hadn't Yilda confided in him either? She felt a knot of fear tighten in her stomach. Had he lied to them about everything? "This *is* a relay station, isn't it?"

"Yes. That's the reason the Speakers *are* prisoners. They are an extremely valuable asset to Nexus. So they're treated very well. But they are isolated here, light years from the circle of Pro-Locutors who make the real decisions—and from the reach of authority. Out here, this far from the Hub, it would be easy to foment dissidence. The Speakers in the dome are not given any tools that might tempt them to redefine the, ah, factional paradigms of Nexus."

"It still doesn't make any sense," Liis said. "Why would they agree to this?"

"They know nothing else. They are cloned here by simple caretaker intelligences. Only they aren't furnished with immortality enhancements. Although they live longer than we do, they age, unlike their counterparts on individual worlds—or at the Hub. That way they're less likely to be obstreperous. Yes. Which also means they're vulnerable." Yilda hefted his rifle. "In all likelihood, ours are the only weapons on this world. The Pro-Locutors wouldn't provide something with which these things could harm themselves."

Liis inclined her head toward the girl, whose right arm jerked suddenly and flopped. A mewling, like that of a baby, emerged from her mouth. "If what you say is true, she could have done nothing to harm us."

"So why did I eliminate her?" Yilda asked the question for her. "Surprise is essential." He swept out a hand to encompass the dome, the forest, the lake, everything. "This whole biosphere is run by rudimentary intelligences. Function as autonomic systems. Yes. Maintain this benign environment, and provide basic services to the Speakers, but none have sophisticated reasoning processes. Nothing that might be turned against the masters at the Hub. Certainly nothing sophisticated enough to understand what we are—or the threat we pose. A detailed record of each Speaker's bio-signature and brain wave pattern is maintained. So the dome recognizes them. But to these intelligences we are simply unimportant electrical impulses, no more significant than the animals that populate this forest. We are, in effect, invisible. That is how we managed to get inside. And that is why I didn't kill her outright. The cessation of her encephalographic activity would have triggered an alarm, one that would have alerted the other Speakers and brought them here."

"And scrambling her mind won't?"

"No. Short of brain death, the intelligences ignore the Speakers."

"That still doesn't explain how these people can possibly defend themselves."

"It is really quite simple." Yilda sighed, as if the point was self-evident. "Once the Speakers are aware of our presence, they will inform the Hub. If the Pro-Locutors consider us enough of a threat, they will provide the Speakers here with instructions to create weapons from the materials at hand. Weapons far more powerful than any we have. There are seventeen more active Speakers here. It is essential we account for as many of the Speakers as possible before they become aware of our presence."

Account for them? You mean wipe out their minds like you wiped out the mind of this girl, Liis thought. But she said nothing.

"Here." Yilda snatched her backpack from the ground and shoved it at her until she was forced to clutch it with her good arm. "We must find the other Speakers as soon as we can."

Liis stood immobile, weighing what Yilda had just said. His explanations were plausible. But she knew he'd lie readily, as Hebuiza would, if he felt it was to his advantage. On the other hand, what did he have to gain by lying to her now? But there was still the question of how he had such intimate knowledge of the dome and its inhabitants. Liis's head ached, as much from fatigue as from trying to make sense of what she was sure were truths mixed with half-truths.

"We must be going," Yilda said. He pulled her toward the place where the girl had broken through the underbrush. "I've eliminated a Speaker. Sooner or later she will be missed. They have shifts when they are required to relay communications between worlds. Three groups of six—if my intelligence is correct. When she does not show up for hers, they will begin searching."

Despite her misgivings, Liis allowed herself to be dragged forward. She turned to take one last look at the Speaker. The girl's eyes had rolled back in her head and her whole body shuddered. Liis wanted to hate her more than she hated Hebuiza and Yilda. Yet all she felt as the trees closed in around her was an inexplicable sympathy, as if this girl were her true ally—and the Facilitators her enemies.

Fifty metres into the forest they struck a path that tunnelled through the thick foliage. Smooth, white rocks lined either side, making it look more like a garden path than a hiking trail.

Without hesitation, Yilda struck off to his right, his strange rifle at the ready. In the reduced gravity, and without the dragging weight of his sled, he took long, loping strides that quickly ate up the distance. Hebuiza stumbled after him, half-hopping, half-running in his exhaustion, his hands wrapped loosely around the short stock of his bolt gun, his head wagging half-heartedly from side to side. Liis had seen him practise with the weapon outside the stasis facility. It used rounds of capacitance darts that not only tore through the bark of his target trees, but also left wide burn marks when they had discharged on impact. In his current state, she was glad she was not ahead of him, the snout of his weapon weaving up and down behind her.

The path twisted and turned, snaking around slight rises and squat, thick-boled trees. Overhead, the canopy was uninterrupted, limbs locking over them like the roof of a vault, allowing only a muted, bottle-green light to filter through. Yilda moved at a double-time pace; Hebuiza staggered after in his awkward gait, trying to keep up, but was already flagging. Liis could understand—she was exhausted herself. Her arm throbbed mercilessly now. She wondered where the small man got his reserves of energy.

Minutes passed, and Yilda disappeared around the bend ahead of them; soon, Liis only caught glimpses of him at a distance, through gaps in the forest. Finally, he was lost to sight altogether. Hebuiza's stride faltered; he stopped, swaying in the middle of the path.

He's finished, Liis thought as she stepped up to him. She felt no pity. Gruffly, she said, "You're blocking the—"

Hebuiza hissed at her, made a slicing motion in the air with his hand to cut her off. He swung his bolt gun around and aimed it at a clump of dense bush. The leaves rustled.

Liis stepped past Hebuiza to get a better look.

Something black exploded from the bush, shot past her and toward Hebuiza; a high-pitched screech pierced the gloom, tore like sandpaper along her nerves. The Facilitator dropped his gun and released his own shriek, reeling backwards, arms flailing wildly to protect his face. The bird—for now Liis could see its expansive, shiny wings beating—banked sharply, narrowly missing him, and streaked off into the forest, making a strange, hollow whistling as it vanished into the gloom.

The Facilitator was on his knees, eyes down, his empty hands trembling uncontrollably. His shoulders heaved and he wheezed as if he were hyperventilating.

Liis heard the thump of footsteps. Yilda ran back around a sharp bend in the trail and pulled up abruptly, his eyes darting between them and the surrounding forest, his weapon swinging around in low, covering arcs.

"A bird," Liis said, her heart still thumping double-time. "A fucking bird." She looked with disgust at Hebuiza.

Yilda swore. He lowered his weapon, and, holding it in one hand, used his other to retrieve Hebuiza's gun from where it had fallen. He shoved the weapon roughly to the other man's chest, and held it there until Hebuiza numbly wrapped his arms around it like a child would clutch a stuffed toy.

"Get up," Yilda said.

Hebuiza rose unsteadily, his eyes averted. He was still shaking.

"We need to stop," Liis said, not out of compassion for the Facilitator, but because she, too, was exhausted.

"We don't have time," Yilda said coldly. "At most we only have a few hours before they'll know we are here." He placed his rifle on the ground and shrugged off his backpack. From one of its side pockets, he pulled out a small, cylindrical container. He popped off the lid with his thumb and spilled several blue capsules into his palm. "Here." He held out his hand. "Stimulants." When no one moved, Yilda shoved his hand right under Hebuiza's nose. "Take it!"

Hebuiza lifted a shaking hand, managed to close his fingers on a capsule. His head swung in long arc from side to side. He placed the pill on his tongue, drew it into his mouth and swallowed.

"You too," Yilda said, swinging his hand toward her.

Liis watched Hebuiza. Already his trembling had subsided. He blinked, looking around as if he had just woken, his shoulders straighter than they had been for days. He swung his weapon into the ready position, his eyes glittering, head for once perfectly still. She wondered what kind of drug could work such dramatic changes in so short a time. Certainly nothing Bh'Haret had to offer. Hebuiza was rocking now with suppressed energy, his feet shifting restlessly. "I'm ready," he said with urgency. "Let's go!"

"Well?" Yilda said.

Reluctantly, Liis lifted a pill from Yilda's palm, placed the capsule on her tongue. The muscles in her throat tightened. She swallowed, but her throat was dry: the capsule stuck and wouldn't go down.

"Good." Yilda snatched up his rifle and trotted off down the path, Hebuiza following eagerly.

Liis waited until they had passed around the bend, then spat out the blue capsule. It glistened on the side of the path. She set out after the Facilitators, forcing her aching legs to move as if they were filled with the same kind of revitalizing energy that possessed Hebuiza's.

They dropped down into a ravine, crossed a simple wood plank bridge over a stream and followed a switchback up the opposite side. Here the path branched, the right fork curving back toward the wall of the dome, the left fork leading toward the heart of the dome.

Yilda took the left.

Almost immediately, the foliage thinned and the path seemed to straighten. The forest dwindled; spotty patches of luminescence overhead became an unobstructed view of the milky-white underside of the dome. Light seemed to emanate from its entire surface, creating an unreal, shadowless world.

Through the trees, a distant line of large white cylindrical structures was visible. They reminded Liis of fuel storage tanks—except they were more massive than anything she'd seen girding the airfields and spaceports of Bh'Haret. Each had to be close to four hundred metres in diameter and perhaps two hundred in height. They stood shoulder to shoulder, with no visible breaks between. Behind the cylinders was a dark background Liis had simply taken to be a discoloured part of the dome; but as the view cleared, she realized it was the steeply-pitched slope of a mountain. It thrust up in the exact centre of the dome, the unbroken line of cylinders ringing it like a fence. Liis craned her neck to follow the slope to the point at which its peak pierced the roof nearly two kilometres overhead.

Passing into an area of rolling fields of tall grasses, they descended into a broad, shallow valley. The cylinders were lost to sight. The stones lining the sides of the path had disappeared, replaced by plants and long-stalked flowers. They crested a rise.

A few hundred metres away were the cylinders. Clinging to their lower portions were plain, squat buildings, composed of grey and brown material. Now Liis could see the buildings clustered about the base of the cylinders in an unbroken circuit that extended fifty to a hundred metres into the surrounding fields. The path they were on led straight to the largest building visible: at four storeys it towered over the adjacent structures. On the side of the dome were two linked gold circles—the only ornamentation evident on any of the buildings.

Yilda picked up the pace and shortly they stepped from the dirt path onto a broad paved surface. In moments they stood at the juncture of that avenue with another one that skirted the buildings, disappearing in either direction around the gradual curve of cylinders. Yilda crossed this last stretch to stand in front of a portico with simple framing members and a plain lintel. Across the opening a translucent material had been drawn. Stepping closer, he poked the material with the tip of his rifle. It flexed, but did not part. He poked it harder, but the material gave less this time, as if the increased force had caused it to become more rigid.

Dropping to his knees, Yilda laid his rifle on the ground and swung his pack off his shoulders. He opened a side pocket and withdrew a clear, flat box. It held dozens of small silver discs, each a few centimetres in diameter. Flipping open the case, he picked one out. Placing it on the ground at the base of the opening, he pressed its top with his thumb. At the centre of the disc a tiny red light went on, then began to pulse, like a beating heart, growing brighter with each beat.

Yilda grabbed his pack with one hand, scooped up his rifle with the other. "Ten seconds to clear," he said. "I suggest you follow me." With that, he turned and jogged back into the field. Hebuiza followed quickly and Liis, glancing at the strobing dot, decided she'd best follow their example.

A dozen metres away from the door, Yilda dropped into a shallow ditch and lay flat. Hebuiza followed suit and, after a moment's hesitation, Liis did too, grunting as she inadvertently jostled her arm.

The roar of the explosion slammed into her. The ground shuddered and shrapnel whistled past. Something ricocheted off her backpack. A cloud of dust roiled around them, choking off the light. For a few seconds, debris rained down. She buried her head under her good arm and prayed nothing sizeable would fall on her.

Someone tugged on her pack.

Liis raised her head; dirt trickled from her back. "Come on," Yilda said. "We don't have that much time before the building starts to repair itself."

She struggled to her feet. Through the swirl of dust she could see a ragged hole had been torn in the wall, its outline shadowed by scorch marks. Yilda had already stepped through the opening, with Hebuiza on his heels. Spitting out the grit that had collected in her mouth, Liis pushed through the tall grasses, and crossed to the wrecked portal.

Inside was a murky, rubble-strewn room.

Liis stood on a smooth floor. Dust and smoke still made a hash of the details. She took a few tentative steps forward and almost bumped into Hebuiza. "Where the hell are the lights?" she asked.

"They won't activate for us." It was Yilda's voice, ahead of her. "Everything here is keyed on the Speakers' bio-signatures. Lights, doors, windows." An amber beam pierced the gloom, sliced past them causing Liis to blink. It settled on the opposite side of the room where a narrow stairwell, wide enough for only one person, descended into darkness.

"They're this way." Yilda's voice had taken on a breathless quality; it quivered with anticipation. "Quickly!" He moved to the head of the stairs and Liis saw that it was the barrel of his rifle projecting a wide beam like a flashlight. "When we find them, don't kill anyone unless you think they'll escape," he said, then turned and began taking the steps two at a time.

"Wait!" Liis called after him. When his light had first swept the room she'd seen several other doors—including wide double doors that looked like they'd been carved from pearl—and another stairway spiralling to her right. "How do you know they're this way?" But Yilda ignored her. His light bobbed from sight. Hebuiza jostled roughly past her, causing her to wince as he brushed her injured arm. With a snarl, he loped down the stairs after Yilda.

"Shit!" Liis shouted loudly to the empty room. "Shit!"

Then she plunged down the stairs after them.

They descended several hundred steps before the stairway ended at the entrance to a long, low-ceilinged corridor. Yilda, who'd been waiting impatiently at the foot of the steps, took off down the corridor the moment Liis's foot touched the floor. Hebuiza followed immediately in his wake, his head almost brushing the ceiling with each of his bounds. The smaller man loped straight ahead, ignoring the frequent branching corridors and arched doorways. Liis struggled to keep up.

Abruptly, Yilda swung left into another passageway, Hebuiza a step behind. Liis was cast into darkness. She faltered, moved cautiously, reaching her good arm out to feel along the wall until she found the junction where the Facilitators had turned.

This new corridor was also dark, the Facilitators already out of sight. Far away, she could hear the pounding of their feet. She stumbled ahead, caught her foot and shouted as she pitched forward. Her palm struck a surface sooner than it should have, skidded until she jammed her fingers painfully into something.

Stairs! she thought before she collapsed onto her side, phantom lights darting in her vision. Ignoring her arm, she pushed to her feet and began feeling her way gingerly along the wall, tapping the toes of her boots against the risers. Her foot pushed into air and she stumbled past the final step onto a landing.

In the distance was a vertical band of bright light. Liis moved toward it, quickening her pace; she sensed the walls falling away, and, by her echoing footsteps, guessed she had entered a sizeable chamber. Opposite her the light grew more distinct and she realized that what she was looking at was the crack of a curtained doorway. A steady hissing grew as she approached the light. Liis parted the drapes, blinking in the sudden onslaught of light and sound. Twenty metres away a waterfall dove through a high, sharp cleft of rock and crashed into a foaming pool. On all sides a steep rock face soared out of view. Slick black rock made up the floor and ran right up to the doorway in which she stood. Liis craned her neck to look up: the underbelly of the dome filled the ragged slice of sky overhead with its pale luminescence.

I'm at the foot of the mountain.

There was no one to be seen.

She re-examined the walls of rock carefully, noticed an opening to the right of the falls, half-hidden by turbulent clouds of mist: the mouth of a large tunnel, its smooth, machined walls trailing away in dark perspective toward the heart of the mountain.

Liis took a tentative step onto the slick-looking surface of damp black stone, fully expecting her foot to slide out from under her. But what she found was that her footing was amazingly firm despite the film of water. She took another step. It felt as if the soles of her shoes adhered to the surface. She moved forward with more confidence, passing through a sudden spray from the waterfall that rose and swirled around her, wetting her face and arms and aching head. She paused, revelling in its coolness for a moment, then jogged forward.

The tunnel was wide enough for ten people to walk abreast. It ran straight, inclining gently downward, and was lined with thick-napped red broadloom. The carpet displayed no signs of water damage; it didn't look wet, even where the mist continually settled on it. No other doors or side-passageways were evident. Although the tunnel was without illumination, a fixed round light, blinking erratically, was visible in the distance. Squinting, she realized the light wasn't in fact blinking; its source was being alternately blocked and revealed by the tiny figures of the Facilitators as they were interposed between her and the source of the light. Liis hurried after them, her steps noiseless on the carpet.

Minutes seemed to pass; her breath grew ragged. Ahead, the

Facilitators fell into the light and disappeared. She knew they had passed into another room. The light grew slowly, took on the shape of a doorway.

Muffled shouts echoed into the tunnel, followed by the distinct *whump* of Hebuiza's bolt gun.

Liis dashed forward. She ran into an empty room and skidded to a halt. It was brilliantly lit, the walls lined with a glowing material that resembled alabaster, fine veins of burgundy marbling its surface. The floor on one side of the chamber was lower by several centimetres and had small dark holes spaced evenly along its length; nozzles sprouted from the wall above. On the other side was a bench; in front of it was a row of hooks on which white robes had been neatly hung. Beneath each garment was a pair of sandals, identical to the ones worn by the Speaker Yilda had shot.

A shower room, she thought. At the far end of the chamber was another doorway hung with curtains like those she'd passed through before. A long protracted groan came from that direction. Liis loped up to the door and jerked the heavy material aside.

A naked figure lay face down at her feet.

A fat man, his paunch spread around his sides like a deflated balloon, beat his bald head rhythmically on the floor. His buttocks jiggled with each convulsion. Overcoming her repulsion, Liis stepped around him and into the room.

It was a hexagonal structure. Wide bands of pastel colours flowed on every vertical surface in hypnotic patterns, softly illuminating the chamber. The motion insinuated itself into Liis's consciousness, wrapping around her like a soothing web, easing her troubled mind. But the scene on the floor belied the peacefulness of the room: twenty metres away, Yilda stood under the cusp of the dome, at the hub of six white couches that fanned out like the spokes of a wheel, all angled so their occupants would face a different wall. A naked, spasming body lay on one of the couches; a second had slid partway off a couch that faced the opposite wall, only a jerking foot and one limp, pale arm was visible. Yilda, the stock of his rifle resting on his hip, its barrel pointing up, turned slowly, apparently surveying his work.

A sound like that of a whimpering child caught Liis's attention. She swung around, saw Hebuiza to her right, near the wall of the chamber. At his feet were three more naked people—only these Speakers had not been incapacitated. They sat on the floor, huddled together, heads bowed, backed up as far as they could against the wall. The one in the middle, a man with a sparse thatch of yellow hair, was clutching at his thigh; blood seeped from between his fingers. He sobbed. Hebuiza swayed above him, the muzzle of his bolt gun centimetres from the man's skull.

"I told you not to damage them," Yilda said.

Hebuiza looked up; his eyes seemed huge in his cadaverous face. "He would have escaped," he said petulantly. "You told me not to let a single one escape."

"Now he'll probably be useless." Yilda sighed. "Show me his face."

Poking the barrel of his weapon under the man's chin, Hebuiza levered the Speaker's head up. The man's eyes were glazed, unfocused, his features contorted with pain. But Liis recognized him instantly. He had Yilda's face.

Liis turned to look at Yilda. With one hand, the small Facilitator hefted his rifle. This time Liis was close enough to hear the faint pop of the weapon discharging; the man with Yilda's face flopped backwards like he'd been hit in the head with a board, then went slack in the arms of the other two Speakers.

"Sweet dreams," Yilda said to his twin.

VIRACOSA · 6 DAYS LEFT

"*You are expected.*"

The words stunned Sav. But the phrase had transformed Josua: he'd gone rigid, the tendons in his neck standing out, the blood draining from his face. He stared at the tiny, phosphorescent words on the comm screen—LINK ESTABLISHED.

"*Viracosa.*" It was the woman's voice again. Her intonation was clear if slightly laboured, as if she were unused to mouthing the phonemes of the language. "*You are approaching Nexus space. Interdiction laws prohibit non-affiliate ships, and weapon-bearing ships, from entering this space. On your current course you will be in violation of both interdictions, and fourteen minor points of conduct, in . . .*" A pause. "*. . . twenty-one point three hours, measured in Bh'Haret standard time. Acknowledge.*"

Sav had set communications circuits to "receive only" mode. With the incoming message a rocker switch on the panel had changed from steady red to a blinking red to indicate that a link for incoming messages had been established. Such switches were standard on all longhaul ships: they were spring-loaded, so that only when pressed and held in place would they turn green to indicate the transmit portion of the circuit was active. Sav lifted a headset from its rest on the side of the comm board, put it on. Then he reached for the switch. But Josua shoved his hand away.

Sav swung his chair around to face him. "What's the matter with you?"

"No!" Josua's face had twisted up. "It's my decision." He curled his hands into fists. The knuckles on his right hand were scraped and bloody, and Sav thought of the smashed panel next to his cell.

"*Request acknowledgement, Viracosa.*"

"We've got to talk to them." Sav tried to keep his voice calm, even. "That's why we're here. We've come to negotiate for the cure. Remember?"

"Negotiate," Josua repeated. Confusion seemed to mingle with his anger, to dilute it. Then his rage dissipated—or, perhaps more accurately, Josua seemed to quash it, swallowing it like a sour pill. "Yes," he said gruffly, unclenching his fists and flexing his fingers. "Of course." Walking unsteadily to the pilot's station, he slumped into the seat. He gripped the armrests on the chair. "Proceed," he said.

Sav pushed down on the switch; it changed from flashing red to green. "This is *Viracosa*," he said.

"*Viracosa, this is Novitiate Lien and Surveillance Platform Aogista 12-42-1031. We have been expecting you.*"

I know, Sav thought irritably. *You already told us.*

"*You are requested to alter your course. Or you will be in contravention of the two major interdictions stated earlier and the following minor ones: entering Nexus space with an unregistered craft; failure to comply with directives issued by a representative of the Pro-Locutor's council; use of an undamped, Level Zero fusion engine in Nexus space . . .*" The voice rattled on through a list of transgressions.

Sav's mind raced. The woman—what had she called herself, Lien?—had said they were expected. Did she mean that she had been tracking them for a long time—or had Liis and the others succeeded in their mission?

"*Viracosa, do you acknowledge?*" The list had, apparently, come to its conclusion.

Until they knew more, it was best to remain non-committal. "We are unable to comply," Sav said.

Silence, except for the soft crackle of background static. Then, "*Please clarify.*"

Josua drew his finger across his throat in the sign to cut communications. Sav said, "One moment," and lifted his thumb. The switch blinked red again.

"We can outrun them," Josua said. "Look." While Sav had his

brief exchange with the woman, Josua had been tapping at the keyboard on the pilot's panel. The screen embedded in the board was filled with several columns of figures. "I've run the data. We've still got enough velocity so that if we cut our deceleration burn now, it's unlikely she could catch us before we reached the Hub. Assuming, of course, she can't squeeze any more gees of acceleration out of her ship."

Sav was confounded. "I don't understand," he said quietly. "Why would we want to outrun them?"

Josua seemed annoyed as Sav's question. "We don't have time to deal with this ship. We need to reach the Hub. To pick up the antidote."

He may be right, Sav thought. There was no telling if a ship set to patrol the perimeter of Nexus space would have the capability of synthesizing a cure. Sav looked at Josua; the other man had crossed his arms and rocked back in his seat. *But it's still only an excuse. That ship out there might be able to synthesize a cure. And Josua doesn't seem to care. He has another reason for wanting to reach the Hub. Something he doesn't want to tell me.*

"Well?"

Sav pressed the transmit key; it changed to green. "Novitiate Lien. Our course has been set for the Hub," Sav began. "We have no fuel reserves." That wasn't true, but then there was no way this woman could know—unless the drones out there had some way of scanning *Viracosa*'s holds. "We are obliged to continue on our course."

"*We will consult Hub authority.*"

On the comm screen the message STAND BY appeared; the transmit switch went red under Sav's thumb as Lien broke the circuit from her end. The Nexus ship was still more than a light hour out from the Hub, so a transmission would take at least one hour there and one hour back—not including the time required to pass the information up the hierarchy where a decision would be made. In all probability, it would be several hours before Lien received her instructions. Sav leaned back in his seat, prepared for a long wait.

But the flashing connect light came back online almost immediately. Sav opened a two-way circuit. "*Your request is denied,*" the woman said.

Josua gripped the arms of his seat. "A Speaker," he hissed. "They must have a Speaker aboard!"

And someone in authority waiting to deal with us, Sav realized. *They had a response prepared.* That seemed to confirm it: Nexus knew about Yilda's party. But had Yilda achieved his objectives?

"*You are not permitted to enter the exclusion zone.*"

"We have no secondary destination," Sav replied, trying to buy more time to think through the situation. "We'll run out of fuel."

"*You are not permitted to enter the exclusion zone.*"

That was it. They had reached an impasse. The only thing left to do was to begin the process they had planned so long ago. Sav began rhyming off the first set of codes he had memorized before leaving Bh'Haret: "One, one, two, four, seven, one, three, two, four." Sweat gathered between the nape of his neck and the collar of his tee-shirt. In a voice that sounded strained and too loud to him, he added, "Any further attempt to interfere will result in the death of a Speaker. Do you copy?"

No response.

Sav waited a few seconds and repeated the sequence. "Do you copy?"

"*Acknowledged. Counter sequence is Beta, Epsilon, Epsilon, Alpha, Rho.*"

Sav couldn't believe his ears. It was the correct response. Yilda's party had made it!

"*Request the transmission of the second key, Viracosa.*"

The codes and responses were the linchpin of their scheme: a prearranged, and seemingly random, sequence of numbers and words. They knew they couldn't trust the veracity of any message the Speakers might pass. Instead, they had devised a series of codes to pass basic information back and forth. Sav and Josua had each been given a dozen to memorize. As a precaution, neither man knew the other's codes, although both knew what Yilda's responses meant. Josua and Sav would alternate passing a key to the Speakers at the Hub who would transmit it to the Speakers at the relay station. Yilda would then immediately return his counter-sequence along the same channel. The one salient difference was that Yilda's codes also had time values attached to them indicating when the next sequence should be forthcoming from *Viracosa*. An inordinate delay—or incorrect sequence—and he would execute a Speaker.

"*Viracosa, we are waiting for the next key.*"

The message Yilda had sent required a confirmation code in three minutes. Sav glanced over at Josua. "Well?"

But Josua seemed lost in thought, staring intently at his board.

"The key." Sav tried to keep the urgency he felt from his voice. "You need to send the next key."

"Yeah," Josua answered, snapping out of his reverie. Picking up his headset from its cradle, he bent the mike in front of his mouth and stabbed the button to patch his line in to the communication channel. He cleared his throat and spoke slowly: "Josua, Sav, Ruen." It was the sequence that let Yilda know that they were about to begin negotiations.

"*Hebuiza, Liis,*" came the response.

Sav shook his head in incredulity. Yilda's scheme seemed to be working. And he'd given them an hour before he expected a response. But where to begin? Perhaps it would be best to find out exactly what they knew.

"Novitiate Lien," Sav transmitted, "do you understand the situation?"

"*We have been apprised of the circumstances at—*" The woman pronounced a word with twisting, guttural syllables Sav didn't understand, but he took it to mean the relay station. "*We have surmised the rest. In contravention of the provisions of the Ascension Program, you wish us to provide an antidote for your plague.*"

"Yes. For *our* plague." The words were galling to say, but Yilda had warned him Nexus would never admit responsibility. They couldn't. An admission they were agents of genocide would unravel millennia of a carefully cultivated image. On worlds throughout the

Polyarchy—and those about to join the Polyarchy—the political repercussions, the uncertainty and consequent unrest, would be devastating.

"*We request transmission of your demands.*"

Sav brought up a list on his screen that Hebuiza had prepared back on Bh'Haret. He read from it: "First, we require the antidote. Second, refuelling for *Viracosa*. Third, safe passage back to Bh'Haret. Fourth, a guarantee that no member of this crew, or the one on the relay station, will be harmed directly or indirectly, by any action Nexus or its agents takes, now or in the future. Fifth, that no punitive action will be taken, directly or indirectly, against Bh'Haret or any of its inhabitants, including those currently in stasis, living off-world or crewing other longhaul ships, by Nexus or its agents, now or in the future. Sixth, Nexus shall assist in every way possible the recovery of Bh'Haret as a viable habitat and with the repopulation of our world by natives still off-world or in stasis. Seventh, that Nexus shall release the entire catalogue of Level IV technology to us and all other non-affiliated worlds . . ." The list went on for several more demands, the final one being that this list, along with a declaration of responsibility, was to be broadcast to every affiliated and non-affiliated world. But this requirement, like many of the other stipulations, was spurious. Part of Yilda's plan had been to put forth several unreasonable demands as a starting point for negotiations. This, he had told Sav and Josua, would allow Nexus to save face by whittling down their demands to the essential first five.

"*Anything else?*"

Was that a hint of sarcasm in the woman's voice? "No. That's it." Sav checked the clock on his screen. "You have sixty minutes to decide. If we do not have a response in this time period, a Speaker will be executed."

"*Copy, Viracosa. Your demands will be passed on to the Pro-Locutors.*" The button changed to a steady red as the channel went into stand-by mode again. Sav released the rocker switch. The outline of the key was impressed deeply on the flesh of his thumb. Sav collapsed back into his seat and blew out a breath.

"That went nicely," Josua said. Sitting rigidly in his seat at the pilot's station, he began drumming the fingers of his right hand on the panel in a steady rhythm.

"Yeah," Sav answered. "No problem."

They waited.

"Viracosa. We are ready to discuss your demands."

The response came back in fifty-three minutes. Seven minutes remained before the next sequence was to be transmitted. Sav, who'd been pacing the narrow aisle between the command panels and the webbing arrayed around the centre of the bridge, hustled as quickly as he could back to the comm station when the request connect signal had flashed. He pulled on the headset and opened the circuit. Josua, still in his seat at the pilot's station, looked on.

"Discuss?" Sav said, out of breath. Sweat beaded on his brow. "What does that mean?"

"In the short time you have given us, we have examined your demands. We agree to accede to several. Others, however, will require more deliberation."

"The next key must be returned to the relay station in—" Sav checked his watch, "—just over six minutes. So you better stop wasting your breath and tell me what you're willing to give us."

"Refuelling. Safe passage. These we can guarantee."

No mention of their first demand: the antidote. "You know those things are worthless without the cure."

"Yes," the woman answered. *"But what you've asked is impossible. How can we provide an antidote to a disease we have never seen?"*

"Then there's no point in continuing this discussion." Sav shot back. "The first Speaker dies in five minutes."

"I have been instructed to inform you that we will do everything in our power to synthesize an antidote. Although we do not anticipate any trouble in synthesizing a molecular nanoagent to disable or repair the deleterious effects of your plague, we will first require tissue and blood samples for analysis. Only upon completion of that analysis will we be

able to confirm a broad spectrum antidote."

Samples. Sav let go of the button and swore softly. Why hadn't this possibility occurred to them? Yilda had told them Nexus would never admit responsibility. Of course they would need specimens. How else could Nexus "cure" a plague they hadn't caused? Sav pressed the switch. "We'll require time to prepare the samples and make arrangements for the transfer." What those arrangements would be, Sav had no idea. But he'd work something out.

"We will begin analysis as soon as we are in receipt of the samples. To expedite the process, we request that you alter course to rendezvous with this platform."

"Yes," Sav said. "It would make up for a bit of the lost time. Please stand by while we plot—"

"This is the commander of *Viracosa*. I wish to talk to the Speaker aboard your vessel." Josua had jacked into the communication circuit.

"I am a Speaker," the woman answered curtly. She sounded annoyed, as if she felt she'd been insulted. *"There is no one else on the platform."*

Sav was surprised that the woman would casually reveal this information. Perhaps she was so confident of her ability to handle the situation that she didn't care what two desperate men from a backwater planet knew.

"We will *not* change our current heading," Josua said coolly, "until we receive the antidote." He signalled Sav to cut the connection.

Sav lifted his thumb. "What are you doing? We can save a couple of hours by changing course."

"A few hours won't make any difference," Josua answered. "And it's too early to begin making concessions."

"Viracosa! Your transmit channel has gone dead. Please respond."

"Concessions? How's that a concession?"

"Can't you hear it?" Josua asked, cocking an ear toward the overhead speaker. "She's upset. She's anxious to draw us away from Nexus space. It makes her masters nervous that we're driving toward the Hub." Josua shrugged. "Don't ask me why. I can't see what sort of threat that we would pose. But, for whatever reason, they feel we are a threat. And anything that makes them nervous increases their desire to negotiate. Now reconnect me."

"*Viracosa. This is Novitiate Lien. Request that you reopen your transmission circuit.*"

Sav pressed the transmit key.

"Novitiate Lien," Josua said calmly, "we're maintaining our current course. Our instruments indicate you've plotted an intercept course."

"*Yes.*"

"Then the transfer of the specimens will take place at the point of interception. We'll put the samples in the emergency docking tube on the nose of our ship. When we rendezvous, you may pick them up there. *You* must retrieve them personally. Your ship is to approach no closer than one thousand metres and *you* must traverse the intervening space alone, with no umbilicals and the minimum of EVA equipment. At no time is a remote, or any other machinery, to leave your ship or enter the tube. If you fail to accept these conditions, we will not transmit the next sequence. Do you understand?"

"*Understood. But given the circumstances, I am required to consult my superiors.*"

"Fine. You have," Josua checked the console, "three and a half minutes to make up your mind."

The STAND BY message appeared on the comm screen as the Speaker killed her transmit channel. Sav released his own switch. He spun his chair around. "*Dammit*, Josua! Why in God's name do we have to let a Speaker into our docking tube? We could have put the samples into a container and expelled them from the airlock."

"What container? We stripped every excess gram out of this ship before we set out. I know. I did most of the off-loading myself. We don't have any airtight sample bags, or a *sealable* bag, for that matter. Just a few torn food pouches. A couple of seconds of vacuum and the samples would be useless."

"What about the dropship?"

"Cleaned out too. Unless you mean you want to send the whole ship over as a giant container. But I don't think that would be a good idea since we'll be needing it to get back down to the surface of Bh'Haret." Josua crossed his arms. "This is the least risky alternative. We can isolate the tube, make a few changes to minimize the risk. It's not perfect, but it's the best we can do given the situation."

"It's nuts," Sav said angrily. "Once in the tube there's no telling what damage this woman might do. She could release nanoagents to take control of *Viracosa*—or us. Bringing this woman aboard will give her precisely the opportunity Nexus needs to sabotage our ship." When *Ea* had left Bh'Haret on its longhaul, nanotechnology had been in its infancy, no more than theory. But Nexus had been successfully engineering on the molecular level for over a millennium. Creating the sub-microscopic nanomachines needed to disable a ship—or a person—would be child's play for them. A single touch from the Speaker might release thousands of invisible molecular machines that would swarm along the tube to infect their ship.

Josua shrugged, unconcerned. "For all we know we're already infected. Do you think Nexus seeded space with those drones and left them toothless?"

Josua's words brought Sav up short. He'd almost forgotten their silent escort. If the drones had the capability, they could have infected *Viracosa* a thousand times over by now.

"We don't have any choice," Josua concluded. "Or, at least not enough time to manufacture another choice."

A Speaker in the docking tube. Sav didn't like it. But he could see no alternative. And Josua was right. Time was slipping away from them quickly. Glancing at the display, Sav saw that only two minutes remained before the next sequence needed to be sent. If Yilda was true to form, he would wait those two minutes, but not a second more. Sav watched the digits count down. When the time ticked past the one minute mark, the LINK ESTABLISHED message reappeared on the screen. Sav enabled the channel.

"We . . . we agree to your conditions." Novitiate Lien's voice had taken on a querulous tone.

For the first time Sav imagined this whole encounter from her point of view. She was being forced to leave the protection of her ship to retrieve the samples. And to place herself at the mercy of two desperate madmen. For the briefest of seconds as he pushed the transmit switch down, Sav almost felt sorry for her.

"Good," Josua replied as soon as the circuit was open. "You've plotted a course with intercept in . . ." he glanced at the pilot's screen, ". . . eighteen point oh eight three hours. Maintain that course and we'll extend our emergency tube prior to intercept. Do you copy?"

"Acknowledged, Viracosa. Please transmit the second key. . . ."

Josua rose, peeled off his headset and dropped it onto the pilot's seat. With a slashing sign across his throat, he indicated Sav should cut the circuit. When the light changed to flashing red, Josua said, "We have to be firm in the beginning. To demonstrate our commitment to this action. It's all part of the game." He trotted toward the ladder below decks. "Now you can transmit the key," he said to Sav over his shoulder. Pausing, he turned back, a strange expression on his face. "Don't worry. You'll see it's all for the best." He grabbed the top rung, swung himself onto the ladder, and climbed from sight.

Sav glanced at the display. There were still thirty seconds left before Yilda would carry out the execution. Pressing the rocker switch, Sav reopened the circuit. Then he spoke the next sequence, pronouncing each word clearly: "'Such is *anhaa-10*'s pleasure,'" he quoted the first part of Ruen's oft repeated mantra.

The response came back within seconds: "'*Pray Blasphemer, for the Dissolution is at hand.*'"

Access to the emergency docking tube was through an escape hatch above the flight deck. Beyond the hatch a narrow passage, crammed with pipes, conduits and the electronics of their communication and navigation systems, led from the inner hull to a dilation lock on the outer hull. On the other side of the lock was the emergency docking tube, a six-metre-long squat silver tube perched on the nose of the ship, the fore and aft sections containing the apparatus for simple air locks. The tube could be telescoped, via a rigid polycarbon-steel umbilical, to a distance of twenty metres.

While Sav continued to engage the woman in negotiations, Josua had gone below decks to prepare blood and tissue samples. Yilda's last message had given them twenty-one hours—the length of a standard day on Bh'Haret—before Josua would have to send the next sequence. Time enough, supposedly, to complete the initial negotiations.

In the midst of a protracted discussion on transferring the fuel, Josua returned from below decks, a sack slung over his shoulder by a single strap. A muffled clanking came from the bag as he hoisted himself up the ladder and undogged the hatch to the emergency tube with one hand while holding a rung with his other. He pulled down a short ladder from the opening and hauled himself up. Metal clanged on metal.

Sav ignored the noise. Instead, he tried to focus on the endless back and forth of his discussion with the Speaker. Nexus had agreed, in principle, to their first five demands, but waffled on several of the others, adamantly refusing to release Level IV technology to non-affiliates. However, they were willing to discuss their role in the revitalization of Bh'Haret. In the last few hours they had been negotiating the finer points of what form their participation might take. For Sav it was hard to concentrate: what point was there to any of this without a cure? And, according to Nexus, that hinged on the analysis of the samples. Doubt had crept into Sav's mind. Was it possible Nexus hadn't seeded Bh'Haret with the plague after all? That they didn't know if they could cure the plague? Or had these uncertainties been purposely planted in his mind by Nexus's steadfast refusal to accept responsibility for the plague? Whenever he tried to sort these things out, his head began to ache.

Novitiate Lien suggested a breather; Sav agreed with barely concealed relief. Massaging his temples, he sank back into his couch. The sounds of Josua's labour drifted down into the cabin. As tired as Sav was, sleep was unthinkable. He decided to keep an eye on the comm board. He brought up a display in the centre of the bridge that showed both craft, and two broken lines representing their courses. The lines intersected just outside the rose-tinted sphere marking the boundary of Nexus space. Staring at the display, Sav chewed absent-mindedly on his lower lip, wondering how Yilda could have overlooked the need to transfer samples to the Speakers. It was out of character. Facilitators spent their entire lives anticipating the moves and countermoves involved in negotiations. Not to have foreseen something so obvious seemed, well, incredible.

Above, the noise finally stopped.

What would Yilda have thought about a Speaker crawling around in their emergency docking tube? But Sav had no means of asking: since the Speakers were capable of altering the content of any message they passed, Yilda had forbid Sav and Josua to communicate anything but the simple, prearranged codes. And their codes were, of necessity, crude, incapable of conveying anything other than the general progress of their mission: contact established, negotiation begun, negotiation concluded. Success. Failure. Their lives had been reduced to a simple binary code, yes/no, on/off, live/die.

Sav checked the clock on the comm board: five hours had elapsed since they'd agreed to transfer the samples. Five more hours subtracted from the time they had left.

A new sound—or, more accurately, the suggestion of another sound, a hum really—filtered down from the tube.

But then Sav realized it wasn't coming from the tube at all. It was coming from below decks. The hum grew until he could hear it distinctly. Propelling himself from his seat, Sav hustled to the ladder below decks and descended quickly. Down here, the noise filled the cabin, vibrating through the floorplates and bulkheads. It was the pumps below the stasis cells cycling up. Sav stared at the status screen next to Ruen's cell. When Josua had disappeared below decks, he'd done more than prepare the samples and collect a few tools; he'd also keyed in the sequence to wake the *patrix* Ruen.

5 DAYS LEFT

The gap continued to diminish. The Speaker's ship closed on its hyperbolic course coming up behind *Viracosa*. Attitude jets, as big as *Viracosa*'s main engines, fired as the Speaker moved her craft into position, the two ships facing one another, nose to nose.

On the display, the point indicators had been replaced by real-time images of the two vessels, now two kilometres apart. *Viracosa* was a centimetre-long narrow wire, unremarkable save for the bulbous feeder tanks on its aft and the long tail of exhaust that lit up the darkness ahead as it continued its deceleration. The Speaker's ship, however, was mammoth in comparison, the mottled grey ovoid at its centre two hundred times the length of *Viracosa*. Its superstructure bristled with antennae, the outer skin of the ship covered with what looked like a metallic furze; dozens of articulated, tapering arms sprouted from the top half of the monstrous egg, most folding back into its underside. Two arms, however, were extended like giant, black mandibles forward of the ship. At their extremities they were mirror-bright silver. Sav couldn't shake the impression that the ship looked like an enormous insect, its mandibles about to close on *Viracosa*.

"One kilometre," Josua said grimly. "That's it." He sat at the pilot's board, his work on the docking tube completed hours earlier. His coveralls were grease-stained, and he had managed to rip them in two places; but he showed no signs of fatigue. He had watched the approach of the Speaker's vessel intently, his chair turned around to face the display.

Ruen sat in the comm officer's couch to Josua's right, his soiled burgundy robes flowing over the arms of the chair. In his right fist he clutched his cane. Maybe it was his age, or perhaps his constitution, but the *patrix* evidently didn't take to stasis well. The skin seemed to sag from his face and his head wobbled slightly. His eyes were unfocused. He seemed only partially aware of his surroundings and occasionally muttered a few incoherent words.

Sav sat in the navigator's couch. He'd broken off negotiations an hour earlier, with the proviso that discussion would resume after the samples had been retrieved and tested. Up to this point, they'd accomplished little other than to establish the parameters for the agreement on the initial conditions. The process had been extraordinarily draining. Although Sav had managed a cat nap earlier during a break in the session, that had been his only sleep since he had woken from stasis twenty hours ago. Everything had taken on the unnatural lucidity of a dream.

"Extend the tube."

It took Sav a moment to remember the command was for him, that that was the reason he'd moved to this station from the comm board. He turned back to the panel, punched up the sequence; the distant whirr of motors was audible through the hatch overhead. At the same time, the display in the centre of the cabin showed one of the mammoth pincers on the Speaker's ship stretching toward them. Sav froze; to his left, Josua's knuckles had gone white as he gripped the arms of his chair.

"I told her one thousand metres!" Josua turned to Ruen. "Connect me!"

The holy man stared at him blankly.

Sav snapped out of his paralysis and was about to scoot across the cabin to the comm board when something happened on the display to stop him: the silver tip of the pincer split open, its sides peeling back like the petals of a flower. Without waiting for Josua's command, Sav swung around and zoomed the view. From the newly formed aperture a tiny figure shot forth, began sailing toward the docking tube of *Viracosa*.

It was a naked woman.

Her body shimmered in the running lights of the two vessels, a faint aura playing over every exposed millimetre of her hairless skin. In one hand she held a canister, presumably to house the samples they'd placed in the tube. If she wore any EVA equipment—other than that protective shimmer—to shield her from the vacuum or direct her movements, Sav couldn't see it. Yet she moved unerringly toward their docking tube, hitting its outer airlock dead centre.

"She's in!" Josua stabbed a key and the air pumps above thrummed loudly as they worked to equalize the pressure in the far end of the tube. Running the lock cycle would take seventy-three seconds; they had stipulated that the Speaker, once in the tube, would have thirty seconds to retrieve the samples before he'd reverse the cycle. In total, she'd be aboard for a little less than three minutes.

"Sixty-five seconds," Josua whispered. A pause. "Equalization."

The pressurization pumps fell silent. Sav counted down the thirty seconds. Right on cue, Josua began hammering keys on the pilot's board.

The pumps didn't come back on. And the command to reverse the cycle required only a few simple keystrokes. Yet Josua typed furiously.

"What's the matter? What's wrong?"

Josua ignored Sav's question. With a final flurry, Josua finished his entry. The pilot's panel lit up; indicators on the navigator's board flickered to life.

What the hell? Sav thought.

Josua pulled his harness over his shoulders and fastened it. It was only then Sav noticed that Ruen had also been buckled into his couch, the material of his robe bunched tightly around him by the straps. Josua punched a final button and the fusion engines died, killing their deceleration. Their world went silent, their gravity fled.

Sav drifted away from his seat, his stomach wobbling. He clutched at the armrest but missed. Ruen sat rigidly, his knuckles white around his cane. His face blanched. Vomit erupted from between his withered lips, fanned out into the zero-gee of the cabin.

Sav recognized the distant sound of their attitude jets firing. The cabin began to rotate. Ruen coughed and sputtered. His cloud of vomit grew, clotting the air. As their ship turned on its longitudinal axis, the air mass dragged Sav along but his inertia kept him from turning as quickly as the rest of the ship. The bridge spun around him.

"Josua!" Sav shouted. "What are you doing?" But Josua was intent on his board.

"Our . . . our time is at hand!" Ruen managed to croak between mostly dry heaves.

The centrifugal force of the ship's rotation made it difficult for Sav to control his movement; he snagged the webbing. A cloud of Ruen's vomit spattered against him.

"Josua!"

But Josua ignored him; he had turned to face the display in the centre of the bridge. Sav craned his neck to follow Josua's gaze. The image showed *Viracosa* swinging around so that its aft would face the Speaker's ship.

The attitude jets flared briefly to halt their rotation. The fusion engines kicked to life. Exhaust plasma from *Viracosa* lashed out; a spear of energy, heated to the ignition temperature of 500 million degrees, engulfed the extended pincer, scourged the forward face of the Speaker's ship. Gravity returned like a punch, throwing Sav to the deck, knocking the breath from him. Drops of vomit pattered around him like heavy rain. On the display, it looked like the Speaker's ship was ablaze. The exhaust stream slewed around the contours of the ovoid, igniting it. There was an explosion amidships and glittering debris spun off into the void, followed by a white plume of atmosphere. The jet of air yawed the Speaker's ship away, out of the torrent of their exhaust stream. Its extended pincer swung like a broken limb. Stunned, Sav watched the gap between the two vessels widen.

"The Dissolution has begun." Ruen had turned to the display. His unkempt beard was flecked with vomit. But his eyes were clear now; he turned his gaze on Sav triumphantly. "Too late to repent," he added with a smirk.

Sav watched *Viracosa* accelerate away from its rendezvous. Behind him, Ruen had fallen into a rapturous chant. Wide-eyed, Sav looked around. Josua had undone his harness and now stood next to the navigator's console. Before Sav could do anything, Josua keyed in a new sequence. Overhead, the explosive bolts anchoring the emergency tube to the ship detonated with a muffled bang. The flight deck shuddered; the clang of the released clamps rang through the cabin. Immediately, Ruen fell silent and all three men craned their necks upward, toward the docking tube hatch, although there was nothing they could see. Metal on metal creaked as the emergency tube was pushed away from its mooring and extended fore of the vessel by the rigid umbilical.

"Now we're safe."

Sav was stunned. Open-mouthed, he watched Josua walk back to the pilot's seat and buckle himself in.

"Safe?" Sav asked, his voice rising. "Safe from what?"

"From them!" Josua waved his hand irritably in the air, a gesture he must have meant to indicate the other ship, the Hub, perhaps Nexus itself. "That Speaker was a pawn. A dangerous one. But a pawn, nonetheless. Our job is to reach the Hub. To get the antidote."

Sav swore softly. *The Hub again.* "But they'd already agreed to our real demands!"

"Don't be naive. We have nothing from them. No fuel. No antidote. Only empty promises. For all we know they might not be able to synthesize the antidote on the vessel out there."

"Not after what you did to it!"

"With any luck." A cold smile lit Josua's features. It enraged Sav; he took a step, and his foot skidded out from under him on the vomit-slicked floor. He grabbed at the webbing to steady himself.

Ruen's eyes fluttered; he began chanting in an unfamiliar dialect—or in gibberish. The holy man's narrow chin jutted up into the air, his knobby arms moving in an intricate obeisance, waving his cane high, eyes open and rolling back as if he were gripped by an ecstatic fervour.

"Shut up!" Sav shouted.

Oblivious, the holy man continued his wheezy glossolalia.

"We had them!" Sav turned his rage on Josua. "And now you've attacked a Nexus vessel."

"I had to," Josua answered, loud enough to be heard over Ruen's rant. "We needed a hostage. One *we* control."

Sav was incredulous. "A hostage? What about the nanoagents she could release? God only knows what damage she's doing right now!"

Josua leaned over his panel to zoom the image of *Viracosa*. The nose of ship and the docking tube, a dozen metres apart, filled the entire display area. The thin shaft of the umbilical, invisible before, now spanned the two. It glowed like a light bulb filament.

"That's the polycarbon-steel umbilical," Josua said, pointing. "It's strong enough to hold the mass of the tube in place. And I've wired it so that it's heated several hundred degrees to prevent any nanoagents from using it as a bridge to infest our ship. The thermal vibrations at those temperatures should break down anything less stable than the polycarbon-steel fibre."

"A burning bridge," Ruen croaked, his voice strained from his chant.

"Unless the nanoagents have been engineered to withstand those temperatures."

Josua shrugged. "True. But it's better than nothing. And the trade off," Josua said, a hint of pride in his voice, "is that we have another hostage."

Sav stared at the image. *Viracosa* was pushing the tube ahead of itself like a shield. But for what purpose?

"The Hub," Josua said resolutely, before Sav could frame the question. "We have to go to the Hub. She's our free passage."

"What?" Ruen asked, licking his withered lips. "It is time?"

"Not yet," Josua answered without shifting his gaze away from Sav. "As soon as our work is completed."

"She can't have much of an oxygen reserve in that suit," Sav said.

Josua shrugged. "The tube has an emergency supply. And I threw in a half a dozen extra cartridges to cover the four days before we reach the Hub."

Four days to the Hub.

A low-grade fever would be upon them within a day of making orbit. If the plague ran its usual course, they would first develop red nodules on the pads of their fingers, then feel woozy and disoriented, as though they had contracted a flu. About forty hours later would be a brief remission. According to Yilda, they would be functional up to the end of that period. It meant roughly three days at the Hub for dealing with the Speakers and acquiring the antidote. After that they would fall into a debilitating, secondary fever from which they would never recover. The only way to extend their time would be to return to shifts in stasis. But Sav thought about the smashed panel beside his stasis cell. He had no intention of leaving himself that vulnerable again. "I'm staying up," he said. "I won't go back into stasis."

"Stasis?" The *patrix* wiped his mouth with the back of his sleeve, smearing more vomit into the flock of his robe. "But the dissolution—"

"No one's going back into stasis." Josua busied himself at the pilot's panel; he cut their fusion engines and they returned to zero gee. Sav's feet drifted off the floor; he clutched the webbing tightly. Josua fired the attitude jets, swinging *Viracosa* about so her exhaust nozzles pointed at the Hub. Then he ignited the fusion engine to resume their deceleration; Sav's feet thumped to the floor. Josua unbuckled his harness.

"The code," Sav said. "We have under two hours to send the next sequence. With the Speaker in the tube, how are we going to do that?"

"Simple." Josua rose and sauntered over to the comm board. Without sitting down, he began tapping keys. Sav recognized the hum of small motors on the outer hull working to reposition the antenna array. "I'm realigning the array to transmit directly to the Hub. We're less than a light hour out, so it should take the message an hour to reach them. Plenty of time for them to pass it along."

Josua finished; he scooped up the headset. The motors fell silent, and a small beep sounded at the board to indicate successful completion of the antenna realignment. Josua pressed the transmit key.

"This is *Viracosa*. We have taken Novitiate Lien hostage and disabled her ship. We remain on course to the Hub where we expect to refuel and pick up the antidote. Any attempt to intercept before we establish orbit will result in the Novitiate's death—and the deaths of other Speakers at the relay station. Once the exchange has been made, we will release the Speaker unharmed." Josua paused, glanced at Sav. "The next code sequence is as follows: Callev, Veddev, Lect." The first three months of the Bh'Haret calendar. "*Viracosa* out." Josua released the key and stripped off his headset. At an hour each way, it would be at least two hours before they could expect Yilda's response. Josua turned to Sav. "Satisfied?"

"No. What if they were telling the truth? What if they didn't manufacture the plague?"

"They did!" Josua's eyes blazed. "They killed her!"

"Her?" Sav asked quietly.

"Her, them." The colour drained from Josua's face, the emotion in his voice now carefully suppressed, deliberate contempt replacing the burst of rage. "Everyone. All of Bh'Haret."

You mean Shiranda, Sav thought. *You're still obsessed with her death. And this attack was part of the payback.*

"I'm going below decks," Josua said. "To get some sleep." Though he now appeared collected, his hands were balled into fists and his arms trembled as if he stood in the middle of a bitter, winter wind. "Wake me when we receive Yilda's response."

Josua made for the ladder. Ruen fumbled to unbuckle his harness. But Josua turned; he caught the holy man's eye and nodded sharply. "Ruen will keep you company," he said, his eyes never leaving the *patrix*. "Won't you?"

Ruen blinked as if trying to absorb Josua's words, then nodded numbly, letting himself back down into his seat. Swivelling to face Sav, he scowled, clutching his cane with both hands. "Company," he said hoarsely, repeating Josua.

Abruptly, Sav understood why Josua had revived the Ruen. To keep tabs on him. *To make certain I don't try to harm him when he's not watching.* Sav looked from one to the other, the two an odd pair, both eyeing him warily as though *he* was the insane one. *They're in this together*, Sav thought. *Josua's frightened of me. Of what I might do. But is he worried enough to want me dead?* He had no doubt the *patrix* would be happy to see the end of him. But Josua? *I could overpower both of them*, Sav thought. *Right here and now. I've got a better than even chance.* Josua wasn't a large man; and Ruen was too old to be much of a threat.

Only there were the codes.

Sav would have to have Josua's co-operation to complete the exchange. As much as Sav disliked it, he would have to abide the situation for a while longer if their negotiations were to continue. But he'd have to watch his back every moment.

On the ladder now, only his head above floor level, Josua paused, turned to Sav. "You look like you could use some rest too."

"I'm not tired." It was a lie, of course. It had been almost a full day since Sav had been revived, and fatigue had settled in his limbs like a weight of sand, made his skull throb. But sleep wasn't a risk he could afford to take.

"Suit yourself." Josua disappeared from sight.

Sav had never felt so tired in his life. Moving across the flight deck, Sav collapsed into the navigator's couch, opposite Ruen.

For a moment he considered what Josua had suggested. He *was* exhausted. Mentally and physically. And Josua's actions had sapped his already slim hopes for the success of their mission. Collecting an antidote now appeared more preposterous than ever. His berth down below had never seemed more inviting. He would settle in, close his eyes, let sleep take him—and to hell with what Josua and Ruen might do.

But then Sav remembered the others at the relay station. Liis and Penirdth and Mira. They were in this too, depending on him. Though he could have cared less about Losson and the Facilitators, he owed the others. He had grown to like Penirdth and felt a kinship to quiet Mira. And there was Liis. His feelings about her were confused. Certainly, he was as close to her as he'd been to anyone else in the last ten years of his life. They'd crewed three missions together. That was all there was to it. Wasn't there?

We made love once.

His throat tightened involuntarily at the thought. She was the first woman he'd been with in years. He wondered if he would ever see her again. Suddenly, he was seized with an intense wave of loneliness, and an equally poignant longing to be back on Bh'Haret, to be home. To be with Liis. The vastness of their separation pierced him. Until this moment he hadn't really thought past what would happen at the Hub. Perhaps he'd been consciously avoiding it. But now the idea of finding the others, especially Liis, and returning to Bh'Haret filled him with urgency.

Only that, he reminded himself, *will be impossible unless I can get the antidote. Sleep is definitely out*, Sav thought. *At least until I can find a way of improving my chances of waking.*

Behind Ruen, at the comm board, the connect light blinked.

Sav stared at it, his heart thumping against his ribcage. Unaware, the *patrix* continued to watch Sav through slitted eyes, his seat turned inward so that he faced Sav across the deck, the light to his back. Gripping his cane in both hands, its tip planted on the floor at his feet, the holy man leaned forward now, as if he sensed the abrupt change in Sav's mood.

Sav forced his gaze away from the flashing light, not wanting to alert Ruen; instead he looked directly at the *patrix* and smiled wanly. The holy man grunted dismissively and spat out of the corner of his mouth. Nevertheless, Sav's mollifying gesture seemed to do the trick. Ruen relaxed back into his couch.

Sav watched the light from the corner of his eye. Only half an hour had passed since Josua had sent his message to the Hub. It was too early for a reply. *Maybe it was intercepted by a Speaker and passed on up the chain of command*, Sav thought. Only the signal was highly directional. Chances of an intercept were small, even if there was a ship manned by a Speaker in the path of the signal.

He frowned, considered the Speaker trapped in the emergency tube. She had said there was no one else aboard her vessel. Perhaps she'd been lying, but it seemed a strange thing to do given her situation. But *if* she was telling the truth—

She has a transmitter.

The notion seemed so obvious that Sav felt stupid for not having thought of it before. The transparent suit she wore had made Sav assume she carried nothing other than the specimen container—as Josua had stipulated. But what did they know of Polyarchy technology? Like the other workings of her suit, a transmitter designed on a molecular level would almost certainly be invisible to the naked eye.

The light flashed; Sav tried hard not to stare at it directly.

I have to talk to her, Sav thought. *Without Josua or Ruen around to listen in.* But how could he do that with Ruen set to watch him with the single-mindedness of a trained guard dog? The moment he tried to establish a link, the holy man would scuttle below decks to fetch Josua.

No time for subtlety, Sav decided. Pushing himself from his seat, he moved across the cabin; a belligerent look flared in the holy man's eyes as Sav approached. Just as quickly as it had risen, the belligerence wavered, going out like a doused fire. "You'd best not try anything," Ruen croaked in a quavering voice, raising his cane. "Or I'll—"

Sav knocked the cane from Ruen's palsied hand; he seized the *patrix*'s windpipe with both hands. Lifting Ruen out of his seat with ease, he felt the fragile bones beneath his fingers move and grind as he dangled the old man above the flight deck.

Ruen's face contorted; his eyes bugged out and a small gurgling noise leaked from between his withered lips. Frail hands flailed uselessly at Sav's arms. Ruen's face turned crimson; he'd gone silent, all the air in his lungs spent. Tears leaked from his bulging eyes and a strand of spittle ran from the corner of his mouth and trickled onto Sav's left wrist. In seconds the old man's eyes glazed over and rolled back in their sockets, showing white half-crescents between quivering lids. His bony arms fell limply to his sides, his entire weight settling on Sav's grip. As light as the *patrix* was, Sav's arms shook with the effort of supporting him.

I could kill him, Sav realized in amazement. *All I have to do is hold on for a few seconds more....*

Sav released his grip and Ruen crumpled to the floor, a heap of thin, jaundiced limbs amidst the folds of his soiled robe. On the holy man's neck were bright red finger marks. Sav let his own arms fall. He prodded the *patrix* with the toe of his boot.

Ruen didn't move.

Sav crouched, felt for a pulse. It was faint, but it was there. Strangely, he felt no relief. Felt nothing beyond the cold knowledge that the holy man still lived. He stood. Stepping over the inert form, he dropped into the seat in front of the comm panel and enabled a two way transmission channel.

"*Viracosa!*" Novitiate Lien's voice burst from the overhead speaker. "*What are—*"

Sav stabbed the key to cut the feed and the cabin instantly fell silent. He swivelled his chair around and pushed himself silently from his seat, almost tripping over the holy man, then running lightly across the flight deck until he clutched the ladder below decks with one hand. Leaning over the semi-circular opening, he craned his head to listen. Everything was quiet. He crept back to the comm panel, stepping carefully over Ruen's prone form, and put on the headset. Lien's voice was carrying on through the tiny speakers.

"*... an act of aggression! You will have to answer to the Polyarchy. And to me!*" A pause. "*Do you hear, Viracosa? Are you there? Answer me!*"

Sav pressed the transmit key. "This is *Viracosa*," he said softly. "What is your status?"

"*Status? You have kidnapped me, attacked my vessel! And you want to know my status?*" This was followed by an outburst of guttural syllables.

No matter that Sav didn't know the language, he understood the intonation well enough. And unless it was a clever act, the Speaker's invective conveyed both an overt indignation—and a bravado designed to hide her fear. The swearing trailed off, and was followed by several sharp intakes of breath, the sort of breathlessness that, Sav realized, often preceded a full-blown panic—she might do herself, or the relatively weak tube, significant damage.

"Take it easy," Sav said in as firm a voice as he could muster in a whisper. "Don't let yourself hyperventilate."

A single hissing syllable returned over the headset, like the start of an angry word. But she bit off whatever she was going to say at the last second. She sucked in a big breath. And another. Her breathing slowed, approached normal.

"*I . . . I am fine.*" Novitiate Lien sounded calmer. Whatever indignation her tone had held before had collapsed.

"Okay," Sav said. "Now tell me if you're in any immediate danger."

"*I only have a small amount of oxygen left. I brought only enough life support for a few of your minutes.*" There was a pause. Then she added, "*That is why I contacted you.*"

"Do you see several short, grey cylinders?"

"*With red markings?*"

"Yeah. Those are cartridges containing an oxygen/nitrogen mix. On the top of each cylinder is a threaded opening with an orange pin in its centre. If you press the pin down, it will release the contents of the tube. Do you understand?"

"*Yes.*"

"Each cylinder contains a twelve-hour supply. And the emergency tube itself is equipped with scrubbers that should be capable of purifying the air you release. Between the two, you should be able to maintain an atmosphere in there for several days."

"*Yes,*" she answered. "*I count seven cylinders.*"

"Good." At least Josua didn't lie about that. In the background, Sav could hear the hiss of gas being released from a cylinder. He waited until the sound stopped. "Now listen carefully."

"*I . . . I am listening.*"

"The commander of this vessel is determined to reach the Hub."

"*Yes,*" she said slowly. "*We already know this.*"

"He believes this is the only way we can be certain of obtaining the antidote and fuel for the return journey." Sav decided it was best not to share any of his own misgivings about Josua's motivations. "That's why he took you hostage. He believes your comrades won't harm us as long as we hold you. But if you can convince the people in charge to get us the antidote before we reach the Hub, I may be able to talk him into releasing you and changing course."

"*You are mad!*" Novitiate Lien's anger had returned. "*How can we give you an antidote when we do not know what we are curing? The samples are here. With me! Do you not remember?*"

Any sympathy Sav had for the woman evaporated. "You created the plague."

"*My superiors tell me we did not.*"

"Then they're lying." Bile rose in Sav's throat, made it hard for him to say the next words. "You murdered millions of innocent people. And now you're too cowardly to take responsibility."

"*No!*" The vehemence of her response caught Sav off guard. "*Not me! I did nothing!*"

"You were only following orders?" Sav said sardonically.

"*The Pro-Locutors tell me nothing.*"

"Ignorance is no excuse."

When she spoke again, the bitterness in her voice was unmistakable. "*I am a Novitiate, patrolling the outer reaches of Nexus space. Alive or dead, I do not matter to the Pro-Locutors.*" Briefly, the channel was silent. "*I do not know who caused your plague. But I am sorry for your people.*"

"Save your pity for yourself. You may need it."

"*So. You will kill me.*"

"We don't want to kill anyone," Sav answered slowly. "We only want the antidote and safe passage home."

"*Then why have you made your ship into a fission weapon?*"

Sav was taken aback. "I don't know what you're talking about." Could this be another of Nexus's tricks?

"*Our drones detected a nuclear triggering device inside one of your fuel tanks. A one hundred and forty-seven megaton release. If detonated, the resulting compressive blast will likely trigger a chain reaction in the deuterium fuel pellets adding significantly to the yield.*"

"You're crazy!" But as he spoke, Sav knew the truth of her words: it was what Josua had planned from the start. All those secretive runs he'd made back on Bh'Haret. The time he'd spent alone on *Viracosa* preparing, as he said, for any "contingency." The way in which he snarled and delayed negotiations by taking the Speaker hostage and attacking her ship. His obsession with reaching the Hub. It all added up. Revenge. He intended to drive a spike into the heart of Nexus.

"If it's true," Sav said slowly, "I knew nothing about it."

"*Ignorance is no excuse,*" she said, throwing Sav's words back at him. "*Perhaps we have more in common than you think.*" Her tone became oddly subdued. "*When my oxygen supply began dwindling, I asked the Pro-Locutors if I could contact you. They forbade it. They told me to wait for permission. By now my oxygen supply would have been spent. I would be suffocating at this moment. And still I have heard nothing. I knew before I was expendable, but it was only an intellectual understanding. Now I know it in my heart. They would have let me die. For all I know, the Pro-Locutors may consider me a liability. Perhaps they were grateful for the opportunity to factor one more variable out of the equation.*"

"I don't understand. They would let you die because of what Josua did?"

"*Possibly. Though I think it more likely that they fear I know too much. The relay station must be a well-guarded secret, for I have never heard a whisper of it before. When I became the intermediary between you and the Pro-Locutors, they told me about the station. So that I could discuss the situation with you in a meaningful way. Perhaps they now regret the decision.*"

"And when they find out you're not dead?" Sav asked. "What will they do then?"

"*I will tell them I found the oxygen cartridges, and managed to determine their use. They may still arrange for my death afterwards. If I survive . . .*" She spoke with an earnestness that surprised Sav: "*We must trust each other if we are both to survive.*"

Sav's first inclination was to laugh aloud. How could he trust her? Her story might be another ploy by Nexus to find out more about the situation aboard *Viracosa*. It was the cornerstone of all hostage negotiation: find a commonality, a point of contact with the captors and establish a rapport. When a victim is no longer faceless, it becomes harder to carry out a cold-blooded execution. On the other hand, Lien's plight could be real, her words sincere. Sav imagined himself trapped in the emergency tube, driving toward the Hub, pinned to the nose of a nuclear bomb. It would certainly provide incentive to co-operate. *We must trust each other*, she had said.

Sav licked his lips, his throat suddenly gone dry.

He made his decision. What he was about to say could bring a swift death—or their salvation. In a hoarse whisper, he said, "I think Josua's mad."

It was out. Immediately Sav felt lighter, like he'd dropped an onerous burden he'd not been aware he was carrying until this moment.

"*Josua?*"

Sav was momentarily confused; then he realized Lien wouldn't know their names. "Josua is the Captain of *Viracosa*. He's obsessed with revenge. I think he plans to go to the Hub and detonate the ship—regardless of whether you provide the antidote."

"*It would make sense. After I reported the discovery of the explosives, the Pro-Locutors assumed the bomb was merely another bargaining tool. When it was not mentioned during the initial negotiations, they wondered if there was more to it.*"

"Can you do anything to defuse the bomb?"

"*I have nanoagents that could be employed. But they are on my vessel which has been disabled. My ship has informed me that it cannot catch us now. Nor do I have anything with me that can help. When I came over to retrieve the samples I was ordered to do nothing that might endanger the negotiations. So I brought only the bare minimum as your Captain requested—a sample cylinder and a basic EVA suit with a few minutes life support.*"

"What about other ships? Or the drones? Can they catch us?"

"*They have been ordered to stay clear. The Pro-Locutors' only concern right now is the relay station. It appears to be of primary importance to them. They will do nothing to endanger the Speakers there. I fear they* would allow the detonation of your weapon sooner than risking action against your vessel. But what about you? Can you not disable the weapon or," she paused here, as if searching for the right term, "*incapacitate Josua?*"

Incapacitate Josua. It had been a possibility he'd considered. Coming from Novitiate Lien, it sounded sordid. He was grateful he couldn't agree. "No. I don't know about the weapon or its trigger, but, yes I probably could 'incapacitate' Josua. The problem is that we each have half of the response codes. If he doesn't send the counter at the right time, the Speakers at the relay station will be executed. I know this for a fact. We need his co-operation."

"Then," Lien said sorrowfully, "*we are both doomed.*"

For a moment, silence filled the cabin.

"Maybe," Sav answered. "And maybe not. First, let me see what I can do about the bomb. For the time being we'll play along with Josua. He doesn't know about your transceiver. I'd feel better if we kept it that way. Let's keep these exchanges to a minimum."

"*Agreed.*"

Sav had a sudden inspiration. "Can you transmit at ten megahertz?" The comm board on the ship wasn't set up to monitor short wave bandwidth.

"*Yes.*"

"Good. Then I'll reconfigure the transceiver in the dropship for the same frequency. We can talk in privacy that way." *And*, Sav thought, *that's also the answer to my problem of getting some sleep. I can dog the airlock to keep Josua and Ruen out of the dropship.* Unlike the hatches aboard *Viracosa*, the hatch to the dropship could only be undogged from inside the vessel itself. "Will you be okay in the tube for a while? I have some things I'd like to check."

"*I . . . I do not like this confined space. But, yes. I think so.*"

"Unless there's an emergency, wait for me to contact you. Understood?"

"*Yes.*"

Sav was about to break the connection when something else occurred to him. "The Pro-Locutors told you about the relay station.

Did they give you any details about the situation there?"

"*Yes. One Speaker is reported dead. Three of your comrades are holding seven more Speakers hostage.*"

"Can . . . can you describe the three?"

"*Two men and a woman. One man is tall and thin and seems to be taking orders from another shorter, balding man. Both have filaments embedded in their skulls.*"

"The woman," Sav asked. "What does she look like?"

"*She is tall, broad-shouldered and has short blonde hair. Her face is scarred heavily with designs.*"

Liis had made it.

"*This woman. Is she important to you?*"

The question startled Sav. "Yes," he said. He added, "They are all important."

"*Even those who did not make it to the relay station?*"

"How did you know there were others?"

The Speaker laughed, a strangely lilting thing. "When I told you there were three of them, you asked me to describe them. If there were only three to begin, you would already know who they were."

Sav said nothing, made suddenly uneasy by the Speaker's insight.

"*My name is Lien,*" she said after a moment, her tone almost apologetic, as if she understood Sav's sudden discomfort.

"Yeah, I know," Sav answered. After only the slightest hesitation, he added, "Mine is Sav."

"*I wish you luck, Sav.*"

"Thanks," Sav muttered. "Luck to you too." Lifting his thumb from the transmit switch, he turned his seat and stared at the *patrix* lying on the floor, his narrow chest rising and falling irregularly, his wheezing breath rattling in his throat. "I think we'll both need all we can get."

After breaking the connection, Sav moved over to the pilot's board. He brought up the status display on the feeder tanks. A bar graph indicated five of the tanks were empty. The sixth was nearly depleted: at the current rate, enough fuel pellets remained for another ten hours of burn. The seventh tank, the reserve, showed full. If Novitiate Lien was to be believed, that would be where Josua had planted the explosives.

Sav keyed in the sequence to run the full diagnostic package on the reserve tank. Everything came up green. But that meant nothing. If Josua had sabotaged it, he would have also gimmicked the sensors to make everything appear normal. There was only one way for Sav to be certain. He'd have to check out the tank itself. With any luck, he'd be able to do it before the *patrix* regained consciousness.

Sav heaved himself to his feet—and stumbled, clutching at the back of his seat to regain his balance. In his fatigue, his legs had nearly betrayed him. The wave of disorientation passed. Releasing the seat back, he stepped over Ruen and made his way to the ladder below decks.

Descending silently through the crew quarters, he glanced at the stasis cells. Josua lay on the pallet in his cell, his back to the room, apparently asleep.

Sav continued down.

The ladder ended in a small antechamber where an airlock led to the dropship bay. Next to the lock was a control panel. Sav pressed his palm on an oversized red button and the door sighed open. He stepped through and the door slid shut behind him.

Walking over to the row of EVA suits hanging on the wall, he unclipped his lamp; where he was going there would be no lights. He trotted over to the corner of the dropship bay where a hatch had been set in the floor; he spun the dogs on the hatch and pulled it open. The engines, always a distant thrum in the background, now became a roar. Sav clambered down a short ladder and past the square propellant tanks and fuel pipes of the attitude jets, until he stood on top of the secondary radiation shield. At his feet was another, smaller hatch leading to the aftmost part of the ship: a crawlspace sandwiched between the primary and secondary radiation shields. Other than going EVA, this service bay was the only point of connection with the tanks. Josua would have been taking a chance had he cut through the tanks outside the ship—it would have left telltale scars that anyone approaching the vessel in a dropship might see. But down here, in the guts of the ship, he would have had the privacy to go about his work. Josua could have cut through the top of the reserve tank, crawled inside and set the fission weapon, then welded the opening shut. He would have worked with impunity, for no one came down into this uncomfortably cramped space unless there was good reason.

Sav undogged the last hatch.

The engines howled in his ears. A blast of heat struck him, made his face bead instantly with sweat. There was no ladder; the primary shield was less than a metre below, concave and set so its edges curved up to meet those of the secondary shield on which he stood. Breaking the smooth curve of the primary's surface were the rounded edges of the seven feeder tanks. Sav lowered himself until he sat on the lip of the opening. Then, sucking in a breath like a diver, he dropped until his feet struck the rounded primary shield. He went down on all fours.

It was like a deafening, vibrating oven. The shield beneath him was so hot, his palms felt like they were being seared. Even his knees smarted through the material of his coveralls.

He clicked on his light and swung it around. The tops of the tanks encircled him; snaking around them were thick bundles of multicoloured cables and square alloy conduits. Perched on the top of each tank were opposing coils of finely wound wire, the heads of powerful electromagnets that controlled the flow of the deuterium microfusion pellets into the ignition chamber. Sav swung his light over to the reserve tank.

A square, metal plate, half a metre a side, had been welded below the electromagnet. The plate had been cut crudely, the ragged edge of the blackened join uneven where metal flowed into metal. At first glance Sav knew the work was far too sloppy to have been performed by an engineering technician. It could only be Josua's handiwork.

It looked like the Speaker had been telling the truth.

He was about to scramble back up through the hatch when he caught sight of the power cable to the reserve tank lying coiled on the floor in front of the tank. It had been severed. Sav played his light over the coil. The circuit board near its base had been shorted out, its surface blackened and melted. The electromagnet feed mechanism was completely useless. *Of course*, Sav thought. *Josua doesn't want the tank being emptied into the ignition chamber.* It would have set off half a dozen alarms if the pellets hadn't fed through properly. This last piece of evidence only seemed to confirm what Lien had said.

Sav hauled himself out of the crawlspace and dogged the hatch. He clambered up the short ladder and into the dropship bay. His breath still came in ragged gulps and he was soaked in sweat.

Making his way over to the tool locker, he pulled the door open—then stared at the empty bracket that normally held the miniature blowtorch. Where the other cutting tools had been, there were only empty spaces. He should have guessed: there was nothing left here that would enable him to begin to undo Josua's work. He shut the door.

What can I do?

Nothing. There's not a damn thing I can do to disable Josua's bomb. Could it be as hopeless as that? Sav rolled the possibilities over in his mind. For a second, his spirits soared as he realized Josua would have had to rig up a trigger for the explosives. *If I could find it*, Sav thought, *I might be able to disable it!* As soon as this occurred to him, he realized there simply wasn't time for a thorough search. And he'd have to be careful in the process not to alert Josua. Sav considered confronting Josua directly. This, too, struck him as a pointless, perhaps dangerous, exercise. What if Josua, in his anger, refused to pass on his half of the codes? Their slim chances of obtaining the antidote would vanish entirely.

There seemed to be no solution.

The creep of exhaustion Sav had been fighting now rallied to numb his senses; his thoughts moved torpidly. *Rest*, he said to himself. *Then figure out what to do.*

Behind him, the dropship hatch was open, as it normally was when the ship rested in the pressurized bay. Sav stepped into the cramped vessel and sealed the door behind. One after the other, he spun the dogs shut and snugged them up, effectively locking himself in the craft. Stepping into the tiny forward cabin, he slumped into the pilot's seat. With an effort, he raised his fingers to the keypad. In a moment he'd tied the dropship's communication software into *Viracosa*'s net, and so to the antenna array on the outside of the vessel. The Pro-Locutors' response to Josua's last message was due in less than an hour. Sav set the local board to alert him the moment it came in. He also modified the board's configuration to monitor transmissions from the Speaker trapped in their emergency tube. That finished, he let himself sink into the padded seat.

Sav closed his eyes.

Disconnected scenes came to him, flashes of memories and half-memories: people he had known, ships he'd served on.

The skirl of the alarm shocked him, dragged him back from the borders of sleep.

A tiny speaker embedded in the control panel crackled. "*Message to* Viracosa *from the Council of Pro-Locutors.*" The voice this time was flat and artificial sounding. "*The next control sequence is as follows: 'Abitef, Miran, Defetesque.'*" Yilda's key: three cities in Bh'Haret's southern hemisphere. The message didn't require a response for another full day. The uninflected voice droned on. "*A ship carrying fuel for your vessel has been dispatched. It is also capable of synthesizing an antidote once biological samples have been transferred. We are awaiting your requirements for the exchange of the fuel and antidote—and for the release of Novitiate Lien. On your current course, rendezvous will be at three point seven three eight million kilometres from the Hub. Closer approach will not be allowed. Request return of the counter sequence. Message repeats. The next control sequence is 'Abitef, Miran, Defetesque.' A ship carrying fuel for your vessel—*"

Sav let the message loop twice more, then killed it. He was about to cut the circuit altogether when Josua's voice filled the tiny cabin. "This is the captain of *Viracosa*." The screen on the dropship's control panel indicated he was broadcasting from the comm board on the bridge. The incoming message had woken him. "Your message has been received. The counter sequence will be returned in twenty hours. We cannot alter course, nor will we make an exchange before we are in orbit around the Hub. Message ends."

The cabin fell silent.

The Hub again, Sav thought wearily. It was becoming harder and harder not to believe what Novitiate Lien had told him.

Sav lifted a leaden arm and checked his watch. 4-17:01. Four days and seventeen hours before the onset of the first symptoms. Four days to the Hub. Two to reach the Pro-Locutors' proposed rendezvous.

It all seemed too quick. And at the same time, excruciatingly slow. There was nothing to do. Except sit here in the dropship and wait. Sav thought about Josua up on the bridge—and suddenly remembered Ruen's prostrate form. He sat up.

What would Josua make of his attack on Ruen? And what would the holy man do when he next encountered Sav? It was something Sav hadn't considered in the rush of the moment. For an instant he felt regret at his precipitate action; then he shrugged it off. Josua probably wouldn't care. His only concern was getting to the Hub. As for the *patrix* himself, Sav would deal with him when he had to.

Sitting back, Sav let his head loll against the seat. He stared through the windscreen at the grey double doors of the outer airlock, a metre past the nose of the dropship. The scene blurred; Sav's eyes fluttered.

"*Sav?*"

The word pierced Sav's consciousness, pulling him from sleep. He thought to sit up, but he was weightless, tumbling from his couch. *Viracosa* ran silently, the thrum of its engines gone.

"*Please respond.*"

Josua's shut down the engines! thought Sav. When the initial wave of panic subsided, he realized that this was the opposite of what Josua wanted. Had Josua's manoeuvres exhausted the fuel prematurely? No. It would have taken time to use up the remaining fuel pellets. *I've been asleep,* Sav realized. *It seemed only like seconds, but I've been asleep for hours.* He spun slowly toward the ceiling of the cabin in zero-gee.

"*What is happening?*" Novitiate Lien's voice had taken on a note of panic, of fear. "*Why have we stopped accelerating?*"

Sav bumped against the ceiling of the cramped cabin. With a practised movement, he tucked his legs and rotated so that his feet thumped against the ceiling. Then he kicked off gently, propelling himself toward a drag bar fixed along the edge of the control panel. Snagging it, he righted himself, feeling a swell of nausea, like a green recruit in freefall for the first time. He ignored the sensation, attributed it to fatigue and stress. Reaching out, he pressed the transmit key.

"This is Sav." He glanced at his watch, saw he had slept ten hours. Why, he wondered, did he still feel so tired?

"*I . . . I am sorry, Sav. I know I was not supposed to contact you. But it has been so long since I talked to you. I wanted to know what was happening. Then the loss of gravity startled me. I thought—*"

"The fuel pellets are exhausted. That's all."

"*Oh.*" She sounded sheepish.

Sav felt irritable; a headache fogged his brain, seemed to settle behind his eyes. "There's no danger," he said. "Except for what Josua might do if he discovers we're in communication."

There was a moment of silence in which his accusation hung between them. Much to Sav's surprise, she didn't respond in anger or fear, but said simply, "*I trust you.*"

Sav felt a stab of shame. "I'm tired." It was all he could think to say.

"*I know. I am too.*"

"You were right," Sav said, his words controlled this time, softened. "About the bomb I mean. It looks like Josua planned this from the start. I think he's determined to detonate it at the Hub." His throat felt thick, and it sickened him to say the next words: "Negotiating for an antidote was only a sham."

"*I see.*" there was a pause. "*I will not tell my superiors yet. Not until it is absolutely necessary."*

Sav understood: if the Pro-Locutors believed there was nothing to be gained from the negotiations, they might decide to destroy *Viracosa*, Speaker and all, before it reached the Hub.

"If we survive, I will do my best to help you find your cure."

She sounded sincere. Sav was surprised to find her simple assurance meant more to him than he would have thought. "Thanks," he said gruffly. "And I'll do my best to see Josua doesn't harm you."

"Thank . . . thank you."

"Try to rest."

"You too."

"Yeah," Sav said, realizing he was still tired, so tired he felt he could fall asleep again simply by shutting his eyes. "I'll try." He cut the connection. Releasing the grab bar, he drifted free. *Rest*, he thought. It sounded so appealing. But first he knew he should check the bridge, find out exactly what Josua had or had not done. Perhaps he should begin his search for the bomb's trigger. But his limbs felt leaden and his brain ached. *Why am I so tired?* he wondered. A shiver ran through him and he closed his eyes, thinking, *I'll rest just for a second*, not intending to fall asleep again.

4 DAYS LEFT

Two discordant sensations swam in Sav's mind: the first was a feeling of detachment, a kind of dizzying displacement from the *moment* in which his physical body was rooted, as if he observed rather than inhabited it; the second was exactly the opposite, a heightened sense of the minutiae of his physical being, of the fine sheen of sweat that coated every millimetre of his skin, of the tiny shiverings that jangled each nerve ending, of the queasy ball growing in the pit of his stomach. His consciousness swung sickeningly between the two perspectives like a long arcing pendulum.

Sav opened his eyes and blinked. He was in freefall.

He turned his head, and the world moved unsteadily, the motion of his skull seeming to drag it reluctantly along. His nausea increased in alarming surges. He decided to remain still. In the periphery of his vision he recognized the shape of a control panel.

I'm in the dropship. His perspective twisted with the rotation of his body.

Then it came back to him: he recalled going between the shields, finding Josua's handiwork, securing himself in the dropship. *I'm tired*, he thought. *A little disoriented. That's all.* But as soon as he thought that, he knew it was wrong. Fear spiked his heart into a fevered beat. *I'm sick.* Lifting his hand, he looked at the pads of his fingers: dozens of small, red nodules had erupted on his skin.

The plague!

Fear banded Sav's chest, making it difficult to draw breath. Holding up his wrist in disbelief, he stared at his watch. 4-2:20. He still had four days and two hours. *No*, Sav thought. *It can't be!*

Yet the tiny red bumps that stippled the pads of his fingers were incontrovertible evidence. The Trojan vector had wound down inside him, had blossomed like a deadly flower into the plague. The disease was multiplying in him at a maddening pitch. Within forty hours he would be in remission. But the respite would be short lived: in a matter of hours black lesions would appear on his skin, and he would begin experiencing intense abdominal pain, nausea, diarrhoea and vomiting. Within a week irreversible cerebral and renal damage would occur, and finally a sudden death from toxic shock, if he was lucky, or the agonizing death of hypovolemia brought on by multiorgan failure. . . .

Panic seized him; he tried to swim back through the air to the couch, but his arms churned uselessly. He managed to snag the arm of the seat and clung to it desperately, squeezing his eyes shut. The wave of queasiness retreated, his heart slowed. Sav opened his eyes again and everything seemed deceptively normal. Except the hard nodules dotting the tips of his fingers. *Maybe*, he thought with a rush of hope, *it's not the plague. Maybe it's something else.* It would be easy to find out. All he had to do was check Josua and Ruen for symptoms.

He launched himself toward the dropship's airlock, the world moving vertiginously beneath him. He managed to open the hatch with awkward fingers and propelled himself to the airlock, slapping the red button to unseal the door. He pulled himself up the ladder toward the crew quarters.

The holy man was in his stasis cell, webbing pulled haphazardly across the opening so that half floated free. Ruen's face was slicked with sweat. Though his eyes were open, they were glazed, feverish. In white-knuckled fists he gripped the bunched material of his stained robe, muttering incoherently between racking shivers. Red nodules speckled the tips of his fingers.

Sav tore his eyes away from Ruen, from the confirmation of the plague, his brain burning red, his limbs trembling with anger and outrage. During the last few seconds the *patrix* had fallen silent, his agitated motion stilled, his eyes closed. Now the holy man began chanting, a low disquieting murmur that seemed to darken the space, to thicken the air like an unsavoury, cloying perfume. The unintelligible plaint grew in intensity, turned into a funerary dirge. A lament for their deaths. It was hypnotic, insinuating its rhythms of despair into Sav's brain.

The chant stopped abruptly; Ruen's eyes snapped open below the arc of his bony brow, swung wildly around until they seemed to catch on Sav. The *patrix*'s irises dilated, then shrunk to pinholes, and he swallowed, the goitre in his neck travelling along his throat like a burrowing animal. He raised himself up on one elbow, straining against the mesh. "I have sinned," he whispered, staring directly at Sav. His tone was filled with righteousness—and self-loathing. "Forgive me," he said, extending his hands through the webbing.

Sav turned and hauled himself up to the flight deck.

Josua was strapped in the pilot's seat, his back square to Sav, tapping steadily at the keypad. The lights of the bridge had been dimmed, and in the centre of the flight deck the display had been activated. At head height, on the opposite side of the bridge, a planet—the Hub, Sav assumed—was represented by a blue point. It orbited a binary star system, two needlepoints of brilliant light that dazzled his vision and made his head ache. In the few moments he'd been on the bridge, the double suns seemed to have shifted their positions slightly. At first he thought his perceptions had been addled by the fever; then he realized that the stars *were* moving. Their orbital period could be no more than a few hours. Although he had understood before the enormous velocities at which these binaries whirled around each other, seeing motion on this scale staggered him. It was the reason Nexus had built the Hub here: to use the gravitational whip of the two stars to fling their vessels into the void like rocks from an unimaginably powerful slingshot.

Sav pushed off from the ladder and drifted toward the navigator's station, still riveted by the spectacle. With an effort, Sav lowered his eyes, focused his attention on Josua's hunched figure across the cabin. Raising his free hand to his forehead to shade against the luminosity of the stars, Sav cleared his throat. Josua seemed oblivious to his presence—and unaffected by the plague. He continued tapping the keyboard as if nothing was amiss.

"Josua," Sav croaked in a hoarse voice, his lips numb and difficult to work.

Josua's hands stilled; he swivelled his seat around. The front of his coveralls was darkened by perspiration. His face and arms shone in the light of the stars. But it was his eyes that left no doubt about his condition: they seemed to have grown in Josua's skull, the iris and cornea merging into black undifferentiated circles, glittering feverishly.

"Hebuiza's watch," Sav said raising his wrist with an effort. "It says we still—"

"No." The double suns of Nexus were reflected momentarily as sharp points in his febrile eyes. "It's wrong."

Sav stared at the timepiece, his thoughts sluggish. He blinked back sweat. "Hebuiza miscalculated?"

Josua fixed Sav with his dark gaze. "No."

"I don't understand. . . ."

"There's no more fuel left," Josua said, as if that explained everything.

Sav's head throbbed. It made no sense. "Why would Yilda and Hebuiza want to mislead us? Why would they endanger our mission? By the time we get to the Hub we'll be too sick to negotiate!"

"Did it ever occur to you," Josua said quietly, "that Yilda might not be interested in the cure."

It took a moment for the words to sink in. "Why?" he managed to say, his voice choked into a whisper.

"Who knows?" Josua answered indifferently. "Perhaps Yilda wanted to use us as a distraction. To keep Nexus occupied." He gazed at the blue marble of the Hub that hung like an unsocketed eye, staring at them. His features tightened. "And now that we've outlived our usefulness, he'd just as soon have us dead." He spoke, it seemed, more to himself than to Sav, his voice taking on a distant quality. "Tie up all your loose ends. That's the way I'd have done it."

In the few moments Sav had been there, the suns had continued their tight orbit; the slightly duller secondary now hung to the right of Josua's head, creating stark, unreal shadows on the left side of his face. "The bomb," Sav said, squinting beneath the light of the star. "Did you plan that together?"

Josua swung his gaze back on Sav, the eye on the unshadowed side of his face brimming with fever, his other a darkened, hollow socket. Thin lines of perspiration rolled down his temples, dripped from his jaw onto his collar bone, and soaked into the ragged collar of his coveralls. He smiled. "Bomb? What bomb?"

"I know about the reserve tank." Articulating his thoughts had become increasingly difficult. Sav spoke slowly, deliberately. "I know what you did down there."

Josua pursed his lips and stared at his feet, as if he was considering the whole question of the bomb abstractly, the way he might consider a problem in mathematics. Sweat fell from the tip of his nose to spatter on the deck. "You didn't, ah, disturb it, did you?"

Sav said nothing.

Josua raised his head until both his eyes were visible. Sav felt himself slipping into the power of Josua's gaze; panic clawed at his chest, and he began to believe that Josua had the ability to reach down inside him, to extract the answer to his question. Although Sav knew it was his own illness befuddling his senses, the illusion was overpowering. He heard a whimper, realized it had emerged from between his lips.

Josua barked out a laugh, relinquished his gaze. "I didn't think you had."

Sav felt his face flush; embarrassment and anger heated his cheeks. His mind seemed to clear. "The bomb," he said. "Was it part of Yilda's plan from the start?"

"No," Josua answered matter-of-factly. He was calm, dispassionate, as if what Sav thought was no longer of concern to him. "I didn't tell Yilda, but I'm sure he had ways of finding out. Of stopping me if he had a mind."

"Then he wanted you to go to the Hub. To detonate the ship."

"It would seem so."

"*Why?*"

No answer.

"Yilda wanted revenge?" Sav paused. "Like you?"

Josua met Sav's gaze, but still said nothing.

"You never intended to negotiate for a cure, did you?"

"No." Josua wiped the film of perspiration from his brow onto his bare arm.

"And the others," Sav said. "What about them?"

"The others?" Josua appeared distracted, puzzled.

"Liis!" Sav blurted. "What about her?"

Shrugging, Josua said, "She's with Yilda, isn't she?"

The knot of nausea in Sav's stomach tightened. *She's with Yilda. The cabin seemed to tilt, to swing in a long, gut-wrenching arc. What chance does she have? That's what he means. To Yilda, she's as dispensable as we are. She might be dead already.*

"It's too late for them," Josua said, as if he was explaining a simple equation to Sav. "It was too late for all of us before we returned to Bh'Haret." His expression became sad, wistful. "Only you were too blind to see it."

Sav shook his head.

"You've got to understand," Josua said, leaning forward against his harness, smiling weakly. He opened his hands, spread his arms wide. "All we have left is this final gesture. Our own Dissolution." He laughed, turning his gaze toward the nose of the ship, toward the Hub. "They'll remember us." Josua's face was a white, bloodless oval; his eyes showed as flat black crescents between pale lids, as if the sockets were empty. He looked more sculpted than human. "They'll remember Shiranda." The lesser star now hung directly above his head, a fiery crown. "I'm afraid I can no longer trust you," Josua said. "Can I?" Reaching in the right pocket of his coveralls, he withdrew a pistol. Sav recognized the grey tape wrapped around its grip, the thick loop of its trigger guard, the nick on the top of its stubby barrel. It was the gun he had pointed at Josua back on Bh'Haret, then heaved into the bushes below the landing pad when he learned that they carried the plague. Josua must have recovered it after Sav had fled into the forest.

Sav pressed himself back into his seat, raised his hand to block out the light of the star. Fear squeezed the air from his lungs.

"You see my dilemma, don't you?" Josua's voice sounded almost gleeful now. "We're working at cross purposes. It would be foolish to give you the opportunity to ruin everything." His finger caressed the trigger lightly, lovingly.

Darting afterimages from the star clouded Sav's vision. "The code sequences. You need them—"

"I needed you to get this far. What does it matter if Yilda executes a Speaker or two? Perhaps losing a few of their precious Speakers will make the Pro-Locutors more cautious about interfering with me."

Sav's fevered head throbbed; sweat trickled into his eyes. The light from the star leaked around his fingers, burned into his mind, lodged there, making coherent thought impossible. Yet Josua stared at him with his eyes wide, unperturbed. How? How could he do that, without shading his eyes from the blinding light of the star?

"Perhaps it will be better for you this way. Sparing you the brunt of the plague."

Sav stared at the barrel of the pistol, his head spinning. There must be something he could do. Although he held himself in the navigator's chair, he hadn't fastened the harness. He was free to move. He glanced at the ladder below decks. Even if he didn't have the proper angle to propel himself directly there, he could kick upwards to the bulwark overhead, spin and launch himself toward the semi-circular opening. The whole thing would take three or four seconds, leaving Josua ample time for several close-range shots. But if he could distract him . . .

"Forget it," Josua said. "You'd never make it."

Sav swallowed. The stars seemed to intensify; they bored into his brain relentlessly, dizzying him. *I can't think with those damn things there!* Sav thought. He was suddenly visited by an image of himself dying under the painful brilliance of the double suns, his final thoughts scattered and incoherent. It was stupid, that at this moment all he could think about was those damn stars. He wanted to turn around and flick off the display, but was afraid Josua might react to the movement. He cursed the stars, the way they befuddled his thoughts and distracted him—

The stars!

Josua raised the gun, aimed it dead centre at Sav's chest.

"You can't shoot me!" Sav blurted. "You'll breech the hull!" He drew himself back, as if he was cowering, and pressed his feet on the floorplate to tilt his seat away from Josua and toward the panel. With his free hand he reached behind the couch, groped for the edge of the board, found it.

The snout of the gun wavered slightly. "That possibility had occurred to me." Josua stared at Sav's chest, then at the bulwark behind.

"There's nothing I can do to get at the bomb," Sav said quickly. "You said so yourself." He inched his hand up onto the board, felt for the keypad, moved his fingers toward the key that would zoom the display. One press would enlarge the projection at the centre of the bridge by a factor of two—unless the operator had keyed in a larger value. Then it would double that. "I can't do you any harm. Let me be here at the end." Clearly Josua had zoomed the display by at least an order of magnitude from the last time Sav called it up, but had he left that value active? Zooming up the suns by a factor of two might not be enough to blind him, to make his aim uncertain. "If I'm going to die," Sav said, "I want to be there. With you and Ruen. You owe me that at least." Without taking his eyes from Josua, he moved his index finger three keys over, then hesitated. Three? Or was it four? He couldn't remember.

"No," Josua said with resolve. "There are too many ways you might mess things up." He shrugged. "The hull's pretty thick. I think I'll take my chances."

Sav's fingertip settled on the fourth key. He pictured the symbol on it, a small square on the left side with an enlarged square on the right. But his finger seemed uneasy, to suggest this wasn't the familiar key. Perhaps he'd been right to start, that it was the third key....

"I'm sorry, Sav." A look of pain flickered over Josua's features, as if he were truly saddened by what he was about to do. But, whatever misgivings he might have had, the gun never wavered. His finger tightened on the trigger, and the hammer drew back the tiniest distance. "I'm sorry," he said again.

Sav jammed his finger down hard onto the fourth key; at the same instant he kicked himself free of the couch. The suns at the centre of the display exploded in a blinding light and he snapped his eyes shut. The report of Josua's weapon followed almost immediately, and pain seared Sav's lower leg, like someone had hammered him with a metal pipe across the shin. Gasping, he spun out of control, crashed into a panel and caromed off. Banging into a bulwark, he began rolling along its surface. Another crack of the gun, but this time the bullet must have gone wide of its mark. With his eyes still screwed shut, Sav flailed with his hands, caught something in his right: the familiar metal cylinder of a handhold. He fought the bright spur of pain that had lodged in his skull and opened his lids a crack. His vision roiled from the shock of light and the intensity of his wound. Through his slitted eyes he saw that he had been thrown a quarter turn around the bridge. He hung above the blazing incandescence of the double suns, the opening below decks now hidden on the other side of the projection. Another shot rang out; flecks of metal fragments from the bulwark behind peppered his neck like tiny, burning needles.

"Damn you!" Josua screamed and fired again. This time the bullet crashed into a display panel below Sav's feet, splintering it with a loud crack. Josua's vision was clearly still dazzled. Two more shots in rapid succession, two more misses, followed by a string of oaths. Shutting his eyes tight, Sav watched the lambent afterimages burn down his vision like shooting stars. He waited breathlessly for the next shot. But nothing came.

Sav held his breath. The agonizing wound in his leg had brought momentary clarity back to his thoughts and sharpened his senses. From the shattered panel below his feet came a crackling noise. The smell of burning insulation filled his nostrils. Bracing himself against the throbbing pain in his leg, Sav tried to focus on the sounds of the bridge.

The soft click of a key. A brief pause, and another click. *He's trying to kill the display*, Sav thought. Except this was only Josua's second flight on a longhaul ship. He'd be guessing at the position of the key, wary of pressing the wrong sequence and causing another unexpected result. *Which*, Sav thought, *should give me enough time.*

Pulling himself into a crouch, he rotated his body until his head pointed directly toward the display; he winced as his feet brushed lightly against the bulwark and an intense pain shot up his wounded leg. He ignored it; he had to concentrate. Opening his eyes an infinitesimal amount, he could make out nothing but the dazzling effulgence—and the faintest outline of the bridge lying across that luminosity like a ghostly imprinting. He changed angles slightly, attempting to line himself up so that when he kicked free he'd pass between the panels of webbing, through the center of the display—and end up on the ladder below decks. His shin throbbed, as if in protest of what he was about to do, but he knew this was nothing compared to the pain that was coming next.

Screwing his eyes shut and sucking in his breath, he launched himself toward the heart of display.

Pain tore up from his shin, rammed an electrified pike up his leg and through his torso, driving its tip of agony into the seat of his brain. He screamed, his lungs emptying out. He clamped his jaw shut fiercely, biting down on his tongue to stifle the sound. He was moving across the cabin blindly, unable to change his trajectory.

Josua fired again, but the shot went wide. Falling into the veil of searing white, Sav extended his hands. Even with his eyes shut tight, the light burned into his cornea, illuminating his eyelids redly, silhouetting dark veins in double images that staggered like drunks. Though he knew it was only a projected image, he had subconsciously braced himself for the consuming fires of the suns. But there were no scourging flames, just something warm and sticky that ticked across his hands and face, tangled in his hair, adhering wetly to his scalp. And then he realized he was flying through globules of his own blood.

Sav's vision darkened abruptly, like he'd passed into the umbra of an eclipse. Opening his eyes a crack, he saw he was through the display; the wall swam toward him. Through the glare he made out the shadowy outline of the ladder leading down to the crew quarters. To his right was a smear of colour that must have been the pilot's board. But the light was still so intense it was difficult to make out any detail, to tell whether Josua was facing the display or turned around toward the board. Sav held his breath, prayed that if Josua was looking at the display his vision was still so overloaded that he wouldn't be able to see the figure drifting a few metres to his left. The ladder drew close; Sav stretched out his fingers to catch at the nearest rung—

The display winked out.

Ahead, the brilliant wall had degenerated into a confusing wash of murky colours and tricky afterimages. Sav waved his hands frantically, trying to feel for the rung that had seemed only scant millimetres away. The palm of his left hand smacked against a rung; he grasped it reflexively, swung his other hand around and seized a side rail. He used his momentum to let his legs swing up and over his head so that he would face down, toward the opening below decks. His good leg thumped against the upper part of the ladder; he fought his momentum, holding his wounded leg rigidly to try to prevent it from striking the wall. But he was only partially successful, and the impact caused another ripple of pain. He grunted, biting off the sound as soon as it had escaped him.

"I heard that!" Josua said, his voice triumphant.

Sav gripped the ladder tightly, not daring to move a muscle, not daring to breathe. The fiery afterimages had begun to subside, and the dark blotches were beginning to resolve themselves into the familiar objects of the bridge. Now Sav could make out Josua's blurry outline, the snout of the gun weaving back and forth like a snake.

"I know you're over there. I can see you."

Sav knew he was lying, for Josua's head was upthrust and moving like that of a blind animal trying to catch scent of its prey. If he was certain of his target he would have fired already. *He can't have many shots left*, Sav thought. *One, maybe two. If he fires and misses, then he knows I'll be out of here before he can reload the magazine. That was why he's hesitating. He's waiting for me to give myself away by moving.* But, Sav realized, it didn't matter: the longer he stayed here, the better Josua's vision would become. He had to move. Tightening his grip, he prepared to launch himself toward the crew quarters.

From below decks Ruen swam up the ladder right toward Sav.

"The Dissolution is at hand!" The *patrix*'s deep voice was euphoric. "Rejoice!" Foul breath wafted into Sav's face as the holy man pulled himself so close their noses were almost touching. Ruen's eyes were wide and glassy, his brow beaded with sweat.

"*Ruen*," Josua shouted. "*Where's Sav?*"

"What?" the holy man sounded confused. The urgency of Josua's words seemed to penetrate his ecstasy. "Why, he's here," Ruen answered, as if he were mildly surprised at the question. "Right above—"

Sav grasped the holy man's thin arms and wrenched them from the ladder; he jerked the astonished *patrix* upward, simultaneously propelling himself down, twisting their bodies round so that the holy man rotated toward Josua.

"Blasphemer!" he screamed as Sav's head passed behind his knees. "You shall be afflicted for daring to—"

The crack of the gun cut off Ruen's words. Sav felt the holy man's body butt lightly against his and heard the sudden exhalation of breath, a huge gasp as if Ruen's lungs had emptied out in massive deflation. Then a wet, strangled noise.

Sav craned his head back; his vision had cleared enough to see the holy man still moving upward, his bony jaw open. Ruen grasped his neck in both his hands as though he was trying to choke himself. His eyes were wide with disbelief. From between his fingers a long elastic rope of blood leaked out, surface tension breaking the red line into small globes that followed in his wake in a wobbly procession.

Sav's momentum carried him into the crew quarters; above, he could hear Josua cursing, shouting incoherently at Ruen. Drifting through the crew quarters to the hangar deck, Sav caught at a rung on the ladder, righted himself in front of the airlock leading to the dropship bay. He hammered his fist against the airlock button and the door recessed into the wall. Pulling himself through quickly, he spun around and pressed the button to seal the airlock. A moment later he was in the dropship, dogging the hatch and then strapping himself into the pilot's seat.

He looked around the tiny cabin.

When he'd fled the bridge his only thought had been to reach the safety of the dropship. Until this moment he'd been running on adrenaline, without any goal other than this one. But here he was, alone, wounded and in the grip of a fever. His thoughts slowed, becoming muddy. *Maybe Josua was right. Maybe killing me would have been a favour.* Was this to be the end, cowering in the dropship, waiting for Josua to detonate the bomb?

No! Sav thought, his fevered brain aching. *Lien said she'd help. She promised.* She was all he had left. If he could rescue her, get away from the ship—

Leaning over the board, he punched in the sequence to power up the engines and open the dropship bay doors. The pumps beneath the decks hummed as they began sucking out atmosphere. It would take twenty seconds to complete the cycle. He glanced down at his wound. There was a blood-stained tear below his knee; a splinter of white bone protruded. He thought he was going to be sick.

"Sav?" Josua's voice piped in over the speaker in the instrument panel. "Can you hear me? I'm watching you on the dropship bay monitor."

Swallowing back his pain, Sav focused on the control panel. Green lights came on across the board as system checks finished successfully. The sound of the pumps had faded with the dwindling atmosphere, and now the final light winked on, indicating pressure equalization. The outer doors split revealing a scattering of alien stars. Sav disengaged the magnetic locks holding the dropship to the deck. A trail of small red spheres drifted in front of his nose; Sav wondered briefly how much blood he had lost.

Halfway open, the doors stopped. "Nice try," Josua said, as the doors reversed their course. "But you should have known I could override your commands from here."

Sav rammed the control stick forward and the craft lurched ahead on the power of its tiny attitude jets, the blunt nose jamming itself into the rapidly diminishing space. Metal screeched on metal, and the whole dropship vibrated so violently in the maw of the airlock doors that Sav thought it would shake apart. The craft canted slightly as the doors pushed together; the cabin was filled with the groans and creaks of stressed metal. If the integrity of the dropship's hull hadn't already been compromised, it would be shortly. In desperation Sav wrapped his hand around the slider that controlled the thrust of the main engines. "Stop the doors!" he shouted over the squealing metal, "Or I'll kick in the engines!" Fired in the bay at full thrust, the ship's exhaust would likely tear *Viracosa* apart.

"After all you've done to prolong your miserable life for a few more hours?" A rivet popped in the bulwark behind Sav and shot across the cabin; in seconds the ship would buckle. "I don't believe you have the nerve."

Sav felt lightheaded, detached, as he pushed the slider to half power and the engines came to life. The craft shuddered and seemed to rear up and strain against the door, widening the gap slightly. Sav focused on the stick, blocking everything else out, trying to keep the ship from slewing off to the side and spinning in a circle like a fiery pinwheel, turning the bay into a deadly inferno. When he felt he had control, he switched the screen to the aft camera: a gout of yellow flame was erupting from the rear of the ship and scouring the inner bulwark, heating the metal until it glowed red and warped.

Josua was screaming hysterically, like he was the one being seared by the flames. "Stop! You're ruining everything!"

"Let me go."

"We'll *die* of the plague! Don't you understand? This is our last chance!"

Everything seemed unreal, dreamlike. Josua's irrational ranting;

the obstreperous control yoke trying desperately to twist itself free of his grip; the roar of the engines, humming and vibrating in the hollow of his bones. He eased the thruster forward a quarter of the way and the nose of the dropship edged ahead half a metre, widening the gap. Then the motor controlling the doors must have overloaded, for the ship lurched forward and, with a horrific screech, burst free of the bay.

The partially melted lens on the aft camera showed a distorted image of *Viracosa* rapidly receding.

"Come back, you thief!" Josua shrieked. "You don't deserve to die with us! You don't deserve to die for Bh'Haret!"

"None of us does," Sav answered, cutting the circuit.

A second later, the request light began to blink furiously. Sav stared at it, fascinated. Confused thoughts drifted in and out of comprehension like the globes of blood that slid in and out of view. He looked at the screen: *Viracosa* was no thicker than his small finger; on its nose a tiny sliver caught the light from the double stars, flashed it brightly. Abruptly, he remembered the Speaker.

Killing the engines, Sav pulled the control yoke sharply; the attitude jets fired, swinging the nose of the craft back toward *Viracosa*. Stars wheeled past, and the brightness of the binary suns swung into view. He raised his arm in reaction, but lowered it a second later. The double stars were still far away, only thumb-sized and dimmed by the polarised windscreen, so that they seemed a pale imitation of what he'd experienced on the bridge. He looked for *Viracosa*, spotted it dead centre, a thin line against the dark backdrop. He pushed the slider forward and the engines kicked in, slowing the dropship, then reversing his course. In moments he began closing.

Ignoring Josua's flashing request light, Sav keyed in the Speaker's frequency, pressed the transmit key. "Lien?"

"*Sav!*" She sounded nervous, but not panicked. "*What is happening? The tube was shaking and I thought it was going to be torn off.*"

Another flight of blood obscured his vision. He batted the bubbles away. He could make out the emergency tube more clearly, a silvered cylinder thrust in front of *Viracosa* and hanging over the double suns of Nexus like an executioner's gleaming blade.

"I'm coming," he said.

"What? What do you mean?"

"I'm hurt." He stared at the protuberant bone, wondering if he should try to push it back inside his leg.

"You are talking strangely, Sav. Are you all right?"

"Yeah," he said, wiping the perspiration off his forehead. "No." He hesitated. "I'm here. What do you want?"

"Sav! You contacted me!"

He tried to focus. "I'm in the dropship." He articulated each word carefully so that she would understand. He craned his neck, watched *Viracosa* draw near. "I can see you."

"You can see me?"

"Yeah," he said, annoyed. What was wrong with her? Why couldn't she understand?

"You've left Viracosa*?"*

"Uh huhn," His tongue thick and unwieldy in his mouth. "I'm coming to get you."

"How? How are you going to do it?"

"Josua shot me." It seemed like something he should share with her. "And Ruen's dead, too, I think. Josua wants to kill all of us," Sav said, then thought to add, "You more than anyone."

"Listen to me, Sav! You are coming to get me. Remember?"

"Oh. Yeah."

"How?"

Sav tried to concentrate, but everything seemed distant and uncertain. "In the dropship." Suddenly he felt ashamed: he had no idea what he was doing, why he was here. "I don't know," he said, tears burning his eyes. "I don't know anything."

"Listen, Sav. I can blow the air lock," Lien said. *"The decompression should throw me free of the tube. My suit has a weak propulsion system, but enough so I can guide myself to your craft if you're near. But I will not be able to catch you if you go past. You must open the hatch and wait for me. Do you think can do that?"*

"No," Sav said, wiping his eyes. "There's no airlock on the dropship."

"Are you wearing a suit?"

Sav looked down. "No."

"Do you have one aboard the ship?"

Sav craned his head; clipped to the back wall of the cabin was the emergency EVA suit. "Yeah."

"Put it on. Then give me the word and we will blow our hatches at the same time and try to get clear before Josua realizes what we're up to."

"Sure," Sav said. It seemed easier to agree than to argue with this insistent woman. He undid the harness and pushed himself toward the rear wall.

The suit was split down the front. It seemed to take forever for him to work both his legs inside, even though his shin had ceased troubling him. At one point he snagged the protuberant bone on a fold in the material and had to free it with numb fingers. After a time (how long had it been?) he managed to accomplish the immensely difficult task. He put his arms into the sleeves, sealed the inner suit and pressed the outer seam closed. Swinging the helmet down over his head, he gave it a quarter turn and pressed the compression snaps down with his thumbs. The display came up, overlaying the bottom third of the visor. It showed the suit was powered up and ready. He felt proud of himself, even though he wasn't sure why he had to put on the suit.

Something was different.

At the far right of the suit display, unfamiliar green digits popped up, a four followed by a colon and then two zeros. Like a stopwatch, the value began counting down like a stopwatch. Sav frowned, puzzled over the curious addition, wondering why it looked familiar. There was some connection he knew he should make, but his brain seemed addled and useless. *A stopwatch.* Counting down like the watches Hebuiza and Yilda had made them, only this one didn't have days, just minutes and seconds. Already several seconds had passed; the display read 3:55.

He remembered the plague, the Speakers. Looking up, he saw

he was closing on *Viracosa*. Obscuring the rest of the ship were the bulbous feeder tanks. He remembered the bomb.

The trigger, Sav thought, trying to marshal his jumbled thoughts. *This suit is the trigger.* Maybe Josua planned to abandon *Viracosa* at the last minute so that he could admire his handiwork from space. Watch the destruction sealed inside this suit before he, too, drove the dropship into its last fiery re-entry. Suddenly Josua's words made sense: taking the dropship had made Sav a thief, stealing Josua's means to detonate the bomb. The clock had ticked down to three and a half minutes.

Pushing away from the wall, Sav drifted back to his seat and grabbed the drag bar fixed to the edge of the control board. "The bomb," he said after fumbling the suit's cable into the board. His words were slurred. Speaking had become difficult. Outside, the slender emergency tube now drifted past. "I . . . I think it's going to blow in three minutes." He cut the engines, fired braking jets. The dropship slowed.

Lien said something Sav couldn't make out, something that sounded angry and frightened. Then she spoke in a calm, measured tone. "*You must open the hatch for me now, Sav.*"

"Yeah," he said, but he wasn't sure what question he'd just answered. He was confused again. It was hard to concentrate. He felt cold and clammy. Like all longhaulers, he'd taken the requisite first aid course, and he recognized the symptoms: *I'm going into shock.* Staring at his leg, he thought sadly, *I should have put a tourniquet on it.* But there hadn't been time. There was never enough time for anything.

Sweat slipped from his forehead and drifted free, clung in tiny round domes to the inside of the visor. Darker, opaque liquid also hung there. *Blood.* He shivered. What was he supposed to do? The hatch. Hadn't she said something about the hatch?

Sav reached forward and keyed in the commands, his clumsy fingers moving automatically, trained from long habit. An emergency alarm blared. He turned around and could see the hatch breaking, the flare of atmosphere being sucked into the void, the rush of bloody droplets being stretched into thin lines that raced toward vacuum. "D . . . done," he said.

"*What's done. You were supposed to . . .*"

Invisible hands clutched at Sav, dragged him back toward the hatch; the cable he'd plugged into the board pulled taut.

"*. . . .tell me first—*"

The connector snapped free, cutting off Lien. Sav tumbled backwards into starstrung darkness. The heavens wheeled around him.

Viracosa came into view, arced across his line of sight, and disappeared. As it swung past Sav for the second time, he saw the hatch on the end of emergency tube spin away silently, a plume of white gas racing after. Impossibly, a naked woman shot from the tube, a miraculous creature of the stars. The edge of her skin was alive with dancing fire. *She burns!* Sav thought. He marvelled at the sight, felt disappointment when she spun from view. *An angel*, he thought.

On his third spin she was nowhere to be seen. In the corner of his visor, the clock showed ninety seconds. *Goodbye*, he thought forlornly. He shut his eyes.

Something seized his arm in a grip so fierce it made him wince. *Go away*, he thought. *Leave me alone*. The pressure persisted.

Reluctantly, he opened his eyes. The dizzying spin of the heavens had stopped. A shadowed face pressed close to his, a faint glow sketching its outlines.

"Liis?"

The figure turned and the shadow fell away; he could see the face was too round, the features too fine, for it to be Liis. It was another woman.

"Your suit," Sav mumbled, stifling his disappointment. "You need a suit. . . ."

Her dark eyes burned with anger and determination, a look that scalded Sav like a brand. The woman wrapped her arms around his chest, cutting off his breath. Sav felt his momentum shift, like he was caught in a current, a strange, otherworldly tug, sharp and persistent. Together, he and the strange woman rotated until they faced a small craft, its rear blackened and its nose battered. The *dropship*, Sav thought, amazed at how different it appeared from outside. They accelerated toward the open hatch.

Before he could fully fathom what was happening, they were inside and in front of the control panel. A connect light on the panel blinked furiously.

"Maybe we should answer that," he mumbled.

But the woman didn't seem to hear him. Instead, she clutched at something near Sav's waist, raised the cable and examined its connector. Sav watched as she began jamming it into the half-dozen jacks of similar size on the board.

With her third stab, a voice erupted in his ear. "—the thrusters! We have to get out of here!"

"I know you," Sav said slowly.

"The thrusters!"

Was that all she wanted to do? Sav reached forward, tried to move the slider up, but it had grown heavier, seemed stuck in its slot. The woman closed her hand over his and pushed hard; the control slid forward easily. The engines fired, and Sav felt himself being dragged back by the acceleration.

Lien managed to grasp both the drag bar in front of the control board and the arm of Sav's suit. She pulled him toward her with an amazing show of strength, then bowed her head over the control board. "How much time?" she asked without looking up.

Sav hardly heard the question; the grip of acceleration had brought the full weight of his wound back upon him. His leg seemed to twist back agonizingly under the stress, and his brain crackled with wrathful bolts of pain. He cried out; tears streamed from his eyes. He felt his limbs flailing, and realized he wanted to get Lien's attention, to let her know how he was too hurt to answer a silly question. But she was intent on the board, her head bowed over the monitor. "How long?" she repeated.

Sav tried to focus; several red droplets had been pulled across the inward curve of his faceplate by the force of acceleration, leaving bloody smears. Others stretched and snapped free, to patter against his face. His eyelids were stranded with red. He tried to ignore everything, to focus on the orange digits. "F . . . five s . . . seconds . . ." His teeth chattered and his whole body seemed to shake uncontrollably. "I think . . ."

She turned, her features twisted up in an irate expression.

But when she looked him fully in the face, her own paled. The anger in her eyes fled; the expression they now held seemed to be a mix of sadness and pity.

"Sav, I'm sorry."

Over her shoulder he could see the magnified image of *Viracosa* on the screen.

She hooked her legs around the arm of the pilot's couch and drew him in, clutching him tightly to her breast. Light flared on the monitor screen, eradicating *Viracosa*. One moment it was there, hanging against a backdrop of stars; the next it had been consumed in a glaring, featureless oblivion.

"Shock wave," she said. "Hold on."

Consciousness returned bit by bit.

At first Sav thought he was back on *Ea*, waking from stasis on the return leg to Bh'Haret. In the background an alarm klaxon wailed mournfully, and he felt the same heaviness of limb, the same sluggishness of thought that accompanied revival. *A dream*, he thought, his heart beating hopefully. *It was a dream!* But was he waking to the beginning of the same nightmare?

"You're conscious." It was a woman's voice, vaguely familiar.

Sav opened his eyes, blinked away the cobwebs. He was strapped into the co-pilot's couch; a naked woman sat next to him in the pilot's seat, studying him intently. She looked grave, her mouth pursed and her brows drawn down in thought. Lifting her hand, she placed it on his forehead.

"No!" Sav said, struggling weakly to push her hand away. "The plague!"

"It's all right," Lien said, corralling his hands in hers, moving them back to his sides. "I do not believe I am in any danger." She returned her palm to his head, smoothing his brow. "Or at least no immediate danger. Nor are you. You have been unconscious for twelve of your hours. Your fever has passed."

It was true that he felt sharper, his thoughts clearer than they had been in days. Just as Yilda had told him he would. "I'm in remission. The fever will return."

"We will be picked up shortly by another vessel. It will have the facilities to cure you."

"*Viracosa*, Josua," Sav said, remembering the blazing light on the screen.

"Dead."

Dead? Sav thought. It seemed unreal.

"When you sealed your suit it set off the trigger for the bomb. We were lucky," she added. "The brunt of the shock wave hit us directly from behind. The engines and shielding plates protected us. I was not sure your primitive technology would stand up to the blast, but it did—for the most part. You will still need treatment for radiation sickness. My skinsuit can only do so much in the way of regeneration."

Sav stared down at his body. He was naked—except for an almost imperceptible shimmer that covered his skin from the neck down. Yet he could feel nothing. Not even the pain of his broken leg. Although the bone still protruded, his shin was amazingly quiescent. And the bleeding had been staunched. In fact, his whole body was as pink and clean as if he had just stepped from a shower. "You put your suit on me," he said.

"Your need was greater than mine," Lien said simply.

"My friends," Sav said. "At the relay station. What happened to them?"

"We do not know. After they were told about the bomb detonating, they severed contact."

"You mean they killed the hostages."

"Yes," she said softly. "We think that is the case. Several were executed immediately, and we have had intermittent contact from others since, those not initially taken hostage. It seems they are now being hunted."

Sav watched her for signs of anger, for the flash in her eyes that would betray her hatred and desire for revenge. But she showed nothing—except, perhaps, for a hint of sadness.

"The Pro-Locutors say they cannot understand why the hostages were silenced. They claim they would have given you what you wanted."

"Do you believe that?"

"I think they are telling the truth."

"It makes no sense," Sav said. "Why would Yilda execute the hostages when it was our only bargaining tool?"

"The Pro-Locutors think he may have been mad, like Josua." She paused. "And there are also whispers of other things."

"What things?"

"Rumours. Things I have overheard. They would be meaningless to you. They don't mean much to me."

"Tell me."

Lien shrugged. "There is talk that the lost Brother has returned. The one consumed by the Twins."

Where had he heard that before? Then Sav remembered the story Yilda had told them. "There was a myth," Sav said. "One of the brothers was thrown into a fiery pit for betraying his twin."

"It is not a myth. The details are uncertain, but this much is fact: the Brothers founded and ruled the Polyarchy for several centuries. One plotted an insurrection, but his scheme was exposed before he could bring it to fruition. When confronted with his sedition, the usurper attempted to flee. When he attempted to use the gravity wells of the double suns of the Hub to escape, his vessel disintegrated in the corona of the primary sun."

Sav's head began to ache. "I don't see what that has to do with us."

"Nor do I. I told you, they are rumours. You have to understand the lost Brother has come to symbolize uncertainty and chaos. Whenever the Polyarchy experiences a setback, his name is invoked.

As if he were a hostile anima guiding those who wish to harm Nexus. Losing the relay station is not a minor matter. Though I do not appreciate its full impact, I sense that it may be the most catastrophic event to befall the Polyarchy since its inception. That his spectre would be resurrected is an inevitability."

"Then I'll be killed. In retribution."

She shook her head. "You are not that important to the Polyarchy now. They are ruthless, perhaps, but never wasteful. You may still play a minor role. They wish to distance themselves as much as possible from the destruction of your planet. You will be cured, then released, as a gesture of their goodwill."

"To do what?" Sav said bitterly, not really expecting an answer.

"Whatever you wish." Her words were abrupt, as if something had angered her. "Stay here as the *guest* of the Polyarchy. Or return to Bh'Haret."

Sav was taken aback; he stared at his bare feet, momentarily lost in thought. *Cured and sent home*. Wasn't that what he had struggled for? Only now there was no reason to go back. Bh'Haret was a dead world. He shrugged and looked up to see Lien watching him intently. "There's nothing for me there."

Her expression hardened; a muscle in her jaw twitched.

Sav resented her reaction. Why should she care whether or not he returned home? "You look like *you're* the one who's lost everything," he said, making no attempt to hide the scorn in his voice.

"I have been privy to information that makes me a danger," she said flatly. "Until now, the relay station has been a well-guarded secret. I can tell they regret much of what was revealed to me. At the least they will strip me of the Speaker's gift so that I am a containable problem; more likely is that I will be destroyed to make certain of the containment." As she spoke she turned her head toward the front of the ship and stared off into the distance, as if she could see the Hub and those who sat in judgement upon her. It was strange, but the expression on her face reminded him of Liis. It was the same kind of emptiness that seemed to have hollowed her out when she'd been spurned by Josua. "I am nothing."

Sav felt ashamed. Reaching over, he closed his fingers around hers. "That's not true."

She turned to him. "I wish it were not so. Speakers have no friends but other Speakers. So now I have no friends at all...."

"We're in this together." And, much to his surprise, Sav realized he meant it. In all the time he'd spent with Josua and the others, he'd never been able to say that because he didn't feel it. Perhaps with Liis he might have—only she'd been too distracted by her own problems to appreciate what he could have offered. "You said the Pro-Locutors wish to make a gesture of goodwill toward me," Sav said. "If I were to vouch for you, might they not reconsider?"

"No." She spoke with certainty. "Unless—" She stopped, furrowing her brow. "That is, if you . . ."

"Go on," Sav urged.

"Bh'Haret," she said abruptly. "If you choose to return to your home world, I could go with you." She looked at him, hope brimming in her eyes. "If you make the request, I believe the Pro-Locutors might be persuaded."

"You want to go back to Bh'Haret with me?"

She lowered her gaze. "My choices are . . . limited. Death or exile."

I can save her life, Sav thought. He stared at the Speaker, turning the possibility over in his mind. It didn't seem so farfetched, returning to Bh'Haret with her. Alone, there had seemed little point in going back. But with Lien, the prospect suddenly seemed far less unappealing. . . .

Or was it another trick of the Polyarchy?

Might this be an attempt to send him back to a dead world with a Speaker to keep tabs on him? Had everything since the detonation of *Viracosa*—or perhaps even before—been carefully scripted to work on his feelings of responsibility and guilt? He looked at Lien, but could see nothing in her expression to answer his doubts. Instead, she looked guilelessly into his eyes, waiting for his answer. He returned her gaze as resolutely as he could, although he was frightened by the uncertainty of his belief in her motives.

"I trust you," she said. "We trust each other, remember?"

"Yeah, I guess we have to. Who else have we got?" *Who else, indeed?* he thought. But despite his assurance, the doubt lingered.

"Your *friend* is alive."

"What?" Lien's non-sequitur startled Sav. "You mean Liis?"

"That is what you called the tall woman, is it not?"

"Yes. What's happened? Why—"

Lien raised a hand. "The situation is not clear. There have been deaths among her party. . . . And that is as much I was told. I doubt anything else will be forthcoming now that your ship has been destroyed."

Sav nodded. "I understand." *Liis is alive*, he thought. *Or was twelve hours ago.*

"I thought you would want to know." She paused. "Before you made your decision."

Sav nodded thoughtfully. "Thanks for telling me."

She squeezed his hand, but so lightly it would have been easy to believe he'd imagined it.

Trust. He studied Lien, a Speaker for the Polyarchy of Nexus, a woman who, if they returned to Bh'Haret, would in all probability be his sole companion until death. There would always be the seed of doubt.

But then trust has to begin somewhere, Sav thought. *Doesn't it?*

THE RELAY STATION · 5 DAYS LEFT

The Speaker was Yilda's twin.

As Yilda had shot him, his two comrades had looked up, horror written in their eyes. In that moment Liis registered the similarity of their faces too. She swung around, stared wildly at the other naked, prostrated Speakers. Men and women alike, they all resembled Yilda: soft, rounded features, with thick lips and high, wide foreheads. It was as if she were looking at Yilda as he might have been as a teenager, a middle-aged woman, a man in his late twenties, a plump, aged woman with grey hair....

And she recalled the disturbing familiarity of the barely pubescent woman Yilda had shot when they'd first arrived. That Speaker, too, had shared these same nascent traits. Liis turned back to Hebuiza who showed no surprise at the resemblance the man bore to Yilda. But then Hebuiza's face was like that of a predator who'd caught the scent of blood; the pupils in his eyes were unnaturally dilated and his nostrils flared. His long thin limbs seemed to tremble with barely suppressed energy—although his head showed none of its usual side-to-side swaying motion. Perhaps whatever stimulant Yilda had fed him had rendered him insensible to anything but the hunt. He still pointed the barrel of his gun at the wounded Speaker, as if daring him to make an attempt to escape, even though the man was naked and unarmed, his mind hopelessly scrambled and his blood leaking copiously from the wound in his thigh.

Yilda rolled one of the incapacitated Speakers off the couch and onto the floor, revealing a large brown stain where the Speaker's bowels had emptied. Using his rifle as a lever, he quickly dislodged the other Speaker. To Hebuiza he said, "Bring one of the functioning ones here."

Hebuiza grabbed the young woman by the forearm; she gasped in pain as he pulled her from the arms of her companion and jerked her to her feet. The other Speaker whimpered and hugged the body of his wounded comrade. Hebuiza dragged the woman, stiff-legged with fear, across the floor to Yilda.

"Put her on the couch."

Hebuiza flung her there like he'd have flung a sack of dirty laundry. She pulled herself into a fetal ball, her small frame shaking. Stepping out from the middle of the couches, Yilda barked out a single word in an alien tongue. The Speaker looked shocked. She buried her head completely in her arms. Yilda jabbed her in the ribs with the snout of his rifle and she let out a yelp of pain. Yilda repeated the word.

The Speaker peeked over her arms, her eyes wide with terror. Yilda spoke again, this time touching his rifle and pointing toward the quivering bodies on the floor. The woman glanced at her comrades and shuddered. She returned her gaze to the dark rifle hovering in front of her and made a puling noise. What followed were more incomprehensible words from Yilda in the Speaker's guttural language, then a pause in which he seemed to be waiting for an answer. After a moment of hesitation, the woman responded with a single, quavering syllable. Yilda gestured, sweeping his hand to indicate the length of the couch. Slowly, reluctantly, the woman unfolded herself, stretching out her thin body. Shivering, she closed her eyes, lying perfectly still, her hands curled into tiny fists, her little breasts flattened. She looked small and pale on the wide couch. Yilda rested the snout of his rifle on her temple. "Watch carefully," he said. It took Liis a moment to realize he was speaking to her. To Hebuiza he added, "And you watch *he* doesn't slip away," inclining his head in the direction of the Speaker still hunkered against the wall.

Hebuiza needn't have worried. The male Speaker seemed to be in a state of shock. His eyes were wide with fright; he looked like he was incapable of rational thought, let alone of escape. Liis turned her attention back to the scene at the centre of the room.

The woman's fists had uncurled and her hands now lay flat on the dark material of the couch. Her small breasts rose and fell with her deep, rhythmic breaths. As Liis watched, the Speaker's face went slack, the fear and tension falling away from it like a loose veil snatched by the wind, making her appear even younger. *No*, Liis thought. *Not younger. Ageless*. The transformation continued apace, changed her features from those of a frightened girl to an exquisite creature, half-human, half-ethereal. A soothing white noise, like the hiss of surf, filled the chamber, obliterating all sound but its own. At first Liis thought it emanated from the woman; but then she realized it had no clearly identifiable source, washing over her in waves from different directions. A diffuse glow spread over the woman's skin and her lips parted in ecstasy. Whatever force infused her, she had given herself completely over to it. Amazingly, she didn't flinch when Yilda placed his hand onto the slight swell of her belly.

Liis glanced at Yilda's face—and was shocked to see he had also fallen into the same kind of trance. His face had gone slack. With his hand still on the woman's belly, he seemed to be teetering on the edge of whatever she was experiencing. Yet he was clearly holding himself apart. Liis watched in astonishment.

Several seconds passed. Then Yilda's eyes snapped open. Yanking his hand away from the woman's belly, he slapped her hard across the cheek; her transcendent expression collapsed, the white noise falling away at the same instant. The woman blinked rapidly like an animal stunned by a bright light. Her gaze fell on Hebuiza, then Yilda, and comprehension seemed to return. Fear reappeared on her face; she clasped her arms around her torso and shuddered. But this withdrawal was only momentary. The woman appeared to force herself to uncoil, as if she were determined not to let her fear master her. There was something else in her expression now that hadn't been there before. *Wariness*, Liis thought. *And hatred*. The woman watched the Facilitators through slitted eyes, raising a hand to cover her reddening cheek.

"That," Yilda said, "is how a Speaker looks when she is transmitting. Her masters at the Hub now know we are here, but little else." He turned to Liis. "In close proximity thoughts pass between Speakers as easily as conversation passes between us. That I do not care about. But if they wish to reach light years out, they must focus their energy as she did. You are not to let her or the other one fall into that state. Strike them to break their concentration. If necessary, render them unconscious. But do not kill them. We need both for the negotiation." Yilda pulled the woman from the couch and onto her wobbly legs; he shoved her back toward the male Speaker. The woman stumbled the first few steps and regained her balance. She walked unsteadily back to her companion and lowered herself to the ground with as much dignity as she could muster. Sitting slightly apart from the male Speaker, she pulled her knees up to her chest, clasped her arms around her shins, and glowered openly at the Facilitators.

"There are eleven Speakers still at large," Yilda continued. "Unfortunately, they've been apprised of our presence by our friends here." He nodded in the direction of their captives. "So it may take me a while to track them all down. If you must sleep, set up watches to spell one another while I am gone. And keep an eye on the corridor outside—I don't believe the others will attempt to rescue their friends, but you should be watchful nonetheless." Yilda started toward the doorway.

Liis stepped in front of him, blocking his way.

"You're one of them."

Half a head shorter, Yilda looked up at her. His eyes were flat black in their orbits, cold and lifeless, indecipherable as a corpse's. The snout of his rifle hovered in front of her face. "These sheep?" Yilda snorted. "No."

"Then you were one of them once. That's how you know all the things you do about this place."

"No."

"You told us the Speakers are prisoners here. Maybe you were too. Only you escaped."

Yilda kept his dead, unwavering eyes trained on her. He gripped the stock of his rifle in two hands. "I do not have time for this. We must secure the remaining Speakers. Before they have a chance to do any harm."

"By destroying their minds?"

"Whatever is necessary."

"You don't begin negotiation by killing your hostages!"

"They're not dead," Yilda answered coolly. "They're disabled."

"Their brains have been fried! They're no good to us or anyone else!"

"You wanted a cure, and *I* will provide one. As long as you continue following my orders. Whether these animals live or die should be of no further concern to you."

"The antidote wasn't the reason we came here, was it? You wanted this." Liis swept her hand out to indicate the scattering of bodies. "Revenge."

"*I* am not the one with revenge in mind."

Liis was taken aback. Was Yilda referring to Josua? "What does that mean? Stop talking in riddles."

"You would do well not to try to understand the motives of a superior intellect. Stick to your childish infatuations."

She felt her cheeks flush. "Answer my question!"

"I do not have time for this nonsense." Yilda snapped the butt of his rifle out; it struck Liis dead centre on her cast.

Comets of pain tore across her vision. She reeled, almost losing her balance, staggering to the wall, shoulder and head simultaneously butting its surface. She groped at it with her good arm to keep from falling. Tears burned in the corners of her eyes.

"I need you to guard the hostages." Yilda's words cut through her agony. "But do not try my patience further." Then he was gone, a short, round figure blurring across her line of vision and out the door.

Within moments the pain receded to a dull throb. Liis touched her cast tenderly, as if she could feel, through its rigid plastic layers, the aching flesh underneath. She ran her fingers along the small depression Yilda's rifle butt had made. The cast seemed to have absorbed most of the damage. Flexing, she felt sore ligaments and tendons stretch; pain shivered up her arm and all the way into her neck muscles, but that was only to be expected. She counted herself lucky to have gotten off so lightly.

Thirty paces away, Hebuiza pried the incapacitated Speaker from the grip of his comrades and dragged him, by his ankles, to a spot several metres away. A smear of blood oozed from his wounded thigh, marking their path. The snout of the Facilitator's bolt gun played back and forth over the two remaining Speakers. The woman watched Hebuiza intently with a mixture of anger and fear; the male Speaker seemed to have withdrawn completely, clasping his arms around his chest and rocking back and forth like an autistic child. As Liis watched, the woman shut her eyes and Hebuiza leapt forward, striking her across the cheek with the flat of his palm. The Speaker didn't cry out, she simply opened her eyes again as if she had expected the slap. She stared unrepentantly at Hebuiza.

The woman is learning, Liis thought. *Testing the limits*. Running her finger along the cast again, Liis felt the indentation. She looked at the Speaker's reddened cheek. *We're no different*, she thought with dismay. For the first time Liis realized how little she'd understood. *I've been sleepwalking through this whole thing.* She glanced at the woman, recalled how she'd braced herself for the expected blow. Was that all they could do? Grit their teeth and wait for the hand to fall?

"Bring me the rope in your backpack."

Hebuiza's voice jarred Liis from her stupor. She looked up.

The Facilitator watched her with a contemptuous expression. "We'll tie them up." He turned back to his captives.

Liis thought about refusing. But what purpose would that serve? *None*, she thought morosely. The time for choices had long passed. If she wanted to live, she had to play out the hand she'd been dealt. Reluctantly, she shrugged her shoulders from the straps and let her backpack slide off; its plastic buckles clacked against the floor.

Hebuiza jumped like a startled animal. He spun around to face her again, his bolt gun levelled. His eyes were still wild, but his head swayed slightly again, as if the drug that coursed through his veins was wearing off. Dark circles made his sunken eyes look more recessed; fatigue deepened every line of his face. He swore loudly and narrowed his eyes. "Hurry up," he said, but his voice held a slight tremor.

Liis turned her back on the Facilitator and squatted in front of her pack. Opening the clasps, she loosened the drawstring and began rooting around inside. Just as she felt the coil of rope beneath her fingers, a movement from one of the Speakers caught her attention. They were to her left, where she could see them only in the periphery of her vision. But she was fairly certain the woman watched her. The hair on the back of Liis's neck crawled; she sensed the Speaker's gaze on her, following every movement carefully. Whirling around, Liis stared at their captive.

The woman's head was bowed, her eyes fixed resolutely on the floor.

Liis felt momentarily disoriented. *Did I only imagine it?* She watched the Speaker, but the woman sat perfectly still. Liis returned her attention to her backpack. The sensation of being watched came back almost immediately. Digging down past the rope, she found the tube of explosives. She lifted out the cylinder, angling it so that its burnished silver cap reflected the scene behind her. The image was distorted, but she was certain the woman's head was up again, and that the Speaker watched her. Still clutching the tube, Liis swung around. This time the woman held her gaze. Only for a second. Then she dropped her eyes. But her intent seemed clear. It was an appeal for help.

Liis stared at Hebuiza's intractable figure, still holding his gun rigidly, then back at the woman whose eyes were fixed on her feet. *Look*, Liis wanted to say to her. *I can't even help myself.* The woman's eyes flickered up, caught at Liis and seemed to impale her with their urgency. *Dammit!* Liis thought, breaking contact. *Leave me alone!* She thrust the cylinder into her backpack, outraged at the imposition. *What right do you have to pin your hopes on me?* Liis got up from her crouch, the coil of rope in her hand, and walked toward Hebuiza.

The woman now stared at her openly, her eyes darting between Liis's face and the rope, her panic growing visibly. Liis tried to ignore her. "Here." She shoved the rope at the Facilitator.

Hebuiza pushed her hand away, his eyes never wavering from the hostages. "Tie them up."

Liis stood unmoving, her arm extended, the rope dangling from her fist. She felt the intensity of the Speaker's gaze burning on her.

"*Do it*," Hebuiza said.

"No." Liis dropped the rope.

Hebuiza turned his large, elongated head; his eyes glimmered angrily in his sallow face. "Pick it up."

"Why should I?"

"Because," Hebuiza answered, "if you choose not to, you will have to bear the consequences of Yilda's displeasure."

"Yilda's displeasure?" Liis felt weary beyond belief; but from this weariness sprang a kind of defiant inertia, an unwillingness to move another step in the direction Yilda seemed to be pushing them. "I'm dying," she said. "What the hell else is he going to do to me?"

"You may live yet," Hebuiza said coolly. "If Yilda chooses to let you."

"He's a *Speaker*!" Anger coursed in her veins, gave her a kind of second wind. "He doesn't give a shit whether I live or die."

Hebuiza's expression was impassive. "He's a Facilitator."

Liis shook her head in disbelief. Could Hebuiza be that thick? *No*, she decided, *not after all we've seen*. He had to be lying. Covering up for Yilda. Even though the evidence lay all around them: it was written in the face of every twitching body. "Anyone can see Yilda's one of them," Liis said. "They're clones!"

Hebuiza shrugged. "A coincidental resemblance, perhaps."

"Bullshit!" Liis pointed to the woman who'd been on the couch. "When she was transmitting you could see Yilda was listening in on the conversation. He can hear them. He could probably have transmitted, too, if he wanted. But he didn't, because he doesn't want the Pro-Locutors to know he's here. Because it's not in *his* interest to do so yet." Hebuiza didn't react; if anything, he seemed bored. "That's how he figured out most of them were in this room. It was like following voices. And that's how he's going to track down the rest." Liis paused, drew a deep breath. "You knew right from the start."

"No. Not from the start. I suspected shortly after he arrived. But it was seventeen days before Yilda admitted to me he was a Speaker." Just like that Hebuiza had dropped the pretence. No explanations, no apologies. But then, he was a Facilitator.

"For God's sake, why didn't you tell us?"

"Telling you would have served no purpose. His purposes always were congruent with ours."

"He's a god damned Speaker! How could his purposes possibly be—"

"He is the Brother. The one consumed by the flames."

The Brother? Why did that sound familiar to Liis? Had Hebuiza talked about Nexus and brothers before? She hadn't really been interested—she'd been consumed by Josua. Her thoughts spun maddeningly like a swarm of flies. "I don't understand. . . ."

"This is Yilda's birthright," Hebuiza said, his words strangely muted for once. "He designed this dome. A millennium ago he ordered it built in secrecy. It was a stepping stone in the expansion of the Nexus empire. But shortly after its completion, his Brother accused him of sedition."

Liis searched her memory, recalled the story as Hebuiza had outlined it so long ago: Nexus founded by identical twin brothers, one of whom perished in a fiery death as retribution for an attempted betrayal. Did Hebuiza honestly believe Yilda was that man? It was insane. "You said he died. That he was thrown into a 'fiery pit.'"

"I said there were apocryphal stories. After his aborted insurrection, Yilda attempted to flee. His ship was damaged. But he and his vessel survived its passage through the corona of the Hub's larger sun. His brother, fearing instability in the empire, promulgated false stories about his death. So Yilda became a fugitive."

"You'd believe any kind of crap Yilda fed you," Liis said in disgust.

"How could he have survived all these years? He'd be four thousand years old!"

"And how old are you?" Hebuiza asked quietly.

"What does that have—" Liis stopped in mid-sentence, suddenly understanding Hebuiza's point. In relative time she was thirty-one. But when she added all the down years spent in stasis on previous longhauls—and the five hundred on the trip here—she'd now be over 866.

"And," Hebuiza continued, "you've achieved this ripe old age without the longevity enhancements available to the rulers of Nexus. Yilda told me he also has a subcutaneous nanoskin that makes him virtually invulnerable. Barring an accident, he could, theoretically, live forever. So it's well within the realm of possibility that Yilda could be the Brother. And given his intimate knowledge of Nexus and of the relay station, I can only conclude he is who he claims to be."

Yilda—the founder of Nexus? Liis swore aloud. A small, balding man who spoke in halting sentences. One who looked more like a minor government official than the ruler of an empire? It was all too much to credit. "Why Bh'Haret? Of all the places he could go . . ."

"Fifteen hundred years gave him time to roam the Clusters. He wandered from system to system, bartering for information and technology, trying to keep a low profile since he feared his brother pursued him. When he arrived at Bh'Haret, he found what he'd been looking for: a planet with a technology base high enough for his needs—and low enough to allow him to slip unnoticed into our society. His intention was to become a Facilitator, and exploit that position to release technological information to us far faster than we would have otherwise acquired it. In effect, he wanted to circumvent the edicts of the Ascension Program he and his brother had originally decreed. With the longevity his bio-enhancements would have given him, he hoped to establish a new empire." Hebuiza paused. "Its heart would have been Bh'Haret."

Liis couldn't believe what the Facilitator was telling her.

Hebuiza sighed, as if at the thought of the lost empire. "But the plague changed all that. Despite Yilda's enhanced immune system, he found he was as vulnerable to the infecting Trojan as we were. His organs will no doubt fare better at fighting off the symptoms, but the disease is in him every bit as much as it is in us. He might last weeks or months longer than we would, but eventually, he will succumb. Like us, he had to procure the antidote—by whatever means were necessary."

"And you believe all this?"

"Yes. I ran the antibody test on him myself."

It still didn't add up. "Look around you," Liis said to Hebuiza. She swept her arm out to indicate the twitching figures scattered around the chamber. "He's destroying the minds of our hostages. How the hell are we going to negotiate now?"

"Negotiation was never part of his plan. Only the pretence of negotiation was. Two functioning Speakers are all that we require for that. And when we've finished with them, they will be *disabled* as well." Hebuiza glanced at the two Speakers; the male Speaker shuddered and averted his eyes, but the woman didn't flinch. "Destroying the Speakers here will unravel the communication in the Right Leg Cluster for decades. It will take decades more to undo the damage. It is Yilda's small way of repaying his brother."

"But the antidote—"

"It can be manufactured here."

Liis blinked. Here. The antidote had been here all along. "What—" She stopped abruptly. "Josua," she said, her breath catching. "Did he know about this *other* plan?"

"Josua?" Hebuiza smiled, curving his lips to expose a row of yellowing teeth. "That fool knew nothing. His mission was never anything more than a decoy to keep Nexus occupied."

"The Pro-Locutors will destroy *Viracosa*!" Liis bunched her hands into fists. "You sent them to their deaths!" She took a step toward the Facilitator.

"Josua wanted to die." Hebuiza's words brought her up short. "Or didn't you know about his little scheme for revenge?"

Liis's stomach knotted. Revenge. *I am not the one with revenge in mind*, Yilda had said before he left. "What do you mean?" Her voice shook.

"Josua rigged *Viracosa* as a bomb. He thought we didn't know. But we did. It was a nice, if unintentional, contribution to the plan. We wanted a distraction and Josua provided a better one than we could have hoped for. We will proceed with sham negotiations to allow him time enough to approach the Hub. If the Pro-Locutors let him get that far, he'll blow the ship, and turn that fat fool Sav and that zealot Ruen into a cloud of expanding radioactive gas." The filaments on Hebuiza's head bobbed as he nodded in apparent approval of Yilda's plan. "Do you think that's Dissolution enough to make the *patrix* happy?"

"I . . . I don't believe you."

"As a precaution," Hebuiza continued, his delight seeming to grow with Liis's dismay, "Yilda planted a different strain of the plague on their ship, one whose symptoms should manifest just *before* they reach the Hub. They now only have enough time to reach the Hub and detonate the bomb, but no window in which to betray us. Tomorrow they'll experience the initial fever."

Liis felt sick. *Josua*, she thought. *Why?* But she knew the answer before she'd asked herself the question. It was for Shiranda. Everything had always been for Shiranda. Liis felt like she was coming unglued. A confusing welter of thoughts dizzied her: memories of Josua, of the blindness of her feelings for him. And of Sav. Poor Sav, who of all them was blameless. What had he done to deserve this? She thought about the days they'd spent aboard *Ea*. Then, abruptly her memories were scattered by an image of *Viracosa* transformed into a ball of radioactive gas, spreading the atoms of the three men into cold vacuum. Her future, if she had one, was here, with Yilda and Hebuiza. *I'm alone*, she thought. *I may as well be dead.* Shaking her head numbly, Liis backed away from Hebuiza. She stumbled, catching her heel on her backpack. The contents spilled out over the floor. She watched dully as the cylinder containing the plastic explosives rolled away with a sad, hollow sound.

"Get back here," Hebuiza said, his deep voice booming in the chamber. He levelled his bolt gun and sighted down the barrel at her chest. "And pick up this rope."

Dazed, Liis stared down the narrow bore of his rifle. Without Josua and Sav, the prospect of survival held no appeal. *I could let Hebuiza finish this right now*, she thought. *Put an end to all the lies. All I'd have to do is go for my gun....* She glanced at her backpack, then up at Hebuiza's face. There was a dark light glinting in his eyes, a cruel smile turning the corners of his mouth. His expression was one of anticipation. As if he were hoping she'd go for the gun.

"Well?"

The shock of the understanding hit her like a bucket of cold water. *He wants to kill me*, Liis suddenly realized. *That's why he told me everything he did. To provoke me. But he's afraid of how Yilda will react if he pulls the trigger.* She glanced at the Speakers, knew they were what had kept her alive thus far: mute witnesses who might later describe the scene to Yilda. *He's trying to create the excuse he needs.* A slow, burning anger churned in her stomach, rose into her gorge. *I won't give him that satisfaction*, she thought. *I'll choose my own time and place.* She took a step toward the rope.

For an instant Hebuiza looked surprised; his eyebrows lifted. "That's far enough."

Liis stopped. "Do you want me to tie them up or not?"

Hebuiza seemed confused; perhaps exhaustion, compounded by the effects of the drug Yilda had given him, clouded his thoughts. But he was clearly unprepared for her reaction. He knit his brows in concentration and took two steps back from the rope and toward the Speakers. "Okay," he said, relaxing his posture and letting the bolt gun slip from its ready position at his shoulder. "Pick it up."

Liis moved forward, stopping abruptly in front of the rope.

Hebuiza lifted the weapon again. "Changed your mind?"

Until this instant Liis had been so intent on the conversation that she'd paid little attention to the Speakers. But now she saw the woman had taken advantage of her confrontation with Hebuiza: unnoticed, the female Speaker had risen to a crouch. She stared fiercely at Hebuiza's back, looking like she was preparing to make a rush. With muscles weakened by years of lesser gravity, and weighing at least a third less than the Facilitator, the Speaker would be committing suicide. But, if what Yilda had told them was true, she probably didn't understand that.

"*No!*" Liis's shout was too late. The woman charged. Hebuiza blinked, then swung in the direction of Liis's gaze just as the Speaker reached him.

The woman ducked, coming in low under the barrel of the bolt gun as it discharged with a chest-rattling *whump*; she hit Hebuiza at the knees, locking her arms around his legs. The Facilitator staggered back two short steps, his stubby rifle waving in the air as he wobbled like a top about to fall. Incredibly, he managed to regain his balance. The woman wrapped herself tightly around his legs. The Speaker was too close for Hebuiza to angle his weapon at her. So instead he lifted his gun so the butt hung over the woman's head. He raised it, about to bring the stock down on her skull. The Speaker stared up, her eyes wide.

Liis sprang at Hebuiza. She threw her good shoulder as forcefully as she could into the Facilitator's side, striking him below his ribcage.

At the moment of impact, the Facilitator grunted loudly. They tumbled to the floor, agony radiating from her injury and burning redly in her brain.

She lay on her back, gulping lungfuls of air, the hurting making it impossible to catch her breath. Air whistled between her lips. After a moment, breaths came easier. She blinked several times to clear her vision. Slowly, she eased herself up onto one elbow.

Beside her Hebuiza lay sprawled on the floor, clutching his bolt gun. His head wobbled slowly from side to side, and his eyes were open, but they swam in their sockets as if he was dazed. A thin line of blood leaked from under the bandage on his right temple. It appeared that, unwilling to let go of his gun, he hadn't been able to break his fall and his head had struck the floor, reopening the wound on his temple. At a right angle to him, the Speaker sat on the floor, her legs entwined in his. She appeared unhurt, but looked shocked, incredulous, perhaps, that she was alive.

Liis rolled over onto her knees; the room spun sickeningly around her. Fighting back nausea, she leaned over and tried to pull the bolt gun from Hebuiza's rigid fingers; but he grasped the barrel and stock with an inhuman strength. No matter how hard she tugged, she couldn't pull it free. Her efforts seemed to penetrate Hebuiza's stupor. He blinked, and his wavering eyes fixed on her. He closed them and groaned.

Liis released the weapon and rose onto wobbly legs. Staggering back to her pack she overturned it, emptying its contents onto the floor. She snatched up her laser pistol and pointed it at Hebuiza. She tightened her finger on the trigger. The woman watched her, wide-eyed.

I can't.

The realization shocked Liis.

She couldn't kill. Not even Hebuiza. For all the contempt she harboured for the Facilitator, she couldn't pull the trigger. She opened her hand, let the weapon clatter to the floor.

Hebuiza groaned again; his eyes fluttered.

Liis looked at the Speaker. She still sat entangled in Hebuiza's legs, a bewildered expression on her face. Stumbling over to her, Liis grasped her by the arm. The woman stared at her obtusely. "Come on," Liis said, hauling her to her feet. "We've got to get out of here!" She tried to drag the woman toward the doorway, only the Speaker resisted, jabbering urgently in her unintelligible language, pointing toward the wall. Liis turned. The male Speaker sat there, his face ashen. Centimetres from his head the wall was scarred black from the discharge of Hebuiza's bolt gun.

"Shit!" Liis said.

Releasing the woman's arm, she hurried over to the man. He stared straight ahead, in shock. The right side of his face bore tiny burn marks where the charge from the bolt gun had brushed him. Grabbing him by the shoulder, Liis shook him fiercely. "Get up!"

The man was insensible. He continued to stare at nothing.

Liis slapped him in the face.

He stared at Liis with incomprehension. "Get up, damn you!" Liis raised her hand again. Cringing, he lifted his forearm to ward off the expected blow.

Liis gripped his upper arm. This time the man allowed himself to be dragged to his feet. She seized him by the wrist and pulled him forward. He moved with a dragging reluctance. They hadn't taken more than two steps when Liis stopped abruptly. She let go of the man's wrist.

While Liis had been trying to jar the male Speaker from his state of inertia, the female Speaker had taken the opportunity to pick up the laser pistol. Now she straddled Hebuiza, the weapon was aimed at the Facilitator's temple. Hebuiza's eyes were open, but he appeared to be confused, his gaze wandering aimlessly around the room, his head swaying from side to side. His mouth gaped open and a string of garbled sounds emerged.

Hatred contorted the Speaker's features into a grimace. For an instant, Liis saw a glimmer of Yilda in her expression, a hint of his haughty corruption. She spoke in her strange, harsh language to Hebuiza, a short sharp word. Then she pulled the trigger.

There was the faint hum of the weapon's discharge. Hebuiza's head bounced against the floor; his body spasmed. The woman, teeth bared in a grimace, pulled the trigger again. Only this time she held it down. A thread of ruby light burned into the side of Hebuiza's skull. Skin blackened and boiled away, hissing and sputtering as it vaporized. Small yellow flames licked out around the point of impact. The filaments on the Facilitator's skull melted and ran down onto his cheek and chin in multicoloured rivulets. The stench of burning flesh mingled with the noxious odour of melting synthetics.

For several seconds the laser hummed. The light stuttered, went out, the battery drained. A single, tongue of fire flickered above the scorched crater in the side of Hebuiza's head for a moment, then sputtered and died. Blood pooled around Hebuiza's charred skull like a crimson halo.

Calmly, the woman bent, pried the bolt gun from the Facilitator's lifeless fingers. Walking over to Liis, she extended the pistol. Liis stared at the weapon, unmoving. The woman shoved the pistol into

Liis's chest. Reluctantly, Liis reached up and took it. The barrel was so hot it burned her hand. The woman slung Hebuiza's bolt gun over her shoulder. Grabbing her comrade's arm, she pulled him toward the door.

The pistol weighed almost nothing in Liis's hand. Suddenly disgusted by the sight of the weapon, she shoved it into her pocket.

The Speakers had already passed through the doorway.

Liis scooped up the things that had spilled from her backpack—a dozen food packets, a medical kit, several battery clips for her pistol, and the tube containing the explosives—and shoved them back in. Behind her, the Speakers' echoing footsteps died as the two passed into the antechamber. Liis stuck her arm through one of the straps and swung the pack over her good shoulder.

With only the briefest of backward glances at the Facilitator's corpse, she hustled after them.

The Speakers had already passed through the antechamber, pausing only long enough to grab their simple robes; by the time Liis caught up to them they were in the broad, arching tunnel, the woman dragging the man along by his hand like a mother might have pulled a dawdling child. Liis sprinted to catch up.

"Wait," she gasped, breathless from her short run. She seized the woman's upper arm. "We . . . we've got to talk." The sound of the waterfall filled the space with its omnidirectional hiss, obliterating her words. But the noise made no difference: even if Liis could make herself heard, the Speakers wouldn't understand her language any more than she could understand theirs. Still, she had to make both of them realize the danger of communicating with the other Speakers. If they were to do so, they would lead Yilda right to them. It was a safe bet the Speakers had already informed their comrades what had transpired in the chamber; and, by default, Yilda would also know. Right now he might be on his way back here.

The female Speaker stared at Liis blankly, waiting. Liis chewed on her lower lip, uncertain how to proceed.

The woman's eyes flickered toward her companion. For an

instant the two Speakers locked gazes and something seemed to pass between them. Immediately, Liis gave the woman's arm a sharp tug, breaking into their exchange.

No! She shook her head sharply; but then it occurred to her that she knew nothing of their culture. A head shake might be meaningless to them—or perhaps mean the opposite of what she intended.

The Speaker narrowed her eyes, a spark of anger briefly illuminating them. She turned back to the man, apparently to resume her communication.

Liis tightened her grip. "*NO!*" Her shout was the first sound she had made since entering the tunnel that hadn't been swept away by the roar of the falls.

The woman looked startled.

"Yilda will find us!" she shouted. "You mustn't communicate by thought. You've got to talk out loud!"

The woman frowned at her.

"Watch!" Liis released the Speaker's arm. Touching her hand to the side of her head, Liis tried to mimic the state she had seen the woman fall into when she was communicating over light years. Liis halted her imitation abruptly, shook her head slowly and held her hands up, palms outward and fingers spread wide in warning. The woman didn't react. Liis touched her lips, extended her hand to touch the woman's. The Speaker flinched only slightly at the contact. Liis pantomimed a conversation by moving her lips. There wasn't the thinnest sign of comprehension on the woman's face; the man stared at Liis as if he thought she was mad.

How can I make them understand?

Liis stooped her shoulders, pushed out her stomach and pouted her lips in a parody of Yilda. Her impression must have been halfway good, for the woman immediately stiffened, narrowing her eyes. "Yilda," Liis said.

"*Ilda*," the woman repeated. She spat in disgust.

Gripping an imaginary rifle, Liis crept around the two Speakers as if she were stalking prey. She paused every couple of steps to cup her hand to her ear as if she were listening. Each time she did so, she fell out of character for an instant to point from one Speaker's forehead to the other. Moving away from them, she halted suddenly, as if something had caught her attention; she swung around to face them, her phantom rifle at the ready, aimed right at them. The man whimpered.

The female Speaker stared at Liis. Then her eyes widened in comprehension. Touching her own forehead, and then her companion's, she raised her hand in warning, as Liis had done before.

"Yes! That's right!"

The woman gave a curt nod; but she closed her eyes as if preparing to communicate.

Liis leapt forward and grasped the woman's arm again.

The Speaker's eyes snapped open. She stared at Liis, but without rancour. Gently, the woman pried Liis's hand from her arm. Stepping back, the Speaker touched her forehead and swept her hand out in an arc, a gesture that seemed to indicate the entire dome. She repeated the movement indicating danger.

She wants to pass the warning on to her friends.

The woman stared at Liis expectantly.

"Okay," Liis said, nodding. "Go ahead."

The Speaker shut her eyes again. At once her comrade fixed his gaze on her as if she'd called out to him. The broadcast lasted no more than a second. Before Liis knew what was happening, the woman was pulling at her companion's arm, dragging him down the hall toward the narrow defile where the waterfall spilled. After a few steps the woman stopped. She turned around. *"Upatal,"* she said, tapping her breastbone with a forefinger.

Liis raised her hand, touched her own chest. "Liis." They regarded one another in silence.

Then the woman set off at a trot, tugging the man into motion behind her.

Liis followed the Speakers, moving out of the tunnel and onto the slick-looking floor, past the waterfall and back into the ring of buildings. Inside, ceiling panels flared as soon as the Speakers entered, illuminating the huge room Liis had previously traversed in darkness. The chamber was bigger than she had imagined: it stretched several hundred metres to either side and was perhaps twenty across. Four doors, hung with dark, pleated curtains, led into the room from different directions. Covering the walls were blue and green pastel paintings—portraits, it seemed—in heavy-looking gilt and silver frames; low, wide benches, resembling stunted pews, had been set in front of each work. The paintings seemed out of focus, depicting smudged figures, sitting on chairs or reclining on things that might have been beds or sofas. The figures were so indefinite as to make it impossible to tell if they were men or women. Upatal turned to the door on the right and jogged toward it. Liis started after her—then halted abruptly. The figures, she realized, were moving. They stirred slowly, as if they were submerged in a thick, viscous fluid. Blurred heads turned to follow Upatal's progress, to gape at Liis. *They're alive*, Liis thought with a shudder. She hustled after the Speakers.

Upatal waited for her at far end of the room. A large picture hung over the door there. Within this frame, a gangly figure had risen to its feet from an oversized divan; it extended a turquoise arm, its fingers stretching the surface of the work, tenting the quivering, transparent surface, adding to the distortion of the scene inside. The thing's jaw worked slowly. Its mouth opened, forming a dark hole, the only clearly defined shape inside the frame. Liis averted her eyes as she passed beneath the groping figure and followed the Speakers out of the room.

They entered a small, carpeted chamber furnished with an oval table and scattered chairs. This time the room had only one other exit that appeared to be made of burnished metal. Liis could see no handle. When the Speakers approached, the door melted away, and they passed through without hesitation. Liis, a few steps behind, saw the air in the opening stir and thicken. She skidded to a halt as the door coalesced in front of her, cutting her off from the Speakers.

The light panel that had been illuminating the room went out, throwing her into complete darkness.

Panic seized her. She struck the surface of the barrier with her fist, the dense material muffling the sound, the sudden movement sending a spike of pain up her injured arm. She sucked in a sharp breath, chastising herself for letting her fear get the better of her.

Yilda warned us, she thought. *Everything here is keyed to the Speaker's bio-signatures. Nothing will work for me—including this door.*

The light came back on and the door atomized at the same time. Upatal, who stood on the other side, reached out and pulled Liis through the opening into a small, empty room. The door rematerialized behind Liis and she felt an immediate sense of relief—not because she was with the Speakers again, but because this substantial barrier now separated her from Yilda. The doors and lights hadn't worked for him. Perhaps it was because he hadn't been cloned at the relay station. The intelligences that had raised Upatal and her companion hadn't overseen Yilda's development. And so they would no more recognize the signature of his brain activity than it would of Liis's. That was why he'd had to blast his way into the building in the first place.

Upatal released Liis's arm; the Speakers moved to another sealed doorway—this time looking like it was made of dark wood—on the opposite wall. As they stepped up to it, the barrier dissolved as the previous one had. Upatal waited until Liis passed through the threshold before she moved on. Liis followed the Speakers as they continued through a perplexing tangle of rooms. Despite her fear, she began to lag further and further behind as exhaustion dogged her; Upatal waited patiently at each door.

Once, at the end of a long, narrow corridor, Upatal stood motionless under the arch of a door that had melted away. Stepping to one side, she waved Liis into the room, then followed her inside. There was no exit. After Upatal entered, the door reformed. Liis's stomach did a flip-flop as the room moved. It took her fatigued brain a moment to realize they were in an elevator. The door dissolved, opening onto a vaulted arcade that dwindled into the distance.

Upatal quickened the pace, jogging down the corridor, turning abruptly through a broad archway into another series of similar rooms. Liis struggled to keep up. She was near the point of collapse. They ran and ran, light panels flaring before them and dying in their wake. Rooms large and small passed before Liis as if in a dream. At one point they rested, and Liis used the moment to discard the dead battery in her laser pistol and snap a new cartridge into the grip.

Occasionally, something remarkable penetrated the haze of Liis's exhaustion: a chamber of brooding figures carved of blood-red stone; a swirling amber fog suspended in the centre of a room, eight tendrils snaking out from its central mass to each of the corners; a dome housing a riot of colourful flora growing only from the upper walls and ceiling, like an inverted jungle; a pyramidal room filled with a tangle of monstrous gears and levers, everything moving in a deafening, inexplicable rhythm. But these sights were forgotten as quickly as they passed from view. Exhaustion made it impossible to think about anything other than placing one foot in front of the other. She stumbled forward. They were in a room that looked like it had been carved from granite; strange, dun-coloured animals (or were they carvings?), no larger than her fist, watched idly from niches in the wall.

It was in a small, empty, hexagonal room that Liis found herself on her knees, her chest heaving, her head swirling. The next thing she knew, Upatal was standing before her, tugging urgently on her good arm, yammering at her in their incomprehensible language. Liis shook her head to show she couldn't go on; the gesture made the room wobble.

"*Aoth*," Upatal said urgently, pointing to the next doorway where her companion stood. "*Ilda!*"

"I . . . I need to rest." The last time she'd slept had been long before they'd entered the dome. And now they'd been running for . . . how long? Liis wasn't certain. But it seemed like hours. If only she could have a few minutes to catch her breath—

"*Ilda!*" The woman tugged on Liis's arm insistently while her companion fidgeted nervously. Liis allowed herself to be pulled to her feet. The room seemed to heave around her like the deck of a ship. Upatal placed Liis's good arm over her shoulder and tried to help her forward. As soon as they passed the threshold of the next door, a brilliant luminescence flared, blinding Liis. Her legs gave out completely; dazzled by the light, she sagged, the dead weight of her body dragging the two of them down to the floor in a slow-motion tumble. She waited for the impact, for the explosion of pain in her arm. Only it didn't come. The Speaker had managed to guide their fall. Liis was on her back, the pale oval of the Upatal's face hovering over her. Far above her was a white ceiling.

"Just a few minutes," she mumbled, the difficult words slurring in her mouth. "Tha . . . that's all . . . I need . . ." She passed out before she could finish her sentence.

Liis opened her eyes on undifferentiated black.

For a second she thought she might be dreaming, and that in fact she hadn't opened her eyes at all. She blinked. The blackness remained. So she sat up—and banged her head.

Momentarily stunned, she groped blindly with her good hand, discovered a rigid, grooved surface curved over her like the roof of a big pipe, preventing her from sitting up fully. In a panic, she swung her hand around, her fingers raking the curve of the wall down to where it met the surface on which she lay. She was trapped in a space not much larger than a coffin. Fear constricted Liis's throat, choking off her breath. She lay back down, closed her eyes, her heart thumping wildly.

Calm down, she admonished herself. Her breathing slowed.

She became aware of a bulky weight pressing down on her thighs. Reaching out with her good arm, she touched the thing, recognized the feel of its material. *My backpack*. The familiarity of it helped calm her. She let her arm fall back to her side.

Only now did she notice the surface on which she lay was damp. It was covered by a few millimetres of oily liquid. Running her finger through the stuff she realized why she hadn't noticed it before: it was warm, close to body temperature—and it had the curious property that it didn't stick to her fingers, or seem to penetrate the fabric of her clothes. It was a disconcerting feeling, the wet on the back of her calves and arms and head, while her shorts and tee-shirt were bone dry.

Sucking in a breath, she listened. Nothing. Nothing, but the sound of her own heartbeat. And a claustrophobic sense of the enclosed space. She let her breath go. *If only I had a flashlight*, she thought. There were still two flares in her backpack, but in this confined space, they'd be worse than useless. She remembered the watch Hebuiza had made.

She pulled it from her pocket. The number 4-06:33 glowed with a bright, anomalous cheer. Just over four days left. The last time she looked, after she'd entered the dome, it had shown five days. She'd been out for the better part of a day. In that time, anything could have happened.

Liis held up Hebuiza's watch, but the light it provided was too feeble to illuminate anything. Transferring it to her other hand, she gripped it as strongly as her weakened muscles would allow; with her good hand, she twisted the base. After a turn and a half, the watch popped open, exposing its works, and casting a dim, but much more extensive, circle of light. Liis raised it like a miniature lantern.

The curving surface above her was incised with parallel narrow channels; crosswise to the channels ran coloured threads. Many of these lines were raised, for the light from the watch cast slim, shifting shadows. Craning her neck, she discovered that a smooth, black barrier closed off the space past her head. She pushed on the obstruction but it was fixed firmly in place. She looked down toward her boots. In the weak illumination of the watch, she saw her backpack—and not much else. She moved her light down as far as she could, was able to make out her boots. Beyond that she could see the glint from another wall like the one above her head. She was sealed in this strange tube. Heart pounding, Liis let her head back down.

I'm going to die here.

The absurdity of this thought struck her as humorous: to come this far to be buried alive in . . . in what? It wasn't a crypt, exactly. Although Liis knew next to nothing about the Speakers' culture, this place looked less ceremonial and more functional. Perhaps it was a service tunnel. If that was true, she should be able get out. She checked the barrier above her head again. There was no handle, button or switch visible, only a soft, nipple-like protrusion at the centre. She pushed the plate in several different places but the cold surface didn't budge. So that left only the one at her feet.

The tube was too narrow to allow her to turn around. Liis pulled her backpack up into the space above her head and, with a grunt, rolled over onto her stomach. Pain shot up, momentarily dizzying her until the ache receded, leaving a ringing in her ears. She wiggled until the soles of her boots touched the barrier. Drawing back her leg, she kicked sharply outward.

With a hollow ring, the plate swung away and air wafted over her thighs. A disagreeable odour, like that of rotting meat, filled her nostrils. Craning her neck, she stared down the length of the tube. Outside was as lightless as inside the tube had been; it was impossible to see anything. She listened, but heard nothing. *If there's anyone out there*, Liis thought, *they'll know I'm here now*. She felt in her pocket for the laser pistol—and discovered it was gone. Placing the watch back in her pocket, she reached for her pack. The battery clips for the laser were also gone. Perhaps the Speakers were smarter than Yilda had credited them.

Picking up the watch, Liis stuck it in her pocket. She grabbed one of the straps from her backpack. Wiggling cautiously, she felt her knees cross the threshold of her prison. When the edge of the tube was against her thighs, the toes of her boots touched a solid surface, half a metre below. She pushed herself out of the confining space and onto her knees, dragging the backpack after her. She dropped it on the floor.

Pulling the watch from her pocket, she held it up.

Liis knelt on a white surface, straddling a shallow groove incised in the floor, several centimetres wide. It ran up to the base of the wall, ending directly below the tube in which she'd been trapped.

In the dim light cast by the LCDs she could barely see the dark maw of her coffin-like chamber, its hatch folded back against a grey wall. Only now did she realize the hatch was composed of a transparent material. She had mistaken the uniform black outside for its colour. Pushing herself to her feet, she saw another hatch directly above the first. A third began above her head. Standing fully, she raised her watch as high as her arm would go. She wasn't sure, but she thought she could make out the ghostly outline of a fourth hatch. Stacked like that, they reminded her of the rows of cells that lined the floors of the stasis facility back on Bh'Haret.

Liis leaned forward, peered through the hatch of the second cell—she had decided now they were not access tubes, but more likely stasis cells—half-expecting to see a body. But it was empty. She ran her hand over the join where the hatch met the wall. Perfectly flush. If she had had her eyes closed, she would never have been able to detect the seam. She straightened, raised her gutted watch, but could see nothing in the dim circle of light other than the bare wall and its column of cells.

Liis weighed her options.

She could wait here; Upatal might return. Then again, she might not. Perhaps the Speaker had abandoned her, believing her chances for survival improved without the added burden of a wounded outsider. If that was the case, Liis couldn't really blame her. Why would Upatal want to help her?

Liis could think of no compelling reason. Yet she wanted to believe the woman wouldn't have abandoned her. Without the Speaker's help, Liis knew she was as good as dead. But with them . . .

Yilda said there was a cure. If I can find the Speakers, make them understand, maybe I can convince them to help me.

There was still Yilda. He was out there, hunting Speakers. In fact, if Upatal hadn't fully understood Liis's warning, she and her companion might already be dead. And Liis didn't fool herself for a moment either: after what had happened to Hebuiza, Yilda would dispose of her as readily as he dispatched the Speakers. Of that she was certain.

I'm going to have to kill him.

The realization chilled Liis. Upatal had coolly held the gun to Hebuiza's head and pulled the trigger without hesitation. Could she do the same to Yilda?

He lied to us all along, she thought savagely, feeling anger burn in her chest. *He let Josua and Sav go to their deaths without a second thought. And he destroyed Bh'Haret, if not directly, then by inviting the wrath of Nexus. He gambled all our lives on his new empire.*

Liis clenched her hand into a fist, suffocating the light of her watch. Her arm ached with a good, sharp ache. It brought things into focus. *He's controlled us through our fear. I can't let him do that anymore.*

She relaxed; the faint illumination of the watch returned. *When the time comes,* Liis thought grimly, *I won't hesitate.*

Despite her bravado, a tiny doubt had lodged in her stomach like a cold pebble. She tried to ignore it. Instead, she set her mind on her immediate problems: finding a way out of this room and locating Upatal. Squatting, she placed her watch on the floor and pulled a flare from her backpack. Although she still had no idea what kind of room she was in, the sounds she made echoed in a way that suggested it was a large space. Large enough, anyway, for the flare not to cause her undue grief.

Liis pushed a protruding tab near its tip, sparking it to life.

Light exploded around her, giving her the briefest glimpse of the room, like an overexposed snapshot, before her vision was completely overwhelmed. She shut her eyes, waiting for her eyes to adjust, trying to sort out in her head the details of what she had seen: in front of her column after column of cells marched upward; before each column a precise groove incising the floor and running off into the darkness; to her right, ranks of machines rising from the floor; and further away, rearing up nearly to the ceiling, a dark looming shape with an overhang, like an immense gallows. But the strongest impression she was left with was that of the extent of the space: it was big, so big that the candle power of her igniting flare hadn't reached out far enough to touch any of the other walls or the ceiling.

Liis opened her eyes. Afterimages, wobbling amber circles and broken red lines, dogged her vision momentarily, then faded. The flare hissed in her ear, casting a wide, pale circle of light, its radius of illumination perhaps twenty metres. Along the wall in both directions the columns of cells repeated at regular intervals. The rank of machines Liis had seen began perhaps ten metres away. They looked more like sculptures. The closest rank appeared to be a row of small dark cubes set atop wide cylindrical pedestals; several metres behind that was a similar row, only here the pedestals supported elongated boxes instead of perfect cubes; in the next rank, the boxes now stretched long enough to resemble small coffins. Beyond that was uncertain darkness. The grooves in the floor ran between adjacent machines in each row, neatly subdividing the ranks of machines into a large, regular grid.

Liis stooped, dropped the flare on the ground, and struggled into her backpack. Scooping up the flare, she raised her arm high and began following the wall, looking for a door. Every few metres she passed a column of the strange cells, an identical groove running out from the base of each column. She stopped to peer into a cell. Empty. Perhaps she had guessed wrong. She could see no possible need for so many stasis cells—after all, Yilda had said there were only eighteen Speakers here. Maybe they weren't stasis cells after all, but served an esoteric purpose which she couldn't possibly fathom. Liis continued walking. She passed column after column of empty cells without finding any sign of an exit—or encountering an intersecting wall.

Five minutes after she had set out, Liis paused when she caught a glimpse of movement. It was on the periphery of the flare's wavering light and seemed to be receding in a steady, mechanical movement through the ranks of machines, toward the centre of the room. Whatever it was, it was tall and dark. Although Liis could only see the base of the thing, it reminded her of the looming hook she'd glimpsed in the initial burst of light from the flare. In a few seconds it was completely absorbed by the shadows. Liis took a step in the direction the thing had gone, then thought better of following it. She had to find a way out of this room, not chase after a mindless machine. Or what she hoped was a mindless machine. She continued walking, more cautiously now, casting backward glances.

Several minutes passed. At one point she realized she'd forgotten her watch on the floor when she'd lit the flare. She thought about turning around and going back for it, then decided to continue, at least for the time being. This flare would burn for some time yet, more than enough to go back, if need be.

At first, Liis didn't notice the glow emanating from the cells. The light they threw was so faint that her own sphere of illumination drowned their glimmer out completely. But suddenly she was surprised to see a stack of tube hatches were already visible—faintly limned as ghostly blue-green circles—just beyond the reach of her light. She looked back behind her and could see, albeit more faintly, the same glow. She held the flare up to the nearest hatch. Inside, a knurled, dark knot, the size of a balled fist, was suspended in a cloudy liquid. A twisting funiculus wound through cloudy fluid to attach to the nipple on the back wall. She checked the tube beneath. It contained a similar shadowy clot.

It's an incubator, Liis realized. *Yilda said they cloned the Speakers at the relay station.* Suddenly she understood why Upatal had brought her here—to hide her. Perhaps to the Speakers this place symbolized safety. But the exact opposite was true: If Yilda was bent on destroying the relay station, flushing the contents of these cells would be one of his priorities.

With a renewed sense of urgency, Liis hurried on; she passed hundreds more active incubators. Now that she was certain of their use, she was baffled by the sheer number of them. Why so many cells if there were only eighteen Speakers here? It made no sense.

Liis moved on. The glow emanating from the cells intensified until it was visible despite the wavering light of the flare. When Liis next paused to look into an incubator, she saw not the clearly formed fetus she was expecting, but was startled to find each cell contained two fetuses attached to a single umbilical—parabiotic twins, the crowns of their foreheads conjoined so that they looked like a mirrored images of one another.

Liis hurried ahead, moving toward the brightening circles. Half a dozen minutes passed.

Abruptly, the cells ahead ceased glowing.

She stopped in her tracks, peered inside the cell beside her. The fetuses appeared to be near the end of the third trimester. Already Liis could detect similarities to Yilda, the weak chins, the watery grey eyes. Even the small round stomachs reminded her of Yilda's paunch. The one nearest her moved, its tiny arm jerking. Liis pulled back in surprise. Recovering herself, she jogged ahead and peered into another darkened hatch. The cell was vacant.

Liis passed dozens more columns of dark, empty incubators.

Then, a few metres ahead, something protruded from the wall at waist height. Hurrying forward, she realized that the lowest cell door in a column was open. She stopped in front of it—and cursed softly. Her watch lay on the floor, where she'd put it when she'd grabbed the flare. *I've been walking in a circle*, she thought. She remembered the giant cylindrical structures they'd seen ringing the mountains and knew now that she was inside one. Stepping up to the cell, she kneed the hatch.

It swung to, sealing silently.

In her entire circuit of the *space*—she couldn't quite bring herself to think of structure this vast as a room—Liis had seen nothing but these cells and the unadorned, grey wall. She recalled how smooth the hatch seam had been. If there was an exit from this place, and it was composed of material identical to that of the wall, it would be impossible to detect—and impossible to open without a Speaker.

Liis lowered her arm; the radius of light diminished.

She could wait here until her flare died—as it must soon—or she could check out the rest of the chamber. She thought about the silent machine she'd seen earlier. It had been moving toward the centre of the room; maybe there was something there. A ramp or a stairway, perhaps.

She struck out from the wall, following the groove that began in front of the column of cells and ran between the ranks of machines.

As she approached the first ring, her light uncovered a fourth circle of similarly shaped machines: elongated boxes, half a metre long and slightly less wide, supported on pedestals. Following the same pattern, the boxes there were slightly longer than those in the previous circle. When she drew even with the objects in the first ring, she realized they had transparent tops. Curious, she stepped away from the groove to peer inside the nearest one. In a cloudy liquid floated twinned fetuses. The single umbilical, however, was gone. There was nothing attached to the children. At least nothing Liis could see. The infants seemed to be drawing their nourishment directly from the fluid which buoyed them.

Liis moved on.

In the next row the fetuses were more mature; in fact, the term fetus no longer applied, for although the twins were submersed in an amniotic-like fluid, they appeared to be fully developed, year-old infants. They stirred, the light from her flare irritating them. The conjoined twins blinked repeatedly. In the third ring the incubators sat on thicker pedestals; here, the infants had shed most of their baby-fat—and seemed less sensitive to the light. Both turned their eyes to stare upwards. The pattern finally broke in the sixth row: the incubators abruptly grew smaller. When Liis passed them, she understood why. Each cell now held only one occupant, a bright pink patch on its hairless skull marking the point of separation. In the ranks after this, the incubators began growing longer again. As she moved toward the centre of the chamber, the sickly sweet odour of decaying meat grew.

She came to a point where there was a gap between the rings of incubators. Here, a second, perpendicular groove, intersected the first one along which she walked. Liis kept straight on. Another dozen rings and she could finally detect the gradual curvature of the circles of incubators. The smell had grown so strong it assaulted her like a slaughterhouse stench. Liis tried to ignore it. She came to the final row of incubators. The containers here resembled narrow coffins. Liis looked in one and found it contained an adolescent male, his size suggesting a young teenager; strangely, he had no pubic hair, and his genitalia were underdeveloped for this age. *Maybe*, Liis thought, *they designed the Speakers this way on purpose. Life here would be far less complicated without sexual tensions.* Briefly, she wondered if Yilda resembled the clones in every respect.

Half a dozen metres beyond this last row, the groove in the floor came to an abrupt end. It was cut off by a trench that curved around the centre of the room. Half a metre deep and roughly three wide, the trench had sloping sides coloured bright yellow, and a flat bottom that looked like it was made of cloudy glass. On the other side of the trench was a ring of low, white benches, like those that Liis had seen in the room of portraits. At the very centre of this chamber, a thick, waist-high pole had been set into the ground. Its flat, circular top glowed a faint amber. Nowhere could she see anything that might account for the heavy, sickening smell of blood and raw flesh.

Liis stared at the trench, reluctant to cross; the yellow sides worried her. She'd been around enough industrial equipment to recognize the implied warning. Yellow meant hazard. But what kind of hazard? There wasn't anything nearby that looked threatening. Nothing that looked evenly vaguely mechanical. Maybe the coloration was merely decorative, although she didn't really believe this. The side of the trench wasn't steep. Leastwise, its slope was gentle enough so that she could stand on it without falling. She decided that if she stepped down cautiously, she could test the bottom of the trench with her other foot to see if it was safe.

Liis took a step onto the yellow slope—and her foot shot out from under her like she'd stepped on ice. With a shout of surprise she tumbled sideways. Instinctively, she flung away the flare and threw out her arm to break her fall; but her palm hit the nearly frictionless surface and squirted out from under her and she collapsed. Under her cheek, the white surface was warm and surprisingly rough, a texture similar to that of fine grain sandpaper. She thought she could detect the faintest of vibrations playing through it.

She raised her head.

The flare lay somewhere in the centre of the room. It raised a corona of quavering light past the far lip of the trench, making the slope on that side appear to be black. Everything was still. It occurred to Liis that the yellow may not have been a caution about dangerous machinery, but might have been a warning not to step on the slick surface. She felt a flush of embarrassment.

With a grunt, she struggled to her feet. Her footing on the rough surface was, thankfully, solid. A few metres away the flare hissed and spat out its gouts of light. Cradling her arm, Liis crossed the trench and sprang up the opposite slope to retrieve her flare.

She stood on an island in the heart of the room. To her right, encroaching on the edge of her light, a ponderous dark shape moved steadily through the ranks of incubators. It was already past the last rank of cells and heading for the trench. She recognized the thing almost immediately: if it wasn't the same machine she'd caught a glimpse of earlier, it was an identical copy. Tall, matte black, and several metres square, it was composed of crossed, structural members. Inside the latticework were two separate columns: the first contained cylinders; the second, oblong boxes. She recognized the shapes.

It's carrying incubators, Liis realized. The thing moved in an eerie silence. There wasn't the slightest tremor in the floor, although the gantry was massive. Its summit was lost in the shadows overhead, and it appeared to be carrying several thousand kilograms of cargo.

As the machine approached, Liis realized it was running along the groove in the floor. The gantry came to a halt directly in front of the trench.

Liis hesitated: should she examine the pole at the centre of the room or get a closer look at this thing? There was no telling how long the gantry might remain here. Or when she might get another chance to see it. She settled on the gantry. The pole, after all, didn't seem to be going anywhere.

Careful to avoid the slope, she hopped down into the trench and leapt back up on the other side in two bounds. She strode over to the machine. At the base of the thing, a metre above the floor, one of the cylindrical incubators had been extended on a semi-circular arm until it hung over the trench. An unseen internal mechanism levered the cylinder up. Its hatch swung open, spilling its contents into the channel.

Liis knew instantly the fetuses were dead. With their shrivelled blue-black skin and bloated bellies it was impossible that they could be anything else. An overwhelming stench assaulted her and she gagged. Now she knew where the smell came from.

For a second the twins lay in a pool of amniotic fluid; then the white floor beneath them rippled. A low-pitched humming began, like that of a heavy motor straining to drive a tremendous mass. The surface of the trench buckled and fragmented into a sea of heaving glassy beads. These shivered into minute particles that sub-divided again, until the surface powdered and fell inward. In the bottom of the channel were hundreds of slowly rotating vertical discs aligned in dozens of rows that curved with the channel. Each disc was a few centimetres thick, and adjacent discs were offset from one another, the whole assembly reminding Liis of a huge paper shredder. And she discovered her impression wasn't that far from the truth. Within seconds, the rollers had consumed the white particles. The shrivelled lump that had been the Siamese fetus rolled until its extremities caught between the discs. Little hands and feet were crunched by the discs; then stubby limbs and bits of loose skin were caught. Over the thrum of the machine Liis thought she could hear bones crunching and cartilage popping. The trunks of the tiny corpses were flayed, the fetuses torn into ever smaller pieces, which in turn were ground between the machined discs with horrifying efficiency.

Liis's stomach knotted; it took every ounce of her will to refrain from vomiting. *They're dead*, she reminded herself. *They were dead before they hit the trench.* She managed to fight back her queasiness.

The incubator had already been retracted and was now moving toward the back of the gantry; a second incubator was being extruded over the trench.

Liis stared at the spot where she had been lying in the trench only moments ago. *Why didn't it open for me? Why wasn't I ground up like the fetuses?* The answer occurred to her almost as soon as she asked the question: like everything else here, those gnashing discs were keyed on some aspect of the Speaker's bio-signatures.

It's recycling them.

Having spent most of her adult life as a longhauler, working in sealed environments, Liis understood the need for this machine: in a closed system, everything had to be recycled—especially organic matter. Here, non-viable clones were dumped into the rollers, their valuable organics ground into constituent molecules to be reused in the next generation.

The second incubator tipped. Its contents sloshed unceremoniously into the trench. This time, mingled with the basso hum of the machine, were distinct snapping sounds: the cracking of tiny bones.

Liis backed away. She had no desire to be anywhere near the trench. And there were at least a hundred incubators in the machine, possibly more. It would take a good hour to cycle through all the containers. The island in the middle of the room, and its strange post, would have to wait until it was safe to cross the trench again. Instead, she decided to follow the rings of incubators, spiralling out toward the wall, looking for anything that might be an exit.

Liis circled, the sound of the shredder a constant companion. After three circuits, she lost sight of the trench. Thankfully, the stench lessened. Shortly after she entered the sixth ring her flare finally guttered and died. In an instant she was in complete darkness. Slipping her backpack off, she fumbled until she managed to extract her last flare. She lifted it above her head, placed her thumb on the tab to ignite it—

—then stopped.

Something had changed in the last few seconds. It was a subtle shift, like the pressure changes one feels moments before a storm breaks. Liis swung her head around, but could still see nothing. But had the darkness itself changed, become a degree less absolute? The hair on the back of her arms stood up.

In a dazzling, silent fury, light burst upon the room.

For several seconds Liis clenched her eyes shut against the brilliance. When she did open them, she had to blink back involuntary tears. She lifted her hand to wipe them from her cheeks—and froze, so overwhelmed was she by the sheer scale of the room in which she stood. The circular chamber was monstrously large, much larger than she had pictured it. As big as a stadium. Several stadiums, in fact. Hundreds of triangular ceiling panels blazed, the dazzling light reflecting off the glossy white floor. Half a dozen towering, black gantries were positioned around the room. Five were stationary, but one moved slowly away from her. On the ceiling, there were hundreds of grooves that mirrored those on the floor, each beginning directly above a column of wall incubators, all converging on a central hub, like spokes.

Liis looked around the room in perplexity, but saw nothing that might indicate why at this moment, of all moments, the lights had chosen to come on. Until now, it had been the Speaker's presence that had activated the ceiling panels in the other rooms. She corrected herself: an *adult* Speaker's presence. Yet, as far as she could tell, she was the only other living being there. She searched the walls, but they were still unbroken; there were no doors visible. Then something occurred to her.

Liis took half a dozen quick steps to the side and scanned the walls to the side of each gantry. From this new angle, an arched doorway, formerly hidden by one of the machines, was now visible. A small figure—Liis recognized Upatal almost immediately—hurried across the intervening space. As she watched, the doorway faded from view, growing translucent, then opaque. Soon, it was indistinguishable from the surrounding wall.

Liis felt a surprising, and almost overwhelming, swell of relief. Stuffing the unlit flare into her pocket, she took long loping strides toward the Speaker, ignoring the tremors of pain that each step set off in her arm.

They met halfway between the wall and the centre of the room. Upatal had Hebuiza's bolt gun slung over her shoulder; she was breathless and appeared agitated. Gesturing to the centre of the room, she seized Liis by the wrist and began dragging her back toward the trench.

"Wait!"

The word brought Upatal up short. The Speaker turned, her brow drawn down in consternation.

Liis pointed at both of them and then at the place where the doorway had been, trying to indicate that they should leave. She was about to attempt her pantomime of Yilda again, hoping to convey the danger of remaining here, when the Speaker seized Liis's hand with renewed vigour and turned toward the centre of the room. "*Ilda!*" she said urgently over her shoulder.

Reluctantly, Liis let herself be pulled along.

After half a dozen steps, Upatal released Liis's hand and, with another anxious gesture, indicated they should hurry. Liis couldn't see where they could possibly be going, unless it was to the gantry. Nevertheless, Liis hurried after. The Speaker ran forward, Liis following closely behind. They approached the trench. Next to it, the gantry still mindlessly expelled its cargo into the maws of the recycler. Upatal ignored the gantry completely. Instead, she ran past it and stepped out over the grinding plates.

Incredibly, she didn't fall.

Although she sagged momentarily below floor level, something invisible buoyed her up. As she sped across the trench, the air thickened around her feet, coalescing into a fog, a tenuous bridge forming above the disks. As soon as the Speaker stepped on the opposite side, the narrow span dissolved, collapsing into thousands of minute particles that showered down and were ground up by the plates.

Liis stood on the edge of the bank, her heart hammering. *Of course they wouldn't let living Speakers stumble into this thing*, she thought. *They'd have safeguards. To distinguish between a living being and a dead fetus.* But, once the machine was going, would it recognize outsiders, like her, as something alive and not to be harmed? She didn't feel like running out over the trench, the way Upatal had, to find out.

The Speaker passed through a ring of structures that looked like children's benches and reached the centre of the room. She turned and gestured impatiently for Liis. Liis shook her head. She pointed down into the trench. Upatal frowned in puzzlement.

I'll have to show her. Carefully extending a leg over the trench, Liis let her foot down until it hung in mid-air above the turning plates. They continued grinding, and the bridge that had materialized to support Upatal didn't form.

Upatal understood immediately. She ran back, the bridge forming almost as an afterthought to her passage over the trench, and seized Liis's wrist again. She stepped back onto the nebulous structure, which hadn't yet had a chance to dissolve, and gently, but firmly, pulled on Liis's arm.

Liis placed a foot on the cloudy surface; centimetres below, the discs spun relentlessly. The bridge provided a solid surface with good traction.

Liis stepped out onto the span and quickly followed Upatal across to the other side. As the Speaker stepped off ahead of her, Liis felt the walkway sag slightly. But she was safely across before the bridge collapsed completely.

Inside the ring of benches a black line on the floor, a final circle, enclosed the centre of the room. Upatal crossed this boundary and made directly for the pole at the very centre, pulling Liis along. With her free hand the Speaker touched the amber disc on top, which turned red.

Liis's stomach fluttered. The air around her seemed to stir. Then she noticed that the walls were moving. *What the hell?* she thought.

Liis realized she'd gotten things backwards. The walls weren't moving; she was. She felt a brief moment of vertigo as she readjusted her perceptions: she stood on a rising platform, its edges defined by the black line she'd seen on the floor. Upatal touched Liis's chest, motioning that Liis should not move. Turning, the Speaker sprinted to the edge of the platform and jumped. Landing on the ground, Upatal sped over the trench and ran back toward the wall.

Liis felt a spasm of anxiety. She thought about following, hesitated. Without Upatal, she wouldn't be able to get over the trench. And the Speaker had clearly wanted her to stay here. The platform rose and Upatal moved further and further away. Then it was too late. The decision had been made for her. The platform was far off the ground and jumping had become too risky. Liis cursed herself for hesitating.

She looked up. Overhead, a dark circle on the ceiling matched the circumference of the platform. At its centre was a small opening, the same diameter at the pole. But there was no shaft into which the platform could ascend. Now half a dozen metres away, the ceiling approached rapidly. Unless there was a safety mechanism, in a few seconds she'd be crushed between the two planes. Heart hammering wildly, she went down to her knees and then lay on her stomach, turning her head sideways.

The space between ceiling and platform diminished to two metres. Then one.

Liis braced herself.

She felt the ceiling touch her shoulder blades. The material gave, like an elasticized film, and the platform slipped through it with no more resistance than a diver might have felt breaking the surface of a pool.

Liis lay on her stomach, staring stupidly around a circle of benches that was identical to the one in the room below.

"Ah. Bit of luck," Yilda said, stepping into view from behind her, his rifle angled down at her face. "Won't have to go to the bother of finding you."

With a strength belied by his appearance, Yilda jerked Liis to her feet, nearly yanking her good arm out of its socket. He shoved her roughly and she stumbled a few steps backwards. He didn't look the least put out by the effort.

Liis could now see this room was a twin to the one below. Only here, the surface of the trench was sealed. And all of the gantries seemed to be busy: one was less than ten metres away, working in the closest rank of incubators; three others were positioned along the wall. Inside their superstructures containers rose and fell; immediately to the right of each machine were several columns of dark holes, emptied of their incubators. *Yilda's destroying the fetuses*, Liis realized.

"So nice to see you again."

Yilda circled behind Liis, keeping his rifle trained on her; she turned to follow his motion. He stopped beside one of the low white benches; above it, three-dimensional projections filled the air, each a simple geometric shape filled with schematics or scrolling text.

"Now, then," Yilda said. "Where are the Speakers?"

Liis said nothing. She looked between Yilda and the busy gantries. He aimed his rifle at the bridge of her nose. "Answer the question."

"I don't know."

"The next level down, perhaps?"

Liis still refused to answer.

"Someone had to start the elevator for you, hey?"

"Upper levels?" Liis craned her neck. Etched on the ceiling was a circle that was identical to the one in which she stood. In this room—and the one below—there had to be a several thousand incubators. If the pattern repeated on the half a dozen or more levels of this building, and in each of sixty-four buildings that ringed the mountain...

"I will only ask you one more time—"

"You're a fluke," she said.

Yilda frowned.

"There are hundreds of thousands of these incubators. Maybe millions. Yet there are only eighteen Speakers at the relay station."

Yilda arched his eyebrows slightly.

"The ability to communicate isn't a product of science at all." Liis fixed him with a stare. "It's a fluke of biology. Nexus doesn't know how to reproduce a Speaker. Except by breeding twinned clones in groups large enough to produce the statistically probable eighteen."

"What you know—or think you know—is of little consequence." Yilda's speech had now completely lost its usual hitches, his pauses and answers to his own questions. "Tell me where the Speakers are."

"Gone."

Yilda advanced until the snout of his rifle pressed against the fabric of her tee-shirt. Liis could feel her heart beat against the cold ring of the muzzle. "Where?"

She hesitated. "With their comrades. They left me behind."

Yilda's fist struck her square across the cheek; she staggered backwards, her legs almost folding under her. Holding a hand against her burning cheek, she watched Yilda advance on her again.

"You're lying. I've accounted for all of the Speakers. They have *no* comrades left. Now then, let's try again. Where are your friends?"

Blood pooled under Liis's tongue; she spat it out. "They're not my friends," she said. Her jaw ached.

"I found Hebuiza. Have to admit I didn't think you had it in you, executing him like that."

"I didn't kill anyone," Liis said. "The Speaker shot Hebuiza."

Yilda lifted his narrow shoulders; Liis jumped back reflexively, expecting another blow. But he was only shrugging. "It makes no difference to me who killed him. What's important is that you were there. You let it happen. So I can only assume you've taken the Speakers' side. Against me. Now that you've demonstrated your willingness to betray me—"

"The woman shot Hebuiza. Then they ran off before I could do anything. I ran after them, but they'd already disappeared. I got lost and ended up here."

"Wrong again," Yilda said with a weary sigh. "You wouldn't be here unless they accompanied you. They were the only way you could have gotten through the intervening doors. They are keyed to admit only those displaying multiple aspects of the proper bio-signature. Which means they would open only for a Speaker bred here." He tapped the snout of his rifle on the platform. "Furthermore, this lift wouldn't have activated without one of them on it or controlling it. Your chances of figuring out the manual overrides are astronomical. I helped design this place and its systems—and it took me the better part of an hour to override the door and bring up the display behind me. Ergo, the Speakers must have been with you when you arrived at the hatcheries, and only moments ago when the platform began to rise."

Liis was dumbstruck. Not because of what Yilda had said, but because she suddenly understood why Upatal had led her to the platform, then jumped off as it began to rise. *She knew Yilda would come to the hatchery to destroy the fetuses. She's been playing me all along. And now she's offered me up as a gift. A sacrificial lamb.*

"You're *still* stalling." Yilda hefted his rifle. "And now I'm becoming *very* angry."

Liis stiffened. Behind Yilda, the dark "O" of a doorway formed in the distant wall, then quickly faded, leaving no trace. But in that brief moment it had been open, a lone figure had slipped through.

"Fleeing is no longer an option," Yilda said, misinterpreting her gaze. "You'd be dead before you took a step. And you've nowhere left to go." He placed the muzzle of his rifle on Liis's left kneecap. "My patience is exhausted. If you don't answer right now, I will shatter your patella. An extremely painful injury. Or so I gathered from one of the erstwhile Speakers."

"They're below." Liis said. "Hiding in the incubation cells." Far off, a small figure darted from the cover of one the distant incubators to the next. Liis fought the urge to stare in that direction.

"Plausible. Not terribly intelligent, really. But plausible. That doesn't explain what you're doing up here."

Behind Yilda, the figure moved between ranks of incubators, closing. Liis was fairly certain it was Upatal. "I wanted to go," Liis said, forcing herself to lock eyes with Yilda. "I made them show me how to work the platform."

"Why?" Yilda furrowed his brow in mock concentration. "Why would you want to do that? You're not much brighter than they are. Why leave a cozy hiding place?"

"Hebuiza told me there was a cure. I wanted to look around. I thought I might . . . I mean I was hoping to find a med machine or something. . . ."

"Stupid woman," Yilda said, the contempt unmistakable in his voice. "You've already been cured. Those capsules I gave you and Hebuiza—they were more than stimulants. They disabled the Trojan. I was afraid I might still need your assistance. But I was wrong."

A hard knot formed in Liis's stomach. *Cured*. She thought about the little blue capsule lying on forest path. *I had it on my tongue—and I spat it out*. Liis stared at Yilda, at the rifle he aimed at her. *He had the antidote....*

In the periphery of her vision, the figure moved closer again, startling Liis. This time, however, she got a good look. It *was* Upatal. Liis suddenly realized she was staring at the place where Upatal had hidden. Yilda frowned, started to turn.

"All this," Liis said. "For revenge."

"Revenge?" Yilda turned back to her; he seemed genuinely puzzled.

"Hebuiza told me. You want to get back at your brother. To disrupt Nexus."

At the mention of his brother, Yilda's face darkened. "As much as I despise my *twin*, revenge was never my motive." He spat out the word *twin*. "But if he chooses to believe I've done this merely for revenge, let him. He always was an imbecile." Yilda regained his composure; he smiled at her. "After all, he let me escape, didn't he?"

"Then why kill the Speakers? Why destroy the fetuses?" Upatal was no more than fifty metres away now, hesitating, it seemed, to risk the next open space.

"I'm not destroying the fetuses. I'm modifying their developmental programming. I'll need them to rebuild my empire."

Liis's mind reeled. "But . . . but you're trapped here," she said, her voice shaking. "You're trapped on this dead rock. Just like the Speakers." Her words rang hollowly in her own ears.

Yilda smirked. "There's no rush now. It'll be decades before a Nexus ship arrives. And I've made arrangements for my departure long before then. I have a ship standing by, waiting for my orders, once I've disabled the orbitals."

He's planned this from the start, Liis thought. Even the blue pills

Yilda had proffered them—he must have had those long before *Viracosa* left Bh'Haret. Liis felt the blood drain from her face. Yilda stood before her, a bow-legged, dissipated-looking man she wouldn't have given a second glance to on a city street. When she spoke, her voice was hoarse, barely above a whisper. "'A convenient plague.' That's what Hebuiza called it back on Bh'Haret." There wasn't a shred of emotion on Yilda's face. Nothing but his galling implacability. "Not convenient for Nexus," she continued. "Convenient for you. It provided you with a group of people desperate enough to help you get here."

Yilda's lips crooked up in a sly, self-congratulatory smile, the figures of his carved teeth showing.

Liis felt sick. "Nexus didn't seed Bh'Haret with the plague." She felt like she teetered on the brink of an abyss. *"You did."*

Yilda bowed from the waist. "A nice touch, don't you think?" His mocking smile broadened. "My witless brother is blamed for the plague. An *outrage* that will work in my favour when I begin negotiating with the worlds in the Left Leg Cluster that are now cut off from Nexus. The new order I offer will seem that much more benign when set against this calculated disregard for life demonstrated by Nexus."

Liis's first reaction was a flash of rage; almost immediately it was replaced by a self-loathing so intense she thought she was going to vomit. *I helped him. He killed everyone on Bh'Haret, and I helped him.* A tremor began in her arms, spread to her chest and legs. Only it wasn't fear that caused her to tremble; it was shame and guilt.

"I'm tired of this chit-chat," Yilda said.

Liis watched his finger tighten on the trigger. Shutting her eyes, she waited for the barely audible pop of his weapon, realizing a split second later that she would be dead before the sound reached her ears. Like everything else that had happened, there would be no warning.

"Then again, you may still be of use."

Yilda hadn't fired. Liis opened her eyes.

In the last few moments, she'd forgotten about everything

except the raw knot of shame and anger in her stomach. Now she could see the snout of Upatal's bolt gun poking above an incubator in the last ring.

Yilda sighed. "If the Speakers feel this same absurd affection for you, then perhaps I can use you as bait. Imagine them, coming across poor, incapacitated Liis, and stopping to help." He reached in the pocket of his shorts and pulled out the clear, flat box of silver discs: the explosives he'd used on the first door. "I designed these microgrenades so they could be detonated either by timers or proximity triggers keyed on the Speakers' bio-signatures. A few planted on you and—well you can figure out the rest for yourself." He rattled the small discs inside their case and stuffed them back in his pocket. "Sadly, you will die when your friends get close to you. But at least your death will serve a useful purpose."

Liis felt like laughing at the absurdity of Yilda's statement. She watched Upatal step out from the cover of the incubator and creep forward, advancing toward them, the bolt gun at the ready. *You're too late, Yilda*, she thought. *I'm already being used. As Upatal's decoy.*

"What are you smiling at?"

Upatal had stopped, raised the bolt gun to her shoulder.

Yilda turned to follow Liis's gaze.

The report from the gun made Liis jump; the muzzle flash momentarily blinded her.

When her vision cleared, Yilda stood before her, swaying slightly, his eyes agog, his mouth open in astonishment. Upatal's shot had hit him squarely in the side of the head. Wisps of smoke rose from his temple; the flesh there was torn and seared, his ear blackened and shrivelled. Yilda's rifle slipped from his hands and clattered to the floor. Stumbling forward, he butted into Liis, his head lolling against her breast, his hands clutching at the fabric of Liis's tee-shirt, closing on fistfuls of material.

Upatal stood perfectly still, the bolt gun levelled. Her lips were drawn tight, her eyes narrowed. Hatred animated her features. With a flick of her head, she indicated Liis should push the Facilitator away.

Liis looked down at Yilda. His eyes were closed; all traces of pain had been erased from his face. He looked as if he were concentrating. But that was impossible. The bolt gun fired a tight array of charged capacitance darts; aside from the physical damage they inflicted, they should have made a hash out of the electrical impulses in his brain when they discharged. *Hebuiza said something about a nanoskin*, Liis remembered. *Could that have saved him?* She stared closely at the shrivelled mess that had been the left side of his face. Oddly, there was little blood. A piece of blackened skin hung down like a crisped sheet of paper. Underneath, something shone. A transparent layer, like a thin plastic film, formed a barrier. Several darts from the bolt gun were embedded in the material. One of the darts wiggled, fell out. Two others began moving.

Yilda's eyes snapped open; instantly he released his grip on Liis's tee-shirt and seized her by the arms, spinning her around. Pain flashed up the nerves in Liis's injured arm, short-circuiting her vision. She screamed in agony.

Yilda's moist breath rasped against the back of her neck. He held Liis in front of him as his shield, fingers like steel pinioning her arms behind her back. Upatal had the bolt gun trained on them, but didn't fire.

Yilda began backing toward the lip of the trench where his rifle lay.

A ruby light flickered in front of Liis's nose; specks of dust in the air sparkled like miniature stars as they ignited.

The crushing grip on her arms relinquished. Liis stumbled forward a step, turned in time to see Yilda vault across the low bench and make an impossibly long leap across the trench. Lines of red light cut the air around him. He threw himself behind an incubator at the same instant Liis heard a discharge from the bolt gun. The round punched a fist-sized hole through the incubator's side; fluid sluiced through the opening and slopped onto the floor.

To Liis's right, the male Speaker stepped out into the open, Liis's laser pistol in his fist. From opposite sides, the Speakers began to work their way toward the incubator where Yilda had taken cover.

Something small flashed through the air toward the male Speaker. Liis dove behind one of the little benches.

The concussion from the explosion caught her mid-leap, knocking the breath from her lungs. She landed hard, felt herself bounce, her body a loose and disjointed thing that tumbled haplessly into the trench. For countless seconds the room revolved above her, the overhead lights burning fervidly in her eyes. She felt battered beyond redemption. She no longer had any sensation in her broken arm, numb and lifeless from the shoulder down; she tried to move her fingers, but they didn't respond.

A second explosion followed, and Liis squeezed her eyes shut. But the trench protected her; other than an abbreviated shock wave that shuddered through the floor, she felt only a mild rush of air before bits of smoking debris pattered down around her like raindrops. She wondered if she was being showered with fragments of the Speaker—then realized a second later she couldn't have been: had a piece of a Speaker landed in here, the machine would have opened up beneath her—and ground her up along with the bit of Speaker's flesh. *I've got to get out of here*, she thought.

Liis tried to sit up. Her body howled its protest. It took an enormous effort and she nearly blacked out, but she managed to raise herself enough to peek over the lip of the trench. The stink of decaying flesh and sickly-sweet smell of blood swirled around her.

In front of her, two metres away, lay Yilda's rifle, a tiny light on the top of its stock pulsing green. On the opposite side of the platform, the floor had been torn up and scorched by the explosion. One bench had disappeared entirely—she guessed it had been thrown into the trench by the explosion—and another had been overturned and split in half by the blast. The display still hung incongruously in the air above the crater. Further away, amongst the ranks of incubators on the opposite side of the platform, a small crater marked the site of the second explosion. Several incubators had been destroyed; others had been breached in varying degrees and their contents now dribbled and leaked through cracks and punctures. The male Speaker, if he was over there, wasn't visible.

She turned her head, trying to locate Upatal. Through the latticework of the gantry she caught a glimpse of movement, saw the snout of Hebuiza's bolt gun poke out. From the corner of her eye Liis saw several more discs spin through the air toward the place where she had last seen the male speaker. She ducked as a chain of concussions roared over her, deafening her.

As soon as the shock waves had passed, Liis poked her head up over the lip of the trench. Gritting her teeth, she threw herself onto the trench's slope, grateful her arm only flopped at her side like something dead, cast clacking against the yellow surface. With her good hand, she snatched at the rifle's shoulder strap, caught it, and slid back into the trench, dragging it after. She braced herself, for the last thing she saw before sliding down the frictionless slope of the channel had been another set of silver discs flashing through the air. This time they had arced to her left, toward the gantry. She crooked her arm over her head against a second set of deafening explosions.

Before the fall of debris had ceased, Liis grasped the rifle in her good hand, her finger resting on the trigger, her thumb on the stock above. Although her grip was awkward, the weapon was light enough for her to balance. Swinging it up and over her head, she aimed it in the general direction where she'd last seen Yilda amongst the incubators and pulled the trigger.

The recoil was almost negligible, the weapon's faint report inaudible over the din in her ears. She jerked the trigger several more times, and was rewarded by the satisfying sound of a booming impact. She had no idea what kind of setting the rifle was on, but at least her rounds were causing damage. She swept the weapon in a wide arc, holding the trigger down, listening to the impacts. Abruptly, the slight recoils—along with the sounds of impacts— stopped as it ran out of juice.

Liis lowered the rifle and examined it. The light on the stock had gone out. She tossed the rifle to one side and peeked over the lip to see what damage it had done.

In front of her was a fan of destruction.

The air was thick with roiling smoke, making it difficult to see anything. The shells of burned-out incubators lay tumbled a half a dozen rows back, small fires burning everywhere. Several lone pedestals still stood but were bent backwards and scored black. One burned brightly at its tip, sputtering like a roman candle. It was hard to believe that Yilda could have survived in the midst of this wreckage. Liis turned to find Upatal.

The last set of blasts had taken their toll on the gantry. The black structure now canted awkwardly to one side, the crossed members near its base broken and twisted. Many of the incubators had been damaged by the blasts, split open inside the tangled structure like cracked eggs. Half a dozen others had been dislodged and tumbled to the floor. They lay in a growing pool of fluid.

From behind the gantry Upatal rose, bolt gun braced on her shoulder, aiming off to Liis's right where Yilda had been. She fired. Liis swung her gaze over—and through a gap in the smoke saw Yilda rise from behind the wreckage of an incubator and dash away, moving with inhuman speed. There was another *whump* of the bolt gun; sparks from discharging projectiles flashed behind his heels. The Facilitator disappeared into the forest of incubators.

Liis heaved herself out of the trench. Ignoring the protests from her battered limbs, she scuttled over to the first row of incubators and hid herself behind a pedestal. It wasn't the best protection, but at least she was out of the trench.

Then Upatal suddenly appeared, heading toward the spot where the male Speaker had been. As she moved, Upatal fired several wild bursts from the hip, strafing the incubators where Yilda had fled, perhaps in the hopes of keeping him hunkered down. Liis decided to take advantage of the opportunity to find better cover. Dragging herself over to the gantry, she collapsed behind the pile of dislodged incubators in a pool of putrid, amniotic fluid.

Centimetres from her face was a round incubator taken from the wall. The tube had been split by an explosion and doubled back on itself so that it looked like a can cut open in the middle with its halves bent back. Inside were twin fetuses lying in opposite sides of the incubator. Whatever had severed their tube had also bifurcated them, sundering their skulls midway, leaving a gaping hole in both. Bits of brain and bone were plastered to the inside walls of the incubator. Liis looked away.

For several seconds the bolt gun had remained silent. Then there was a shout, followed by a single shot from the gun. This was answered almost immediately by a new series of explosions. The concussions boomed, drum-like, inside the incubator halves.

Silence again.

Liis waited, holding her breath. Nothing. She decided to hazard a look.

But before she could rise up high enough to peek over the incubator halves, Yilda's voice rang out from the centre of the room.

"Your friends are dead."

Liis stiffened.

"A shame, really. They had more spunk than I believed. Perhaps I might have been able to make use of them."

Upatal's dead. Liis was shaken. Even though the Speaker had used her, she felt the stab of loss.

A movement from the interior of the incubator caught Liis's attention. Through the transparent hatch at the end she had a partial view of the platform. Raising herself on one arm—and doing her best to ignore the vile stink—she inched forward until she could see the centre of the room. Yilda stood there in plain sight, the left half of his face blackened. His white tee-shirt was holed by laser burns. Yet for all of that, he appeared unhurt.

"I know you're unarmed. I've accounted for all the weapons." In one hand he held Liis's laser pistol; in the other he clutched the bolt gun Upatal had been carrying. "You almost had me," Yilda said conversationally. "I used up the last of my explosives on the Speakers." He strolled toward the channel. "But it was a mistake to throw away my rifle. If you had had enough patience you would have discovered that it only requires a few moments to recharge itself." Yilda slung the bolt gun over his shoulder and hopped down into the channel. "In fact, I'd be happy to demonstrate now that it is fully recharged." He walked over to where Liis had dropped the rifle.

Liis pulled the fetus nearest her out of the broken incubator and pinioned the little body under her chest; its jagged skull protruded from under her chin. She settled her weight on it and there was a muffled cracking; something wet and sticky seeped through the front of her tee-shirt. Liis plunged her hand through the hole in its skull; she dug her fingers around a fistful of brain. Twisting her wrist sharply, she pulled and a wet chunk came free with a tiny sucking sound. She rolled over and sat up, bits of grey matter dripping from her hand. Ten metres away, Yilda bent to retrieve his rifle.

With a grunt, Liis heaved the soggy mess.

The lump hit Yilda as he straightened. It struck him on the thigh and fell to the bottom of the channel, leaving a grey and pink smear on his shorts.

For a split second the Facilitator frowned as he stared at the stain; then his face went white as the floor sagged beneath him and the low thrum of the machine suddenly welled. He shrieked and spun toward the near bank. But it was already too late. The disintegrating surface of the channel wouldn't give him any traction. He stumbled forward like a man caught in quicksand, fell onto the yellow slope. His left arm slapped down on the floor and the laser pistol flew from his grip. He slipped from sight.

A high-pitched whine went up from the discs. It sounded as if the dynamo powering them was straining against tremendous resistance.

Struggling to her feet, Liis staggered over to the trench.

Yilda was still in the channel.

Or at least something that resembled Yilda. Most of his skin had been flayed, leaving a transparent, human-shaped sheath filled with stark white bone, red ropes of muscle tissue, and shadowy internal organs. In a dozen places Yilda's nanoskin was caught between straining rollers. Competing forces tore at the protective material, trying to pull it in different directions. Liis watched the skin being drawn tighter and tighter, flattening everything inside until the ribcage cracked and folded, organs began to rupture, and the thicker bones of arms and legs bent backward against the tops of rollers. The jaw of the thing—Liis couldn't think of it as Yilda anymore—gaped open. Large, glassy eyes goggled and were pushed back in their sockets as the head was compressed. A single, piercing cry rose above the whine of the machine.

He's still alive, Liis realized in horror.

Inside the transparent skin, the skull split open and the face collapsed into a flat parody of itself. In seconds everything inside the nanoskin had been squeezed into an unrecognizable reddish-pink mass.

The whine of the machine grew louder until it seemed to pierce Liis's eardrums like a spike. Drawn out now to exaggerated proportions, the nanoskin resisted for perhaps another second. Then, it ruptured, ripping down the middle and spraying out its contents in a low wide circle, bits of Yilda spattering wetly against Liis's shins and knees.

Upatal was alive, after all—barely.

Liis found her amongst the wreckage on the other side of the platform. The Speaker was unconscious, her face ashen, breathing raggedly, her robe holed and stained pink in several places by fragments from Yilda's microgrenades. Blood seeped from a jagged tear in her forehead. Next to her lay the mangled body of the male Speaker, eyes wide open with shock or surprise, one arm splayed at an unnatural angle, his mid-section awash in blood where a piece of shrapnel had gored him.

The medikit in Liis's backpack was ill-equipped to deal with serious injuries; she did what little she could for Upatal. She applied pressure until the bleeding stopped. Then she cleaned the Speaker's wounds with an alcohol swab, covered them with sterile gauze patches and bandages. There was nothing in the kit that would have allowed her to probe for the fragments that were lodged in the Speaker's body. As Liis worked awkwardly with her one good hand, she remembered how she'd tended to Josua's wounds when he'd been hurt back on Bh'Haret.

Surprisingly, the memory evoked no reaction. Josua was dead.

There was nothing more she could think to do for Upatal. Liis stood.

The room around her was alive with movement. Everywhere she looked, small metallic creatures scuttled, snagging bits of debris, dragging them over to the channel where they nudged them onto the frictionless slope. The debris slid down into the trench and accumulated on the white surface, apparently waiting to be recycled when the next fetus would reactivate the rollers. The gantries had all moved as well, their priorities altered, Liis assumed, by the damage done to the incubators. Articulated arms, previously hidden amongst their superstructures, had swung out to grapple larger fragments. A second gantry had already positioned itself next to the damaged one and seemed, in concert with hundreds of the swarming devices, to be disassembling it piece by piece. No doubt the parts would be recycled, and a new gantry constructed.

Ignoring the activity, Liis hurried through the ranks of incubators until she reached the place where the twins were first separated and placed into their own cells. Standing in front of one, she drew the laser pistol from her pocket, aimed at the transparent panel and pulled the trigger.

The material was tougher than it appeared. It took several minutes of sustained cutting to make a hole wide enough to draw out the infant.

Liis reached in with her good arm; the liquid was warm and slightly oily. Clutching the baby by its ankles, she pulled it from the incubator. Fluid trickled from its nose and mouth and ears. Its tiny chest heaved. Laying it face down on top of the incubator so that its head lolled over the edge, Liis swatted it lightly on its tiny buttocks. The infant coughed and began to howl.

Liis picked the child up, cradling it next to her chest, and walked over to where she'd seen Upatal slip through a door. Slowly, she moved around the periphery of the room. When the wall next to her darkened, she stopped. She stood there, the child bawling in her arms, as the arch of a doorway formed.

EPILOGUE: THE RELAY STATION

Under the pale illumination of the dome, a tall woman hurries along something more than a path, but less than a dirt road, clutching a naked, wailing infant to her chest. The light is failing, as it had been for a long time before she emerged from the broad door of the hatchery.

An eerie twilight clings to the fringes of the forest. Under the canopy of trees, it is already pitch black. The woman and child pass the treeline and are swallowed by night.

They descend into a ravine, cross a small wooden bridge that spans a dark stream, and ascend the opposite slope.

She stops, places the infant on the ground and pulls a cylindrical object from her pocket. The child's puling grows as the woman raises the object above her head.

A circle of wavering light springs up from the tip of the flare, shocking the child into silence. But the respite is only momentary: in seconds its wail resumes. The child's cries follow the woman as she moves away, pursuing her into the forest. Bent low, the woman fixes her eyes on the path, ignoring the wails.

The wavering light makes an impossible hash of things, creates counterfeit shadows that flee as soon as she steps up to them. Over and over she tells herself not to hurry; to be patient, to be thorough. To make as much use of the light as she can. A few steps ahead, she spots something, and her heartbeat quicken. The woman rushes toward it.

Another false alarm: bits of stick, a shadow. She curses, resumes her search.

Behind her, the child has fallen silent.

Alien trees loom, press in from all sides on her fragile bubble of illumination; it is easy for her to imagine they resent her presence and would like nothing more than to crush the intruding light. She is seized by an urge to flee the forest. To run back to the light and warmth of the hatchery.

But she suppresses this impulse; to accede to it is to surrender. And she has come too far for that.

She fixes her mind rigidly on the task at hand. Moving ahead, she scans the path carefully, painstakingly, searching for her salvation.

EPILOGUE: THE BROTHER

The sudden onslaught of pain was a ripping agony; Yilda's twin felt as if the meat was being torn from his bones. He staggered to his feet, clutching his head. Tears streamed from his eyes. Distantly, he was aware of the other Pro-Locutors in the room with him, some real, some virtual, watching in shock. Through the burning sheets of pain he felt helping hands grasp him, lay him on the floor and restrain his arms and legs. Protocol forgotten, a welter of messages flooded his mind, questions concerning his well-being and their own fears. He closed them off, shut them out. He had to focus his attention on this attack.

It was unlike anything he had endured in his long life; savage in its intensity, hatred aimed solely at him, driving a spike into his brain. He had no time to marshal a response, to assay a counter attack. It was all he could do to keep the other mind from completely overwhelming his, from destroying his final barriers and annihilating the kernel of his sanity. He had dealt with strong minds before, but never anything so immensely powerful—so suicidal in its intent on destroying him.

And he understood why: light years away, it was already dying an agonizing death. It had used its own pain to bolster the attack, to span an improbable distance and find his consciousness. With a monumental effort of will, he held on.

The other mind shattered his defences. Like a firestorm, it swept through his brain. He convulsed as his neurons overloaded.

Goodbye, brother, he heard the other's last thought.

Bound together for the final time, the twins' millennia of memories flared and burned up like tinder.

ABOUT THE AUTHOR

Robert Boyczuk is the author of *Horror Story and Other Horror Stories*, a critically acclaimed short story collection about love, grief, and loss, which is also available from ChiZine Publications. His website is located at: boyczuk.com.